RAP
SUPERSTAR

DEBRA CLAYTON

WWW.URBANBOOKS.NET

Clayton

Urban Books
6 Vanderbilt Parkway
Dix Hills, NY 11746

©Copyright 2005 Debra Clayton

ISBN **0974725-4-4**

First Printing January 2005

10 9 8 7 6 5 4 3 2 1

This is a work of fiction. Any references or similarities to actual events, real people, living, or dead, or to real locals are intended to give the novel a sense of reality. Any similarity in other names, characters, places, and incidents is entirely coincidental.

Chapter 1

"Richmond, Virginia, where the hell are you?" twenty-four year old rap star, Animalistic yelled as he strutted across the stage. "If you're in the house, make some fucking noise!" His eyes scanned the massive crowd that filled the coliseum. Giant waves of bodies moved simultaneously to the music blasting from the huge speakers. The crowd roared.

"I can't hear you! If you're loving this shit, make some fucking noise!" He ran across the stage to another section of the audience. The crowd roared again. He walked over to the edge of the platform and looked down into the thousands of hands that frantically reached up for him.

This is the shit, he thought as a huge smile danced across his pretty-boy baby face. Although he collapsed into bed almost every night from exhaustion, the fans, the money, and the endless array of available pussy made it all worthwhile.

He ripped off his T-shirt and revealed the hard, ripped muscles of his chest and abs. His sweat-drenched body glistened. The crowd went crazy. He threw the shirt into the mob of fans chanting his name. Audience members dove over each other and fought to possess the coveted souvenir.

He hurried over to the left side of the stage. As he stood at the edge, he shouted, "Farmville, Virginia, where the fuck are you? Let me hear you make some noise!"

Screams filled the air. He laughed when a girl in the front row lifted up her T-shirt and exposed her breasts to him. This was nothing new. He would probably fuck her before the night was over if she was clever enough to get backstage. If she wasn't, another young lady would be the recipient of

1

savage lovemaking.

"Let's get fucking crazy!" He screamed into the microphone then walked over to a table, picked up a bottle of Evian water and guzzled it. He poured the rest over his body to cool himself down.

The music changed. Two scantily clad female dancers raced onto the stage and took their positions. The crowd went wild when they recognized the music of his current number one single. Right on cue, the dancers gyrated to the beat that pounded through the arena. He licked his lips and darted back and forth across the stage as he spit out the lyrics to his multi-platinum single.

> *And you and me, and me and you,*
> *Rolling on twenty-inch dubs,*
> *Hitting all the hottest clubs.*
> *You riding in my limousine,*
> *You checking my bling-bling.*
> *Your nigga likes to roam.*
> *Like McCauley, he left you home alone.*
> *Yeah, your nigga ain't shit.*
> *He's so fucking lazy.*
> *That's why I got your legs up in the air,*
> *Fucking you like crazy.*

He strutted over to one of his dancers and grabbed her from behind. Arrogance danced across his face as his hand slithered over her full, round breasts then crept down between her thick, man-eating thighs. He molded his body against hers as they gyrated to the nasty beat of the music. After he dragged his tongue up her neck, he bent her over, gave her three quick thrusts from his hips, then abandoned her as he raced back to the front of the stage. The men hooted and hollered while the women screamed.

> *I'm Animalistic,*
> *Don't go ballistic.*
> *Never seen a nigga rhyme,*
> *So damn futuristic.*
>
> *Niggas don't know,*
> *How I flow so sweet.*
> *Damn, spread your legs, baby.*
> *I think it's time to eat.*

The audience went crazy. He stood at the edge of the stage as his whole body bounced to the beat. His 6-foot 8-inch frame was drenched with sweat. His baggy jeans hung low on his waist, exposing his cotton boxers. Bursts of fire shot up from the stage and illuminated the dark arena. He continued to spit out lyrics as he gave his hyped fans what they wanted. He would be performing again for another sold-out crowd in two days.

Ten hours later, Animalistic rolled over in his bed. He looked at the naked woman asleep next to him. Her silky black curls spilled all over her pillow, and although he couldn't see her face, he remembered her. Carla, he thought as he recalled her name. She was a good fuck and gave good head too. She was a freak. He smiled as he thought about the night before. Some of things he had done to her were considered illegal in many states.

He glanced over at the clock. It was 6:00 in the morning. He didn't have time to hit it again. The bus would be pulling out for Greensboro, North Carolina in less than two hours. He reached over and gave one of her buttocks a quick

3

squeeze before he slid out of bed. A nice, swollen ass was one of his biggest weaknesses; Carla had the kind that made a brother want to sleep in it all night.

He grabbed the empty condom wrappers off the nightstand and tossed them into the trash as he made his way to the bathroom. After a quick shower, he awakened the sleeping beauty. He thanked her for a good time, gave her a kiss on the forehead, and sent her on her way.

***

Twenty-one year old Randi glanced at her watch. It was 10:05 at night. She had another fifty-five minutes before she could leave work. It was a long night. Her feet ached from the black stiletto heels that she wore. Her tiny black leather skirt and white tuxedo shirt were not as neat and tucked in as they were three hours ago. Strands of her jet-black satin curls, once pinned up nicely, fell gently around her face. Her back ached from the large, round trays that she carried high above her head.

Although a few of the customers were extremely pleasant and the tips were more than respectable, the feeling of going nowhere fast plagued her. After working at Alexander Deveraux's, an upscale restaurant and bar, for the past two years, she had slowly begun to let go of her dream of becoming a writer. *A raisin in the sun,* she thought as she remembered the Langston Hughes' poem, "A Dream Deferred." Back in high school, it was just a reading assignment. Recently, the poem had become a painful reminder of her own shortcomings

Three years had passed since she had graduated high school with hopes of going to college and obtaining a career as a writer and filmmaker. Due to her family's economic situation, they couldn't afford to finance literary desires. Finances, along with the problems she had with her ex-fiancé, Eric, were enough to stall the pursuit of her dreams.

Eric was very controlling and overbearing. They had been high school sweethearts and he was her first and only lover. She had given herself to him completely, so when he had demanded that she forget about college and just be his wife, she succumbed to his wishes, and they were engaged. He gave her very little room for her friends and family, and she couldn't even look at another guy. Her family continuously warned her about him, but she was too consumed by him to listen. She convinced herself that the only reason he wanted to control her was because he loved her so much and didn't want to lose her. It wasn't until after she found out he was cheating on her that she saw him for what he really was. It was then that she tried to walk away from him. And it was that same night that he changed her life forever.

"It's not that bad," Mike, a co-worker said as he handed her the plate of food.

Realizing that she must have gone back to her dark place again, Randi quickly forced a smile as she grabbed the plate. "No, it's not," she said then hurried out of the kitchen to wait on more customers

As she buzzed around their tables, she did her best not to reveal her emptiness. She wore her pleasant but manufactured smile, which she kept readily available for days like this.

"Do you need any change?" she asked her customer as she picked up the money for the bill.

"No, sweetie," the elderly lady answered. "You keep the change. You have been an absolute pleasure."

"Thank you." Randi smiled. "You have a good evening."

"You too, darling."

Randi hurried back into the kitchen to turn in her money. Soon after, her best friend Kathy burst through the double doors.

"You're not going to believe this."

"What's wrong?" Randi was concerned. Maybe Mr. Allen had threatened to fire her again. Kathy was always getting into trouble at work.

"Guess who's here. You're never gonna guess who's here." Barely able to contain her excitement, she resembled a 3-year-old who had to go potty.

"Oh." Randi lost interest. "Who?" she asked dryly as she continued to count her money.

"No. Guess," Kathy insisted.

Randi sighed as she looked at her friend. Kathy was about to come undone. *Poor child*, Randi thought. Although Kathy got hysterical whenever a celebrity dropped by, Randi never paid them much attention. She wasn't gaga over Hollywood the way Kathy was. She thought the rich and famous were a bunch of spoiled brats who expected people to baby-sit their every need. She wasn't impressed with their status or their egos. She also knew that part of her resentment toward them was because they had achieved their dreams and she was just about to give up on hers.

"Kathy, I'm tired and I want to go home. I don't feel like guessing." She shifted her weight from one foot to the other in an attempt to relieve the throbbing pain.

"Come on," Kathy begged.

Randi sighed again. She knew that it was someone big by the way Kathy was acting. "Um . . ." She feigned interest.

"Animalistic!" Kathy blurted out. "Animalistic is here!"

Randi looked at her in disbelief. "Yeah, right. And of

all the fancy places he could have chosen to eat at, he somehow ended up here where I just happen to work." She was his biggest fan and Kathy knew this. Randi knew that Kathy was a notorious prankster, and this was just another opportunity to stick it to her. She wasn't going to fall for it this time. Although she gave Kathy's words no validity, she smiled inwardly as she turned and placed the money in the register. She wouldn't mind seeing his pretty bad-boy face tonight.

"Well, tonight's your lucky night, girl. He wants to meet you."

Randi laughed. "You know, I've got those papers on the Golden Gate Bridge if you're interested."

"No shit, Randi. He's really waiting to meet you," Kathy tried to convince her.

Bull, Randi said to herself, but decided to play along with Kathy's game. "Okay, Kathy, I'll bite. What does Animalistic, the future father of all my children, want with me?"

"Hell, I don't know, girl," she said as she grabbed Randi's arm and tried to pull her along. "But you sure as hell better not let him leave without meeting him." She tugged harder.

"All right, all right." Randi gave in as she pushed Kathy off of her. "I'll go, but you better not be playing with me."

"I promise you I'm not."

Randi narrowed her eyes as she stared at Kathy for another second or two. What if she was telling the truth? What if her future babies' daddy was out there waiting to meet her? Okay, she decided, being at the restaurant was believable, but him wanting to meet her was impossible.

"What the hell are you waiting on?" Kathy asked. "Come on." She grabbed her wrist and started pulling again. "You don't want to make him wait too long."

Randi followed as Kathy dragged her through the crowded restaurant. They navigated through the tables until they reached his.

At first glance, Randi couldn't see him because he was surrounded by his entourage and a group of autograph seekers. When one of his boys saw Randi and Kathy, he nudged Animalistic. He quickly looked up, made eye contact with Randi then turned his attention back to his fans.

"Oh my God," Randi whispered when she saw him. "It's him, it's him." She thought she might pass out. She looked at Kathy in disbelief. "It's him, Kathy, it's, it's—"

"See, I told you, girl. I wouldn't bullshit you over anything like this." She smiled excitedly

After signing a few more autographs, Animalistic rose to his feet. Randi looked up at him in amazement as he towered over them. When Kathy realized that her friend was in shock, she leaned over and whispered in her ear, "Breathe, Randi."

Randi nodded and repeated, "Breathe, Randi," never taking her eyes off the man of her dreams.

He smiled broadly, revealing all thirty-two of his perfect, professionally whitened teeth. He extended his hand. When Randi extended hers, he took it and brought it to his baby-soft lips. His eyes stayed on her face as they smiled mischievously down at her. "Animalistic." He introduced himself.

"I'm, um, I'm . . . " She tried to think of her name.

"You're Randi." Kathy assisted.

"Yeah, I'm Randi." Her voice cracked out of anxiousness. She cleared her throat and tried again. "Randi

Jacobs." She tried to remain calm, but inside she was doing cartwheels. She wanted to turn tail and run. How could she be meeting Mr. Animalistic while looking like a tired, run-down mess? She was embarrassed by her appearance.

He tried to make eye contact, but her shyness forced her to look away. This gave him the opportunity to size up the merchandise. His eyes roamed her body as they openly took inventory of her assets. One corner of his mouth curled into an approving smile.

"Randi Jacobs." He repeated her name. "You are fine as hell." He looked at her like she was the Last Supper and he hadn't eaten in days.

Randi forced a smile as she tried to ignore his roving eyes. "I'm a big fan of yours," she managed to get out.

"Really? I guess you'll be checking us out tomorrow night." He gestured for her to have a seat.

"I can't," she said to the invitation to sit down. She wished that she could because her legs were beginning to buckle.

"What about the show? You gonna be there?"

"I'm um, I'm working tomorrow night." She stumbled over her words. "I tried, I um, I had to work, I—"

"What time do you get off?" He looked at one his boys and gestured for paper and pen.

"Um, I . . . " She looked around nervously as if she was searching for someone who knew the answer to her question.

"Eleven," Kathy piped in and rescued her friend. "She gets off at eleven."

"Peep this. We're having a small party in my hotel room after the show. You could stop by and have a little fun."

"A party?" she asked as she tried to focus on what he was saying. Kathy nudged her excitedly.

9

"Let me give you the hotel name and the room number and I'll put your name on the list." One of his boys passed him the paper and pen. He scribbled the information and handed it to her. "You are gonna check us out, right?" he asked.

"Um, yeah." She nodded. Although she tried to relax, her body betrayed her. When she reached for the slip of paper, her hand was trembling.

Noticing that her friend was quietly losing it, Kathy stepped in and took the hotel information. "I'll hold onto this." She smiled then pretended to whisper, "I think she's in a little bit of shock right now."

"I see." He chuckled. "Can I count on you to make sure she stops by?"

"Oh, she'll be there." Kathy nodded confidently.

"Thanks."

"Oh shit," Kathy said as she grabbed Randi by the arm. "Here comes mister asshole. We've got to get back to work."

"I'll see you tomorrow night," he called after Randi as she was dragged away.

Randi stared back over her shoulder at him as Kathy pulled her. She couldn't believe she had just met her future babies' daddy.

His eyes followed her. He studied the way her hips swayed. She didn't posses the full, voluptuous ass and thighs of the women he was accustomed to fucking, but he was sure that she could handle him.

"Nice piece of ass," one of the guys from the entourage said.

Nice, he thought. *Very nice*. His smile broadened. He would be knee-deep in that tomorrow night.

Chapter 2

The next day, after she took care of her last customer, Randi anxiously rushed home to get ready for the party. She was still having a hard time believing that she had met Animalistic and that she was going to one of his parties. Kathy had to keep reassuring her that the previous night had actually happened.

After a quick shower, she slipped on the little black dressed she had picked out the night before. She stared at herself in the mirror and hoped that the dress wasn't too suggestive. It had taken her three hours to pick out that dress and now she was second-guessing it. She quickly slipped the dress off and began rummaging through her closet. She wanted to impress him, to make him say *damn* when he saw her. Now she wished that she had gone out and bought a new outfit for the night. After trying on a few more outfits, she ended up in the first one she had picked.

She nervously set her hair and applied her makeup. She had never been to an after-party before, and she wasn't sure what to expect. She had heard about some of the things that went on at parties like this one, but she was sure that they couldn't be as bad as they sounded. People had to be exaggerating about how raunchy they got. And even though wild parties weren't her scene, she couldn't give up this chance to hang out with an idol.

Randi knew that her mother would kill her if she found out she was going to a party like this one, much less hanging out with what her mother called a "gansta rapper." To make the situation worse, she was going alone. Kathy had made plans to be out of town for the weekend and couldn't go with her.

Once she was completely dressed and ready to go, Randi headed for the door. She reached for the doorknob then paused.

"I can't do this," she said, shaking her head. She stared down at her hand on the knob. "What if I'm just one of a hundred women that he invited to this thing? What if he doesn't even remember me?" She let go of the doorknob, turned around and leaned against the door. "What am I thinking?" she whispered. "I don't know him. I don't know anyone that's going to be at this party." She closed her eyes and she could see her mother scolding her. "Randi Lynette Jacobs, if you don't get in there and wash that crap off your face and take off that skimpy dress, I'm gonna skin your hide." Then she could see Kathy riding her. "Girlfriend, if you don't get your ass to that party and have hell of a good time, I'm gonna remind you every day of your life just how fucked up you are."

"Okay, okay, okay," Randi said as she opened her eyes. She turned around and grabbed the doorknob again. "Sorry, Mom," she apologized as she took a deep breath, opened the door and left for the party.

Within 30 minutes, she was at the hotel. She took a deep breath to calm her nerves as she stepped onto the elevator. It didn't work. Her heart pounded wildly as she rode up to the eighth floor. You can do this, she told herself.

When the doors opened, she stepped out of the elevator and noticed a group of people gathered in the hallway. Most were women. She hesitated as she wondered if all the women were there to meet Animalistic. Was she just one of many that he had invited? She bit her bottom lip as she contemplated running back into the elevator.

Then she thought about Animalistic, the way he

looked at her, the way he kissed her hand and smiled down at her. He was so perfect. And even though she didn't like men ogling her, Animalistic was different. He could do no wrong in her eyes. She had to do this. She would have to put away all of her shyness and inhibitions just for one night. He didn't even have to talk to her. Just being in the same room with him for a few minutes would satisfy her for the next ten years.

She began to walk down the hall to room 809 where the small mob congregated. The women made futile attempts to get into the room, but two security guards kept them at bay.

"What do I have to do to get in?" one of the women asked the guard as she pushed her body up against his.

He smiled at the other guard knowingly and responded. "What are you willing to do?"

"I'll show you my tits," the woman offered. She cupped her breasts through her flimsy, see-through blouse.

"I can see tits all day. What else you got?" he asked.

"Well, let's go around the corner and I'll show you what else I have to offer." She stroked his face with one of her scarlet red fingernails and pursed her matching red lips at him.

The first guard nudged the other with a silly grin on his face and asked, "You got this, man?"

"Sure, man. Go ahead." He gave him one of those *go and get her* slaps on the back. He would get the next one. The guard followed the woman down the hall and around the corner.

Randi had heard about women giving favors to the security guards just so they could see the performers, but she never expected to see it happen right there in front of her. Maybe this party was a little raunchier than she initially thought it would be. Her good girl sensibility told her to turn tail and go home, but the fan side of her told her that she'd better not leave until she had at least seen Animalistic. She

13

focused on the remaining guard as she managed to push her way through the crowd. After being shoved by a few angry fans, she reached the guard and nervously stepped up to him. "Um, uh, Animalistic invited me," she finally managed to get out.

"Yeah, you and every other chick here." He sounded as if he was already bored with her.

"Yeah, but um," she stumbled over her words, "he um, said he would um, put my name on a um, list."

"Yeah, yeah. What's your name?" he asked as he looked down at his clipboard.

"Randi Jacobs." Her heart pounded. What if she wasn't on the list? What if he had forgotten about her? She was sure he ran across hundreds of women. Surely, he wouldn't have remembered her. She started biting her bottom lip again as she waited for the guard. She prepared herself to hear "Sorry, but you can't get in."

He looked down the list of names on the paper he held. "Randi Jacobs," he repeated. "You're right. Your name is on the list. I guess you're his candy for tonight." He chuckled.

"What?" She grimaced at his statement.

"Never mind. You can go in."

"Aw, hell no!" one of the other women said. "My name's on that damn list too, and I've been waiting here for over an hour."

"Now, I've told you three times already that you're not getting in," the guard said.

"Well I've offered to hook you up."

"Honey, you ain't even fine enough to suck my dog's dick."

"Bitch!" the woman snarled at him.

"Take your simple ass home," he said as he opened the door for Randi to enter.

Randi tried to ignore the words between the security guard and the angry woman. She silently prayed that she would see Animalistic and he would remember her.

She took a deep breath as the door opened wider and loud music poured out of the room into the hallway. The thumping beat of 50 Cent's "In Da Club" made the room vibrate. She cautiously stepped inside, unsure what to expect. The door closed behind her. The aroma of pot filled the air. Half-naked bodies gyrated wildly to the beat of the music.

Randi was not a social butterfly, so she immediately looked for a safe haven to retreat to until she could work up the nerve to mingle. She saw a seat in a corner, quickly moved over to it and sat down.

The party resembled a giant orgy as bodies smashed up against each other, simulating sex acts. She could barely tell where one person ended and another one began. A few feet away, she noticed a group of people sitting on a couch passing a joint around. When they caught her spying on them, they held it up in her direction in an attempt to offer her a hit. She quickly shook her head and looked away.

Expensive alcoholic drinks fueled the outrageous guests. Women disappeared into the back rooms with two and three men at a time. One of the rappers who had performed earlier with Animalistic was with a woman over in a corner. The half-naked woman pushed her full, round behind up against his crotch. His hands gripped her rotating hips as he dry-humped her.

Where was Animalistic? She scanned the room for him. Her excitement about seeing him was slowly dwindling. She debated with herself whether she should stay or leave. He was the reason she was there. Although she was anxious to see him, the environment she was in made her very nervous.

While most young women her age enjoyed going out

and partying all night, she would have been satisfied curled up in front of the television watching movies or dreaming of seeing her own movies onscreen. She could either watch movies all day or spend hours in front of her computer pounding out stories and scripts that she hoped would make it to the big screen one day. Yes, writing was her passion, but hanging out with wild men and loose women was not her thing. Drinking and getting high was no desire of hers as well. She had seen how the influences of drugs and alcohol had strained her parents' marriage and her relationship with her father until he managed to break away from it.

She sighed as she thought about her father and his warnings to her about drugs and alcohol. He would be so disappointed in her right now. She clutched at her purse as she contemplated her next move. Either she could move around the room to find her future babies' daddy or she could head straight for the door to make her exit. Before she could make up her mind, one of the other rappers known as Cooney noticed her and stumbled over. She thought he was going to end up in her lap.

"Damn, baby girl, why you sitting over here all alone?" His speech was slurred. Before she could answer, he grabbed her hand and pulled her to her feet.

"Let me get a look at you," he said as he spun her around. "Damn, damn, damn, damn." He shook his head. "You make a nigga wanna fuck you and eat you at the same time." The stench of alcohol and pot seeped out of him and filled her nostrils.

Repulsed, she pulled away. She resisted the urge to slap him, but the look on her face revealed her anger.

"Hey, bitch, come here. Don't you know who the fuck I am?" He grabbed at her as he stumbled and almost fell. "I'm the m-man," he stuttered. "The man w-with the f-fucking plan."

"Hey, hey, Cooney. What's up?" a familiar voice cut in. It was Animalistic. He walked toward them. "Leave the lady alone."

Randi was relieved to see him as she straightened her clothes and tried to gather her composure.

Cooney looked at Animalistic. "What's up, my nigga?" He grabbed Animalistic's hand and shook it. "This bitch don't know who the hell—who the fuck I am."

Randi kept quiet. She had seen her father drunk enough times to know that it was a waste of time to try to talk to someone in this condition. But she was sure that giving him a swift kick in his nuts would have made her feel a lot better.

"Calm down, Cooney," Animalistic said as he patted him on the back. "This is a guest of mines. She's here to see me."

"For real, man? No shit?"

"No shit."

"All right, all right. I-I'm sorry, man." He took one last long and degrading look at Randi. He wobbled. Randi felt naked as his eyes invaded her. "Well, you tear that ass up for old Cooney-Coooooon." He howled as he stumbled away.

So, he did remember her, she thought as she stared up at him.

Animalistic quickly apologized. "Forgive him. He's fucked up right now."

"Thank you," she said nervously. "He scared the crap out of me."

"He's harmless." He chuckled as he thought about her choice of words. He had never heard anyone over the age of fourteen use the word *crap*.

As he looked down at her, he hoped she wasn't as innocent as she sounded. Now it was his time to blatantly

17

undress her with his eyes. He flashed another thirty-two at her as he smiled approvingly. "Damn, baby, but you do look good."

Randi felt self-conscious. Maybe her dress was sexier than she initially thought. He finally took his eyes off her body long enough to look her in the face.

"You want a drink? We've got Cristal, Moet, beer."

"No, thank you. I don't drink."

"Really?" He was surprised.

"Long story," she said as if she read his mind. She smiled up at him. He was more beautiful than he was the day before. Her heart was pounding wildly again.

"I guess you don't get high either then?" he asked, his head cocked to the side.

"No."

"Good. Me neither." He was impressed. "But I do have to get my drink on," he said as he lifted his glass.

She smiled again. She felt shy.

"Well, Miss Randi Jacobs, what do you say we go in one of the back rooms?"

"For what?" He wasn't gonna try to sleep with her, was he? She wasn't that type of girl.

He knew what she was thinking. "C'mon. It's noisy as hell out here, and I'd like to hear every word you say," he explained. "We could have some privacy." He gave her a *you can trust me* smile.

"I, um . . . " She hesitated. Was she really gonna say no to him? "I—"

"C'mon." He reached for her hand. "I promise I won't bite." He smiled. "Not unless you want me to."

She laughed nervously. "Okay." She followed him as he led her through the bumping and grinding bodies to one of the empty bedrooms. Once inside, he closed the door and

18

locked it.

"So we won't be disturbed," he explained when he saw the worried look on her face.

Randi watched him as he walked over to the bed, reached into his pocket and pulled out a colorful array of condoms. He tossed them on the bed then pulled off his shirt revealing his smooth, tight muscles. Without a word, he began unfastening his pants.

"Hey, wait a minute." Randi stopped him. "What are you doing?"

He looked over at her and smiled. "Getting ready to fuck you like you've never been fucked before."

Her mouth dropped open. "Are you serious?"

"Hell yeah. Now, take your clothes off, unless you just wanna suck my dick."

She became disillusioned by him that very moment. She had tried to ignore all the indications that he was a jerk, but she no longer could. He was a jerk. "I don't believe this," she mumbled as she shook her head. "I thought you were—"

"Believe it, baby. You're getting ready to fuck a superstar." He chuckled.

"I don't think so." She stared at him, feeling stupid. She knew he was no angel, but she didn't expect this.

"What's the problem? I'm gonna use protection."

"Protection." She shook her head again, looked up at the ceiling then back at him. "I'm sorry, but I'm not her."

"Her? Who's her?"

She smiled as she decided to forget about the fact that he was a rap superstar and instead focus on the fact that he was a full of himself jerk. "You know my mother raised me to be a lady, so I'm not going to get to raunchy with this, but I'm not the one who's gonna be sucking your dick tonight."

"What your momma raised you to be is frigid. Damn,

girl. Chill. Don't be so uptight, baby." He gave her a half-ass smile.

"Uptight? I don't even know you. Besides, your mother, if you have one, should have taught you how to act like a gentleman, even if you were raised by dogs."

"Roof-roof, baby," he barked at her. "Now c'mon, baby girl, let this dog give it to you like you never had it before."

Damn, this wasn't the same sweet-faced, could barely talk girl he met at the restaurant yesterday. She definitely didn't have a hard time finding her words tonight. He didn't mind, though. If she wanted to play hard to get, he could deal with that. If she wanted to put up a little fuss before dropping the panties, he could deal with that too. He knew it was all an act to make her feel better the next day. That way, she couldn't say she gave up the pussy too easy. It was all a game. He'd play along with her for a little while, but if he wasn't knee deep in her within the next twenty minutes, he'd have to pull another chick off the bench.

"Are you serious?" she asked. "Can you be for real?"

"Hell yeah. Now, come over here and get some of this." He reached for her.

She stepped away. "Not even," she said, placing her hand on her hip and narrowing her eyes. "You keep your hands off of me."

"You don't know what you're missing." He added, "Girl, I could fuck you so good that it would make your momma and grandma cum."

"That's nice. That's real nice." She didn't know whether to slap him for insulting her mother and grandmother or to laugh at him for such a weak line. Humility was obviously not his strongest feature, she thought as she turned and walked toward the door.

"Where you going?" He sounded surprised. Women never turned him down.

"I'm leaving. This isn't what I had in mind. I don't sleep with people I don't know."

"Do you know how many women would love to be in your position right now, how many women would love to fuck me just so they can go back and tell their friends about it?" Damn, he hadn't worked this hard since . . . Hell, he had never worked this hard. This bitch was acting like her pussy was made of gold. "I'm giving you the opportunity of a lifetime."

"While you're stroking your ego, why don't you reach down there and stroke yourself, because it ain't happening."

"Listen, if you don't want none of this, then I'm not gonna force you. I don't have to beg for it and I sure as hell don't jack my dick. I fall in pussy every day." He opened the door for her.

Fall in pussy every day, Randi thought. *Not mines.*

There was a girl dancing in the hallway. She looked in their direction when the door opened.

"It's just too easy for me to have to work for it. Besides, it's not like you got the only pussy in North Carolina. Pussy's everywhere," he continued. He looked at the girl then back at Randi. "Well, what do you know? More pussy." He smirked.

He looked at the girl. "Hey, ma. Come here." He held his hand out. She walked over to him and took it.

"You wanna fuck a superstar?"

"Only if it's you, daddy." She smiled.

"Well, tonight's your lucky night."

"No. Tonight's your lucky night. You just traded up." She slipped into the bedroom as she gave Randi a wicked smile.

"Just like that," Randi said.

21

"Just like that." He smiled. "You just missed out."

"No, baby." She smiled. "You just missed out. You are about to get into something that every man at this party has probably already been in."

"Fuck you, bitch!" the girl said to Randi.

"No, you're not fucking me, honey. You're fucking him." She grabbed the door and pulled it closed for them. Satisfied with herself, she held her head up high and left the party.

The next day, Animalistic sat on his tour bus as it pulled out of the hotel parking lot and turned onto High Point Road. He wore a small grin on his face as he thought about the night before. The smile wasn't for the girl he fucked but for the one that got away.

"Randi Jacobs," he said under his breath. He rolled her name off his tongue. Boy, she was feisty, he thought. She was fine as hell too. Evidently, she thought she was too fine to give up the pussy. He smiled at the way she handled him. His mouth played with a toothpick that he held between his teeth.

The bus pulled to a stop at a red light. He thought about the way Randi's hips swayed when she walked away from him. Did she intentionally tease him only to tell him no later? He thought about the way her dress clung to her body. Prick tease. He thought about her round face and her caramel skin. He remembered the way her big brown eyes narrowed when she informed him that she wasn't sleeping with him, and the way her red, pouty lips curled as she expressed no interest in him. He chuckled to himself.

"Randi Jacobs." He whispered her name again. "Miss Randi Jacobs from Greensboro, North Carolina. I could have shown you a good time. I guess you'll never know."

22

One of his boys sauntered up and sat down next to him. "That was some nice piece of ass you had up there last night. You know the one in that little black dress that Cooney was trying to get with. I saw you take her to the back. Was it as good as it looked?" He grinned.

"Don't know, man. Didn't hit it," he admitted.

"Didn't hit it? You pussy. Nigga, what's wrong with you? Tell me playa-playa ain't losing his touch." He looked at him in disbelief. If nobody else got the pussy, Animalistic did.

"Naw, man. Now, don't get me wrong. I got some pussy last night," he bragged, "but not hers. She was a quote-unquote good girl." He made quotation marks with his fingers.

His friend laughed. "All them hoes up in that piece, there were no good girls there last night."

"Oh, yes there was." He smiled and repeated to himself. *Oh, yes there was.*

"Oh yeah? Well, what in the hell was she doing up in there last night?"

"She was a fan," he said aloud. *But I thought she was just another piece of ass.*

Chapter 3

"Where my niggas at?" Animalistic bellowed out as he raced on to the stage of the Bi-Lo Center in Greenville, South Carolina. The sea of people roared as the number one rapper in the country emerged. Smiling at their response, he raced over to the left side of the stage and screamed, "Are my niggas in the house?" He stared out into the audience as he awaited their reply.

The men returned with a resounding "Hell yeah."

"I can't hear you!" he shouted as he put his hand to his ear. "Let me hear my niggas make some noise!" The men howled even louder.

He ran over to the right side of the stage and yelled, "Do my ladies run this muthafucka?"

The women screamed, "Hell yeah!" as they frantically jumped up and down and reached for him. This was one hell of a rush. He had no need for drugs. Performing was his drug of choice. His fans kept him high. He stood at the edge of the stage and shouted, "Let me hear you say the ladies run this muthafucka!"

"The ladies run this muthafucka!" they screamed back at him.

"Again!" he yelled.

"The ladies run this muthafucka!"

"Again!" he demanded as he leaned forward with a hand up to his ear.

"The ladies run this muthafucka!" they began to chant. "The ladies run this muthafucka!"

"Aw hell, no you don't!" He cut in. "The only thing y'all run is your damn mouths!" He laughed.

The men began to hoot in agreement while the women

24

started booing.

"Naw, naw, man. I'm just kidding y'all." He laughed. "You know I love my ladies. Without the ladies, niggas wouldn't know how to act."

The women began to scream and holler again.

"Now, for my ladies, just because I love you so much and I want you to be satisfied tonight, I'm gonna tell your niggas what they need to do when they get you home tonight." He ran to the center of the stage. "Now, fellas, can you hear me?" he yelled.

The men roared.

"Now, this is what you say to your lady tonight when you get her home." He looked at his DJ, gave him a quick nod, then looked back to his fans. After the music started booming through the arena, he sauntered around the edge of the stage as he bounced his head to the beat and began to freestyle.

> *You got a phat-ass booty,*
> *And a tiny-ass waist.*
> *Now, sit your sweet-ass pussy*
> *Down all over my face*

The women squealed with excitement as he licked his lips and continued.

> *Now ride my tongue, baby,*
> *And hold on to my knees.*
> *You grinding so deep, baby,*
> *a nigga can't even breathe.*

> *Now shake it, jiggle it.*
> *rattle it, then roll.*

Now, hold it still, girl
And feel how deep my tongue can go.

The women went into a screaming frenzy as he paused and squatted on the edge of the stage. He reached down and touched a few of their hands. They frantically pushed and shoved one another as they tried to get to him. So as not to start a stampede, he stood back up and continued his stroll around the stage.

"Now, to all my niggas. Now that I got all your ladies' panties nice and moist, I'm gonna help you brothas out. Once you've licked her and sucked her and tongue-fucked her, now that she's done creamed all over your face, this is what you say to her."

Now, drop to your knees
And return the favor.
Can I stroke your tonsils?
Deep-throat it, baby.

The men went crazy as they shouted out "Hell yeah!" in agreement.

"All right, all right." He laughed as he sprinted to the rear of the stage to grab a bottle of water. After guzzling it down, the music changed. His dancers raced onto the stage and took their positions.

Animalistic reemerged from the shadows and yelled into the mike, "All right, people. Let's get this muthafucking party started!"

Two hours later he shouted, "Greenville, South Carolina, I love you!" then disappeared into the darkness. The sounds of his roaring fans followed him as he hurriedly pushed his way backstage to get to his dressing room. *Another satisfied customer,* he said to himself as he moved down the hallway cluttered with people.

"Great job, Anthony," someone called out to him.

"Thanks," Animalistic responded without looking to see who it was.

"Damn, nigga, you did your thing," Cooney said as he slipped past him.

"Well, you know how we do, nigga." He laughed as he brought his elbow up to Cooney's chest.

"Ya know."

"You know your shit was tight too, nigga."

"Hell, I'm just trying to be like you, man." Cooney laughed.

"Practice makes perfect."

"You sick, nigga." Cooney chuckled.

"Yo, man, I'll holla at you later," Animalistic said as he started back down the hallway again.

"Holla."

He paused a couple more times to speak to people and sign a few autographs for fans who were working backstage.

"Yo, yo, Anthony," one of his security guards called out as he was passing by.

Animalistic stopped to see what he wanted. "Yo, man, what's up?"

"These young ladies have been waiting back here all night to meet you." He grinned as he gestured to the three scantily dressed females who stood anxiously next to him.

"Damn," Animalistic muttered when he saw the three beautiful girls. Barely wearing enough clothing to cover their tits and asses, he couldn't take his eyes off their nearly naked bodies. He sauntered up to the three beauties. They looked like they were ready to jump his bones. He licked his lips as he imagined what they would look like riding his dick all night.

"Hello," one of the girls said seductively as her eyes traveled over his glistening bare chest.

"Damn, baby. Y'all make my tongue hard," he said as he finally pulled his eyes away from their curvaceous bodies and looked up to their faces. "Triplets?" he asked when he realized that all three girls looked exactly alike.

"We're identical," one of the girls answered. "I'm Mia, and these are my sisters, Tia and Kia."

"Nice to meet you ladies." He grinned

"Hello," they replied.

"The pleasure's all ours," Kia said as she stepped up to him and placed her hand on his chest. She brought her lips to his ear and spoke softly. "I hope your tongue's not the only thing we make hard."

Before he could respond, he felt the tip of her tongue tracing over the edge of his ear. This gave him shivers. Damn, he was one lucky-ass nigga, he told himself. He grabbed a handful of her ass and pulled her closer. The smooth, round buttock in the palm of his hand made his dick hard. He pulled her hand from his chest and placed it on his crotch. She groped the thickness in his pants and marveled at the size.

"Damn, nigga, what you packing?"

Jealous that their sister was getting all the attention, Mia and Tia moved over to where the grab-fest was. Mia grabbed at his ass while Tia went for the crotch.

"You think you can you handle all three of us?" Mia asked as she nibbled on his earlobe.

"With what he's packing, we may not be enough for him," Tia responded as she gently squeezed the swollen bulge in his pants.

Animalistic grabbed another handful of ass and

squeezed. "Ladies, why don't you come by my suite tonight and I'll see if I can handle all three of you?" Tonight was going to be the ultimate. He wasn't gonna just fuck three beautiful women at one time; he was gonna fuck identical triplets. His niggas were gonna hate the hell out of him.

"That sounds like a plan," Mia said as she slid her hand across his six-pack and up to his chest. Tia purred as she brought her lips up to meet his in an attempt to kiss him.

He pulled away. "No, baby doll," he said. "No kissing, no kissing at all," he informed them. That was his one of his rules for the women he slept with. He didn't kiss them or eat them, and he didn't fuck them without a condom. He didn't know where they had been, and he wasn't gonna put his mouth on them or dip his dick in them without protection. While most of the women had no problem with his rules, a few tried to give him a hard time about them. Nevertheless, in the end, he always got his way.

"No problem, daddy," Tia replied. "Just fuck us right and we'll be happy."

Two hours later, Animalistic was hitting the three sisters like a freight train. His body glistened with sweat as he plowed into Mia doggie-style. She'd cry out every time he went deep. He'd back off a little then start pounding again. The other two sisters played with themselves or with each other as they waited for their turn to come around again. Sweat poured down his body as he worked on his fourth nut. His dick was sore, but it was still hard, and he wasn't gonna stop until it went down. He had never been so turned on before this night. Fucking three women at once gave him a hard-on that he couldn't get rid of. He felt like the Energizer bunny. He kept going and going and going. Mia finally announced that she could take no more so, he grabbed Kia and went to work on her again.

A few hours later, unable to sleep due to all the bodies crowding his space, Animalistic climbed out of his bed. Wearing nothing but his huge ego, he walked over to the window and looked out into the night. *Man, tonight was the shit*, he told himself as he looked back at the three naked women who still lay asleep in his bed.

Those girls were freaky as hell, and there was nothing they wouldn't do. He wasn't sure what he enjoyed more; fucking one of them in the ass or watching the other two eat each other out. Now they looked like three angels. Two hours earlier, they were trying to fuck his brains out—or was it the other way around? He wasn't sure, but he knew his dick was sore as hell. *Too much fucking,* he told himself. Damn, and he had to piss too. *This isn't going to be fun.*

A few minutes later, Animalistic was sitting in a chair watching the triplets sleep. Although this was the wildest thing he had ever done and he should have been pleased with himself, he was starting to feel like this was not such a big accomplishment anymore. What had he really done? He had just fucked three women who would have probably fucked any man that came along. They were hoes. Where was the challenge in that? Anybody could fuck a ho. He wanted a challenge, someone he could conquer.

Then he thought about the girl he met in Greensboro. Randi was her name. He was surprised that he still remembered it. He couldn't remember the name of the girl he fucked most nights, but he could remember Randi. She was the one who thought she was too cute to give up the pussy. Now *she* was a challenge. If he had fucked her, then he would have conquered something.

Then he thought about it longer. No, Randi was not the type of girl you try to conquer. She was the type of girl that you settle down with. She was the kind of girl you took home to meet the folks.

He thought about the way he treated her, the way he disrespected her, and the way he disrespected her mother and grandmother. She deserved better than that. He was surprised that she didn't slap the shit out of him for the way he had acted. He knew that his mother would have. He glanced over at the clock. It was nearly 6:00 a.m. He would be leaving to go back to L.A .in a couple of hours.

Chapter 4

Two weeks later, Animalistic maneuvered his black Lexus coupe through the unfamiliar streets of Greensboro, North Carolina. Struggling to follow the directions that Kathy had given him twenty minutes earlier, he asked himself why he was doing this. It had been four weeks since he had run into the young lady that he couldn't get out of his head. No matter how hard he tried to forget about her, Randi Jacobs kept easing back into his thoughts. Whenever he was with one of his many groupies, Randi Jacobs seemed to be there, watching him, judging him, making him feel empty afterwards. And no matter how great the sex was, how freaky the groupies were, he still felt dissatisfied.

Maybe it was the guilt that was eating him up inside. He felt like shit for the way he had treated her. He remembered the disappointed and disgusted look on her face when he revealed his true intentions to her. He remembered how her beautiful brown eyes lost their smile when she saw who he truly was. And now, a month later, the reflection of himself in her eyes was a disappointment to him.

Maybe, just maybe, he thought, if he could talk to her again, apologize for his actions, maybe he could get back to his life without her haunting him another second. Maybe if he could make those pretty brown eyes smile up at him again the way they did when she first met him, then he could get on with his life. He didn't know if it would work, but it was worth a try.

He glanced over at the bouquet of yellow roses that lay on the seat next to him. *Women like roses, don't they?* he asked himself. He hadn't done much apologizing to anyone, much less a woman. The only woman he had ever given flowers to was his mother. He hoped Randi liked flowers. He hoped she'd accept his apology and get out of his head.

***

Randi was exhausted. She finally had the night off and she wasn't about to do anything constructive. Donned in her favorite bunny-covered pajamas and a do-rag around her head, she looked more like an elderly woman than a 21-year-old. She didn't care. She wasn't trying to impress anyone. She was chilling with Martin Lawrence and Will Smith and they didn't mind her attire. She had paid her $3.50 at the local Blockbuster, and Martin and Will were hers for the entire evening. As she sat on her bed and painted her toenails, she watched the bad boys.

There was an unexpected knock on her door. After she paused the movie, she waddled up the hallway to answer it. Maybe it was her next-door neighbor who borrowed everything but never returned anything. Randi wondered what she wanted now. When she opened the door, she was completely taken aback. It wasn't her bothersome neighbor in her doorway; it was Animalistic accompanied by a beautiful bouquet of yellow roses.

He smiled when he saw her. As he surveyed her appearance, he realized that she hadn't expected company. Still, in bunny-covered pajamas, with a do-rag around her head and cotton stuck between her toes, she was beautiful. He couldn't deny that.

Randi opened her mouth but remained speechless. She was angry as well as stunned. What was he doing there? After the way he had treated at the after-party, he had some nerve to show up on her doorstep. Maybe he hadn't insulted her

33

enough, she thought. Maybe he was there to show her that he could be an even bigger jerk than before. She tried to speak again, but still her words abandoned her.

Noticing her loss for words, he decided to speak first. "You just open the door for anybody?"

Ignoring his question, she went straight for an explanation. "What are you doing here?" she asked, placing one hand on her hip like his mother used to do when she was preparing to hear some bullshit.

"I wanted to apologize," he started as he tried to hand her the roses. "These are for you." He hoped that she would accept them. All of a sudden, he was becoming nervous.

His *I'm the shit* attitude was starting to dwindle as he stared down at her *take no prisoners* expression. He hadn't accounted for nervousness. Who was she? She had no right to make him nervous. She had no right to judge him for his way of life. He was Animalistic. He was a rap superstar. Still, he had to admit that the way she looked up at him made him feel a little uncomfortable with the way he lived.

She looked down at the roses, then up at him. "Apology accepted," she said then closed the door in his face.

Okay, this isn't going to be that easy. He knocked again.

Randi stared at the door as she debated whether to open it again. Although she knew he was a jerk, he was still Animalistic. He was still one of the biggest rappers out there, and he was standing at her door with a bouquet of roses for her. She was both intrigued and put off by him. She bit her bottom lip as she contemplated opening the door again. After the incident at the after-party, she was sure that if she ever set eyes on him again, she wouldn't give him the time of day. But now . . . Now that he was at her door, now it was different. It was easier said than done.

He knocked again. She didn't respond. She just stared at the door, wondering what to do.

Animalistic stared down at the roses again. He had flown all the way from L.A. to apologize, and she wouldn't even open the door for him. He was getting impatient. Who the hell did she think she was? *Fuck that bitch,* he said to himself. He didn't need the aggravation. He was Animalistic, rap superstar. He didn't need to be begging for this chick's forgiveness. He threw the roses down at her door and started walking away.

Just as he was about to head down the steps, he stopped. *What am I doing?* He was pissed off because she hurt his ego again. That was what had got him in this mess in the first place, his big-ass ego. So what if she didn't throw the door open and welcome his apology with open arms? What had he expected? He had treated her like shit. He deserved much worse than a door closed in his face, he told himself. He decided to check his ego and give Randi the apology she deserved. If he didn't, he knew he wouldn't be able to get her off his back

Sucking it up, he turned around and walked back to the door. He picked up the roses, straightened them up, and knocked on the door again. "Randi, can you just hear me out?" he called out.

Randi stared at the door and started biting her nails. He remembered her name. It was a month later and he still remembered it. She was sure he ran across hundreds of women, yet somehow he remembered her. Why was he really there? What did he want from her? Why was he banging on her door?

"Please," he said. "Just give me ten minutes. I don't blame you for not wanting to talk to me, but I came all this way to apologize. Can you please just give me ten minutes of your time?"

Ten minutes, she thought. What harm could it do? It was just ten minutes. She'd listen to what he had to say and then he'd be on his way. After all, he did come all this way to say he was sorry. She opened the door and looked up at him.

Relieved, he smiled. "I'm sorry." He tried to give the roses again.

She ignored them. "What do you want from me?"

"I want to apologize."

"Well, you have." She stared up at his face. He didn't look as arrogant as he did a month ago. The mischief in his eyes was replaced with a serious, almost somber look.

"Well, I was hoping that I could talk to you."

"Ten minutes, right?"

"Ten minutes." He nodded.

Randi took a deep breath and stepped outside, closing the door behind her. She walked over to the railing and looked down at the parked cars. She saw a black Lexus coupe. She had never seen it before, and assumed that it must have been his. *Pretty modest for a rapper.* She thought he would have driven something a little flashier, like the rappers she had watched on *MTV Cribs*. So, he wasn't a showoff. That was nice, she thought.

He leaned on the railing next to her. "I just wanted to apologize for the way I treated you at the party." He looked over at her.

She didn't respond. She just continued looking out into the parking lot.

"I treated you like you were just a piece of ass and that was uncalled for. I should have been able to look at you and realize that you weren't like the other women at the party," he said in an attempt to explain his behavior.

"And how were the other women?" She already knew

the answer. She saw how they acted at the party.

"You know—loose, easy."

Some excuse, she thought. If he had come all the way to her doorstep to apologize, he should have come up with a better excuse than that one. "So, you're saying that if you had known that I wasn't easy, then you wouldn't have disrespected me?" She finally turned her head toward him and looked up at him.

"Yeah," he admitted.

"Maybe it's just the way I was raised, but shouldn't all women be respected?" She was sure that it had to be difficult for him to be a gentleman when he was surrounded by the type of women that had been at the party, but he didn't have to be so crude when she turned down his advances.

"Well, when I rehearsed it in the car on the way over here, it sounded smoother than it does now."

"You do have a mother, don't you?" She turned the rest of her body toward him. "Or are you just the result of an evil genius with a test tube and a mischievous plan?"

"Ouch," he said. He looked down at her. Five feet six inches was probably as high as she reached, but she had some gumption about her. "No, no evil genius here. I'm the product of a loving mother and father."

She couldn't tell.

"Your loving mother raised you to treat women like you do?" She knew she could have been nicer, but she didn't want to let him off that easy.

He smiled. "My mom would string me up if she saw how I treated women," he admitted. His mom would have also liked her.

"Women should be treated with respect, not like some hole for you to shove your dumb-stick in."

He chuckled at her choice of words, but agreed with

37

her. "True, but shouldn't these women respect themselves?"

She hesitated but then nodded. He was right. Women had to respect themselves if they wanted to be respected by others.

"Women throw themselves at me every day."

"You mean you fall into pussy every day." She knew her mother would have shoved a piece of soap down her throat if she heard her language.

"I'm sorry. I shouldn't have said that," he said.

"Why? That's what you do, right? Fall in pussy every day?"

He chuckled. Now his words were coming back to bite him in the ass. "You were at the party. You saw how the women acted. How can I show respect for a woman who's willing to give head to a security guard, a complete stranger, just so she can get in a room to sleep with me, another complete stranger?"

He made a good point, and it showed on her face. He smiled when he saw that she could appreciate his position.

"So, you treat women like crap because they lack self-respect, but why did you treat me the way you did when I told you I wasn't going to sleep with you? Did you enjoy insulting me?"

"No. I just thought you were playing hard to get," he admitted.

"So, I can say that's the reason you're here now. You think I'm playing hard to get and you like the challenge."

"No," he quickly said. "Not at all." He wanted to make sure she knew that wasn't the reason for his visit. "I just thought you deserved an apology. And because I was so rude to you, I thought the least I could do was deliver it in person."

That was nice, she thought as she looked away at the porch light. She watched as the moths and bugs congregated around it, and figured that he drew women to him the same way. They couldn't help themselves.

He walked over to the apartment building and squatted down, leaning against the wall with his knees bent. He laid the roses down next to him and rested his arms over his knees.

Could he be telling the truth? she wondered. Could he be sincere? She wasn't sure if she should be so quick to believe him. Nevertheless, he did seem like a different person. He didn't seem like the same person she met at the party.

She studied him. He was beautiful, she thought. The porch light revealed the smooth, hazel-brown skin of his face. It was flawless. His curly black hair was brushed up on top of his head. The tapered sides were trimmed short, but the top was longer. They started out as waves and ended up as curls. His lips were full, bow-shaped. He had a thin mustache that lay just above those perfect lips, traveled down the sides of his mouth and under his chin. Then there were those teeth; she couldn't forget those thirty-twos.

"You plan on staying for a while?" she asked when he got comfortable on the porch. She didn't like him getting too relaxed. Ten minutes wasn't that long. She got the feeling that he would try to squeeze a little more time out of her.

"Seems like you don't plan on letting me off the hook," he said.

"Why do I have to let you off the hook? You've apologized and I've accepted. What more do you want from me?" She looked at his hands. They were huge. He had a little bling-bling going on.

"Why don't you sit down?" he asked. He wasn't ready to leave.

"Why are you really here?" She was sure he had underlying motives.

He paused as he finally realized his true motives. It

wasn't the fact that he was trying to get her out of his head so he could move on with his outrageous lifestyle. It was the fact that he wanted her in his head. He had never met a woman like her and he wanted to find out more about her. He wanted to see what made her different. What was so special about her that she could say no to him? He sighed as he debated whether to tell her the truth about his reason for being there.

She waited.

"The truth is I can't get you out of my head. From the moment I saw you at the restaurant, I was like damn, that girl is fine as hell. I gotta get with her. And then you showed up at the party looking so damn perfect." He paused as he wondered if he should go on. He knew that if his boys could hear him now, they'd call him the pussy that he was acting like. But his boys weren't there, and they didn't know how he was feeling. If he was gonna say it, he might as well say it all. "When you shot me down at the party, that hurt, but my ego was too big to admit it. From that point, it seemed like you were haunting me and shit. I couldn't get you off my mind. I tried not thinking about you, but you're always there. I guess what I'm trying to say is that I like you and I want to get to know you better," he finally admitted. "I want to see what you're all about."

She stared at him. *He likes me?* That would be flattering if he was the guy she thought he was before she had become disillusioned at the party. Now he was just a guy who would do anything to get in her pants.

He waited for her response, but she gave none. She just watched him. "So, you're not going to say anything?" he asked. He hoped he hadn't just made an ass of himself by revealing what was going on inside him.

She hated that he was sitting there on her porch causing confusion in her life. A month ago, she thought this man could do no wrong. Yesterday, she still considered him the biggest jerk in the world. And today he was asking her to accept the fact that he liked her and wanted to get know her better. How could this one man cause so much chaos inside her head? "I don't get you," she finally responded. "I know you're a famous rapper and all. I was one of your biggest fans, but you can't treat me like crap one day and then say I like you the next. You can't drop by with roses and expect this to make it all better. I don't know what you want from me. I really don't. But if this is a nice, more civilized way to try to get me in your bed, it's still not going to happen."

She paused as she considered the fact that he had traveled all that way to apologize to her. It was more than she would expect out of anyone, especially him. She continued, "But if you are sincere in your apology, then I sincerely accept it. But that's as far as it goes." She was ready to go back inside now. This was too confusing for her to deal with. While part of her wanted to believe him, the other part of her wanted to guard her against any of his underlying intentions.

As she started walking back toward her door, he quickly stood up. "Randi."

She turned and looked up at him.

"I'm not trying to get in your pants." He hesitated then continued. "I was hoping we could go out sometime."

"Go out," she repeated softly, barely audible. "No, I don't think that would be a good idea."

He stepped closer to her, so close that he could see his reflection in her eyes. "And why not? I think I could learn a lot from you."

"But I don't think I could teach you anything."

"I'm sure you can." Their eyes connected. *So, this is how a good girl acts*, he thought. She was totally different from the women he ran into on a regular basis. He wondered if she knew how rare and special she was.

41

"So, what do you say? You be my teacher?"

He had a piece of lint on his silk shirt. She reached up and picked it off him while trying to ignore the smooth, brown skin of his exposed chest. He smelled delicious.

"Like I said, I'm sure I couldn't teach you anything." She slowly turned and started to walk away from him.

"Well, can I at least call you?"

"I don't think that would work either," she replied. "I've got to get back inside." She moved over to her front door.

He watched her. Although she said no, he didn't feel defeated. At least she wasn't slamming the door in his face. That was a big step in itself. He would give her some time to think about it, and he would try again.

He picked up the roses and handed them to her. "These are yours." His eyes twinkled. He felt a little more confident than before.

"Thanks." She took the flowers and smelled them as she looked up at him.

"Think about my proposition," he added.

She wasn't promising anything. "Good night." She opened her apartment door. She didn't know his true intentions, but she wasn't taking any chances. The draw to him was too strong, and she knew she could get herself in a whole lot of trouble fast if he wasn't on the up and up.

"Good night."

She left him standing outside.

Inside, she put the roses in a vase and arranged them neatly. Was he really interested in her? She wondered as she stared at the beautiful flowers. She carried them into her bedroom and set them on the TV stand. After she restarted the movie, she climbed into the bed and tried to get her mind off her visitor.

Her eyes traveled up to the roses. She sighed. She didn't know what to think about Animalistic. He had insulted her then traveled thousands of miles to say he was sorry. She knew she'd have to give him credit for that.

Her telephone rang. She rolled over and picked up the receiver. "Hello?"

"Hey." It was a man's voice.

"Who is this?" she asked.

"Anthony."

"Anthony who?"

"Anthony Talbert." He laughed. "Animalistic. I thought you were a big fan. You should know my real name," he teased.

She was a big fan, and she knew more than just his name. She knew his real name was Anthony Lamar Talbert, born November 21st, 1980 in Des Moines, Iowa. She knew that his favorite color was green, favorite food was Rib-eye steak and favorite sport was basketball. She also knew that he would rather have been a singer than a rapper, but he didn't feel that his voice was strong enough. What she didn't know was why he was pursuing her. "How'd you get my number?" She was curious.

"Your friend Kathy gave it to me when she gave me your address."

"Well, what is it that you want now?" He was persistent, she thought.

"Just wanted to say good night, that's all."

"Good night," she said.

"Hey, slow down. What's the hurry?"

"I thought you just wanted to say good night."

"I did, but you don't have to be in such a hurry to get me off the phone."

"I don't know what you want me to say."

"Tell me how I can get a date with you."

"You've got thousands of women who would give their right arm just to go out with you. Why are you interested in me?"

"Because you're different, and I want to get to know a nice girl. I've never met a woman like you before. You intrigue me."

"Before the party, I thought you were mister wonderful, but now I don't know who the real Anthony Talbert is. You don't respect women, and you don't even respect yourself."

"Respect myself? What do you mean?" Although he could admit that he hadn't always been on his best behavior when it came to women, he had never thought that he lacked self-respect.

"The way you treat women is not only disrespectful to them but to yourself as well. Have you ever thought about what these women really wanted from you? You think you're using them, but aren't they using you too? And don't you think you deserve better? Don't you think you deserve someone who is genuinely interested in you and not your status, your bling, your cheddar?"

He thought about her words. He used women and women used him. Hell, he knew he was fine, but he also knew that the sistahs he dealt with wouldn't give him a second look if he wasn't worth millions. Maybe she was right. Maybe he did deserve better. Maybe he deserved someone who *would* genuinely care about him and not his cheddar.

At twenty-four, he had slept with more women than he could remember. They didn't care about him, and he didn't care about them. He had blindly given himself to so many faceless strangers. Had he been so caught up in the whole rap game of fucking every beautiful woman who came along that

44

he had lost his respect for himself?

"Are you still there?" she asked, interrupting his thoughts.

"Yeah. I was just thinking about what you said." He sounded different, and she noticed the change in his mood. She wondered if her words would truly have an affect on him. She hoped they would. No matter how bad he had treated her and countless other women, he was a gifted rapper and she felt that he deserved better than he had given himself. "Good. Now, can I get some sleep?"

"Oh yeah, sure. Can I call you again?"

She was confused about how she felt about him. She was torn between the person who knew better than to give into a womanizer and the person who still thought he was the finest thing that walked on Earth. She chose to go with her good sense. "It's probably better if you didn't call me anymore."

"Okay. I'll call you this week," he said before he hung up. He didn't want to give her a chance to respond. He smiled at the thought of her as he maneuvered his rental car through the streets of Greensboro to get back to his hotel. He would be heading to Atlanta for a show the next night.

Chapter 5

A few nights later, after performing at another sold-out show, Anthony sat in his hotel room in Charlotte, North Carolina. Perched on the edge of his bed, he watched as the blonde's mouth went up and down on his swollen manhood. Her sparkling blue eyes stared up at him as she nursed vigorously on his shaft. Placing one hand on the back of her head, he pushed her down, encouraging her to take more of him into her mouth. Without hesitation, she did. He moaned as he felt the tip of his penis slipping down into her throat.

"Damn, baby." He marveled at her skill as he leaned back and closed his eyes.

This was not how he had planned his evening. After his show, Poppi, Li'l Bit and Cooney had tried to convince him to hang out with them at the after-party, but he decided he would stay in. Randi had been on his mind and he wanted to give her a call to see if she had considered his invitation to go out sometime.

Upon returning to his room, he found Tammy, the beautiful blonde who was now sucking his dick, lying butt-naked and spread-eagle in his king-sized bed. His first thought was to fuck her good and hard, but then he thought about Randi. He remembered what she had said about him respecting himself, so he decided to ask Tammy to leave. But as he watched her lying there playing with herself, he decided that pussy was pussy and no self-respecting man was gonna turn down pussy from some fine-ass freak who was finger-fucking herself right there in front him. Minutes later, he had his dick shoved down her throat.

Realizing that he was about to cum, Anthony pushed

his hips up as he tried to drive himself deeper down her throat. He pressed harder on her head and began to moan louder. She nursed relentlessly.

"Suck it, baby. Suck my dick," he growled. "Oh shit!" He cried out as he came in her mouth. Without missing a stroke, she continued sucking until he was completely drained.

A few hours later, Anthony again sat on the edge of his bed. This time, he was not consumed by pleasure. This time, confusion had taken over. He pushed his hand through his hair as he thought about what he done a few hours earlier. He looked over at Tammy. She was still asleep. He thought about the sex with her. Even though it was wild and uninhibited, even though it was just the way he liked it, he still wasn't satisfied. *What do I want?* he asked himself. What was he looking for? Whatever it was, he definitely hadn't found it between her legs.

He sighed as his mind quickly slipped back to Randi. *She did this,* he said to himself. She was the culprit. She had infiltrated his life, and she was the one causing all of his confusion. Now he knew what she meant when she stood outside his bedroom door at the after-party and told him that it was his loss. She knew she had something special that he couldn't find in just anyone.

Until Randi, he thought that all women, with the exception of his mother and aunts, were whores. He thought the only thing they were good for was sucking his dick and fucking him any way he wanted. But then there was Randi. In his twenty-four years of living, after sleeping with countless strangers, he had never met anyone like her before, and he didn't think he ever would again. His occupation didn't leave much room for finding a nice girl like her. Running into her at Deveraux's was pure luck. She was a one of a kind, and he had to have her. He couldn't let her just walk away from him.

Debra Clayton

He stood up, slipped on his boxers, and glanced at the clock by the bed. It was 3:17 a.m. Although he had promised to call, he suddenly had an urge to see her. Greensboro was only a two-hour drive from Charlotte. If he left within the next few minutes, he could be there before 6:00 a.m. He wasn't sure how she would to respond to him just showing up on her doorstep again, but he didn't care. He needed to see her.

Chapter 6

Randi rolled over in bed and looked at the roses. They were in full bloom. She thought about Animalistic and smiled. Maybe with the right supervision he could be reformed. She laughed softly at the mere idea that he could change. She had a better chance of becoming the president of the United States, and she hated politics.

She glanced at her alarm clock. It was 7:58 in the morning. She rolled back over onto her back and stretched. Her thoughts remained on Animalistic. She hated to admit it, but she liked him. She liked the fact that he came all that way to apologize to her. Although she still questioned his motives, she had to admit that she was impressed by his attempt to smooth things over. She also had to admit that she was a bit disappointed when he hadn't called like he said he would. Although she told him not to, she hoped that he would. She wanted a sign from him that there was some truth in the things he said to her the other day. A call would have made him more believable.

Her telephone rang. She rolled over on her stomach and picked up the receiver.

"Hello," she managed through a yawn.

"Wake up, sleepy head," a male voice said. She recognized it.

"Animalistic?"

"Anthony. Call me Anthony," he answered. She could hear the smile in his voice.

"You weren't expecting me to call?"

"No, not really," she answered as she tried not to reveal the slight joy she was feeling because he had called.

"What are you doing?" he asked. He was happy to hear her voice again. He could also tell that she wasn't pissed anymore.

"Trying to sleep." He didn't need to know that she was thinking about him, she thought.

"Sleeping in on a beautiful day like this?"

"I don't know how beautiful it is, but I do know how early it is."

"Get up and go to your front door," he directed.

"Why?"

"Do you always ask so many questions? Just go," he teased.

She slipped out of bed, wondering what he was up to. "Okay, okay, I'm going to the door." She complied as she walked down the hallway to her living room. "I'm at the front door."

"Now open it."

She opened it. "It's open."

"Go outside and look in the parking lot."

She walked out onto the porch and looked over the railing. What was she looking for? She didn't see anything special, just cars. "Okay, I'm outside," she informed him.

"Are you looking in the parking lot?"

"Yes." Her eyes continued to scan the lot. They stopped when she saw the door of a cream-colored BMW open. She didn't recognize the car. A man stepped out talking on a cell phone. She did recognize him. It was Anthony.

"What are you doing here?" she asked, still on the telephone.

"See, there you go again with all the questions." He chuckled. She wore her pajamas with the bunnies again. He would have to get her some Victoria's Secret.

Randi tried not to smile as he walked toward the

building. She tried to fight it, but she couldn't deny that she was happy to see him again.

"So, what are you doing here?" she repeated into the telephone.

"I came to take you to breakfast." He walked up the stairs. "You do eat breakfast, don't you?"

"Yes, I do." *Don't you smile at him when he gets over here,* she told herself. He looked as fine as ever. She bit her bottom lip as he approached.

They both hung up their telephones.

"Good. I'm starving." He towered over her. She looked so tiny, maybe a size six. A size medium in Victoria's Secret would probably fit her.

She looked up at him and forced her face to remain expressionless. "And you're so sure that I'm going to have breakfast with you."

"No, but I'm hopeful."

"I guess I do have to eat." She studied his face and saw that mischievous sparkle in his eyes as they smiled down at her.

"Shall we?" He held his hand out toward her apartment.

"Come on in." She led him inside. "Have a seat. I'll be ready in a minute."

He didn't sit. He walked around and surveyed the living room. She stopped and watched him.

"Go ahead. I promise I won't steal anything," he teased as he paused just long enough for her to leave the room.

After she disappeared down the hallway, he resumed his snooping. First, he flipped through her CDs, checking out her assortment of music. Her collection included artists such as Montell Jordan, Maxwell, Jagged Edge, Joe, Boys II Men, and R. Kelly. She was into love songs. After he flipped through a few more CDs, he found all four of his on the bottom. He smiled. He assumed that he was also on the bottom of her list. He would work on that.

Next, he moved over to her bookcase. She was an avid reader. He was impressed. The only people he knew who read were his mother and his older brother. He looked over the titles. She had a lot of how-to books. Most of them were about writing novels and screenplays. Next to them she had a collection of fiction. Some of her favorite authors included Terry McMillan, Marcus Major, Michael Baisden and Eric Jerome Dickey and Carl Weber. He thought about her sitting alone each night reading. *She must get lonely*. He would work on that as well.

He wondered if she was single. He had assumed that she was. Maybe she had a man stashed away somewhere. He scanned the room for signs of a significant other. There were none. He smiled. Maybe she had room for him. Maybe she didn't want room for him. Maybe he didn't care. She intrigued him, and he wanted her. All he had to do was figure out how to make her want him.

He walked over to her computer. On the desk lay some typewritten papers. He felt a little devilish as he picked up a sheet and read. It was a poem. He chuckled at the title, "Chocolate Lollipop," and assumed that she must have one hell of a sweet tooth to write about candy. Soon after he began to read, he realized that candy wasn't the object of her fixation.

> *Long, tapered fingers,*
> *Urging my body closer,*
> *Tongue dancing across my belly,*
> *Each stroke becoming bolder.*

The flickering of its tip,
Uncensored and savagely wild,
You lick and suck and taste me,
I'm your lollipop; you're my child.

How many licks will it take,
Before my walls surrender?
Just how desperate is your tongue,
To taste my creamy center?

My trembling chocolate thighs,
Swollen, honey-dipped hips,
Caramel folds of womanhood,
Each aching for your kiss.

"Damn." He licked his lips and continued to read.

"Excuse me." Randi snatched the poem away from him. "That's private."

He looked down at her tiny frame. "I'm sorry. I didn't know."

Embarrassed, she picked up the remaining papers off her desk and tossed them into a drawer.

"I didn't mean to pry," he said when she turned around and faced him.

"I didn't mean to snatch them from you," she explained. "It's just they're personal, that's all." She didn't want him to see that side of her. She didn't want anyone to see it. Although she was shy, it was in her writing that she became uninhibited and free, that she could explore many worlds and personalities. She didn't have to be the boring Randi Jacobs who led a mediocre existence. Instead, she could make love to strangers, live in exquisite mansions, and foil the enemy's plans. In her writings, she could be the seductress who drove men mad or the villain who couldn't be captured or a powerful executive ruling a corporate empire. Her writings gave her power to say what she couldn't express in the real world, allowing her to take chances with her heart. Anthony had stumbled into a part of her world that she wasn't ready to share yet.

"Did you write it? He wondered if she had chocolate thighs, honey-dipped hips, and caramel folds of womanhood.

"Yes," she admitted. She was sure her face was crimson by now.

"That was tight as hell." He smiled. "I mean you've got skills, girl. You should be writing my rhymes."

"Thanks." She smiled back nervously.

"Does that smile mean you're gonna let me take you to breakfast?"

"Yes."

"Good. Now, where can we find something to eat at around here?"

"There's an IHOP down the street if you like that."

"Sounds good to me." They walked over to the front door. "I think I passed one on the way over here."

Minutes later, they were in traffic.

"Is this yours?" she asked as she watched him maneuver the car through the busy streets.

"No, it's a rental."

She turned and looked out the window. He glanced at her, hands folded in her lap and legs crossed at the ankles. She even sat like a lady.

"So, what are you doing down in Greensboro again?" she asked as she continued to stare out the window.

"We had a show in Charlotte."

"But this is Greensboro, not Charlotte."

"I had you on my mind, so I decided to drive down and see you."

She looked at him. "You drove down here to see me?" She was surprised and flattered.

"It was only a two-hour drive. I drove down last night after the show and got a room." He knew he was scoring brownie points.

She smiled inwardly. He had made two trips to see her in less than a week. Maybe this guy was sincere. Maybe he was on the up and up. She turned back to her window.

"So, you're a writer, huh?"

"I try."

"You in school?"

"Can't afford it."

Hearing the sadness in her voice, he glanced over at her. "You need some help?"

Surprised by his statement, she looked over at him. Was he offering to help her? She smiled at his kind gesture but felt that she couldn't accept it. "No, I think I'll be all right," she said. "But thanks for the offer."

"Well, it's no problem for me. I'd be willing to help you out. No strings attached."

"Again, thanks but no thanks," she said as she turned to look out the window again. Although she knew that he had more money than she dared dream about, it didn't diminish the magnitude of his offer. He barely knew her and he was willing to help her with school. She'd definitely have to give him credit for that.

"Well, if you change your mind, let me know."

She nodded as her mind wandered to her ex-fiancé, Eric. He hated her writing. He hated anything she did outside of loving him, and he did whatever he could to discourage her.

But Anthony knew about dreams. He had followed his, and he was a star because of his relentless pursuit of it. Now he was not only encouraging her not to give up on hers, but he was offering to help her finance them as well. That meant a lot coming from him, because he knew the struggle.

"So, what else do you write about besides getting ate out?" He looked over at her and wondered if she wrote from experience.

She blushed. " 'Chocolate Lollipop' isn't about getting ate out. It's about love."

"Love." He chuckled. "Yeah, about a woman who loves to get ate out."

"You're hopeless." She smiled.

"No, you're hopeless. Here I thought you were this sweet, innocent young lady, but in reality you are a closet freak," he joked.

"I'm still a lady." She was starting to relax.

He looked over at her. "I know you are."

Twenty minutes later, they entered the restaurant and waited to be seated. When the hostess approached them, she couldn't take her eyes off Anthony. Randi wasn't sure if it was because she recognized him or because he was so fine.

"Smoking or non-smoking?" the hostess asked as she studied his face.

"Baby?" He looked at Randi.

She shook her head.

"Non-smoking," he informed the hostess.

"Follow me."

He put his hand on the small of Randi's back as the hostess led them to their table.

They took their seats and the hostess handed them their menus.

"Don't I know you from somewhere?" the woman finally asked.

"No, I don't think so. I'm not from around here." He looked at Randi and smiled.

"Are you sure? You look—" Her mouth dropped open. "I know you. You're that rapper, Animalistic. My kids love you."

Anthony smiled. "That's me."

"Can I get your autograph for them?"

"Sure. What do you want me to sign?" he asked as he watched Randi and wondered what she was thinking. She wore no expression.

The hostess handed him a menu to sign.

"What's your kids' names?"

"Jessica and Corey."

He scribbled a message to the kids and signed his name.

"Thank you." She smiled. "My babies are going to hug my neck for this."

"Not a problem." After the hostess left, he looked at Randi. "Sorry about that."

"No problem. You just made two kids' day." She smiled but quickly looked down at her menu when he tried to make eye contact.

Seconds later, the waitress hurried over. She looked as if she needed a bib to catch her drool.

"Hello," she said in the sexiest voice she could find. She ignored Randi.

"Good morning." He looked up at her.

"Are you ready to order?" She stooped down beside him.

"You ready, baby?" he asked Randi.

"Yes." She ordered three eggs with pancakes, no meat.

57

He ordered the Breakfast Sampler. After the waitress wrote their order, she bent over to give him a full view of her large, round breasts.

"Do you see anything else that you'd like to have?" She smiled seductively.

Even after what she witnessed at the party, Randi still found it hard to believe that women acted this way toward a complete stranger.

Embarrassed by her disrespect for his date, Anthony gently took hold of the waitress's elbow. "I don't mean to be rude, but if you can't have a little more self-control, then maybe I need to speak with your manager about getting another server." His voice was stern but not angry.

The waitress stopped smiling and stood up. She looked down at Anthony. "Well, excuse me," she said, placing her had on her hip. She looked at Randi, rolled her eyes then walked off.

Randi was impressed with the way he handled the situation. Maybe he had been listening to her. Maybe he wasn't the same guy she met over a month ago. "You pissed her off," she said.

"She'll survive." He chuckled.

"You may have just lost a record sale."

"Maybe so, but I didn't drive up here to talk about her. I came here to talk about us."

"Us," she repeated. What was he talking about? There was no "us."

"Yeah, us. You, me, us."

The waitress returned with their drinks. He took a sip of his tea then continued. "You don't know this, but from the first time we met, you have done nothing but cause me confusion." He smiled as he reached for a packet of sugar and opened it.

"Me?" She laughed. "You're the one causing all the confusion. One minute you got me thinking you're the biggest jerk in the country and the next minute—" She paused.

"And the next?" He urged her to continue.

"And the next minute I'm second-guessing my opinion of you. Now you're acting more like the guy I wanted to meet," she admitted as she watched him add the sugar to his tea and stir it.

He chuckled. "Well, you can credit yourself for getting a brotha to change."

"Oh really? And why's that?" she asked after taking a sip of her water. She was happy to see that she had a positive influence on him. She hoped that he was sincere.

"Well, since I met you, jumping into bed with all these different women isn't as fulfilling as it once was."

"I'm sorry," she apologized. So, he was still a ho, she thought. Well, at least he was honest about it. She gave him points for that.

"Don't be." He tasted his tea again. "I've just realized that something's been missing from my life."

"Really, what?"

"A good woman to make me leave these hoes alone."

"Hoes?" She frowned at the term he used.

Realizing that he may have offended her, he quickly chose another word. "Women." He smiled apologetically.

She smiled back. At least he was trying.

"You see," he continued, "after our last conversation, I realized that you were right. I do deserve better. These chicks out here don't dig me for me. They try to get at me because I'm Animalistic. They don't know who the hell Anthony Lamar Talbert is, and they don't want to know. They're just there because of the fame. And I admit that was okay before. That is, until I met you. Those girls satisfied my ego, but they did nothing for my soul."

"Wow," she said. "Good for you." She was proud of him for wanting more than just a warm body.

"Well, that brings me to my point."

"And what point is that?"

"Well, since I'm trying to be a respectable man, I'm looking for a nice, respectable young lady to put on my arm."

"And?"

"And I wanted to see if you were interested in accepting that role."

"You're not serious, are you?"

The waitress returned with their food. "Can I get you anything else?" she asked. She was still smarting from Anthony's last remark to her.

"No," they answered.

"And why not?" he asked after the waitress left.

"Because you're Animalistic. You're a big name rapper. You could date anyone. Why would you want to see someone like me?"

"Not someone *like* you. You," he said as he poured ketchup on his eggs.

"But why me?"

"Because you're Randi Jacobs and I like you."

"But I'm a nobody. You could be dating Alicia Keys or Ashanti or somebody like them."

After swallowing a mouthful of eggs, he responded. "First of all, Alicia and Ashanti are cool peeps, but they're not what I'm looking for. Second of all, and most important, you, Randi Jacobs, are not a nobody. You're a future writer that's gonna knock this world on its ass. You are also a self-respecting, take no shit, beautiful woman that put this nigga in his place. You are the first and only woman that has gotten this brotha to stop and take a look at himself and the way he's living. Besides that, I think you're cute as hell. Damn, girl, you make a nigga wish he could sing so he could serenade you and shit."

"Stop it." She blushed.

"So, what do you say?"

"Anthony," she managed when she finally stopped smiling. "I am flattered. Truly, I am, but I can't see you like that."

"And why not? You got a man?"

"No," she admitted.

"The niggas here must be crazy as hell."

"Why do you say that?" she asked as she took a bite of her pancakes.

"To let you run around here single."

"Oh." She smiled.

"So, why are you single? Why don't you have a man?"

Her smile slowly melted away as she pulled her eyes away from him and looked down at her plate.

He saw the change in her demeanor and wondered if he had opened a wound. "Hey, what's up? You okay?" He touched her hand.

She looked up at him as she thought about Eric. "I'm okay," she whispered, trying not to reveal her feelings.

Now he was really curious. He wanted to know what was causing the heartbroken look she wore on her face. "What is it?" he pried.

It had been a year since she had seen Eric, but the memories of what he did to her still brought her pain. They had met during their junior year in high school. He was an all-around jock. The guys envied him because he could pull the honeys, while all the girls fought to be the one on his arm. Although Randi thought he was a dream just like all the other girls, she was consumed with her writing and had little interest

61

in dating. Eric, however, decided that Randi was the one girl he wanted to sport on his arm. They started dating and quickly became the envy of the school. Everyone thought they were the perfect couple.

If only they knew, Randi thought as she remembered the relationship. They started off as all normal couples do. He treated her very well, but shortly after she gave him her virginity, he became possessive. He started demanding that she spend all her free time with him. He wanted her to give up her friends and her dreams of going to college for him. When she refused, he grabbed her, slammed her up against the wall, and choked her until she gave in. She knew that she should have walked away then, but he promised that he would never hurt her again, so she stayed. A few days later, he dropped to his knees and asked her to marry him. Without hesitation, she accepted.

A year went by and Eric had kept his word. He never physically abused her again until one fateful night. That night, Randi received a call from a woman saying that she was pregnant by Eric. Devastated, she immediately confronted him. Without hesitation, he admitted that he had a baby on the way and that she'd better get ready to be a stepmother to it. It was then that she decided that she could do better. She told him that she was leaving him. Eric, however, refused to let her walk away so easily. After several futile attempts to get her to stay, he went mad. He began beating her, promising her that if he couldn't have her, then nobody would.

Randi swallowed hard as she remembered how close she came to dying that night.

"Hey," Anthony said as he squeezed her hand. He could tell by the expression on her face that she was no longer with him.

Realizing that she must have slipped away somewhere,

Randi quickly apologized. "I'm sorry."

"Talk to me," he whispered.

She slowly pulled her hand from underneath his. "I'm sorry. I can't." It was too painful to talk about, and too much to share with him so soon. She looked down at her partially eaten breakfast.

"He must have been some asshole," he said with a little attitude.

She looked back up at him and gave a slight smile to his remark. "Yeah, he was."

"Did he hit you?"

"Can we not talk about this?"

Anthony took her response as a yes to his question, *Coward*, he thought. Any man that would lay his hands on a woman was a coward. "Sure." He forced a smile. He wished he could track this guy down and beat the hell out of him, but Randi wanted to change the subject, so he let it go. "Now, let's get back to talking about you and me."

"There is no you and me."

"Not yet, but there will be." He winked.

She smiled at the thought of them dating. It had been over a year since she had seen anyone. The fear of getting into another relationship like the one she had with Eric paralyzed her. She didn't trust her judgment when it came to men, so she pretty much kept them at bay.

But Anthony was different. The idea of being his girl was flattering. Who wouldn't want to date him? But then she thought about his lifestyle. With all the traveling and all the groupies and all the temptations, how could a man like him be faithful to a woman like her? He had been with hundreds of experienced women, while she had only been with one man. She didn't know if she even knew how to please a regular man, and she definitely knew that she couldn't please a man like Anthony who had been with the best. She remembered when they were at the hotel and he asked her if she was gonna suck his dick. Although it was insulting when he said it, it was slightly funny now. He was expecting her to suck his dick, and she didn't even know how to give a blow-job. *Boy, he would have been disappointed,* she thought.

Anthony glanced at his watch. It was getting late and he had to get on the road. "Well, I gotta get going. I've got two hours to get back to the hotel before they take off."

Disappointed, Randi picked up her purse. "So, you're ready to go?"

"Not really, but I gotta. I can't miss the rest of my tour." He stood up. "You gonna get that?" he asked, referring to the check.

Randi looked up at him, but before she could respond, he laughed. "Just kidding."

He picked up the check, paid the bill and they left.

When they arrived at her apartment building, she looked over at him after he parked the car. The idea of being his girl was enticing, but also ridiculous. She knew she couldn't even consider it. With her issues with trust and his issues with women, they wouldn't make it past the first day. She'd be accusing him of cheating before the ink dried on their agreement. Still, she was flattered that a rap star—not just any rap star, but superstar Animalistic—had wanted to date her. This was one that she would have to tell her grandkids about one day. She smiled at the thought.

Anthony watched her smile. He wondered what she was thinking about. He hoped that she was considering his proposition. Their eyes met. He wanted to lean over and taste her soft smile. For the first time in years, he had found someone that he was willing to throw out all the rules for. His no kissing policy was voided when it came to Randi. Not only would he kiss her, he'd even eat the hell out of her. *Whoa, boy,* he told himself. He was way too far ahead of himself. Maybe he should wait until she agreed to a second date before he started picking a china pattern. He chuckled at his own thoughts. *China patterns, where in the hell did that come from?* They weren't getting married; he was just bucking for another date.

"I better let you go," she finally said.

"I guess I should be hitting the road. Stay right there." He jumped out of the car, hurried to her side, opened her door, and helped her out.

"And you said you didn't know how to treat a woman like a lady," she teased.

"You make me wanna be a better man." He closed the door and walked her to her apartment.

"Thank you for breakfast. It was nice." She looked up at him.

"Thank you," he said, "for obliging me." He kissed hand.

Those lips, Randi thought, were softer than they looked, and they looked featherbed soft.

"I do want to see you again, Randi," he informed her.

"That would be nice, but I told you—"

"Shhh," he whispered, placing his finger on her lips. "I'm not proposing marriage, just another date."

"We'll see."

He smiled down at her. "Yes, we will."

She turned to open the door and he stopped her. "May I?" He gestured for her keys. She handed them to him. He opened the door then gave them back to her.

"Thank you." She hesitated in the doorway.

"Good bye, Miss Randi Jacobs."

"Good bye, Anthony." She smiled.

He returned to his car. *You don't know it yet, Miss Jacobs, but you're gonna have a hard time getting rid of me.*

Chapter 7

When he got back to his hotel in Charlotte, the guys were already coming out and loading the bus. One of the other rappers known as Li'l Bit, saw him and came to meet him.

"Hey, dawg, where've you been?" Li'l Bit asked.

"I had some business to take care of."

They walked over to where the other guys were.

"Man, you missed a phat-ass party last night."

"Was it off the chain?"

"Hell yeah, man, and the pussy . . . The pussy was so damn fine it was ridiculous."

"Well, I didn't do too bad myself. Got back to my room last night and there was this chick waiting for me butt-ass naked," he said with a laugh.

"Nigga, you ain't even gotta go out looking for the pussy. The pussy just come to you."

"Well, you know it, nigga." He looked at his watch then walked over to the side of the bus and handed the driver his bags.

"I ain't mad at you, dawg," Li'l bit said with a laugh. "Now, check this out. These chicks were asking for you last night. I told them you'd be rolling down to Raleigh, so they gonna drive down to party with us tonight after the show."

"Good looking out."

"No problem."

Poppi walked over to them as they headed into the hotel so Anthony could return his car keys. Poppi was one of the older rappers. He was married and had two kids. While Anthony wanted to hide his feelings for Randi from the other guys, he felt it was safe to tell Poppi how she was getting under his skin. He knew Poppi wouldn't ride him for catching feelings for this girl.

"So, where were you this morning?" Poppi asked. "Did you go see that girl?"

"Yeah, man. I saw her," he admitted.

"Who? That ho you fucked last night?" Li'l Bit asked.

"What ho?" Poppi asked, a little confused.

"That nigga had some bitch waiting for him butt naked when he got back to his room last night."

"Randi?" Poppi asked.

"No, not Randi," Anthony answered.

"Did you fuck her?"

"Hell yeah, he fucked her. That nigga ain't married. He ain't got no muthafucking ring on his finger," Li'l Bit answered.

"Nigga, I ain't talking to you. I'm talking to Anthony. Did you fuck her?"

"Yo, man, don't jump on my back about this shit."

"I guess that means you did." Poppi looked at him with disappointment. "Nigga, you need help."

"Muthafucka, don't judge me. What am I supposed to do, give up pussy cold turkey for some chick?" Anthony asked as he tried to defend himself. "Like Li'l Bit said, I ain't got no muthafucking ring on my finger."

"Hell, I didn't know she was just some chick. I thought you were feeling this girl. I guess I was wrong. I guess she's just another piece of ass to you."

"Nigga, get outta my face. Go home to your muthafucking wife!"

"Don't worry, nigga, I will," he said as he walked off, shaking his head.

"Yo, Anthony, don't worry about that nigga." Li'l Bit laughed. "He so whipped that I could have sworn that I smelled his wife's pussy when he walked by."

"I'm not." He returned his keys to the girl at the front desk and she gave him a receipt. Who in the hell did Poppi think he was? Sure, he liked Randi. He liked her a lot, but was he supposed to stop living just because he liked her? They hadn't made a commitment to each other. Hell, he didn't even know how she felt about him. He made up his mind that until he knew that he and Randi had something solid, he was gonna continue to live it up.

Later that night, after the concert, Anthony and his boys sat in the VIP room of Club Afterthoughts. He quietly sipped on a glass of Cristal as he checked out the local talent. Only the finest women were allowed back in the VIP room. And from the looks of it, Raleigh, North Carolina, had no shortage of beautiful women. Perfectly applied makeup, not a hair out of place hairdos, professionally manicured fingers and toes, and the tightest, tiniest, most expensive outfits wrapped around young, taut bodies were the order of the day. He enjoyed watching his boys as they slapped, grabbed and groped perfectly shaped asses. The sistahs giggled nervously as they pretended not to be offended by the guys' roaming hands and vulgar language. *Anything to get with a baller,* Anthony thought.

He had seen this scene play out in front of him hundreds of times. The only difference now was that normally he would have been grabbing handfuls of tits and ass too. His original plans were to go out, get drunk and fuck some little honey all night long, but Poppi had ruined that for him.

He couldn't forget about the conversation they had earlier that morning. He remembered calling Randi "some chick." That was a mistake. Randi was more than just some chick, and he knew it. He knew why Poppi was giving him such a hard time. If he was gonna pursue Randi, then he had to do it right. He had to stop fucking every woman that cocked her legs open in front of him.

He knew it would be hard, but if Poppi could be happily married and still be in this business, then Anthony could at least try to control his hormones. He chuckled to himself as he thought about giving up all the pussy for a woman he wasn't sure was even feeling him. Caught up in his thoughts, he didn't notice the leggy beauty who had approached him.

"Hi, Animalistic," she said.

He looked at her. She wore a red form-fitting sequined mini-dress that revealed her perfect 36-26-36 figure. Her honey blonde hair tumbled down her bare shoulders, accenting her flawless, hazel-brown complexion. She was definitely the type of woman who could get him into trouble. He stood up and smiled. "Yeah, what's up?"

"I've been subtly trying to get your attention all night, but you appear to be immune to my charm." She smiled seductively.

"I'm sorry. My mind was somewhere else," he said as he sipped his drink and studied her full, inviting lips. He was sure she could suck a mean dick.

"I noticed, so I decided to try a more direct approach." Stepping closer to him, she placed her hand on his chest. "How about you buy me a drink and keep me company?"

"What's your name?"

"Misha Taylor." She smiled.

"I'll tell you what, Misha," he said, looking around for a waitress. When one looked his way, he signaled for her to come over.

She quickly responded. "Yes, sir."

"How about bringing another bottle of Cristal for Miss Misha Taylor?" he said.

The waitress nodded and hurried off.

"Cristal." Misha smiled. "My favorite."

"My pleasure," Anthony replied. "Do enjoy," he said as he set down his glass and sauntered away. He smiled as he thought about how easy it was to walk away. Maybe leaving all the women alone wasn't gonna be as hard as he initially thought. He was sure that a woman like Randi was worth the sacrifice. Suddenly, he felt the urge to call her.

To avoid causing a disturbance, he slipped out the back of the club and went back to his hotel room. Once inside his suite, he made himself a drink and debated whether to call her. He glanced at his watch. It was after midnight. Maybe she would still be up; maybe she was sound asleep. Either way, he had to talk to her.

After he put down his drink, he pulled out his cell and dialed her number. The telephone rang three times then the machine picked up. *Where the hell is she this time of night?* he asked himself as he waited for the beep.

"Hey, Randi, it's me, Anthony. I was just—"

"Hello," Randi said.

"Hey," he said again. "I was just leaving a message. I thought you weren't home."

"I just got in from work." She was surprised but happy to hear from him so soon. "So, what's going on?" She sat down on her couch, tucking one leg under her.

He walked over to the couch and sat down. "Just got in."

"So, did you make it back in time?"

"Yep." He smiled as he leaned back on the couch.

"No after-party?" She was curious.

"Actually, I went out for a little while, but I got to

thinking about you, so I left early."

"I hope thinking about me didn't ruin it for you."

"Naw, I wasn't really feeling the party anyway."

"You're not sick, are you?"

"No, not sick. I just needed to chill a little. Performing every night is stressful."

"I'm sure. So, when do you come off tour?"

"We've got two weeks to go."

Randi stood up and went into her bathroom. "Well, that's not too far away. Maybe you'll be able to get some rest."

"Hardly. Right after that I gotta go to New York to shoot a video for my new single."

She turned on the water in the bathtub. He could hear it.

"What are you doing?" he asked.

"Running my bath water."

"You want some company?" he teased as he pictured her naked in a hot tub of water. He licked his lips.

"Sure, come on in." She walked into her bedroom and sat on her bed.

"You wouldn't be saying that if I was right there." He chuckled.

"You're right. I wouldn't. There is something about you being over a hundred miles away that gives me a sense of security." She laughed.

He leaned forward on the couch. "Check this out. In two weeks, I'll be in New York shooting my video. How 'bout I fly down after the shoot? We could have a late date after you get off from work."

She smiled at the thought of him flying back down to see her again. "That would be nice."

"Is that a yes?"

"Yeah, why not?" She unbuttoned her blouse.

"What time should I pick you up?" He tried to hide his excitement.

"Ten o'clock. Is that okay?"

"Ten's great."

"Well, I better get off the telephone before my water turns cold." She slipped off her shoes.

"Okay, I'll let you go."

"Good night." She unfastened her skirt and let it fall to the floor.

"Good night." He hung up his cell and walked over to the bar. After he finished his drink, he went into his bedroom. He wanted to impress her. It couldn't be an ordinary date. He had to make that night special.

Randi slipped off her stockings, bra and panties then lowered herself into the hot bath water. It felt good against her skin. "Mr. Anthony Talbert," she whispered. He was coming back to see her again. She smiled. She couldn't wait to tell Kathy. She closed her eyes and slid deeper into the tub until the water rose up to her neck.

Chapter 8

The next morning while the fellas were boarding the tour bus, Anthony pulled Poppi to the side. "Yo, man, can I holla at you for a minute?" he asked.

Poppi handed the driver his bags and turned to look at Anthony. "Yeah, man. What's up?"

"Yo, man, I um . . . " He looked down at Poppi. "I wanted to apologize to you about yesterday."

Poppi smiled. "No problem, nigga. I was way out of line."

"No, man, you weren't. I know what you were trying to say, and I appreciate you trying to look out for a young brotha like me."

"No prob."

"Oh, and for the record, Randi's not just some chick. I like her, man. I like her a lot, and I really wanna see what can happen with her, you know?"

"Yeah, I know."

"So tell me, man. How do you do it? How do you stay faithful with all these hoes running around here chasing after us?"

"I just remember what I have at home. You know Cindy and the kids are all I got. I'm not willing to risk it for some chick who just wants to get fucked by a superstar."

"Is it always that easy for you, man?"

"Hell no. You see these chicks out here. Fine as hell and probably could fuck my brains out."

Anthony laughed. "They sure can."

"I get tempted, nigga, but when I think about some other nigga fucking Cindy, I say hell no. When I think about some other nigga living in my house and my kids calling him

Daddy, I say hell no. So, when those hoes try to get with me, I say hell no."

"Nigga, you crazy." Anthony chuckled.

"But seriously, man, if you get with Randi and she gets your heart, man, and then you start thinking about fucking up, you think about her being with somebody else, giving your loving to someone else. Then when these hoes try to get with you, you'll be able to say hell no too."

"That's some powerful shit, man."

"Hey, pussy is a powerful thing, but love is more powerful. When you fall in love, you'll know what I'm talking about."

"Thanks, man."

"So, you think Randi is the one for you?"

"I don't know, man, but I'll tell you what." He paused. "I can't get her outta my damn head."

"That's the way it's supposed to be, nigga." Poppi laughed.

Later that week, Randi and Kathy met at the mall so Randi could buy a new outfit for her date with Anthony.

"How about this one?" Kathy asked as she held up a red strapless mini-dress.

Randi frowned. "That's too suggestive."

"Oh really? And what does it suggest?"

"It suggests that he jump my bones."

"And that's a problem because . . . "

"I don't want him jumping my bones."

"Why the hell not? Lord knows you could use some dick by now. You haven't had a good fuck since—" She stopped herself.

"Since when?" Randi asked with a hurt look in her

eyes. "Since Eric raped me."

"Randi, I'm sorry," Kathy quickly apologized. "I didn't mean that. Baby, you know I didn't mean that."

"Maybe you're right."

"No, no I'm not. I'm stupid, stupid, stupid. Forget everything I just said and listen to me now. What Eric did to you was fucked up, but that was over a year ago, baby. You don't deserve to be locked up. He does."

"I just can't do this."

"Yes, you can, baby. Anthony seems like a great guy. He offered to help with school. He wants to support your dream. He's nothing like Eric."

"I know, but—"

"No buts. Anthony obviously wants to be with you, and you've been loving him from so far away. Now it's your time to love him up close. Don't let Eric fuck this up for you. You hear me?"

"It's not just about the rape, Kathy. I gave up everything for him. My friends and family, my dreams, and then I find out he's having a baby with someone else. After that, how could I trust somebody like Anthony, who lives so far away, surrounded by beautiful women all the time? How do I trust somebody like that? And what about the fact that I haven't been with anyone since the rape? What if we do make it to that level and he wants to make love to me? What if I can't?"

"I know you're scared, baby, but you just have to take it slow. Take your time and take it slow. And if you do make it to that level and you're still scared, then tell him. Tell him what you've been through, and if he really cares for you, he'll understand and you two can get help. There are things that you can do to get through this. Just stop running so damn much, okay?"

Randi nodded.

"Good. Now that we got the inside straight, let's work on the outside." She reached over and picked up a cream-colored suit. "How about this? It doesn't say *jump my bones.* It says *I'm a lady, so treat me like one.* What do you think?"

"Yeah, that's nice." She smiled softly.

"Good, now come here." Kathy pulled Randi to her and hugged her tightly. "You can do this, Randi. I know you can."

Chapter 9

A week later, after her shift was over, Randi rushed home to get dressed for her date. She washed her hair in the shower and allowed it to air dry. It poured down her shoulders into tiny curls. She slipped on the cream-colored pantsuit that she had purchased. It fell gently over her curves. As she applied her makeup, she thought about the conversation she had had with her friend. Kathy was right. She could do this. After all, it was only a date. He hadn't proposed. And although she hadn't convinced herself that she would continue seeing him after their date, she couldn't deny that she was feeling him.

Take it slow, Randi, she told herself. *Take it really slow. Don't get caught up in his fame and his money. You're going out with Anthony Talbert, not Animalistic.* Just as she put on the last touches of her makeup, there was a knock at the door. She looked at her watch. It was 10:00 exactly. He was punctual, and she liked that.

As she headed for the door, her heart started to race. She was both nervous and excited about seeing him again. *Calm down,* she told herself. She stood at the door a second before she opened it. *It's only a date,* she told herself. *It's only a little date.* "Then why are you so damn scared?" she whispered. She took a deep breath then opened the door.

Anthony stood there so tall and commanding. He was beautiful. He wore a tan, super-soft silk and cashmere Armani suit. He didn't look like a rapper; he looked more like a male model. His eyes lit up when he saw her. He smiled approvingly. They stared at each other in silence for a second or two.

"You look beautiful," he said as he started to get nervous.

"Thank you." She blushed. "You look very nice too."

"Oh, um, these are for you." He handed her a bouquet of white roses.

"Thank you. They're beautiful." She took them and stepped back for him to enter. "Let me put these in some water and I'll be ready to go."

He watched her as she went into the kitchen. Her suit fit her perfectly, accentuating her waist and hips. *Damn,* he said to himself. He could see his confirmed bachelorhood going down the drain with this girl, and he didn't mind.

Neither one of them said a word as they headed for the car. Once they slipped inside, Randi finally spoke. "Is something wrong? You're quiet."

He looked over at her. "You make me nervous," he admitted.

"Nervous. Why?" She was surprised.

"Not counting breakfast, it's been six years since I've been on a date," he explained as they pulled off into the night.

"Six years," Randi repeated.

"And the fact that you're so damn perfect scares me. I don't want to fu—I mean screw this up."

"Thanks, but I'm hardly perfect."

"What's wrong with you then? From where I'm sitting, you look perfect to me." He looked over at her.

She blushed again. Twice in one night, that was a record. "I don't cook."

"We'll work on that." He smiled and turned his eyes back to the road. "I've made reservations for us, so I hope you're hungry."

"I did eat a little something at work."

"You didn't think I would take you out and not feed you, did you?" He chuckled and began to loosen up.

"It wouldn't be the first time." She smiled.

"Really? Then you've been going out with the wrong guys. You're with the right one now."

Randi became puzzled when he turned into the parking lot of a small, independent airport.

"Hold on." He got out of the car and ran over to a man who stood in the parking lot smoking a cigarette.

Randi watched as they exchanged a few words. The man threw his cigarette down and stepped on it before he climbed into a small Beech Jet 400. Anthony ran back over to the car and opened her door.

She got out. "What's going on?" she asked.

After he closed the door behind her, he slipped his hand into hers and led her over to the jet.

"You aren't afraid of flying, are you?" he asked. "I know it's small, but it's safe."

"No, but what are you doing?"

"We've got dinner reservations in one hour in Atlanta."

"Atlanta? Are you serious?"

"Yep." He started up the stairs of the jet and pulled her along.

She pulled back. "But I—"

He stopped and turned around to face her. "What's wrong?"

"Are, are we really doing this? Are we really flying to Atlanta for dinner?"

"Yes, ma'am."

"But this is so unreal. It's like something out of a movie."

"Well, it's real, baby. It's just one of the perks of dating a rap star, so get used to being treated like a princess."

"I can't believe this is happening." She smiled.

"Are you impressed?"

"Yes."

"Good. So, are we doing this?"

"Yeah." She nodded as her smile grew bigger. "Yes, yes, we're doing this."

"Ladies first." He stepped back and held his hand out so she could go up.

They climbed into the small aircraft. Although Randi had flown before, she had never been inside a private jet. She looked around. It was small and cozy. The interior was a pale, relaxing color from the walls to the carpet to the soft leather captain's chairs that surrounded a small table. The plane included a small refrigerator and a flat-screen TV to keep passengers fed and entertained during their flight.

Randi smiled as she took in all of this. This was some fancy lifestyle, she thought as she took a seat in one of the captain's chairs. The comfortable seat was so large that it almost swallowed her tiny frame. Anthony sat down across from her.

"You want something to drink?" he asked.

"No, thank you." She looked around the plane then back at him. "This is really, really nice."

"This is what I flew down here to see you in," he said.

"Really? I guess you fly a lot."

"Not really. We travel on our bus when we're doing concerts, but for special occasions like this, I rent a jet."

"This is a special occasion?" she asked.

"This is our first official date."

"Oh. You've gone through a lot of trouble for this date."

"It's worth the trouble, and I hope there's many more."

She smiled nervously as she watched him. He was so charming and so handsome and so rich. She had to keep reminding herself why she couldn't just drop her defenses and go for it. "Maybe."

The jet ride was smooth and quick. After they landed, they got into another car and drove to the restaurant, which appeared to be closed. There were only two cars in the parking lot, and the building appeared almost completely dark.

"We must be too late. They look closed," she said.

"Let's hope not." He got out of the car, walked over to her side, and opened her door.

When they reached the restaurant, the front door was unlocked. They stepped inside. The restaurant was quiet and empty. In one of the corners was a small round table with a candle flickering in the center. It was set for two. Anthony put his hand on the small of her back and guided her through the room to the table. He pulled the chair out for her and she sat down then took his seat across from her.

"You planned this?" she whispered.

He nodded with a smile.

A second later, a waiter came out and filled their water glasses. He gave them menus and took their drink orders. Randi watched Anthony while he looked over his menu. She didn't know what to think. This guy was definitely trying to sweep her off her feet, and he wasn't doing a bad job of it.

He looked up and caught her watching him. "What's wrong?" he asked.

"I just can't get over tonight. I can't believe you did all this." The candlelight danced across her face. She was smiling.

"I can't believe you did all this," he whispered.

"What?" She didn't understand.

The waiter reappeared with their drinks and took their orders.

"What did I do?" she asked after the waiter left.

Their eyes met. "You knocked me off my feet. I'm just trying to return the favor."

Girl, if you blush one more time I'm going to pinch you, she told herself as she felt herself turning red again.

"This place is beautiful," she said as she looked around.

"You like it?"

"Yeah, I do." She paused. "It must be really nice to be able to afford to do all this."

"It is. Money is great. Success is wonderful. But you know, at the end of the day, it doesn't matter how much money or fame you have. At the end of the day, when the fans have gone home and the coliseums are closed, when the groupies have gotten what they wanted and you go home, you're alone."

"So, you get lonely?" She never thought about that side of fame.

"Yeah, I get lonely sometimes."

"I just assumed that with people constantly clamoring after you, you wouldn't get lonely."

"What about you? You ever get lonely?" he asked.

"Yeah, a lot."

"Two lonely hearts in search of love, meet finally face to face."

"The happiness and joy I'd lost, I've found in your embrace." She finished the line for him.

Impressed, he smiled. " 'The Longest Night' by Mr. Montell Jordan. You're good."

"Well, I've been a fan of Montell's for about as long as I've been a fan of yours."

"Well, it's a good thing I met you before he did."

"Actually, I know more about you than Montell."

"Well, impress me then."

"Okay. Let's see. You were born Anthony Lamar Talbert to a Paul and Sylvia Talbert in Des Moines, Iowa. You are the youngest of two kids. You have an older brother named Michael. Although you would rather be singing, you broke into the rap industry in 1998 when you were only eighteen. Your first CD was *Now Hear This,* which went platinum. In 2000, you released *All I Need* and then in 2002 you released *This Way Us,* both of which went multiplatinum. In 2004, you released *A Lover and a Fighter,* which has also reached multi-platinum status. Of all your songs, 'You Know How We Do' is your favorite, and your least favorite is 'Roll With Me.' So, how am I doing?"

"That was an impressive body of knowledge. And I mean impressive body."

"Why, thank you." She smiled and nodded.

"You know, I'm looking at you and I'm wondering why you listen to my music. The way you look, the way you talk, the way you carry yourself, it's hard to believe that you listen to hip-hop."

"I know. I get that a lot. The thing that draws me to hip-hop is the lyrics. Since I'm a writer, words are very important to me, and some of the hip-hop songs have the most incredible lyrics. I mean, some rappers have got crazy skills when it comes to their lyrics. Rappers like Tupac, Fabolous, Lloyd Banks, Eminem, and of course yourself. Your lyrics are nasty."

"Nasty. I like that." He took a sip of his wine. "So, are you enjoying yourself so far?"

"I am."

"So, this isn't the worst date you've ever been on?"

"Hardly. My worst date . . . " She shook her head.

"Tell me about it."

She watched his smile as she thought it over. "When I was about seventeen, this guy took me to his house and we watched television in his living room."

"And?"

"His parents were in the other room watching porn and getting high. They asked us if we wanted to join them. He said yeah and I said no, then I ran for the nearest exit."

By the time she finished, he was laughing out loud. "Are you serious?"

"As a heart attack."

He took a sip of his wine, sat back and watched her. She needed to laugh more often.

"So, what about you? What was your worst date?" he asked.

He thought for a moment. The waiter returned with their food.

"I never really had a bad date, but I did have a bad morning after."

"Tell me." She leaned forward.

"I was about sixteen and I took this girl out. We slept together on our first date. The next morning when I woke up, I was burning," he confessed.

"Eeww." She made a face. She was surprised by his honesty.

"From that point on, I've always used protection." He cut into his steak.

"At least you learned something from it," she teased as she took a bite of her salmon. "So, have you ever had your heart broken?"

"Never," he said after swallowing.

"I guess that would mean that you've never been in

85

love before." She watched for his response.

He looked up from his food. "Never." He waited to see what she was going to say.

"Man. So, nobody's ever gotten to you, huh?"

He looked her in her eyes. "You get to me."

She stared back. *You get to me,* she thought. She finally tore her eyes away and focused on her food.

"I didn't mean to make you uncomfortable." He sensed her uneasiness.

"You didn't." She looked up at him and smiled. "I'm just not ready for any of this."

"Why not?" What was she running from?

"I've just got a lot of personal issues that I need to work out."

"Like what?"

"They're personal."

"Talk to me, Randi."

"I can't," she insisted.

"What in the hell did he do to you?"

"I'm not ready to talk to you about it yet. I'm just not ready."

"Okay, okay, I won't pressure you. It's just that I'm starting to catch feelings for you, and you just keep pushing me away."

"Just give me some time."

"I can try, but I have to know that I'm getting somewhere with you. I have to know that you're feeling something."

"I am," she admitted.

"Now, that's what I'm talking about."

After they finished dinner, soft music began to play. *Right on cue,* Anthony thought. To their left, a spotlight came on and lit up the stage. Singer Kevin Rivers stepped into the light and began to serenade them with love songs. His first song was Ruff Endz's "Someone to Love You." Randi's mouth dropped open as she looked at Kevin then Anthony, who smiled as he watched the expression on her face.

"I can't believe you did this," she whispered as she stared at him. No one had ever done anything like this for her. She was overwhelmed as she fought to keep herself from crying.

Without a word, Anthony stood up, moved to her side, and held out his hand for her. She took it and stood up. He gently pulled her to him. Her arms automatically went up and around his neck as she pressed her head against his chest. His arms encircled her waist; his hands rested on the small of her back. They swayed to the slow rhythm of the music. His body felt hard and strong as she lay against him. His scent filled her nostrils. He smelled delicious, she thought. She felt surprisingly comfortable in his arms.

So, this is what it feels like to hold her, he thought. She felt so tiny and fragile. He held her gently as if not to break her. She was so different from the women he was used to and he liked her frailty. He wanted to protect her. He wanted to wipe away all her bad memories and replace them with nights like this one. He wanted to keep her and never give her back. His lips came down next to her ear.

"Can I keep you forever?" he whispered. His breath was warm on her skin.

She looked up at him and wondered how she had gotten there. She wondered how, after so many nights of crying and so many nights of screaming and so many nights of loneliness, she had ended up in this wonderful man's arms. Was he real or was he just another one of her characters that had somehow come to life, if only for one night? Maybe she had written this scene herself. Maybe she had placed herself in his arms. She didn't know how she had gotten there, but she knew that she did want to stay there forever. "Yes," she responded. "Yes, you can keep me forever."

Anthony brought his hand up to her face as he thought about his no kissing rule. There were no rules when it came to Randi, he told himself. He slowly dragged his thumb over her lips as he wondered if they tasted as sweet as they looked. Slowly, he lowered his head, pulled her face closer, and allowed his lips to gently brush over hers. Patiently, cautiously, he kissed her as he waited for her response.

Randi slightly parted her lips as she kissed him back. She marveled at the tenderness in his touch as his tongue entered her mouth to taste her. Wanting more, he pulled her closer and their kiss deepened. He felt himself slipping away as he savored the sweet warmth of her mouth. *Remarkable,* he thought as his hand slid down to the small of her back and pressed her hips to his. He felt himself becoming aroused and he fought the urge to let his hands explore more. Fearing that he would offend her, he slowly, reluctantly pulled away from her.

Randi stared up at him in awe. He had kissed her. She had been kissed by Animalistic. She couldn't believe it. She couldn't believe the sweet, warm tenderness that his lips held. She couldn't believe how gentle and non-invading his hands were on her body. Over a month ago, he was asking her for a blow-job; tonight he gently held her in his arms and kissed her like he was her prince charming. She could really fall for him.

"That wasn't too much for you to handle, was it?" He hoped he hadn't gone too far.

"No." She shook her head.

"Good." He pulled her back into his arms and they began to dance again. " 'Cause I could really get used to kissing you."

"Me too," she whispered as she allowed herself to melt into his arms.

After they danced for what seemed like hours, he said in a barely audible voice, "I guess I should be getting you home." He didn't want the evening to end, but he knew that he couldn't keep her out all night.

Reluctantly, she pulled away from his arms.

"I guess you should," she agreed. She looked up at him. How could this man be the same guy she met at that party? He had changed so much. She turned away, picked up her purse and they left.

They reached the jet and boarded it.

"Tell me about your family," he said once they were in the air. "Are your mom and dad still around?"

"Yeah, but they aren't together. Dad lives in Virginia. That's where I'm from originally. Mom lives in North Carolina. She moved us there when she left my father," Randi answered.

"Was it hard when they split up?"

"Yeah, it was, but I got over it. When you're young, you're very resilient."

"Good. They get along?"

"Yeah. I think they get along better now that they're divorced."

He laughed, watching her as she pushed her hair away from her face and smiled at him "Damn, you're beautiful, girl," he said.

She blushed again and pinched herself.

"What was that for?" he asked.

"For blushing," she admitted.

"Do I make you blush?"

"Yes."

"Does that mean you like me, just a little?"

"Just a little." She smiled.

After they got off the jet, he drove her home.

"Sorry I got you home so late." He apologized as they stood in front of her apartment door.

"Don't apologize. I had a great time." She looked up at him with her key in her hand.

"May I?" he asked, taking the keys. She watched as he unlocked the door. She was sure he would invite himself in, but he didn't. He turned back around and handed her the key.

"I guess we'll be going out again?" He looked down at her.

"I guess so," she said with a smile.

"I'll check my schedule and call you this week. Maybe we'll be able to set something up." He brought his hand up to her cheek, caressing it. He looked into her eyes as if trying to see her soul. "I guess I have to say good night," he whispered.

"Would you like to come in for a little while?"

"Actually I would, but the way I'm feeling right now, holding your hand and talking wouldn't be enough for me," he said as he fought the urge to satisfy his own desires. He didn't want to rush her. *Walk away, man,* he told himself. *She's not ready for this.*

"Okay, I understand."

"I'll call you," he said as he pulled his hand away from her face.

"Okay," she managed to mutter.

He turned and walked away. She watched him as he disappeared then she entered her apartment.

Once in her bedroom, she slipped out of her clothes and climbed into bed. *Tonight was perfect,* she thought. He had made her feel beautiful. She thought about their dancing, about how good it felt to be in his arms, pressed up against his body. His cologne still lingered on her skin. She was surprised by his behavior. He was a perfect gentleman the whole night.

She lay in the darkness and thought about him. Then in revelation, she sat up in the bed. What was she doing? She wasn't supposed to let things go this far. He was so smooth that he had slipped in under her radar. She realized that she was letting herself fall for this guy. She couldn't do that. She couldn't fall for him. It was too dangerous. She had to regain control over the situation. She couldn't get caught up. She knew what she had to do.

The next day, Randi told Kathy everything that happened on their date.

"So, when is the next one?" Kathy asked.

"He said he would call me, but I can't go out with him again."

"Not because of Eric?"

"It's everything. It's the groupies and the intimacy and the trust issues. If I fell in love with him, Kathy, and he cheated on me with one of those groupies, I'd die."

"He's obviously feeling something for you. Why would he cheat on you?"

"Eric felt something for me but he cheated on me. And what about the sex? How am I supposed to be able to satisfy someone who I may not be able to have sex with? And if I can sleep with him, then how am I supposed to be able to satisfy someone who's used to being with a lot of experienced women? My only sexual experience was with Eric. I would never be able to keep Anthony satisfied. And why should he go without when he has all these beautiful women ready and willing to do anything that he asks of them?"

"You can't live life like this, Randi. You're not even giving him a chance. Because of Eric, you've already written this guy off. He's really trying, and you keep pushing him away. Randi, you've been alone for over a year now. You haven't let anybody get this close to you since Eric. You need to stop this."

Randi continued to listen to Kathy as she scolded her.

"Girl, I love you. I think you're beautiful and you're one of the kindest people I know, but you have to get over this. Give this guy a chance."

"I can't. I just can't."

"Eric really did a number on you, didn't he?"

"You were there. You saw what he did to me." She cringed as the memories of that evening came flooding back.

She could still feel the painful blows against her body as he pummeled her. She could still taste her own blood which covered her face, and still see him unfastening his pants just before he forced himself on her. She could still feel his hands around her neck when she tried to scream for help, and then everything went black.

She remembered waking up in the hospital with a broken and bruised body. She suffered from cracked ribs, a broken jaw, blackened eyes, and a concussion. The police charged him with simple assault. He only got a year and a half for nearly killing her.

"Yes, I was there," Kathy said. "I found you, and I'm the one who dialed 911. I saw what he did to you. I thought you were dead.

"Your body healed, but your heart didn't. I see what he's doing to you now, Randi. He's killing you every day by killing all possibilities of you ever being happy again. Let him go, Randi. Just let him go."

Randi swallowed as she tried to keep herself from

crying. She knew Kathy was right, but she wasn't ready to get back out there, to put her heart back on the line.

"I've gotta go, Kathy," she lied. She didn't want to talk to her friend anymore.

"Randi, don't hang up."

"I've gotta go." She hung up, pulled her knees to her chest and wrapped her arms around them, as if in an attempt to protect herself. She took a deep breath, closed her eyes and bit her bottom lip. She continued trying to hold back the tears but she couldn't stop them. They swelled up behind her eyelids, seeped out and trickled down her face. She knew she couldn't see Anthony anymore. She just hoped that it wasn't too late.

Chapter 10

The crowd roared as Anthony dashed off stage after his last performance. He had agreed to do the last-minute performance for the Atlanta "A Home for the Homeless" benefit concert only after he couldn't set up another date with Randi. It had been three weeks since their date in Atlanta, and even though he called nearly every day, he couldn't get a straight answer from her about why she couldn't go out with him again. She always said that she was busy, but he knew it was a lie. He was the one with the busy schedule as he raced off to shoot videos, perform at events, and record his latest CD. If he could find time to see her, then surely she could take a break from her job to make time to see him.

He pushed his way through the crowd backstage as he tried to make sense of her actions. One minute she was in his arms kissing him, and the next she was running away from him. His patience was wearing thin with her inconsistencies. He wanted to talk to her and find out what was really going on with her. As he slipped past the other performers, he ignored their attempts to get his attention. His mind was on Randi.

Once he reached his dressing room, he darted inside and went straight for the phone.

"Hello," Randi said as she answered the phone.

"What in the hell's going on, Randi? Did I do something wrong?" he asked.

It's him again, she thought. She could tell he was not in a good mood, and she knew it was because of her. "No."

"Listen, I've been calling for three weeks now to get another date with you, and you keep brushing me off. What's up with that? I thought we had a good time."

"We did. I had a wonderful time, but—"

"Then why are you avoiding me? You told me I could keep you forever."

"I know, but I was just caught up in the moment. I didn't mean it."

"So, you don't care about me?"

"Why are you doing this, Anthony? I told you I have issues to work through. I don't need all of this pressure on me."

"Well, I'll tell you what I don't need, Randi," he said, becoming even more heated. "I don't need you to keep jerking me around like this. I'm running all over trying to get to you. I've given up all these hoes to be with you, and all you can do is push me away and say you don't need the pressure. I don't have to put up with this shit. Do you hear me?"

"I never asked you to put up with me, Anthony. I never asked you to call. I never asked you to come by. I never asked you for anything. You're the one who insisted on being a part of my life."

"Well, I'll tell you what. You don't want me in your life, then I'm gone. Is that what you want? Huh? Is that what you want? You want me to leave you the hell alone?"

"Yes," Randi said as tears streamed down her face.

Anthony slammed down the receiver. "Fuck!" he yelled. He paced the floor as he tried to figure out what to do next. Why in the hell was she acting like this? He had to get out to get some fresh air. He headed for the door. If she didn't want to be with him, he knew somebody who did. He knew plenty of women who would love to be in her place. He knew plenty of women who would love to be in his bed. He didn't need this shit from some country-ass chick in North Carolina.

A determined Anthony stepped out into the night air. The streets were still crowded as performers waited for their limos and security held back star-struck fans who struggled to get a good glimpse of their favorite performers.

"We love you, Animalistic!" a group of young women yelled as they frantically tried to get his attention.

He gave them a quick wave of acknowledgement as he waited for his driver. The girls went crazy when they saw that he had noticed them. His driver pulled up and he slipped in the back seat of his limo. As he sunk down into the seat and enjoyed the benefits of his wealth and fame, his mind quickly went to Randi and their conversation. He didn't have time for her silly excuses. He was tired of trying to chase her down. If she wanted him out of her life, then he was ghost. She wouldn't have to worry about him anymore.

As the driver pulled the limo out into traffic, Anthony told him to stop near a group of young ladies standing near the curb. The driver pulled over, lowered his window, and gestured for the girls to come over.

"Mr. Animalistic has requested your company," the driver informed the one that Anthony had picked out. "Are you interested?"

"Oh yes," the girl squealed with excitement as her friends clamored around her with the same enthusiasm.

The driver slipped out of the car and walked the young lady to the back door of the limo. Anthony sat back and took in all the excitement. He wondered why Randi never got that excited about him. He knew that she had to have something that she was hiding inside her that wouldn't let her just enjoy him. He knew that she must have been hurting inside, but if she didn't open up and share, then he could do nothing to help her. He had to move on.

The driver opened the door and the young lady peered inside. Her eyes grew large with excitement and she looked at Anthony. She could barely believe her luck. Anthony gestured for her to come in. She quickly slipped into the leather seat of the limo. "Oh my God," she mouthed, but nothing came out. She was in awe as her eyes absorbed the luxuries of the limousine.

"What's your name?" Anthony asked as his eyes traveled over her curvaceous figure, which her tiny black dress barely covered. She would do for tonight, he thought. She was just what he needed to get his mind off of Randi.

"Asia Tyler." She smiled. "I'm a huge fan of yours. I just love your music."

"Thanks," he said as he brought his eyes up from her plump, round breasts to her angelic face. Although she looked like an angel, he was sure that she was not one. "So, Asia Tyler, you want to get fucked by a superstar?"

Asia smiled confidently. She knew his intentions before she stepped into the limousine. He wouldn't be the first rapper she fucked, and she didn't plan on him being the last. "Why the hell not?" She crossed her legs, showing him just enough skin to whet his appetite.

"Now, that's what I like," he said with a smile. "A woman who knows what she wants."

A few minutes later, Anthony and Asia had checked into a nearby hotel. He didn't have time to take her back to his hotel. He wanted to fuck her as soon as possible.

"Just let me freshen up," Asia said

"Go ahead. I'll fix us some drinks," he said as he walked over to the mini bar. "What are you drinking?"

"I'll take a Fuzzy Navel," Asia said as she slipped into the bathroom.

"Cool," he said as he fixed their drinks. He started to think about Randi, but quickly tried to push her out of his head. He didn't want her anywhere around tonight. If she didn't want him around, then he didn't want her. He was gonna have a good time tonight. He was gonna fuck Asia like he should have been fucking all those groupies that he had given up for Randi. Did she not know what he had given up for her? Did she not know how much he had sacrificed and how much he cared for her? Women were throwing pussy at him left, right and center, and all he got from Randi were excuses why she couldn't see him again. He definitely didn't need that shit. What he needed was a blow-job and a good fuck.

***

Kathy entered Randi's apartment. Randi was sitting on the sofa with her knees pulled up to her chest, hugging her legs. Her tear-covered face was swollen. Kathy walked over to her and sat down. She pushed Randi's hair back out of her face. Randi blinked, and more tears raced down her face.

"You didn't have to push him away, baby," Kathy said. She felt sorry for her friend. It was obvious that she was falling in love with Anthony, even if she wouldn't admit it.

"This is for the best," Randi whispered.

"How can you say that? Look at how you're hurting now. How is this for the best?"

"Six months from now, it would hurt worse. Six months from now when he decides that I'm not enough for him; six months from now when I'm madly in love with him; six months from now when he wants to walk away from me, it will hurt a whole lot worse than it does now."

"Baby, you can't look at it that way. You've got to believe in the relationship. You've got to believe in you and him. You gotta love, baby, like you're never gonna get hurt."

"Well, it doesn't matter now. He's gone. He's gone out

of my life." Her lip trembled as she started to cry harder.

Kathy slid over next to her and pulled her into her arms. "I'm not leaving you alone tonight."

***

"I hope you're ready for me," Asia said as she stepped out of the bathroom wearing nothing but a smile.

Anthony turned around and looked the leggy beauty as she walked toward him. Without a word, he handed her a drink. He didn't want to talk. All he wanted to do was fuck her like she had never been fucked before.

"Why aren't you undressed?" she asked as she took her drink.

"I'm just moving a little slow tonight, that's all."

"Well, I hope you're not moving too slow." She took a sip of her drink then set down the glass. "Now, let me make you a little less restricted." She started unbuttoning his shirt. As she revealed the smooth skin of his chest, she covered it with soft, wet kisses.

Still nursing his drink, he closed his eyes as Asia squatted in front of him and started working on his belt. He thought about Randi. She should have been the one undoing his clothes. She should have been the one that was getting ready to make love to him. It should have been her hands on his bare skin, not Asia's. The sound of his jeans being unzipped made him open his eyes. He grabbed Asia's hand as he looked down at her.

Surprised, she looked up at him. "Is everything okay?"

Suddenly, he felt like he was doing something wrong. He didn't want to do this. Randi was hurting, and instead of finding out what it was that she was going through, he was up in a hotel room with some chick whose name he couldn't even

99

remember.

He didn't really want to fuck this girl. He wanted to find Randi and make her tell him what the hell was going on with her. He wanted to find out why she was really running away from him and make her stop. He had to talk to her. Before he truly walked out of her life, he had to see her. He had to talk to her face to face and make sure this was what she wanted. He wasn't ready to give up on her yet. He wasn't ready to give up on them.

He put his glass down and pulled Asia up. "I'm sorry, sweetie, but I have to leave."

"Right now?" She looked puzzled.

"Yeah, right now. It can't wait."

"Just like that? You got me standing here butt-naked in front of you and you're telling me that you have to leave."

"I gotta go take care of some business. The room's paid for, so enjoy."

"I don't believe this bullshit," she said, placing her hand on her hip. "I coulda been fucking Kobe Bryant by now."

"Thanks for understanding." He pulled up his zipper and left. He had to hurry back to his hotel and pack. He was going to Greensboro, North Carolina.

Chapter 11

A couple of hours later, a loud banging on the door awakened the girls. Randi rolled over and looked at the clock. It was 2:38 a.m.

"Who in the hell could that be?" Kathy asked as she sat up in the bed and looked over at Randi.

"I don't know." She climbed out of bed, slipped on her robe, and hurried down the hall. Kathy followed.

"Who is it?" Randi asked midway through a yawn.

"It's me. Anthony."

"Anthony," she whispered as she looked at Kathy. "What is he doing here?" She didn't want to see him. He said he was gone out of her life, and now he was back. Why was he back? Why was he trying to make this so hard for her?

"Open the door, Randi," Kathy said.

"I can't. I don't want to see him."

"You need to talk to him. He wants to talk to you."

"Why doesn't he just leave me alone?"

"Because he cares about you." She grabbed Randi's arm. "Listen, if you don't open the door, I will. I promise you, Randi. I will," she threatened. She hated putting her friend in that spot, but she felt that Randi wasn't thinking clearly. She was too emotional to know what was best for her. If she wasn't going to willingly talk to Anthony, then Kathy would make her.

"Randi, you might as well open the door. I'm not leaving here until I talk to you. I've come too far to leave without seeing you," Anthony demanded. He was tired of accommodating her. She was gonna have to put up with him until he was satisfied with her explanation for running away from him.

"At least hear him out, Randi," Kathy urged.

Randi stared at Kathy. "I can't."

"You can."

She stared down at the doorknob.

"I've got all day, baby," he informed her as he prepared himself to take a seat outside of her door. "You can either open the door, talk to me and get it over with, or I can sit out here all day long waiting for you. It's up to you."

She looked at Kathy. "What am I supposed to say to him?"

"Tell him how you feel. Tell him what's going on inside you. He deserves that. Don't just shut him out."

Kathy was right. Anthony had been so patient with her. He had taken time out of his hectic schedule to see her and to show her an incredible time. He was putting so much effort into being with her. The least she could do was talk to him.

"Talk to him," Kathy said.

"Okay." She nodded. "I'll talk to him."

She opened the door. The look on his face revealed that he was more than frustrated with the situation. She understood. She was frustrated with herself as well. She knew she could have handled the situation better than she had. She should have just stayed away from him. She should have just refused to go out with him, but her heart and her head were in constant battle over what she should do about him.

Without saying a word, Anthony walked past Kathy and Randi and took a seat on the couch. He picked a magazine off the coffee table and started flipping through it.

"I was just leaving," Kathy said as she touched

Randi's arm. "You talk to him and explain everything to him."

Randi nodded.

While Kathy disappeared into the bedroom to get dressed, Randi walked over and sat down across from Anthony. She watched him as he continued to feign interest in the magazine articles. They both sat in silence as they waited for Kathy to leave.

Minutes later, Kathy reentered the living room fully dressed. "Hey, guys, I'm gonna let myself out. Randi, I'll talk to you later. Anthony, it was good seeing you."

"Wait a minute," Anthony said as he tossed the magazine back down on the coffee table and stood up. "Let me walk you out."

He walked Kathy to her car while Randi waited for him.

"Anthony," Kathy said before getting into her car. "She really cares about you, even if she won't admit it. She's just scared. But no matter what she does, don't leave here until she tells you what's going on."

He nodded. "Thanks, Kathy."

After Kathy drove off, he ran back upstairs to Randi.

"Okay, now tell me what the hell is going on," he demanded as he sat back down. He was tired of handling her with kid gloves. His patience was worn, and he was sick of playing games. He stared at her as he searched her small face for an answer. "I know you care about me. Why the hell do you keep running from me?"

She could hear the frustration in his voice. She couldn't blame him for what he was feeling. "It's like I told you, Anthony. I have a lot of issues I need to work through."

"No," he said as he stood up and looked down at her. "That's weak. That's too weak an answer. I didn't fly all the way over here to hear that same weak-ass excuse. I deserve more than that. What in the hell is going on?" he demanded.

She looked up at him and shook her head. "It's so much, Anthony. It's so much." She bit her bottom lip as she tried not to cry.

He knew she was hurting. He knelt down in front of her and took her hand. "Baby, what the hell did he do to you?" He searched her eyes for an answer.

She quickly turned her face away from his, but he placed one hand on her chin and gently guided her face back to his. "Talk to me, baby," he said. His voice was much softer.

Randi's lip quivered as tears swelled up in her eyes. "He took everything away from me," she finally managed.

"How? What did he do?"

"We were high school sweethearts," she said as she wiped away the tears that were perched to race down her cheeks. "I know it sounds like a cliché, but we were."

"Okay." He nodded.

"He was really possessive. I gave up my family and friends and my dreams for him."

Anthony gently squeezed her hand to reassure her that it was okay to go on.

"We got engaged and moved in together." She swallowed. "One day, while he was at work, I got a call from a girl saying she was six months pregnant by him."

"Damn," Anthony said as he watched the pain on her face.

"He didn't even deny it." She blinked, and more tears spilled down her cheeks.

He reached up and gently wiped the tears away with his thumb. "I am so sorry," he whispered. "He was an idiot, baby." He was beginning to understand her pain.

Randi closed her eyes tightly as she remembered that night. She didn't want to fall apart in front of him. As she tried to regain strength, she opened her eyes and looked at him. She was unsure whether she should tell him the whole story, but she wanted to. She wanted him to understand why she couldn't be with him. "I tried to leave him that night," she continued. "But he wouldn't let me."

Anthony quietly listened.

She brought her hands up to cover her face. She knew she was about to break down, and she didn't want Anthony to see her. "He tried to kill me," she whispered as her hands began trembling and tears raced down her face.

"Damn," was all he could say as he pulled her into his arms. She buried her face in his chest as she wept. He squeezed her trembling body against him.

"He beat me and raped me and tried to kill me." She sobbed as she clung to him.

Anthony closed his eyes and kissed the top of her head as he felt a rage building in him. He clutched her to him as he tried not to lose it. How could a man hit a woman? How could he rape a woman? Women were the weaker sex. Only a coward would do this. Only a punk-ass coward would put his hands on a woman. The longer he held her trembling body, the angrier he grew. He wanted to find this guy. He wanted to find the guy who had caused her so much pain, the guy who had damaged her heart and her soul and her spirit.

As Randi's crying began to diminish, he loosened his grip on her. He stroked her hair. Now he understood why she was hurting so much. "I'm glad you told me," he whispered.

She slowly pulled away from him and looked up at him. "Do you understand now why I can't be with you?

"I understand why you're hurting so much, but it doesn't change the way I feel about you. I still want to be with you Ran—"

"You don't understand," she cut him off.

He stared down at her tear-stained face. He was confused. "Then make me. Explain it to me."

"After what I've been through, how could I trust you? How would I be able to trust you, Anthony? I've only been with one man, and he cheated on me and then raped me. You're constantly on the road, surrounded by beautiful women who are willing to do anything for you. I don't know if I could satisfy you. I wouldn't even know how to satisfy you. I don't even know if I could be intimate with you. You've had all kinds of women, Anthony. Why would I expect you to be satisfied with me?"

It all finally made sense to him.

"I could fall for you. I could really fall hard for you and what—" He paused, tilted her face up to his and shook his head. "Damn, it, Randi. I've already fell. Don't you know that?"

"But what about my issues?"

"They're our issues, and we'll work through them one day at a time. I don't want you and me anymore. I want *us*. I want to be with you. Just give us a try, Randi. We'll take it slowly. I won't put any pressure on you. You set the pace and I'll go with it. I'm just not ready to let you walk away from this. Just give us a try."

"And you're willing to put up with my insecurities?"

"Yes. Baby, I have never met anyone like you. You are the only woman that wasn't mesmerized by my stardom. You are the only one that wouldn't lower your morals just to appease me. You treated me like a regular guy, and I appreciate that. I know why you want to be with me. It's not because I'm Animalistic. You want to be with Anthony Talbert. All these other chicks want to be with the rapper. You want to be with the man. I trust you. And I've never been able to trust any of these other women. You also push me to be better than I was. You made me reevaluate the way I was living, and all in all, you make me wanna be a better man. Baby, you make me a better man."

"I did all that?"

"Yes. I put away my whorish ways because I want to be with you. No one else could make me do that."

He was telling the truth and she knew it. She had seen the changes in him. It was the changes that made her want to be with him. He had grown so much since their first encounter.

"So, what do you say, Randi? Give us a try?"

"And we'll take it slow?"

"As slow as you want it, baby. I won't rush you. Any time you feel uncomfortable with the rate things are moving, just let me know and we can slow it down even more. Okay?"

"Okay." She nodded and smiled.

Anthony kissed her they embraced.

After Anthony finally released her, she looked up at him. "Do you have to leave?" she asked. It had been so long since she had seen him. She missed him and wanted him to stay longer.

"Not 'til about six in the morning. Do you mind if I stay? I haven't had any sleep."

"No." She wanted him to stay.

"Do you mind if I lay down with you?"

"I um…" She became uneasy at his request.

"I just want to hold you, that's all. Nothing else."

Seeing the sincerity in his eyes and hearing it in his voice, she knew she could trust him. "That's fine." She smiled.

Anthony followed Randi as she led him to her bedroom. After taking off her robe, she climbed into bed and slid under the covers. Anthony slipped off his shoes and climbed onto the bed next to her, however, he lay on top of the covers. He didn't want to make her too uncomfortable. *Take it slowly,* he told himself. He lay on his back and gently pulled her over to him until she was in his arms. She rested her head on his chest and draped her arm around his waist.

Her body molded against his perfectly, Anthony thought as he held her. He had never held a woman like this before. This was so different from what he was used to. Normally he would just fuck, nut, roll over and fall asleep. This was what he had been looking for all this time and he hadn't even known it.

"Randi," he whispered.

"Yes."

"So, where is your ex now?" He wanted to make sure this guy was long gone. He wanted to make sure he wouldn't hurt her ever again.

"He's serving an eighteen-month sentence."

"Eighteen months," he said in disbelief. "Is that all he got?"

"Yeah. They charged him with assault, but not for the rape. He denied raping me, and they said since we lived together at the time, the rape was too hard to prove."

"You'll never ever have to worry about me hurting you like that. I would never put my hands on you like that."

"I know," she whispered as she closed her eyes. She marveled at how surprisingly comfortable she felt lying there in his arms. It had been a lifetime since someone held her like that. She could do this forever, she thought.

The next morning when Anthony awoke, he realized that they changed positions. Randi had rolled over and curled up. He had curled up behind her with his arm draped around her waist. She was still asleep. The warm feelings of the night before seeped back into his memory. He smiled and gently squeezed her. He glanced at the clock. It was 8:00. His flight had left two hours ago. He knew Thomas was going to be pissed, but he didn't give a damn. Thomas would just have to get over it.

He carefully pulled his arm from around her waist, trying not to disturb her. He rolled over onto his back, then on to his other side and slipped out of the bed. She stirred slightly but didn't wake up. He paused for a few seconds, watched her sleep, then disappeared into the bathroom.

After he relieved himself, he washed his face. Minutes later, he walked over to her side of the bed and stooped down in front of her. She snored lightly. He chuckled. She didn't look like the snoring type. He gently pushed her hair back, exposing more of her face then leaned over gently kissed her forehead.

"Thank you," he whispered. He left the room only to return with a note to place on the pillow.

When Randi woke up, he was already gone. She felt a twinge of sadness. He was probably in the air by now. She smiled when she spotted the note he left for her.

Good morning,

Sorry to leave you like this, but I had to get an early start. You looked so peaceful sleeping that I didn't want to wake you. Thanks for such a wonderful night, and thank you for trusting me.

I'm leaving my home and cell numbers in case you need or just want me. I'll call you.

***

"So, where the hell were you this morning?" Thomas barked when Anthony entered his office. Thomas was a stout man. He stood about five feet six inches, and was just about as wide as he was tall. He was a chain smoker. Although he had tried to give up smoking a few times, he finally resigned himself to the fact that he was a slave to nicotine. He blew his smoke into the air as he stubbed out his cigarette in the glass ashtray on the edge of his desk.

"I had some business to take care of." Anthony took a seat on the leather couch.

"Listen. We can't have you disappearing into thin air. We needed you to be here. We booked the studio for you four hours ago and you didn't even show up." He stood up, walked around to the other side of his desk, and lit up another cigarette. He pulled on it and looked down at Anthony as smoke poured from his nostrils like an angry bull.

"I told you, man. I had some personal business to take care of." Anthony leaned back on the couch and folded his hands behind his head as he stretched out his long legs.

"You're not doing drugs, are you?"

Anthony laughed. "Man, you're crazy. You know I don't touch the stuff. I get high off life, nigga." He leaned forward, rested his elbows on his knees, and clasped his hands. He looked up at Thomas, who towered over him, while he took another puff of his cigarette. "I just got me a little honey, that's all."

Thomas looked up at the ceiling in frustration, then back down at Anthony. "Look, man. You don't need no woman. All of these little hoes running around here after you. Why would you need a woman?"

"I don't want any of those other women. They can't do nothing for me."

"Three months ago they were sucking your dick. Now they can't do nothing for you."

"Man, that shit's over with. I'm in love."

Those were not the words that Thomas wanted to hear.

"Aw, hell no," he said as he put his cigarette out and sat down next to Anthony. "Now, why you want to go and say some shit like that? You don't know nothing about love. It's just lust. The pussy's good. I understand you think you're in love, but man, there's other good pussy around here. Hell, you've had the best pussy in the business."

"Look, man. You don't understand. It's not about sex. I haven't even slept with her. She's just . . . " He looked off into space as he tried to find a word to describe her. "She's just everything—everything I need, everything I want."

Thomas looked at him in disappointment. This nigga was fucked up. He hadn't even gotten the pussy yet, and this girl had his nose wide open. "You ain't fucked her and she got you running around here like this already? What she put on you, roots?"

"Naw, man. She's just a nice girl. She's everything, man. She's perfect." He smiled at the thought of her.

"Listen. She can be everything and perfect and all that good shit. Just don't let her fuck up your career."

"All right, man. I'm straight." Anthony looked at him. "You don't have to worry about me, nigga."

"I better not." Thomas stood up and lit another cigarette. "You and I are a team. Don't fuck me over for some little honey."

"Sure thing, man," Anthony said. He wondered what Randi was doing. "So, what's on the agenda for today?"

Chapter 12

As soon as Randi got off the airplane and entered the airport, she spotted Anthony. He had invited her to Des Moines to meet his parents and attend their thirtieth wedding anniversary party. She had agreed, though she was nervous about meeting his family.

He stood at a window with his hands in his pockets as he watched the airplanes arrive and depart. As if he felt her presence, he turned around when she approached him. He smiled and walked over to meet her.

"Hey, baby." He hugged her. His arms felt good around her. She missed him. They hadn't seen each other in two weeks. He kissed her on the cheek.

He stood back to look at her. Damn, this girl had a hold on him. "How was your flight?" He took her carry-on bag.

"It was a little bumpy." She smiled anxiously.

"You look nervous." He hooked his arm in hers as they started toward baggage claim.

"I am. I don't even know what I'm doing here."

"You're here because I asked you to be here."

"But meeting your family . . . "

"Relax. They won't bite." He chuckled. "Actually, they can't wait to meet you. I told them that you were an aspiring writer/director and now Mom keeps going on and on about it. She used to write when she was younger, which is where I get my skills from."

"Skills," Randi said teasingly. "You've got skills."

"Well, let's put it this way. If it wasn't for my writing, I wouldn't be rapping, then I wouldn't have met you. So yeah,

I say I've got skills." He laughed.

They stood at the carrousel and waited for her luggage.

"I hope you're hungry. Mom cooked this big meal for you."

"That's it." She pointed to her luggage as it came toward them. He grabbed the bag.

"Let me take that." She took the carry-on bag while he carried the other. "Why'd she do that?"

"Do what?"

"Your mom." They turned and headed for the car. "Why'd she cook a big meal for me? I'm already nervous as it is."

"She wants to talk to you. Get a chance to know you before the rest of the family sinks their teeth into you and rips you apart."

Randi raised her eyebrow.

"I'm just kidding." He nudged her. "Relax. You got nothing to worry about. They're gonna love you."

As they continued through the airport, Randi started noticing people staring and pointing at them.

"Randi," Anthony said as he glanced over her shoulder and gripped her luggage tighter.

"Yes," she said as she looked up at him. He wore a worried look on his face. Then she heard an unfamiliar sound.

The sound, however, was very familiar to Anthony. "Are you a good runner?" he asked as he continued to stare over her shoulder.

"Yes, why?" The noise was getting louder and closer. She turned around only to see a herd of screaming fans racing toward them. "Oh my God," Randi whispered. She had never seen anything like it before.

"That's why," Anthony said. "Run!" he yelled as he grabbed her arm to get her moving. She nearly fell down as he pulled her. "Run, Randi!" he yelled.

After getting her footing, she gripped her carry-on and they raced through the airport. Anthony held her hand tightly as they dashed in and around other passengers. His legs were so long that he was practically dragging her along. Randi kept glancing over her shoulder at the crowd of fans that appeared to be growing in size the farther they ran. She didn't know how much longer they would have to run before they could escape his fans, but she knew that her legs couldn't endure much more of this chase.

Anthony was used to the mobs of fans. His long legs gave him a huge advantage over them. However, he knew that Randi was slowing and that if he didn't find refuge soon, he'd have to throw her over his shoulder to keep them moving along. He quickly began to search the area for a safe haven to hide from the fans. Recognizing their dilemma, a quick-thinking airport employee got their attention and signaled them to enter a door marked EMPLOYEES ONLY. Without hesitation, Anthony dragged Randi over to the door and they slipped inside.

Once inside, Randi dropped her bag and slid down against the wall until she was sitting in the floor. She struggled to catch her breath while Anthony and the employee peered outside the door and watched the screaming mob race right past them.

"Thanks, man," Anthony said to the employee as he tried to catch his breath.

"No problem, man. That shit was crazy."

"No shit," he said and squatted down next to Randi. "Baby, are you okay?"

She nodded, still breathing heavily. Although she was in good shape, she had never run so hard in her life.

"You sure?"

"Yeah," she finally managed. "I'm okay." She took a few more swallows of air. "Is it always like this?"

"Not all the time. I guess I should have warned you."

"Yeah." She smiled. "I would have packed lighter."

"I thought I was gonna lose you a few times." He chuckled.

"You and me both." She laughed. "I don't know how you do it."

"Practice, baby." He grabbed her hand and pulled her to her feet. "Now let's get the hell outta here."

With a disguise and help from the employee, Anthony and Randi finally reached the car. He slid down into his seat and looked over at her.

"Are you ready to meet the parents?"

"After that run, I'm pumped for anything."

"Good." He smiled, started the car, and pulled out into traffic.

Randi watched him as he maneuvered the white Lexus coupe through the busy streets. He saw her from the corner of his eye.

"What are you looking at?" he asked, not taking his eyes off the road.

"You."

"Why?"

"Because I can't believe I'm here. I can't believe I'm actually . . . " She hesitated.

"Can't believe you're actually what?"

"I can't believe I'm actually putting my trust in your hands."

That was the next best thing he could have heard from her. He looked at her as he reached for her hand, brought it to his lips, and kissed it.

"Yes, you can trust me," he whispered as he placed her

hand back in her lap. He didn't let it go.

She looked down at their hands entwined and smiled.

It didn't take long for them to reach his parents' house. The impressive two-story brick home with a circular driveway was a present from Anthony. He purchased it for them when he released his first CD.

As he pulled into the driveway and parked, he looked over at Randi. "They're good people."

"Just don't leave my side."

He chuckled. "Mad dogs couldn't drag me away from your side."

Randi wasn't worried about mad dogs. She was worried about being abandoned in a group of strangers.

His mother met them at the door. Anthony looked just like her.

"Mom, this Randi Jacobs. Randi, this is my mom."

"Hello, Mrs. Talbert."

"Hello, Miss Jacobs."

"Just call me Randi."

"Then you call me Sylvia. Mrs. Talbert is my mother-in-law's name." She laughed. "Come on in." She stood back for them to enter and gave Anthony an approving nod.

They went into the living room and sat down. Sylvia gave him a *get out of here* look, but he pretended not to see it.

"I'll bet you're tired from your flight," she said to Randi.

"Just a little." Randi smiled nervously.

"Anthony, don't you have something else to do?"

"No." He knew what his mother was trying to do.

His mother gave him another look, but he acted like he didn't see that one either. Finally, she just came out with it.

116

"Why don't you leave Randi and me alone so we can get to know each other better?"

"I can't, Mom."

"Anthony Lamar Talbert, if you don't get your narrow behind out of here right now . . . " she said through clenched teeth.

Randi found this amusing. Anthony stood up and looked at Randi. "Sorry, baby. Gotta go."

"Is that all it took for you to abandon me?" Randi laughed.

"She used my full name. When Moms uses the full name, you know she means business."

"Abandon? You're not afraid of me, are you?" Sylvia looked at Randi.

"I'm just nervous."

"Don't worry, dear. I don't bite."

Randi laughed. She felt a little more relaxed. "That's what your son has been telling me ever since I met him."

"He hasn't bitten you yet, has he?" she teased.

"Not yet."

"Let me know if he does." She put her hand on top of Randi's. "Anthony, you go get her bags out of the car and put them in the second bedroom at the top of the stairs."

"Okay, Mom." He shrugged his shoulders at Randi and left.

"So, you really do exist," Randi said to Sylvia.

"What do you mean, child?"

"Well, when I first met your son, I thought he was the product of an evil genius."

She laughed. "Was he that bad?"

"He was that bad."

"And you're with him?" She raised her eyebrow.

"Well, he had to do a whole lot of back pedaling to get

117

me to this point."

They both laughed.

"Well listen, dear. I set you two up in two different rooms. I hope you don't mind not sleeping together while you're here."

"That's fine, Mrs. Talbert—I mean Sylvia."

"So, you must be very special, Randi. You're the only girlfriend Anthony's ever had, and definitely the only woman he's ever brought home."

Hearing his mother call her Anthony's girlfriend nearly knocked her over. She had never considered the reality that she was his girlfriend. *What else could I be?* she asked herself. She was meeting his parents.

"You're all that boy talks about when we can get him to call," she continued. "I can't get him to shut up about how wonderful you are. I think you're good for him."

"Thank you. I'm crazy about him."

"He says you've been through a great deal of pain." Her eyes softened.

"Yes, ma'am, I have." She was surprised that he had told his mother about her problems. She wondered just how much of her pain he had revealed.

"Well, Anthony's a little wild and a little high strung, but all in all he's a good boy." She smiled as she squeezed Randi's hand then stood up. "Now, come on in the kitchen so I can put you to work."

Randi laughed as she followed his mother. She liked her already.

When they entered the kitchen, Sylvia swatted her husband on the behind as he stood with his head in the refrigerator.

"Hey." He pulled his head up to see who assaulted him and saw Randi. "Was that you being fresh, little girl?" he asked.

Randi smiled. "No, sir."

He stood up all the way, and it became clear that Anthony got his height from him.

"Not before dinner," Sylvia scolded as she checked the pots on the stove.

"She's no fun. I'm fifty-six years old and you would think I wouldn't have to put up with this," he teased. "I'm Paul, Anthony's old man." He closed the refrigerator door and extended his hand to Randi. When she reached to shake it, he pulled hers up to his lips and kissed it.

Like father like son, she thought.

"And you must be the beautiful, funny, ambitious…" He stopped for a second to remember. "Oh yeah, and intelligent Randi Jacobs, to use my son's exact words." He winked at her. "If I was twenty years younger, I'd—"

"You'd still be too old for her. Now, stop flirting with your son's girlfriend." Sylvia poked fun at him. She checked the food in the oven.

Anthony came back downstairs and joined them in the kitchen. "You're not mistreating my guest, are you?"

"If your mother wasn't in here supervising, I'd steal her from you." Paul laughed. "After thirty years of marriage, you'd think she'd let me have some fun."

"After thirty years of marriage, you shouldn't remember what fun is." She pulled the roast out of the oven and placed it on the counter. It smelled delicious.

"Randi, you wash your hands and help me set the table for dinner."

"That's right, Mom. Get her trained for me," Anthony said with a big grin.

Randi and his mother both shot him a glance.

"Sorry." He laughed, holding his hands up in mock

surrender. "Come on, old man. Show me that garden you're so proud of," he said to his father. The men left while the women set the table.

"Thirty years. That's a long time to be married," Randi said. She wondered how they made it.

"Well, it wasn't all peaches and cream. Sometimes it got hard, real hard."

"Really?" Randi placed the plates on the table while Sylvia added the silverware.

"Yes, but you have to remember; anything worth having is worth fighting for. And boy, did we have to fight to keep this marriage together."

"You look so happy."

Sylvia stopped what she was doing and looked at Randi. "We are, and one day you will be too." She smiled. "Just be patient. It'll happen."

After dinner, Randi decided to head upstairs to bed. She was tired.

"I'll walk you up." Anthony got up from the table. She followed him upstairs. "So, what do you think?"

"I think they're just as crazy as you are."

"I'll take that as a compliment."

"I like them. They make me feel at home. Now I know where you get all your charm. Your dad is a shameless flirt."

"And proud of it."

They reached her bedroom door. "Here we are," he said.

She turned and looked up at him. His eyes smiled down at her as they stood in silence and gazed at each other.

"I guess I'll see you tomorrow," she finally said.

"I guess you will."

"Good night."

"Good night." He kissed her forehead.

She went into her bedroom and closed the door behind her. Anthony ran back downstairs to see what his parents thought about her. They sat in the den. His father smoked a cigar.

"So, what do you think?" he asked as he entered the room and took a seat next to his mother. He valued their opinion.

"I'd chase after her," his father said between puffs. "She's a good-looking woman."

He looked at his mother. "Mom?"

"I think you did good, son. She's a lovely girl. Thank God you didn't bring one of those hoochie mamas home." She laughed.

"What do you know about hoochie mamas?"

"I see those half-naked women running around in your videos, showing all their stuff and shaking booties all up in your face like they ain't got good sense. Boy, if you brought one of those girls home with you, I would lock both you and her outside."

"I know you would, Mom."

"Randi's a nice girl. You be nice to her." Sylvia knew her son had lots of women after him and that they were tempting. He was young and immature. She knew it would be easy for him to blow this.

"I will, Mom," he promised.

Chapter 13

The next morning, there was a light knock at Randi's door. She sat up in the bed.

Anthony cracked the door open and poked his head inside the room. "Good morning. I didn't wake you, did I?"

"No. Come on in."

He walked over to the edge of her bed and sat down. "How'd you sleep?" he asked

"Good. It's really quiet around here."

"I know. That's because we're so far out in the country."

"It must have been nice growing up here." She climbed out of the bed, walked over to the window and looked out over the land. It was beautiful. Their backyard included a duck pond, a garden, and a small orchard.

"I didn't grow up here. I grew up in a tiny two-bedroom apartment in the middle of the city." He walked over to where she stood. She wore short pink pajamas.

"It's beautiful out here, isn't it?" He looked out the window.

"Yes." She glanced over at him. He was already dressed in a white tank and royal blue shorts. "What time did you get up?" It was only eight o'clock.

"Six o'clock."

"Every morning?"

He sat down on the window seat and looked up at her.

"Yeah, ninety percent of the time."

"Why so early?" She sat down next to him. Her leg rested against his.

"So much to do. Life is too short to sleep it away. You

gotta get up, get out there, and savor every day."

"You sound like a television commercial."

"I know." He chuckled. "Well, it's just you and me today until six. That's the time the party starts."

"Where is everybody?"

"Mom and Dad are putting together a few last minute details and they've got to go get all dolled up for tonight, so they said that we were on our own. You won't meet the rest of the family until we get to the party tonight."

"Then I can go back to bed." She smiled.

"No." He stood up and pulled her to her feet. "Get dressed so we can get out of here. I'm gonna take you to where I grew up at and let you see all the elements that created the man you see standing here before you today."

"Only if you insist on showing me how you became such a mess," she teased.

"I insist. I'll make breakfast, and you can come on down when you're ready."

After he gave her a tour of his old stomping ground, they visited a few of his old friends. They told her stories about him in his Jheri-curl and braces days. To back up the stories, they pulled out photos and embarrassed him even more. Randi doubled over with laughter, tears forming in her eyes.

Anthony sat back and watched as she interacted with them. Her face glowed. She was happy. Suddenly he had an urge to grab her, hold on to her, and steal her away from the rest of the world.

Later, they returned to his parents' home. His parents were not there, but left a note saying that they had already left for the hotel, the party would be in the ballroom, and they would see them there.

Randi and Anthony decided to go ahead and get dressed. Anthony was finished first so he waited downstairs for her. He stood in the living room and flipped through a magazine in his black gabardine and silk Versace suit, looking as if he should be strutting down a runway. Then, as if he felt Randi's presence, he turned around to watch her descend the stairs.

She was breathtaking. Her hair poured down over her shoulders. She wore a little sexy black dress that hugged her body and melted over her curves. Anthony instinctively licked his lips as he went to meet her. He couldn't believe how beautiful she looked.

"You look stunning," he said, unable to take his eyes off her. He took her hand, spun her around to get a better look, and smiled approvingly.

She blushed. "Well, you don't look too bad yourself."

"This old thing?" He pretended to straighten up his suit. "Thank you." He held out his arm for her. "Shall we go, madam?"

"Yes, we shall." She played along and took hold of his arm.

They arrived at the party promptly at 6:00. The ballroom was beautifully decorated in hunter green and gold, the colors his parents used at their wedding thirty years earlier. The colors were everywhere, from the tablecloths to the centerpieces to the balloon arch over the table for the guests of honor.

Beside the dance floor sat the DJ station, a podium where family members and friends could make speeches about the couple, and a fully stocked bar. After dinner, the guests would celebrate with a wedding cake that was an exact replica of the one Anthony's parents had thirty years before.

It took Randi a minute to take all this in. She was happy for his parents. They had made it. She wondered how they knew they were soul mates, how they knew they belonged together. She wondered if she and Anthony belonged together. As if he could see what she was thinking, he nudged her, slipped his hand into hers and gently squeezed. She squeezed back as she smiled up at him.

Guests who hadn't seen each other in years stood around socializing and trying to catch up. Through the crowd, Anthony spotted his older brother, who he hadn't seen in almost a year.

"I want you to meet my brother," Anthony said as he led Randi across the room. As they approached Anthony's lookalike, he saw them and grinned.

"Hey, baby brother." He grabbed Anthony and hugged him.

"What's up, man?" Anthony said when he stepped back.

"You, man."

"Yo, Mike, I want to introduce you to my friend." Anthony put his arm around Randi. "Mike, this is Randi Jacobs. Randi, this is my brother, Michael. We call him Mike."

Mike looked at Randi and smiled. "Nice to meet you." He took her hand, brought to his lips, and kissed it. He cut his eyes at Anthony. "Baby brother, you better look out or I'm gonna have to steal her from you." He chuckled.

"Get in line. Dad's already tried but failed miserably."

"That's because he's an old man. He doesn't have the energy it takes to steal a woman like this away." He looked back at Randi. "How'd you end up with this P. Diddy wannabe?"

Randi laughed. "I don't know. I was running. He was

chasing, and he finally caught me." She smiled up at Anthony.

He squeezed her waist. "So, where are Mom and Dad?" he asked as he surveyed the room.

"Anthony. Anthony, is that you?" A plump lady bounded up to him. She grabbed him and hugged him, kissing him on the cheek.

"Aunt Betty," he said when she let go. "How you been?"

"I'm just fine. You look a little thin. Who is this young lady?"

"This is my friend, Randi Jacobs. Randi, this is my Aunt Betty. On my mom's side." Aunt Betty was the Ma Bell of Des Moines. She knew everything, and she told everything she knew.

"My, she's a pretty little thing. But you do need to pick up some weight, dear." She touched Randi's arm then turned back to Anthony. "I'm so glad you're here. Sylvia wasn't sure you were going to make it, you being a big rap star and all. Speaking of rap, I need to talk to about those lyrics. You really should clean that stuff up. Didn't we raise you better than that?"

"Yes, Aunt Betty."

Randi smiled. He sounded like a scolded little boy.

Aunt Betty fidgeted with his suit. "You trying to be like that Puffy man and that Jay something or other. You're a good boy. You don't need to have such a dirty mouth. Promise your Aunt Betty you're gonna clean up your mouth. You're too pretty to have such ugly words coming out of it."

"Yes, Aunt Betty."

Mike and Randi laughed at the way his aunt reprimanded him.

"Can I have your attention?"

They looked in the direction of the podium. The party

coordinator stood at the microphone and announced, "It's time to eat, so if everybody would take their seats, we'll say grace and then you can help yourself to the buffet."

Everyone had assigned seats. Anthony and Randi, along with Mike and Aunt Betty, were assigned to the guests of honor table. When they reached the table, his parents were already seated. Anthony walked over to them, kissed his mother on the cheek, and shook his father's hand.

"I'm proud of you guys," he said. He went back over to Randi and helped her with her seat.

"Thank you," she said as he pushed her chair in behind her.

He sat beside her, and Mike sat on the other side. During dinner, Mike and Anthony caught up on what each was up to. However, Anthony noticed that Mike was more interested in talking to Randi and getting to know her better.

"Randi wants to be a writer," his mother told Mike. He had done a little writing himself.

Anthony watched as Randi and Mike talked. Mike was more suitable for her than he was, he thought. Mike was older, more settled, and hadn't slept with the hundreds of women he had. Mike was ready to settle down, get married, and have children. Anthony hadn't thought about settling down until he met Randi. He knew she was the one, and he didn't intend to let her get away.

After dinner, Sylvia and Paul moved to the front of the room where guests made speeches and presented gifts. Anthony and Mike had to offer words about their parents, and now it was Anthony's turn. He stood up and walked to the podium.

He cleared his throat, smiled at his parents then informed the crowd, "I promise I'm not gonna rap."

Everybody laughed. He caught a glance of Randi. She

smiled.

"I've known these two people for over twenty-four years now, but I still find myself speechless when I try to explain what they mean to me and what this day means to them. Being a rapper, I guess that's pretty bad. I'm supposed to be able to freestyle, so while I'm not gonna to rap, I am going to just look at these two people and tell you what I see." He looked at his parents. They held hands.

"When I look at these two people I see love, peace and joy. I see heartache and pain, laughter and tears. I see struggles and overcoming, I see forgiveness and faithfulness. I see respect and adoration. I see wars and surrenders. I see patience, virtue, and happiness. I see mountain peaks and low valleys. Mom and Dad, we all know there can't be peaks without valleys or sunshine without rain. But whatever you've been through, you've made it through. When I look at you, I see a strong and powerful marriage. I see where I want to be one day. So, I must say that I'm proud of you. I love you, and I respect you. And Mom, I have to say that if after thirty years of marriage you can still love this man, then maybe some special lady could learn to love me the same."

He walked over and kissed his parents. Everyone clapped. He glanced at Randi. She looked like she approved of his speech. Maybe one day she could love him, he thought. He made his way back over to her and sat down.

"Did I do good?" he asked.

"You did great." She squeezed his arm.

After the speeches and a few more introductions, the DJ started playing music. He began with Al Wilson's "Show and Tell" at the request of Anthony's parents. They danced the first dance alone. Later, the older guests joined the couple as the DJ played a few more oldies but goodies.

"Do you want something?" Anthony asked before he

ordered himself a drink.

"Water."

"Can I get an Icehouse and bottled water?" he requested. After the bartender brought the drinks, Anthony threw some money in the tip jar.

"Are you having a good time?" he asked as they watched the older folks dancing.

"Yeah. Your family is great, and your Aunt Betty is crazy."

"Every family has one."

"Well, at one point I thought she was going to pull out a switch, make you drop your pants and whip you." She smiled and took a sip of her water.

"It wouldn't be the first time. Aunt Betty got my rear end a whole lot of times. She'd get me, my neighbors would get me, and then they'd call my mom and she'd get me when I got home." He took a swallow of beer.

"You must have been a bad kid."

"I was." He chuckled.

"Who was worse, you or Mike?" She looked up at him. Yeah, he was a bad boy. The one Momma warned her about.

"I was. Mike's always been a good guy. He followed all the rules. Dotted his I's and crossed his T's. Never got in any trouble. Probably a lot like you."

"But you stayed in trouble."

"Yep. Never knew how to avoid it. Trouble just followed me around like a shadow."

Mike walked over to them. "Now, you can't hog this lady all night." He laughed. "Share."

"C'mon, man. I don't see her every day. My time with her is precious. Go harass someone else."

"I'm not harassing you, am I?" Mike asked Randi.

"No." She smiled

"Well, let's go dance." He took her by the arm.

"I really . . . " She looked at Anthony.

"C'mon. He doesn't mind. You don't mind, do you, baby brother?" He took Randi's water and set it on a table.

"If she doesn't mind," Anthony answered.

"Good." Mike pulled Randi onto the dance floor. She looked back at Anthony as if begging for help.

Anthony watched as Randi and Mike danced. She was an excellent dancer. He wasn't thrilled about seeing her dance with another man, even if it was his brother. Mike was still a man and he was single. He was the competition.

Randi's body moved to the music as if it were her natural rhythm, as if the music were her heartbeat. Each step was so precisely executed. She was beautiful, and she moved beautifully. When the music ended, Anthony thought they would stop dancing, but they didn't. They continued on to the next song.

He walked around socializing, trying to ignore what was happening on the dance floor, but Randi had unintentionally caused a scene. Her technique and style of dance made people stop to watch her. She was obviously unaware of her audience as her body devoured the music.

Anthony paused and watched them again. Mike was having too good a time with his woman, and although they never touched during their dance ritual, their bodies spoke to each other.

Anthony went to the bathroom and hoped they'd be finished when he returned. He was disappointed to see them still on the dance floor. His mother caught a glimpse of the worried look on his face and walked over to him.

"Hey, baby" she said. "Is everything okay?"

"Oh yeah, Mom." He forced a smile. He hated to

admit that he was jealous of Randi dancing with his only brother.

Sylvia stood beside him and watched what was happening on the dance floor. "Randi is a good dancer."

"She is."

"You'd better be careful. I think your brother's in love," she teased.

"It looks like it."

"You'd better go and rescue her." She knew that this woman had to be special to have this effect on him. Mike fell in love every six months, but Anthony had never fallen in love before, and she didn't want Randi to get away from him.

"I can't do that. Then I'd look like a fool," Anthony said.

"No. You'd look like a man in love."

"It's that obvious, huh?"

"That obvious. Now go and get her."

Anthony walked across the room to the dance floor and danced behind Randi. She turned around. He placed his hands on her hips as they moved to the rhythm. Mike continued dancing behind her until Sylvia approached him. She slid in between Mike and Randi and danced with him.

Randi liked the way Anthony's body moved. She saw him dancing in the videos, but these movements were different. His hands on her hips made her feel sexy. She held her hands up in the air as he pulled her closer. Their bodies almost touched. She looked up at him and smiled devilishly.

She is so sexy, he thought.

She turned in his hands and pushed her back up against his chest. He felt her behind barely touching his groin as their bodies moved in harmony.

"I didn't know you could move like this," he whispered against her ear.

131

She turned around to face him. "There's a lot of stuff about me that you don't know."

"How about sharing?"

"Maybe one day."

After a few more songs, the DJ announced that the next song would be the famous Cha-Cha Slide.

"I can't do that." Randi started to leave the dance floor.

"Sure you can. Come on." Anthony pulled her back.

"I don't know how," she insisted.

The music started and the crowd rushed to the dance floor. They started moving.

"Watch me. I'll show you." He moved her out of the way of the other people.

Mike grabbed her other arm. "C'mon, Randi, you can do this."

She watched them and clumsily tried to mimic their movements. The brothers encouraged her until she finally got the routine down. All three of them began to move in synchronized steps. They had a good time.

After the song, Randi sat down while Anthony went to get her some more water. Mike walked with him.

"So, what's the deal with you and Randi?" Mike asked while they stood at the bar and waited for the drinks.

"What do you mean?"

"You introduced her as a friend. What type of relationship do you have with her?"

"She's my girl," he answered after he got his drinks.

"Yeah right."

"She is."

"She's not your type."

"Not my type? What's my type?"

"You know what you're used to. Don't forget you told

me about all those women." They walked over to the side so they could have more privacy.

"I don't mess with those girls anymore," Anthony said.

"Anthony, please. All those women throwing themselves at you and you not hitting it. You used to get head from a different girl every night."

"Man, I've changed. I haven't been with another woman in months. I'm in love, man."

"Love? You crazy. You wouldn't know love if it bit you in the balls."

"For real, Mike. I'm in love with Randi."

"For real?" Mike still didn't believe him.

"You've met her. She's perfect. She's all that I want but more than I deserve. I've got plans for me and that girl."

"And you're serious, baby brother?"

"I'm serious."

"What about her? Is she in love with you?"

"I don't know, man. She's been thrown a few times, and she's afraid to get back up on the horse. Some nigga did some crazy shit to her."

"Once bitten, twice shy, huh?"

"Yep. So I'd appreciate if you'd stop trying to push up on her."

"Okay, but I know you. If you mess up, I'll be right there."

"I ain't trying to mess this up," Anthony told him.

"Well, go do your thing, baby brother."

After a few more songs, the DJ slowed it down with Luther Vandross and Cheryl Lynn singing "If This World Were Mine." Randi was talking to a couple of his cousins when Anthony walked up behind her.

"I want to dance with you," he whispered in her ear. He apologized to his cousins for stealing her away and pulled her over to a corner.

"I thought you wanted to dance."

"I do. Right here. I don't want to know that anybody else is in the room. Just you and me." He pulled her to him. His arms went around her waist, his hands rested on her lower back.

"You be careful with those hands," she teased as she laid her head against his chest. She loved this song, and being there in his arms felt so right.

He pulled her closer as they swayed to the music. She could hear his heartbeat, and although they barely moved, it pounded uncontrollably.

He started to sing so lightly that she could barely hear him, but it didn't matter. He just felt and smelled so good. This was perfect. She looked up at him as he sang to her.

He brought one hand up and held her face. Then he gently rubbed his thumb across her lips. They were so soft, just waiting to be kissed. He caressed her cheek as he tilted her face up to him. He lowered his head and his lips barely grazed hers. When he felt her respond, he kissed her softly and slowly. She parted her lips as she felt his tongue enter her mouth. *She tastes so sweet she could give a nigga a toothache,* he thought. He kissed her deeper as if trying to taste her soul. Randi's arms tightened around him as she held him closer. He dropped tiny kisses on her cheek and chin, before he reluctantly pulled away.

Randi opened her eyes and looked up at him. They stared into each other's eyes.

"What was that for?" she whispered. She still held onto him.

"Because you looked like you needed to be kissed."

"Oh, really?" She raised an eyebrow.

"Really."

134

"And what does needing to be kissed look like?"

"Like you look right now." He lowered his head and kissed her again.

"Hey, you two. Get a room," Mike said as he approached them. They pulled away from each other and laughed.

"What's up, man?" Anthony asked.

"The Soul Train line has just started. You know you can't miss that."

Anthony looked at Randi. "Shall we?"

"We shall," she replied.

The next morning, Randi got up, showered, and got dressed. After she packed, she went downstairs into the kitchen. Sylvia sat at the table drinking coffee and reading the paper. Anthony and his father piddled around outside in the garden.

"Good morning, sleepy head." Sylvia looked up from her paper. "We saved you some breakfast."

"Thanks." Randi picked up the plate of food they had left for her, and put it in the microwave.

"Did you have a good time last night?" Sylvia asked.

"I did." She stood by the microwave and waited for her food.

"You're going to have to visit us again."

The microwave started beeping.

"I'd like that." She took her food out and sat down at the table with Sylvia.

"I think you're good for Anthony."

"You think so?" She took a bite of her food.

"Yes, I do. You're a nice girl, a good girl; exactly what he needs."

135

"Anthony's been out there." She took a swallow of water.

"He has. Nevertheless, I think he's met his match in you. I see the way he looks at you. He's a changed man."

"You know he tried to sleep with me the first time we got together," Randi confessed.

"Did you slap the soup out of him?"

"No. But I did run as fast as I could to get away from him," Randi answered between bites of food.

"But he caught you."

Randi thought for a minute. "I guess he did." She stopped smiling.

"Don't look so sad, honey. Falling in love isn't as bad as it seems." She touched Randi's arm as she stood up from the table. "Anthony's not perfect. No one is. I only hope you can appreciate the way he feels about you." She walked over to the sink.

Randi stood up and followed her. "How does he feel about me?" She handed Sylvia her plate.

Sylvia rinsed it off and stuck it in the dishwasher. "He loves you, dear."

"He loves me." She looked at his mother in disbelief.

"Can't you tell?"

Anthony and his father entered the kitchen. "Hey, baby." Anthony kissed Randi's cheek. "Did you sleep well?"

Randi looked at his mother then up at him. "Yeah, I did." She forced a smile. Did he really love her like his mother said? Was he feeling the same way that she felt for him? She couldn't think about it now. "Good morning, Paul," she said to his father.

"Good morning, sweetness." He winked at her.

Anthony looked at his watch. "I guess we better get you to the airport. Your plane leaves in about hour and a half."

"I guess you're right."

Anthony went upstairs and got her bags. Randi thanked his parents for a wonderful time and for their hospitality, then Anthony took her to the airport. Her flight would leave at 10:00.

"You didn't say much in the car," he said after they checked her bags. "Is something wrong?"

"No." She smiled as she thought about what his mother had told her.

"Did my mom say something to you?" he asked as he adjusted the ball cap he wore to disguise his identity.

"No, she didn't." She looked into his eyes. "I really had a wonderful time. Thank you for inviting me."

"I hate to let you leave." He pushed some stray hairs back off her face.

"I hate to leave."

"Then don't. Fly with me back to L.A."

"You know I can't do that."

They called her flight number for boarding. She looked around at the gate then back at him.

"How about in two weeks? You can come and stay with me for a couple of days. See what it's like to live in my world."

"It sounds good." She would love to visit him in L.A.

"Good. I can show you around, introduce you to my peeps. I'll even take you to the studio."

"Okay." She agreed

They called her flight number again.

"I've gotta go."

"I know." He pulled her to him, kissed her and hugged her tight. He didn't want to let her go. "I love you," he whispered as he released her.

She stepped back from him, not sure if she believed her ears. She wanted to tell him that she felt the same way, that she had been in love with him for weeks, but she feared that by admitting it, their relationship would move a lot faster than she was ready for. She looked into his eyes then turned and walked away from him. She hadn't said a word, he realized. He had blown it. It was too soon for her.

He watched as her pace slowed and she turned around. She walked back toward him. She didn't care if the relationship was moving too fast. She wanted him to know. She wanted the whole world to know. A tear raced down her face and she quickly wiped it away as she approached him. Her arms went around his neck as she pulled him down to her. His mouth covered hers. She kissed him as if it was the last time. Finally, she pulled away.

"I love you too," she whispered against his lips before completely releasing him. She turned and walked away. This time she did not turn back.

Anthony smiled. She loved him too.

Chapter 14

Two weeks later, Anthony was picking Randi up at LAX airport. "I missed you," he said when met her. He grabbed her in an embrace.

"I missed you too." She stepped back and looked up at him.

A couple of weeks had passed since they last saw each other. She was happy to be there. They collected her bags and headed for his place.

She looked out the window of his pearl white Escalade at the beautiful sights of L.A. She felt his hand on hers and looked over at him. He smiled. He couldn't believe she was actually there.

It wasn't long before they arrived at his apartment. He opened the door to let her inside. Her mouth dropped as she entered the living room. It was huge.

"This is an apartment?" She looked around. "This is bigger than my mom's house."

The room was beautifully decorated. It was simple but elegant, nothing like she would expect from a single man's apartment. The walls were a slate blue, accented by the dark blue drapes pulled open to allow the sunlight in and reveal a spectacular view of the city.

The room, decorated with expensive leather furniture, was complete with a 46-inch television, a fireplace, and a semi-circular bar.

"Anthony, this is beautiful," she told him.

"It's what I call home. Come on. I'll show you to your room, and then you can take a look around." She followed

139

him down the massive hallway.

"I don't usually have company," he said as they passed the first door. "This is my bedroom." They kept walking. "Mom and Dad may come up and stay a day or two with me, so I have a second bedroom." He got to the second door, opened it then stepped back to allow her to enter.

The walls were a rose color. In the middle of the bedroom was a four-poster queen-sized bed covered with a pale yellow comforter decorated with a rose pattern to match the drapes and lampshade. The white furniture gave the room an elegant touch.

"So, did you do all this decorating yourself?" she couldn't help but ask.

"Hardly." He chuckled. "I got my mom to come down and decorate it for me. If I had decorated it then all you would see is black and leather."

"Your mom has good taste."

"She must have. She likes you a lot." He set her bags in a corner. "Go ahead and make yourself comfortable. You can look around if you like. I need to make a couple of telephone calls."

"Okay."

He went back into the living room and got on the telephone while Randi explored the rest of the apartment. She cracked open the door to his bedroom and stuck her head in. She wasn't sure what to expect— maybe whips and chains— but instead, she found another tastefully decorated room. She entered it and admired the décor in comforting shades of green.

A hunter green leather recliner sat near the window. Maybe he liked to sit back and watch women strip for him, Randi thought. She wondered how many women had been guests in his bedroom.

She peeked inside his bathroom. The floor was tile green marble. He had a sunken Jacuzzi tub and a separate glass-enclosed shower. There were his and hers marble sinks and a walk-in closet.

Curious, opened the medicine cabinet. He had all the usual, as well as a box of condoms. She picked up the box and looked at it. *Magnum,* she thought. *So, he's got it like that.* She smiled as she put the box back.

When she returned to the living room, he was just getting off the telephone.

"So, whatcha been doing?" he asked when he saw her.

"Just checking out your place."

He pulled her into his arms. "What do you think?" He pushed her hair back from her face as she looked up at him.

"It's nice. I'm impressed."

"Well, thank you," he said before kissing her. "I've missed you so much, girl."

The telephone rang and he answered it. Randi sat on the couch and waited for him to finish his conversation. After he hung up the telephone, he told her that it was his manager. They had been trying to get some studio time to work on his new album. The studio would be available in half an hour. They had to meet Thomas over there for a couple of hours. He would show her around when they finished.

When they got to the studio, Thomas Day, along with his producers, Irvin Douglas and Warren Martin, were already there.

"This is where it all happens," Anthony said as he opened the door for her. "This is where they make me a star."

The men stood when they saw Randi. Anthony introduced them.

"So, this is the famous Randi Jacobs." Thomas shook her hand. His eyes strolled up and down her body without any shame. "It's nice to meet you."

"Nice to meet you." She pulled her hand away from his. She didn't like the way he leered at her.

"This shouldn't take too long." Anthony kissed her on the forehead. "Go ahead, sit down and relax." He went into the booth while his producers went back to the mixing console and started talking to him.

"Why don't you come over and sit next to me?" Thomas suggested as he patted the space beside him on the couch.

Randi agreed and sat down. She tried to focus on what was going on with Anthony in the recording booth, but something about Thomas made her feel uneasy. In the booth, Irvin gave Anthony a few instructions then he put on his headset. Warren started the music. She liked the beat.

She felt Thomas's eyes on her. "Anthony is a lucky man," he said.

Randi looked at him as he licked his lips and grinned. He reminded her of the Cheshire cat in *Alice in Wonderland*.

"I mean damn, baby. You got your shit together."

"Thank you." She forced a smile. She wasn't sure if he was giving her a compliment or coming on to her. As Anthony started rhyming, she turned her attention back to him and tried to focus on his lyrics.

> *Girl, your ass is wearing them jeans,*
> *Like the skin on a grape,*
> *And though I'm peeping your talent,*
> *Make no mistake.*
> *Brothas sweating you hard,*
> *All up in your area,*
> *'Cause we feelin' you, girl.*
> *Damn, you wifey material.*

You make me wanna settle down,
Get a legitimate gig.
Make me wanna buy a ring,
Have 2.5 kids.
When you step up in the club,
You cause mass hysteria.
Brothas don't know how to act,
'Cause you wifey material.

I see you licking your lips,
And smiling with your eyes.
The swivel in your hips,
Got a nigga hypnotized.
We all trying to see if
We fit your criteria.
No more playas for life,
Shit, you wifey material.

Thomas slid closer to her. "You know I own that boy right there. A sistah like you don't have to settle for the help when you can have the owner," he whispered in her ear. His breath was hot on her face and it stank of cigarettes. "Let me know when you feel like fucking a real man."

"Get lost, you creep," she muttered as she stood up. Anthony looked over at her to see what was wrong. She mouthed the words to him that she would wait for him outside as she pointed to the door. He nodded. She left the room.

Thomas leaned back on the couch with a big grin on his face. *She won't be around here too long*, he thought. Anthony didn't need her in his life. She was bad for both him and his career. His rhymes were getting soft. He was turning into a little punk-ass nigga for this ho who wouldn't even give up the pussy. No, Thomas thought, he wasn't throwing away his golden egg-laying goose just because this trick had his boy's nose wide open. He would do whatever it took to make sure she didn't stick around.

Randi paced in the hallway, wondering what was Thomas's problem, before she decided to venture outside to get some fresh air. The sun seemed hotter in L.A than it was in North Carolina. It beamed down on her skin. A cool breeze came by and gave her a little relief from the heat. After a while, Anthony came searching for her.

"What are you doing out here?"

"Just wanted to get some fresh air." She tried to smile.

"Thomas didn't say anything out of the way to you, did he? He can be an asshole sometimes."

"No," she lied. She didn't want to tell him that Thomas had come on to her. She didn't want to cause any controversy.

"So, what did you think about the new song?"

"I liked it. I didn't hear much of it, but I did like the beat and what I heard of your lyrics."

"Well, we've gotta lay down one more track and then we'll be able to leave. It's hot out here. Why don't you come back inside and get in the air?"

"I will in a minute."

He studied her face. "Are you sure you're okay?"

"I'm fine," she assured him. "Now, go back and finish what you have to do."

"I won't be long," he said before he went back into the building.

Randi went back inside a minute or two later to get out of the heat. She took a sip of water from the fountain and waited in the hallway for Anthony.

Some time later, Anthony and the rest of the guys emerged from the recording room. They were laughing, obviously happy with the results of their work.

"That shit was as tight as hell," Irvin said. "And I'm feeling those lyrics."

"At the rate you're moving, man, we can get that album finished before Christmas," Warren said.

"Well, I'd like to see it drop before then." Thomas looked at Anthony. "If you can give us some more of your time, we can make it happen."

"I'll see what I can do." Anthony walked over to Randi and put his arm around her.

"Check this out," Thomas said. "I'll see you at the pool party today, right?" He looked at Anthony.

"What pool party?"

"Marvin Sadler is having a party today at his place. You were invited. I thought I told you."

"Naw, man. I don't remember anything like that."

"Well, he's working on his new movie. He's considering you for a role, so you gotta be there." He pulled out a cigarette and lit it.

"I got plans with Randi today."

Thomas took a draw off the cigarette. "Bring her. I'm sure she has a bikini." He smiled at her. "You can't miss this opportunity. All the big-name rappers are into the movies now. P Diddy, Ja Rule, DMX, LL, even Bow Wow. You gotta to keep your name out there." He took another draw on his cigarette and blew the smoke up in the air.

Anthony looked down at Randi.

"It's okay," she said.

"Are you sure you don't mind? We don't have to."

"Sure you do." Thomas edged in.

"I don't mind. We're in your world, right?"

He nodded. "We'll just stop by for an hour or two and then we'll have the rest of the day to ourselves." He looked at

Thomas. "What time does it start?"

"Two o' clock."

"You guys gonna to be there?" Anthony asked Irvin and Warren.

"Hell yeah," they said in unison.

"Beautiful women in bikinis, you don't have to twist my arm," Warren said with a smile.

"That's what I'm talking 'bout," Irvin added.

"You know where his place is?" Thomas asked.

"Yeah, I know. I'll be there," Anthony answered

Anthony apologized to Randi as they drove back to his place to get their swimsuits.

"It's all right. This should be nice." She put her hand on his.

Back at his place, Randi put on her bikini and wore it under her shorts and T-shirt. Anthony just wore his swimming trunks and a T-shirt. When they got to Marvin Sadler's place, Randi's mouth dropped open. It was a mansion. She had never seen a place like it in real life, only on television or in the movies. It was a pale yellow, southwestern-style mansion with a red terracotta roof. The circular driveway was packed with luxury cars from Ferraris to Porsches to Jaguars to Bentleys.

People actually live like this in real life, she thought.

Anthony looked over at her and saw the look of astonishment on her face. "Breathtaking, ain't it?"

She looked over at him. "Never in my wildest dreams could I have dreamed up a place like this. I mean, I know that people live like this but I, I . . . " She couldn't find the words to describe it.

"I know," he said. "First time I saw a place like this, it blew my mind to think that one day I could live like this."

Two valets approached and opened their doors. Anthony gave his keys to one of them and walked around to

Randi's side of the car. He took her hand and led her up to the mansion.

The butler opened the massive door and instructed them to follow. Randi looked around at the huge foyer with two spiral staircases that met at the top. The marble floor was so polished they could see their reflections in it. The sunlight danced off a huge crystal chandelier hanging above them.

Randi tried not to look starry-eyed, but she wanted to drink up as much as she could as they walked through the house to the back. The rooms were enormous. Beautiful, one-of-a-kind paintings decorated the walls. Drapes made of fabrics from the most exotic places in the world covered the windows.

When they got to the pool area, Randi was even more taken aback. The place was swarming with beautiful women and men, all dressed in the tiniest swimsuits. There was an Olympic-sized pool where a couple of people played water games. Models lay out in lounge chairs, trying to catch some rays. Off to the side were two square-shaped Jacuzzis filled with people laughing and drinking champagne that came from the bar where the most expensive alcohol flowed like water. Other guests sat beneath huge palm trees that provided shade from the sun, or enjoyed the exotic foods spread out on the enormous buffet table. A DJ entertained them all, pumping out some of the latest and hottest music in the hip-hop industry.

Anthony's arm tightened around her waist. "You want something to drink?" he asked.

"Yeah," she said as she continued to take in the view.

They walked over to the bar where he ordered her some water and himself a glass of champagne. Just as Anthony handed her a bottle of Evian, she spotted Thomas walking toward them. He wore bright orange swimming trunks, shamelessly revealing his hairy back and potbelly. It was so large that Randi hoped there was a doctor around just in case he went into labor.

"You made it," he managed to say with a cigarette wedged between his thin lips.

"Only for an hour or two," Anthony reminded him.

"C'mon. I want you to meet Marvin." He pulled the cigarette from his lips as they followed him. "This could be good for your career."

They approached an older man sitting in a chair with a beautiful woman on his lap. When he saw them, he signaled the girl to get up, then he stood.

Thomas introduced them. "Marvin Sadler, this is Anthony Talbert, a.k.a. Animalistic. Anthony, this is Marvin Sadler."

Anthony removed his arm from Randi's waist and shook Marvin's hand. "This is my lady, Randi Jacobs."

Marvin shook her hand then turned his attention back to Anthony. "I'm interested in putting you in my latest movie."

"Why don't you two talk shop and I'll entertain Randi here?" Thomas offered as he gave her one of his wicked smiles.

"That's okay," Randi said. "I'll be all right on my own."

"You sure? Thomas can keep you company." Anthony didn't want her to feel stranded.

"I'm sure," she answered, trying to avoid Thomas's gaze.

Anthony leaned down and kissed her. "I won't be too long."

"Okay." She walked over to the one of the lounge chairs by the pool and sat. Anthony sat down with Marvin to discuss the movie, but kept his eyes on her.

Randi took a couple sips of water as she watched the people in the pool play volleyball. She got splashed a couple of times and the water felt good. A few minutes later, she decided to take a dip in the pool to escape the heat. She slipped off her sandals and stood. She pulled off her T-shirt, unfastened her shorts and let them fall to her ankles to reveal a sexy little black bikini.

Damn, Anthony said to himself when he saw this. He no longer heard what Marvin was saying.

She picked up her clothes, folded them, and laid them on her chair. When she started to get into the pool, one of the guys who was already in swam over to help her.

"Thanks." She took his hand and lowered herself into the cool water. Anthony watched intensely.

The stranger introduced himself. "My name is David Daniels."

"Randi Jacobs."

"Are you new? I haven't seen you around at any of these parties before."

"I'm not in the business. I'm just here with my friend."

"So, this friend of yours, male or female?" he asked.

"Male." She smiled.

Marvin finally got Anthony's attention. "I've got a script that you can take home, read, and then you can call me with your thoughts."

"That sounds good," Anthony answered, eyes still glued to Randi and her new friend. Marvin realized that Anthony's mind was elsewhere.

"Go ahead and have fun. I'll have one of my people give you the script before you leave."

"Thanks." They stood up and shook hands.

Anthony walked over to the side of the pool. Randi had gotten rid of her friend and was swimming by herself. He slipped off his shoes and pulled off his shirt. Just as he was about to get into the water, a beautiful model approached him. Randi emerged from below the water and watched them.

"I just love you, Animalistic," the model said. "I've got all your CDs. You're so damn hot." She pursed her red lips.

"Thank you," Anthony said.

"I'm trying to get into this movie. Maybe we'll be working together."

"Maybe."

She touched his chest with her matching red fingertips. He stepped back from her. "I don't think that's a good idea," he said.

"Well, can a sistah at least get a hug? I'm harmless." She smiled seductively.

He could tell by the devilish smile on her face that she was far from harmless. *Dangerous* was a more appropriate adjective to describe her.

"I don't think that's a good idea either." He had never turned down so many women since he met Randi.

He lowered himself into the water and waded over to her. The model looked at Randi and rolled her eyes before she walked away.

He put his hands on Randi's hips. "I love your bikini."

"You don't think it's too much?" She rested her hands on his arms and looked up at him.

More like too little, he thought. "No," he said. "It looks great on you. It really shows off your—"

"Don't say it." She smiled. "So, how did it go with Marvin?"

"Good. He's gonna give me a script to read so I can see what I think about it. You having fun?"

"Yeah."

He looked over at the Jacuzzis. One of them was unoccupied. "Let's get in the hot tub," he suggested.

They climbed out of the pool and headed the tub. Jason Novice, a video director, stopped them.

"Hey, Anthony, who's this?"

"This is Randi Jacobs. Randi, this is Jason Novice. He's only the hottest video director in L.A."

"Check this out, Randi. I've been watching you. Do you do videos?"

Randi was flattered. "No." She smiled.

"Well, I'd be interested in putting you in a few of my videos. What do you think?"

She looked up at Anthony, and before she could answer, he spoke up. "Randi's not interested in doing any videos."

"Let the lady speak for herself," Jason protested.

"I may be interested," she said just to get under Anthony's collar for speaking for her.

"Randi, you're not interested in anything like that," he said.

"Here's my card," said Jason. Randi took it. "Give me a call tomorrow."

"I'll get with you later," Jason said to Anthony before he walked off.

"You aren't really serious about that, are you?" he asked as they went back to the Jacuzzi and climbed in.

"Why not?" She sat between his legs and felt him slip his arms around her waist. His hands rested on her stomach.

"I just don't picture you as a video girl, that's all." Two of his fingers circled her belly button.

151

"Would you protest if I did it?" She rested her elbows on his thighs.

"No. I couldn't. I'd have to respect what you want to do."

She liked his response.

He leaned over and kissed her on the jaw. The fingers on her belly button had started to cause a stir inside her. She parted her legs slightly as if giving him an invitation. As she laid her head back against his chest, she closed her eyes. The thumping sound of 50 Cent's "Twenty-one Questions" pumped through the air.

"I wouldn't do it anyway," she said.

"I thought you said you were interested in it."

"That was just to get your goat since you spoke up for me so fast." She smiled.

"Get my goat?"

"It's an old country saying that means to bother you, get under your skin."

"You're already under my skin." He kissed her ear and gently tugged on it with his teeth.

Her heartbeat quickened as she felt one of his hands drop below her navel. His fingers brushed against the edge of her bikini bottom and played with the elastic band as he gently massaged her belly. He wondered what her response would be if he slipped his fingers down into her bikini. She felt him become aroused as his manhood began to press against her back.

He pulled her tighter against him as his fingers continued to debate whether it was all right to travel even farther down. She opened her legs a little wider and he saw this as an invitation. He slowly slipped his fingers below the waistband and waited for her to stop him. When she didn't, he edged his finger a little farther. He felt the curly hairs of her pubic area. He hadn't touched a woman like that in so long it was ridiculous.

She let out a little moan. It had been a year and a half since someone had gotten this far with her. He inched his fingers down as he thought about her poem and licked his lips. His tongue craved to taste her caramel folds of womanhood.

"What are you two kids up to?" Thomas asked as he walked over to them.

They both jumped, startled back into reality. Anthony quickly pulled his fingers out of her bikini bottom and she automatically closed her legs. Thomas puffed on a cigarette.

"How can you smoke those things in this heat?" Anthony tried to sound calm.

"Can't help myself." He kicked off his sandals. "Mind if I join you?" he asked. Without waiting for a response, he lowered himself into the water directly across from them and started talking about business.

Randi closed her eyes again and laid her head against Anthony's chest. He had lost his erection. The vibration of his voice made her doze off.

"Little lady's not used to this lifestyle," Thomas joked.

A short while later, Thomas left and Anthony awakened Randi. Drowsily, she looked up at him. He kissed her temple.

"You ready to get out of here, baby?" he asked.

"Yeah."

They climbed out of the Jacuzzi and found some towels on a nearby table. After drying themselves, they slipped back into their clothes. Before they left, Anthony caught up with Marvin and got the script he promised. Because Randi was tired from the jetlag and the hot sun, they picked up some takeout, rented a couple of movies, and headed back to his apartment.

After a shower and dinner, they lay on the couch together and watched the movies. Within a few minutes, they both fell asleep.

Hours later, Anthony woke up. Since Randi was still asleep, he decided to put her in bed. He carefully slid from behind her and climbed off the couch, trying not to wake her. Gently, he picked her up in his arms and carried her down the hall to her bedroom. He attempted to lay her down without waking her, but he wasn't successful.

Her eyes opened as he lowered her onto the bed. Her arm instinctively went around his neck to keep herself from falling. When he laid her down, she didn't let go, forcing him to remain leaning over her. His face was so close to hers that she felt his warm breath on her skin. He looked into her eyes when he realized she wasn't letting go. She stared back, not sure of what she was doing.

Seconds, which seemed like minutes, passed before he slowly lowered his mouth onto hers. He kissed her gently at first, as if he were savoring her lips. When he felt her respond to him, he kissed her deeper. He pushed her lips apart with his own as his tongue entered her mouth. She felt the weight of his body lower down onto hers as he lay on top of her.

She kissed him as she drank from his soul. Her hands moved over his back and she arched her body against his. He brought his hands up to her face and held it as his mouth traveled down to her chin then along her jaw-line then to her neck. She felt the hardness of his manhood against her thigh as he pushed himself up against her. They both wanted more. Finally, he raised his head and looked down at her.

"Can I make love to you?" he asked with his lips barely touching hers. His eyes probed hers for an answer.

She stared up at him. "Yes," she whispered.

"Are you sure?"

"Yes. I'm sure."

He hesitated for a moment. "Wait right here," he said before he kissed her again and got up. He left the room, returning a few seconds later.

Randi was puzzled by this until she saw him lay a condom on the nightstand. He climbed back onto the bed and gathered her in his arms. Slowly he peeled away her clothes, replacing them with long, hot kisses until she lay naked in front of him. He continued to explore her body with his hands and mouth. She arched her back as she felt his mouth cover her breasts. He nursed gently on them before his lips traveled down over her ribs and belly. He paused at her belly button, his tongue probing her flesh while his fingers gently teased her ribs.

When he started moving below her belly button, she protested "Don't." She barely whispered. No one had ever done that to her before.

He raised his head to look at her. She stared back. He gently spread her legs and lowered his head. He heard her gasp as he tasted her with his tongue. He never imagined that she would taste so sweet. *Caramel* was not the word to describe her sugary insides. She closed her eyes. Her hands slowly slid down to his head as her body began to move against his mouth. She felt his tongue entering her, teasing her, driving her crazy. His skilled tongue worked with perfect precision, tasting every crevice of her treasure. She moaned against her will as his mouth continued to savor her sweetness. Then she felt him insert his finger as he continued to tantalize her with his tongue.

"Oh God," she whispered as he inserted another and gently worked it in and out of her.

He felt her legs begin to tremble as she clutched at his head. He pressed his tongue against her clitoris as her body shook uncontrollably. When he felt her go limp, he raised his head and gazed down at her beautiful body.

He stood up, removed his clothes and released his swollen manhood, which had been straining against his pants. He reached for the condom and slipped it on without taking his eyes off her. Slowly, he climbed between her opened legs and lowered himself on top of her.

She felt his hardness pressing against the inside of her thigh. He kissed her gently, sliding one hand down to her thigh and spreading her legs open wider. As he began to enter her, he felt her body tense up against the pain.

"Are you okay?" He looked into her eyes.

She nodded as she tried to relax. He pushed himself all the way inside her.

"Damn," he whispered. "You feel so damn good."

She felt herself opening up around him. He waited patiently for her body to relax and accommodate him. Slowly, he began to move against her as his mouth traveled from hers down her jaw then to her neck. He moaned as her body responded to his.

Although he had slept with hundreds of women, nobody ever made him feel like he felt with Randi. They moved in a slow, rhythmic motion together. Their pace quickened as their passion built. Her fingers clutched at his back as she reached another climax. His body became tense as he drove himself deeper and deeper inside of her. He held her as if he was holding on for life.

"Oh God." He moaned. "Oh God, Randi." His entire body became rigid as he shuddered. She held him tightly as he collapsed on top of her. Gently, she stroked his head as he lay exhausted. His breathing began to calm down as he pulled his fingers through her hair.

"I love you so much, Randi." he managed to whisper

against her ear. He raised his head up and kissed her deeply.

"I love you too," she whispered as she looked into his eyes.

He rolled off her and pulled her into his arms. After he pushed her hair away from her face so he could see her, he tilted her head up and forced her to look him in the eyes.

"I'm going to make you happy," he promised.

"You already have."

He pulled her face to his and kissed her as he caressed her cheek. She lay her head on his chest. As he fell asleep, she lay in his arms and listened to him breathing. She closed her eyes and felt his heartbeat. Before she fell asleep, she thought, *I hope this wasn't a mistake.*

Later that night, she awakened to an empty bed. She looked over at the glowing numbers of the alarm clock. It was 3:35 in the morning. She wondered where Anthony was. After lying in the dark for a couple of minutes, she pulled on her robe and went to look for him. She found him in his bedroom, sitting on his bed, playing video games on his PlayStation II. He looked like a little boy as he focused intensely on the game.

"You want some company?" she asked as she stood in the doorway.

He looked over at her. "I didn't mean to wake you. Come on in."

"You didn't." She walked over to the bed.

"I couldn't sleep," he explained. "You want to play?"

"I don't know how." She sat on the bed next to him.

"No, come here." He took her hand and pulled her around to sit between his legs. He put the controller in her hands and instructed her. After he pulled her hair back and kissed her neck, he watched her play.

He wasn't going to blow this, he thought. He wasn't

going to let Randi Jacobs out of his life.

When Anthony awakened later that morning, Randi was standing in front of the window, looking out over the city. Still naked, he climbed out of bed, slid up behind her, and slipped his arms around her waist. He kissed the back of her head.

"What are you thinking about?" he asked with his face in her perfumed hair.

"I've got to leave today," she whispered sadly.

He inched her robe down, revealing a little bit of her shoulder, and replaced it with a kiss. "You don't have to. You could stay."

"I can't." She felt his fingers pull her robe open as his tongue traced from her shoulder up to her neck. One of his hands traveled across her belly up to her breasts. He teased the nipple with his fingers.

"Why can't you?" he asked as he gently bit her ear before his tongue darted inside. His hand slid down between her legs and his fingers delicately probed the folds of her womanhood until he felt her moistness.

What is he doing to me? Randi thought as she felt his finger inside of her. Her legs became weak. She needed him.

"Why can't you stay with me?" He asked as his tongue continued to explore her ear.

"I can't."

He turned her around, cupped her face in his hands and kissed her feverishly. Next he slipped the robe all the way off her shoulders and let it fall to her feet. He picked her up, wrapped her legs around his waist, and carried her to the bed. Slowly, he laid her down and allowed his body to rest on top of hers.

"Open your eyes, Randi," he whispered against her lips. She did. He wanted her to see who was making love to her.

They didn't say much in the car on the way to the airport. Anthony kept looking over at Randi as she stared out the window. He didn't want her to leave. They checked her bags then sat down and waited for her flight. She rested her head on his chest and closed her eyes. She tried to remember everything that had happened that weekend. She didn't want to forget any second of it. Well, maybe she could discard the parts containing Thomas.

His hand moved up and down her back in an attempt to make her feel better. His schedule would start becoming hectic for the next few weeks, with the work he had to do on his new album and the movie role he was considering. He didn't know when he would get some free time to see her.

They called her flight number for boarding. She hesitated then stood up. He stood up and pulled her into his arms.

"You don't have to leave, Randi. You can stay here with me," he whispered against her hair. He held onto her, not wanting to let her go. Inside of him, it felt as if his heart was being crushed.

They called her flight number again.

"I have to go," she murmured against his chest.

He still didn't let her go. Instead, he squeezed her even tighter as she sobbed against him. He stroked her hair.

"You don't have to go, baby."

"I have to go." She pulled away from him. He wiped the tears from her face.

"Don't cry." He kissed her eyes, her nose, and her cheek until he found her mouth, where he stayed and drank from her. "I love you," he whispered

"I love you." She pulled herself out of his arms, turned around, and walked away without looking back. She knew that if she had, she wouldn't have been able to leave.

Anthony watched as she gave her ticket to the attendant and walked into the tunnel that led to her plane. He sat down in one of the chairs and wiped his eyes.

This was hard, he thought. Love wasn't supposed to make him feel like this.

Chapter 15

"You whore," Kathy said playfully when Randi told her that she had slept with Anthony. "Was it good?"

"It was nice." She tried not to sound too whorish.

"How do you feel about the situation now? Do you think you can handle it?"

"I don't know. It was so hard saying goodbye to him yesterday. I do love him, and he says he loves me. I just hate being away from him."

"Girl, you've got it bad."

"Don't I know it."

"So, when are you going to see him again?"

"I don't know. He's got a pretty busy schedule for the next few weeks. He's going to try to fit me in."

"Well, I'm happy for you. He's the one, Randi. I can tell."

"How can you tell?"

"Because you gave him the bootie." Kathy laughed. She was so happy that her friend had fallen in love.

***

Anthony stood in the studio booth with a headset on. He listened to the beat and tried to focus on the task at hand. However, his mind would slip back to Randi and how good she felt, how good it felt when she put her fingers on his skin, how sweet she tasted. He remembered how her eyes lit up when she looked up at him, how her legs felt wrapped around his waist, and how his heart ached when she walked away from him at the airport.

Talking to her every day was not enough. He wanted to see her and hold her and kiss her. He wanted to make love to her in every way. He was so engrossed in thought he missed his cue to start rapping for the third time in a row.

"What the fuck are you doing?" Thomas barked as he ripped his cigarette out of his mouth. "Get your shit together, nigga."

Anthony ignored his outburst and kept his eyes on Irvin and Warren. "Give it to me again," he said.

They started the music. He nodded his head to the beat and licked his lips. He hit his cue this time and spit out the lyrics, but they were not raw enough for Thomas.

"Hold up, hold up!" Thomas yelled. The music stopped. "Get that bitch out of your head and do your damn job."

Anthony ripped the headset off and pointed at Thomas. "Fuck you, nigga. Fuck you!" he shouted as he paced the floor of the booth. He threw the headset against the wall and tore open the door. "I'm outta here."

Irvin hurried over to him. "He didn't mean nothing by it, dawg. Calm down." He put his hand on Anthony's shoulder to stop him from leaving.

Anthony looked over at Thomas, who calmly pulled on his cigarette and blew the smoke up into the air.

"Sorry, dawg. I was out of line." He took another puff on his cigarette before putting it out in an ashtray. "I know you're in love, man, but you can't let that fuck up your career. We've been doing this shit for over six years now. Don't fuckin' throw it away."

Anthony took a deep breath and exhaled.

"Let's finish this so we can get the hell out of here," Irvin suggested.

"All right, man," Anthony agreed and returned to the booth. He got another headset and waited for his cue. This time, he started rhyming the way Thomas wanted him to rhyme.

***

A few days later, Randi pulled up to her apartment building at 11:35 at night. She had just gotten home from work. Slowly, she climbed the stairs to her apartment. She was tired. When she turned the corner, she noticed someone sitting on the porch outside her front door. She hesitated.

The first person she thought of was Eric, and her heart began to thump against her chest. She gripped the edge of the handrail and prepared herself to run. But as the person stood, his face got closer to the porch light, and she realized that the stranger was Anthony. She let out a sigh of relief as she tried to calm herself down.

He walked toward her and pulled a bouquet of white roses from behind his back. He presented them to her.

"What are you doing here?" she asked excitedly.

"So many questions." He laughed as he scooped her up in his arms and kissed her.

They could barely get inside the apartment before they had ripped each other's clothes off. He picked her up, carried her into the kitchen and sat her on the table. He pushed her down until she lay on her back, then he spread her legs. His mouth covered her womanhood as he savored the taste of her warm flesh. Randi closed her eyes as his full, strong lips and agile, skilled tongue took her to ecstasy. After she climaxed, he entered her. He closed his eyes as he felt the warm wetness of her body envelope him. Slowly, gently he made love to her. He gripped her hips as he buried himself

163

deeper.

"Damn, Randi, what the hell are you doing to me?" he moaned just before he spilled himself inside of her. Nearly spent, he picked her up and carried her to the bedroom, where he made love to her again.

A while later, all of his energy was drained and she lay on top of him. His long fingers gently traced up and down her buttocks. He loved the way they fit in his hands.

"Randi."

She lifted her head and looked at him. "Yes."

"I don't like your hours."

"What do you mean?"

"I don't like you coming home this late at night. Like tonight, for example. I could have been anybody. What would you have done if I had tried to attack you?"

"Run, scream, I guess."

He pushed his hand through her hair. "It's not safe." He hated the thought of losing her to some craziness.

"I know, but what else can I do? The earliest I can get off is ten."

"You could quit. Let me take care of you. I think I make enough money." He smiled.

"I'm sure you do, but I can't."

"You can't take money from me?"

"No, I can't."

"Independent woman," he said as he continued stroking her hair. "If you and I were married, you'd still insist on working?"

"I don't know." She changed the subject. "How long can you stay?"

"I've got to leave first thing in the morning. Thomas is already biting my head off for being over here now."

"You like him?" she asked.

"He's all right. He brought me a long way. I owe him a lot."

"No. Your talent brought you a long way. He owes you a lot."

"Getting back to your work schedule, what are we gonna do about it?"

"I don't know."

"Can you get another job? Somewhere you don't have to come home so late at night."

"I like my job. Besides, if it wasn't for that job, I wouldn't have met you."

"Score one for the job."

Chapter 16

A few weeks later Randi was back in L.A. with Anthony. She sat in his car with a blindfold over her eyes as he drove. He had a surprise planned for her.

"Where are we going?" she asked. She felt silly riding around with a blindfold.

"You'll see when we get there. Be patient." He put one of his hands on hers.

She felt good about their relationship. When they were apart, she was a little worried about the distance that separated them, but his daily telephone calls assured her that they would be okay.

After they drove for about thirty minutes, she felt the car slow down, turn off the road and stop. She heard a buzzing sound then the car began to move again, but this time much slower.

"I hope you're not trying to kidnap me," she teased.

"I am." The car stopped again. "We're here," he announced as he got out and walked over to her side. He took her hand and helped her out. She heard the car door shut behind her. He held onto her arm and guided her. After a few more steps, they stopped.

"Are you ready?" He moved behind her.

"Yes." She could barely stand it.

He loosened the blindfold then stopped. "I don't think you're ready," he whispered in her ear.

"Anthony," she scolded.

He removed the blindfold and she opened her eyes. In front of her stood a beautiful, 10,000 square foot, $2.9-million brick mansion. Her mouth fell open as she looked at the house then looked up at him.

"So, what do you think?" He squeezed her hand.

"It's beautiful." She looked back at the mansion. "What are we doing here? Are you buying this?"

"Come on." He took her hand and they walked up to the mansion. He removed a key from his pocket and unlocked the door. They stepped inside.

"Oh my God," she said as she looked around.

The foyer was massive, with a beautiful custom-designed hardwood floor and an exquisite chandelier.

"Could you live in a place like this?" he asked as he watched her reaction.

She looked at him in disbelief. "What have you done?"

"Come on and let me show you around." He gave her the grand tour of the six bedrooms, four and a half bath mansion, describing every room to her. There was even a kidney-shaped pool, a sauna for twelve, a tennis court and basketball court.

"This is where we'll be able to watch movies," he said as he showed her the media room. He picked up a remote control from the wet bar and pushed a button. A huge movie screen descended from the ceiling.

"Tell me what's going on."

"Not yet." He led her up the spiral staircase. "This is the master bedroom. Check out the view. "This house sits on twelve acres of land," he continued, sounding like a tour guide. "It has an orchard and a manmade pond."

She walked over to the window and looked out. The landscape was beautifully manicured. She could see the pool, the tennis courts, along with a pond and a detached four-car garage. She couldn't believe this place. He stood behind her with his arms wrapped around her waist.

"Do you like it?" he asked.

She turned in his arms to face him. "Yes, I do," she

167

answered, still confused. "Are you buying this place?"

"Yes." He finally answered one of her questions. "For you." He reached into his pocket and pulled out a small ring box as he got down on one knee in front of her. He took her hand and cleared his throat. Randi put her free hand over her mouth in disbelief and started crying.

"Randi, you're everything to me. When you're away from me, I go crazy. When you're with me, I am weak. I never imagined being in love, much less loving someone the way I love you. I can't picture myself without you. I know this is quick and we've only been together for about three months, but I know that you're the one for me. Baby, you make me want to be a better man. You're all that I want and more than I deserve." He paused. "Will you marry me?"

By the time he finished, Randi was sobbing uncontrollably. He nervously fumbled with the ring box as he opened it and took out the platinum princess-cut three stone diamond ring. He slipped it on her trembling finger and waited for an answer, but she couldn't stop crying. She was in shock and couldn't believe this was happening. She didn't know what to say. He stood up and held her tear-covered face in his hands, tilting her head up forcing her to look at him.

"I don't know what to say." She finally managed to speak.

"Say yes," he said.

"But . . ."

"You love me, don't you?"

She nodded.

"And I love you."

"We . . ."

He brushed the tears from her cheeks with his thumbs. "I can't stand being away from you. You can quit your job, move here with me and I'll take care of you. You won't have to work. You can go to UCLA, take your writing classes and become a famous writer. All you have to do is say yes."

"This so sudden." Her heart pounded.

"If I ask you a year from now, would you say yes?"

"Yes."

He lowered his forehead until it touched hers. "Then all you have to do is say yes now."

"Yes," she whispered.

"Yes?"

"Yes." She nodded as she began to cry even more. "Yes. Yes. Yes."

He rained kisses all over her tear-soaked face before his mouth landed on hers. She could taste her own salty tears from his lips. Their kiss deepened as he crushed her body against his. He slowly pulled away from her.

"There's something else." He took her hand and led her downstairs.

Randi wiped the tears from her eyes. What more could it be? He led her to the garage and opened the door. They stepped inside. In front of her sat a silver Jaguar.

Randi's mouth dropped open. "No." She whispered.

"Yes," he answered as he watched her.

"Anthony!" she cried.

He pulled out the keys and attempted to hand them to her. She just stared at them. He placed them in her hand. "Why don't you take me for a ride?" He opened the car door for her.

Chapter 17

After the initial shock, Kathy agreed to be her maid of honor. They were married six months later on the grounds of their new home.

Initially, Randi's parents weren't pleased with both the facts that they got married so soon and that she married a rapper. However, after they got to know Anthony, they realized that their love was genuine and he wasn't the bad guy they saw in his videos.

On the other hand, Anthony's parents were thrilled from the start. They adored Randi and thought that she was perfect for him.

Anthony had arranged to fly Randi's guests over and set them up in hotels. All of his friends and family were there, including his manager.

Thomas told Anthony that he thought the marriage was a mistake. He told Anthony that although he liked Randi, she made him soft and his music had suffered because of her.

The guest list included some of the biggest names in the business. Uninvited guest included die-hard fans and the paparazzi. Some sneaked in by pretending to be the wait staff for the reception, while others scaled the fence that surrounded their estate. Security caught most of them and escorted them out.

At the reception, Cristal flowed like water. Anthony spared no expense in making sure that Randi had the best of everything. He even arranged for Michael Daniels, Randi's favorite R&B singer, to perform for her. Before the night was over, the infamous Cha-Cha Slide was played, and everybody got up and danced. This time Randi knew the steps.

After the reception, Randi and Anthony said goodbye to their family and friends. They slipped away from their guests in a stretch limousine and made their way to the airport. From there, they boarded a private jet and headed for their honeymoon in the Bahamas.

Two weeks later they returned home. Randi immediately enrolled in classes at UCLA where she majored in creative writing, while Anthony left for a two-month tour. Thomas threw it together at the last minute. Anthony only had two weeks to spend with his bride in their new home before he had to take off.

Randi was a little disappointed that he had to leave so soon, but she understood. She was married to a rap superstar. He was in demand. He couldn't just sit at home babysitting her. Still, she felt that Thomas had set up the tour on purpose. She knew that he wasn't her biggest fan, so she tried not to complain or cause problems between him and Anthony.

While on tour, Anthony managed to call every night to make sure she was fine and to let her know what he was up to. He said that the tour was great, and that every show had been sold out. He promised to be home as soon as he could.

A couple of times, he flew Kathy over to spend some time with Randi. Anthony gave Randi a few credit cards so she could start decorating the mansion. During Kathy's visits, they would spend the day shopping. Kathy made her laugh. And when Randi felt down about Anthony being away, Kathy constantly reminded her of how much he loved her, how much he needed her, and he was only doing his job.

Anthony had a hard time dealing with being away from her also. He rolled over in his bed to reach for her, but she wasn't there. He held on to the memories of what she smelled like, what she tasted like, and how she felt. He carried her picture in his wallet so he could remember her smile.

While all the other rappers were out at after-parties, he was up in his hotel room on the telephone with Randi, discussing the events of their day. He didn't tell her about the women because he didn't want to add to her insecurities.

The women were relentless. They didn't care that he was married. They continued to throw themselves at him. While some stowed away on his tour bus, others attempted to sneak into his hotel room to seduce him. They offered him everything from blow-jobs to anal sex to some of the freakiest things he had ever heard of. Although tempted, he remained faithful to Randi. He knew that even though these women offered him the time of his life, he had his platinum princess at home. He wasn't willing to throw that away for anything or anybody.

***

The hot, steamy water raced down Randi's naked body as she stood in the shower and rinsed her hair. Anthony would be home in two weeks, she thought happily. She couldn't wait to see him. Living off telephone calls for the last month and a half was unbearable.

She hummed a little tune that she had heard earlier that day and couldn't get out of her head. All of a sudden, the shower door opened and there stood Anthony. At first, Randi just stared at him in disbelief. Still fully dressed, he stepped into the shower and pulled her into his arms. He kissed her feverishly and began to remove his clothes. She helped him. Once he was naked, he pushed her back against the shower wall. His hands slipped down to her hips and picked her up. He opened her legs, wrapped them around his waist, and entered her slowly. Her hands clenched at his back. An involuntary moan escaped her lips, and he began to move in that old, familiar rhythm that she loved.

"I've missed you so damn much," he whispered against her ear. He drove himself deeper and deeper inside of her until they climaxed and collapsed in each other's arms.

Afterwards, he carried her to the bedroom where he made love to her over and over again until they were exhausted. Randi held onto him the entire night. She didn't dare let him go.

The next morning, he took her again. He could not get enough of her. As they lay in the bed enjoying the afterglow of their lovemaking, the telephone rang.

"Hello?" Anthony answered.

It was Thomas and he was furious. "What in the hell do you think you're doing?" he barked. He was so loud that even Randi could hear him.

"I'm enjoying my wife's company." Anthony smiled as he looked over at her.

"You owe me two more weeks!"

"I don't owe you shit." He reached over and gently squeezed her thigh.

"You're a fucking pussy, you know that? Now you're gonna to take your black ass back on the road and finish your tour!"

"No. What I'm gonna to do is make love to my wife one more time before I get up and cook her breakfast." He hung up the receiver and pulled Randi into his arms.

Chapter 18

During the next year, Anthony was only away from home a couple of days at a time. He refused to leave Randi for an extended period. Whenever she was out of school, he took her on the road with him.

Randi knew that the friction between Anthony and Thomas was building. They argued a lot about his schedule, and about what he was and wasn't going to do.

"You're throwing away everything we worked for, for this bitch." She overheard Thomas tell this to Anthony.

Anthony stormed out of the room and refused to talk to Thomas for a couple of weeks. Numerous times, Thomas tried to apologize, but Anthony wouldn't accept it. Anthony told Randi that when his contract was up, he was dropping Thomas and moving on. He only had two years left.

Thomas tried to smooth things over with Anthony by inviting him and Randi to a party at his place. Randi didn't feel well that night. She had an upset stomach, so she stayed home. She urged Anthony to go and work things out with Thomas. She felt guilty because she knew that she was the source of all of their disagreements. Reluctantly, he agreed to attend, but insisted that she call him on his cell if she needed anything.

"Kathy, I just took a pregnancy test," Randi blurted out later that night as soon as Kathy answered the telephone.

"What?" Kathy asked.

"I just took a pregnancy test. I've been sick for a few days now and I'm two weeks late." She was excited. "So, I

174

bought this test today and I just took it."

"Are you pregnant?"

"I don't know. I'm waiting for the results. I just didn't want to do it by myself."

"How much longer?"

"Thirty seconds."

After thirty seconds, Kathy said. "Well, don't keep me waiting. What does it say?"

"I'm pregnant!" Randi squealed. "I'm pregnant." She jumped up and down.

Kathy joined in the squealing.

"Are you ready for a baby?" Kathy asked after they calmed down.

"Yes."

"What about Anthony? Do you think he's ready?"

"I don't know. I know he wants kids, but Thomas is giving him a hard time about me. A baby right now is just going to make it worse."

"Don't you worry about that fat ass Thomas. This is you and Anthony's life. Thomas is just gonna have to get over it. When are you going to tell Anthony?"

"Tonight, when he gets home from a party. Thomas is trying to smooth things over between the two of them."

"Let me know how it goes."

Randi was so excited that she could hardly contain herself. She was living a dream come true. She was in school for her writing, married to the best man in the world, and now she was about to have his baby.

She couldn't wait to tell him as she paced around the room and tried to come up with the words to tell her husband that they were expecting. She hoped that he would be as happy as she was. Overwhelmed with excitement, she couldn't wait another second and decided that she would go over to the party and tell him.

***

Anthony looked at his watch. It was 11:15. He wondered how Randi was feeling. He sipped his champagne and watched Thomas's lips as he tried to talk while holding his cigarette in his mouth. Anthony wasn't listening to him, and he wasn't feeling the party.

He interrupted Thomas. "Man, I'm gonna head on home. You know Randi's not feeling good."

"Naw, dawg. You can't leave yet. Just give her a call or something. We've got some serious stuff going on tonight."

"Naw. She's got an upset stomach. I feel bad for leaving her tonight."

"Maybe she's feeling better now. Go give her a call. She might decide to come on over and join us."

Reluctantly, Anthony agreed and walked down the hall to Thomas's study to use the telephone. He sat on the edge of the desk and dialed the number. While he waited for Randi to answer, a beautiful woman walked in. He looked over at her as she approached him. She was scantily dressed, and he felt like tossing some clothes her way. The answering machine picked up.

"Hey, baby, it's just me. Just wanted to see how you were feeling. I guess you've already gone to bed. I'll be home in a few minutes," he said. His eyes remained on the woman, who now stood boldly in front of him. She smiled seductively. He hung up the telephone.

Before he could say a word, she started. "Thomas wanted me to check up on you to see if you needed anything."

"No thanks." He picked up his glass.

She took it from him and drank the remaining

176

champagne.

"Anything." She raised an eyebrow.

Anthony smiled. He was flattered. His eyes traveled down to her breasts.

"Naw, I'm straight." Her silicone implants resembled two over-inflated balloons.

She moved closer and pressed her body against his. "That's what I'm hoping," she said. Her hands rested on his thighs.

He gently pushed her away and stood up. "I'm flattered, but I'm also a happily married man."

"That's fine. I won't tell if you don't." She pulled her dress up and revealed her black lace thong and two perfectly round, caramel cheeks.

Anthony told himself not to look but he did. *Damn,* he thought. *She's got a phat ass.*

"You like?" she asked. She could read his expression.

"I've got a sick wife at home. I need to check up on her," he said.

She pushed him back down on the desk and stood between his legs as she pressed herself against him again.

"She's asleep," she said. "Let's not wake her."

He became aroused. He hated that other women besides Randi still turned him on.

***

The drive was only thirty minutes, but it seemed like it took forever to get to Thomas's house. The driveway was filled with cars. This was some party, she thought as she got out of her car and went inside. The party reminded her of the one she went to when she met Anthony. Music blasted from the speakers and half-naked women gyrated to the beat.

Debra Clayton

She didn't see Anthony but spotted Thomas. Maybe Anthony was headed home. She wondered if they worked things out. She walked over to Thomas to ask if Anthony was still there.

***

"I gotta get out of here." Anthony told the woman as she slid her hand down to his crotch and grabbed his swollen manhood. She smiled at this.

"Damn, you must be happy to see me." She gently squeezed him, feeling the thickness. "Really happy," she added as she slid down his body until she was squatting in front of him. She unfastened his pants.

"Don't do that," he said, but he didn't try to stop her. *What in the fuck are you doing?* he asked himself. *Stop this bitch.* He didn't move.

She pulled out his swollen manhood and smiled up at him before she slipped it into her mouth.

"Shit," he said as he stood up to stop her.

She wouldn't stop. She slipped his pants down around his ankles and pushed him back against the desk. The things she did with her mouth were incredible.

He thought about Randi. He thought about how much this would hurt her, how much it would break her heart if she knew what he was doing. He tried to walk away, but his body wouldn't let him. He closed his eyes. *Nigga, you're fucking up,* he told himself. *You're fucking up.*

***

"Hey, Randi." Thomas smiled as she approached him. He seemed a little too friendly. After all, she knew he hated

178

her. "I thought you weren't feeling good."

"I wasn't, but I needed to see Anthony and it couldn't wait. Is he still here?"

"Yeah. He's in my study. He wanted to make a call. Go right down the hall and it's the second door on the left." He was all too eager to help her.

"Thanks." She headed in the direction he pointed.

Thomas was pleased. This was better than he had planned.

When Randi got to the door, it was closed. She knocked lightly then opened it. What she saw almost knocked her down. Anthony was leaning against a desk with his pants down around his ankles. A woman was down on her knees in front of him, giving him a blow-job. Anthony's eyes were closed until he heard the door open. He jumped up and looked at Randi like a deer caught in headlights.

Randi couldn't speak. She felt as if the room was spinning. She couldn't believe her eyes. This had to be a cruel joke. This couldn't be real.

The woman continued to give him head. Randi stumbled backwards, shaking her head. She was in a daze. Her body started screaming inside. How could he do this to her? This was her husband. This was the man she loved more than life itself. This was the father of her child.

"Randi!" Anthony broke the silence as he shoved the woman off him and onto the floor.

"You bastard!" the woman screamed as he struggled to pull up his pants.

Still dazed, Randi turned and bumped into the wall. She grabbed onto it to try to steady herself. Tears raced down her face as she felt her heart being crushed. She stumbled into the hall like a drunk and began to run.

Anthony chased after her, calling her name. He knew

he had really fucked up. The look on her face was indescribable. He had never seen it before, and never wanted to see it again.

Randi clumsily raced down the hall and back into the crowd of people as she tried to find her way out. Tears clouded her vision as she pushed her way through. She couldn't breathe. She felt like she was drowning as she gasped for air. She could still hear Anthony as he continued to call after her.

When she reached the front door, Thomas grabbed her arm. "Randi, are you all right?" he asked. Inside, he was thrilled. *Good old Anthony.* He hadn't let him down.

Embarrassed, Randi couldn't look at him. She pulled away and hurried out of the house. She ran to her Jaguar and fumbled with the keys before she could get the door unlocked. Once opened, she jumped in the car and locked it. Again, she struggled with the key as she tried to put it in the ignition.

Anthony raced up to her car and tried to open the door. "Randi! Open the door!" He beat on the window. "Open the door, baby!"

She finally managed to get the key in the ignition and started the car. Although tears clouded her vision, she sped off and left him standing in the driveway, screaming her name.

Anthony jumped in his car and chased after her. What in the hell was he thinking, jeopardizing his marriage for a blow-job? He couldn't get the look on her face out of his head. The look in her eyes reflected the pain that he had put in her heart. She was hurt and he was to blame. He was no better than Eric was.

***

She didn't know how she managed to get home

without getting herself killed, but she did. She ran up the stairs and into her bedroom where she started breaking things. She grabbed one of his gulf clubs and swung it like a baseball bat at everything she could see. She wanted to break everything he owned the same way he had broken her heart.

She went to the cabinet filled with all of his awards and started swinging. The glass shattered and his music awards fell to the floor. She knocked all of his gold and platinum records off the wall. Then she moved on to his cologne and the DVD system.

She trusted him, and this was how he repaid her. How many times had this happened? How many times did she sit at home waiting for him, missing him while he was off fucking someone else? She was a fool. Why did he do this to her? Why did he insist on ruining her life?

She swung the clubs at their wedding pictures, his PlayStation, the vase that held the flowers he sent her just because. He should have let her walk away from him when they first met. Why did she let herself fall for him?

Anthony heard the sound of breaking glass when he ran into the house. He raced up the stairs, taking them two at a time.

"Randi," he called as he entered the bedroom. She swung around to see him. He was nothing but a blurry vision to her.

Without thinking, she raised the golf club and swung at him. He dodged.

"Randi!" He tried to get the club from her and she swung at him again.

"I hate you!" she screamed. "How could you do this to me?"

"I'm sorry, baby. I swear this was the first and only time." He knew that he deserved an ass whipping.

She looked at him. Tears streamed down her face. Her breathing was ragged. He had no idea of what his infidelity had done to her.

He knew she was tiring, so he tried to take the club from her again. She swung at him with all her strength. He dodged and when she spun around, he grabbed her from behind. His arms wrapped around hers as he held them to her side. He wrestled the club from her and threw it against the wall.

"How could you?" she screamed through her tears. "How could you do this to me?" She struggled to get away from him. He held her tight.

"Baby, I'm sorry. I didn't mean for it to happen. I swear." He tried to explain.

"I hate you!" She was powerless against him as he held her captive in his arms. "Let me go!"

"Let me explain," he pleaded. "Let me tell you what happened."

"I know what happened!" The more she struggled, the tighter his grip became.

He pulled her down to the floor as he leaned up against the wall, never loosening his hold on her.

"While I'm at home waiting for you, you're running around fucking everybody!"

"No, Randi. This was the first and last time." He tried to explain. "I wasn't going to sleep with her. It was just a blow-job. And I didn't mean for it to happen."

"What happened? Did you trip and your dick fell in her mouth? You told me you fell into pussy every day. I guess you're falling into mouths too."

"I fucked up, Randi, but it never happened before. I swear this was the first time. I was trying to call you. Thomas sent her in there. I think he set me up, baby."

"So, he's the one that stuck your dick in her mouth." Randi's body began to tire as she slowly stopped struggling. "Oh God!" She cried out. "Oh God! Why did you do this to me? You're supposed to love me. You promised me you would never hurt me." She sobbed uncontrollably. "You promised me, Anthony."

"I know, baby, but I fucked up. I fucked up bad. I swear I fucked up," he repeated as he rocked her in his arms. That was the only way he could describe it. He had fucked up.

Her body ached from crying. His tears streamed down his face onto hers as they cried together. He was determined not to let her go.

She couldn't get the image of this woman with her husband out of her mind. Randi cried until she was exhausted. Hours passed before she finally fell asleep.

Anthony didn't know how to fix it, but he knew he couldn't lose Randi. She meant everything to him. He pushed her hair back and looked down at her swollen, tear-stained face. How could he have done this to her? He closed his eyes and leaned his head against the wall. He knew that this could very well be the end of his marriage.

Chapter 19

When Randi woke up the next morning, his arms were still wrapped around her but he was asleep. She thought about the night before. Maybe she had a nightmare. Maybe she hadn't caught her husband with another woman. When she looked around the room at all the damage she had caused, she knew it wasn't a dream, and all the pain came rushing back. She carefully slipped out of his arms, packed her bags and left him sitting on the floor, still asleep.

Anthony awoke to find Randi gone.

"Fuck," he said as he got up off the floor. He saw that her bags were gone. She left him. The only place that he knew she would go was to Kathy's. He called her and frantically paced the floor while he waited for her to answer the telephone.

"Hello?"

"Hey, Kathy. It's Anthony." He stopped pacing and tried to sound calm.

"Hey. I hear congratulations are in order." She sounded cheerful.

"Congratulations?" He thought she was being sarcastic. Randi must have told her everything. "What are you talking about?"

"The baby."

"Baby? What baby?" He was puzzled.

"Randi didn't tell you? I thought she told you." Kathy didn't understand why her best friend, who was ecstatic last night about being pregnant, hadn't told her husband the good news.

"Randi didn't tell me what?"

"She took a pregnancy test last night. It was positive. She thought she was pregnant. Maybe she's not. Maybe that's why she didn't tell you."

Anthony sat down on the edge of the bed and closed his eyes. It all fell into place—the upset stomach, the tiredness. That's why she came to the party last night. She came to tell him she was pregnant, that he was going to be a daddy. He had fucked up royally. He knew he was in jeopardy of losing his wife and his child.

"Have you talked to her today?" He had to find her.

"No. The last time I talked to her was last night. That's when she told me about the baby. Is anything wrong?"

"No," he lied. He looked around at the room. It was shattered like their world, he thought. He noticed their wedding pictures, lying in cracked frames all over the floor. "But if she calls you, could you call me and let me know?"

Now Kathy was worried. "Where is she, Anthony?"

"I don't know," he admitted. "She left me." He pushed his hand back through his hair.

"Why? What happened?" She knew her friend was in trouble.

"Could you just let me know if you hear from her?"

"Sure." She wouldn't push him.

"Thanks." He hung up the telephone and picked up one of the wedding photos. It was a picture of them kissing. He poured the shattered glass onto the floor and set the picture back on the nightstand. Where in the hell could she be?

Twelve hours later, Randi arrived at Kathy's house.

"What's wrong?" Kathy asked as she grabbed her and pulled her into the apartment.

Randi looked drugged. Her face was swollen from

crying. Her head ached. She didn't answer.

"Anthony called looking for you. He said you left him."

Randi didn't want to talk about it. She knew that if she did, she would start crying again. "I need to lie down," she finally muttered.

"Okay," Kathy said. She wanted to help her friend, but didn't know how.

Randi went into the bedroom and lay face down with her, head turned away from the door. She was dying inside, and she didn't know what to do to save herself. She didn't want to save herself. She just wanted to lay there and die.

Kathy came into the room a couple of times and tried to get her to eat or drink something, but Randi was unresponsive.

***

Anthony stormed into Thomas's office. He was busy with some other clients, but Thomas stood up at the sight of him. He knew that the shit had hit the fan. Thomas asked his other clients to give him a minute with Anthony.

"You set me up," was the first thing Anthony said.

"I don't know what you're talking about." Thomas played dumb.

"You sent that bitch in there to fuck with me and then you sent Randi to catch me." He paced the office, his nostrils flaring like a raging bull.

"Listen, Anthony," Thomas said calmly. "I may have set you up. Fact is, I sent the bait, but you're still the one who shoved your dick down her throat, not me. Randi showing up like that was something that I hadn't anticipated, but boy, it was perfect timing." He grinned.

Anthony stopped pacing and looked at his manager. "Why?" he asked. "Why would you do that?"

"Being in love isn't good for your career. You won't go on tour. You can't be away from home too long. You've lost your edge. You've become a lovesick idiot since you met that bitch." He reached for a cigarette.

Anthony snatched him up by the collar and shoved him against the wall. He pushed his fist into Thomas' windpipe.

"That woman that you're so quick to call a bitch is my wife, and she's carrying my child. If I don't get them both back, then you're a fucking dead man." He let him go.

Thomas crumpled to the floor, gasping for air, and Anthony walked out of his office.

***

Randi awoke to the sound of the telephone.

"Hello?" Kathy said.

"It's me again," Anthony said. "Have you heard from her yet?"

"Yeah, she's here."

"Thank God." He felt a wave of relief. "Is she all right?"

"She's just laying there in the bed. She won't even talk to me. What's wrong with her, Anthony?"

"Don't let her leave. I'll be there as soon as I can get a flight."

"I'll tell her."

"Thanks."

"Bye." She hung up the telephone then poked her head in the doorway to see if Randi was awake. "Randi," she whispered.

She didn't answer.

Kathy walked over to the bed and knelt down in front of her. "Baby, you're breaking my heart. Tell me what's wrong."

Randi just looked at her friend. She couldn't tell her. She felt like such a fool. How could she have let this happen? How could she have been so blind? Her eyes began to well up with tears. She turned her head so her friend couldn't see them.

Kathy rubbed Randi's back. "Anthony's on his way."

Randi rolled over onto her side, with her back against Kathy, and curled up into the fetal position. She cried silently as tears soaked her pillow.

Twelve hours later, Anthony knocked on Kathy's door. Randi could hear the voices. She wanted to get up and run, but her body betrayed her. She couldn't move.

"Hey," Kathy said to Anthony.

"Can I come in?" he asked.

"Sure. You look like shit."

"How's she doing?"

"Not good. She won't eat. She won't drink. She won't even talk to me. All she does is lay there and stare at the wall. Last night she cried for hours."

"You think she'll talk to me?"

"I don't know, but you can try. Maybe you can convince her to eat something. This starving herself can't be good for her or the baby." She looked at him hard as she tried to figure out what was wrong. She knew that he loved her, but he had fucked up somewhere along the line.

"Anthony, you didn't hit her, did you?" She remembered what Eric did to her friend, how he left her there to die.

"No," he said immediately. "I would never do that."

"Then you fucked around on her." She was afraid of what his answer would be.

He didn't say anything. He just stared at her.

She knew the answer. She closed her eyes and turned her head away from him. She had gone to bat for this guy. She was the one that kept pushing Randi to him when she wanted to run. She looked back at him. "How could you do some shit like that?"

"I know I fucked up, but it wasn't something that I planned."

She held her hand up to his face. "Forget it. You need to be talking to Randi."

"Where is she?"

"She's in the second room on the left."

Randi heard him walking down the hall. He poked his head into the room as if he was waving a white flag.

"Hey, baby," he said with hesitation.

Randi lay motionless and looked at him. The sight of him made her want to cry, but she refused to do so. She had cried enough over him. He wasn't worth another tear.

He cautiously entered the room and moved over to the bed where she lay. He knelt down beside her.

Kathy was right. He did look like shit. She hoped he felt like shit too.

He gently laid his hand on her stomach. She knew he knew about the baby. His thumb traveled gently back and forth across her belly. Two days earlier that would have turned her on, but now the thought of him touching her made her feel sick. How could he put his hands on her after what he did? How could she let him after what she saw?

She couldn't get the image of that woman giving him

head out of her mind. The way he stood there enjoying it made her angry. If she was a real woman, she would have beaten the hell out of both of them. Instead, she curled up and crawled away like a struck dog with her tail between her legs.

His thumb moving back and forth irritated her. She pushed his hand off her belly.

"I'm sorry" he apologized nervously. He looked down at the floor then back at her angry, pain-filled eyes.

She could tell he had been crying. His eyes were red and swollen.

"Kathy told me about the baby. I'm happy about it."

Randi silently stared at him. She hated him. She hated the sight of him. She hated the scent of him. She hated his presence.

"You need to eat." He was worried about her and the baby's health. "Kathy says that you're not eating but you need to."

She didn't respond.

"Randi, say something. Talk to me. Curse me out. Slap the shit out of me. Do something."

She still didn't respond.

"Baby, I love you and I'm sorry. That was the first time that happened. I've never cheated on you before. I swear." He tried to make his case. "I've got no excuses for what I did, but I was drinking and Thomas admitted to me that he set me up. You know he's been trying to break us up since we got married."

She knew Thomas didn't like them together, but that was no excuse to blame him for this. And if he did set Anthony up, that was still no excuse for him to stick his dick in this girl's mouth.

He continued. "I only went into his study to call you. I wanted to check up on you because I knew you were sick. I didn't even want to go to the party. I went to call you, but you didn't answer. I thought that maybe you had gone to bed so I just left a message. That woman came in afterwards. When she started coming on to me I tried to stop her."

Randi didn't want to hear this.

"I tried to stop her, but I didn't. I swear, baby, it just happened. I didn't go to the party expecting this."

Her eyes began to well up with tears. Although she tried to hold them back, she couldn't. She blinked, and the tears rolled down the sides of her face.

"I'm sorry, Randi. I swear it'll never happen again. I promise you, baby. And as soon as I can get out of my contract with Thomas, he's gone."

Even if he was telling the truth, Thomas hadn't undone his pants. Anthony still had the option to walk away from this woman, but he didn't. And what was worse was the fact that he enjoyed it.

"Randi, please say something."

She didn't. She just lay there like a rag doll. She slipped from being angry to being sad again. This was her husband. This was the man that she loved ridiculously. This was the father of her child. How could he have just given himself to a complete stranger? How could he have so much disregard for their love? Didn't he love her enough to say no, to just walk away? How many more times had this happened? How could she ever trust him again?

He finally sat down on the floor beside the bed with his back against the wall. He didn't know what to do, but he knew that he wasn't leaving there without her. To him, it didn't matter much that she wouldn't talk to him. Just being close to her again was good enough. They sat in silence for quite a while before he started talking again.

"Randi, we can make it through this. We've got a baby

on the way. We can do this." He looked over at her. She didn't move.

Kathy knocked on the door and stuck her head in. "How's it going?" she asked Anthony. She carried a tray of food. He looked up at her and shook his head.

"Well, I fixed her something to eat. Maybe you can get her to eat it." She placed the tray on the table next to him.

He stood up over Randi. "You need to eat, baby."

She didn't move.

He leaned over the bed and pulled her lifeless body up. After he propped her up against the headboard, he picked up the tray and sat on the bed in front of her.

"Are you going to eat?" He held out a spoon for her.

Kathy had fixed her some soup and crackers. Randi just looked at it. She didn't feel like eating. She didn't feel like living.

"You've got to eat something," he said, still holding the spoon out for her. She just sat there looking as if she had been drugged.

Determine to make her eat, he scooped up some soup with the spoon and attempted to feed it to her.

She slowly lifted one of her hands and reached for the spoon. He carefully gave it to her so she wouldn't spill it. She brought it to her mouth and sipped. Almost automatically she lowered the spoon back into the soup and brought it to her lips again. She couldn't taste it; she couldn't smell it; she couldn't even feel its wetness. She was numb.

Anthony smiled as he watched her. When she finished, she dropped the spoon into the bowl. He handed her a glass of ice water. She took a sip. He took the glass from her and set it back on the table. He was happy to see some life in her. She wrapped her arms around her knees as she drew them up to her chest and began to sway. He watched her as she gently

192

rocked herself back and forth like a child. Her face was sad and lost. He could see what he had done to her, how he had drained the happiness from her body.

He reached out and touched her arm as if he was afraid he would break her. He already had.

"Randi." He gently squeezed her arm. She stared into his eyes. Had he lost her forever? "I need you to come home with me. Let me take care of you."

She only stared.

"I don't want to lose you," he continued. "I can't lose you and the baby."

She tried to see her husband. She tried to see the man she loved. All she could see was that woman giving him head. She looked away from him so he couldn't see her cry as the tears began to flow from her eyes. She rolled over and curled up like a baby with her back to him. This hurt so bad. When was it going to stop? She cried softly in her pillow.

Anthony climbed in the bed and curled up next to her. He put his arm around her waist and tucked his fingers under her. He held her like he had held her hundreds of times before, but this was different. This time he held her like he was afraid to let go.

Twenty minutes later, Randi jumped up from the bed and ran into the bathroom. Anthony followed. She leaned over the toilet and threw up. He held her hair back and helped her steady herself as her body heaved and spewed out everything she had eaten. He ran some cold water on a washcloth and helped her wash her face.

Anthony sat with Randi around the clock for the next two days. He held her when she cried, apologized to her every chance he got and tried to convince her to come home. It had been a one-sided conversation, but on this day, Randi finally spoke. She lay curled up on the bed and he stood by the window looking out.

"Why?" she whispered.

Not sure if he was hearing things, he turned around and looked at her.

"Why was I not enough?" she asked. Her voice trembled.

He walked over to the bed and sat next to her. Staring into her eyes, he wished he could make it all go away, erase everything that had happened in the last few days. But he couldn't. He had fucked up, and he had to face the consequences.

"You're more than enough, Randi. You're everything."

She couldn't understand. "If you wanted oral sex, I could have . . . "

"It's not about oral sex."

She slowly sat up. "What am I doing wrong?"

"Nothing, baby." He looked up at the ceiling and tried to figure out why he let this happen. He looked at Randi, whose eyes searched his for an answer. "I was too cocky, and I let her get too close."

She didn't understand.

He continued. "When I'm out on tour, women are throwing themselves at me constantly."

She braced herself.

"They throw themselves at me constantly, but I resist them, all of them. I kept a safe distance and avoided letting myself get in situations that I may not be able to get out of. That's how I've been faithful to you. That night I did go into Thomas's study to call you. You weren't home. The girl came in and started hitting on me. Instead of getting away from the situation, I got cocky. I thought I could handle it. I figured that I'd enjoy a little attention from another woman and then I'd just walk away. I wouldn't have to touch her. She wouldn't have to touch me. I'd just let her flirt a little and then I'd walk away." He watched Randi's reaction to his explanation.

She had none.

"But she got too close. She started pushing up on me, rubbing on me, and by the time I realized that I couldn't handle what was going on, it was too late. I had let it go too far." He bit his bottom lip. "I got aroused. My head kept telling me to walk away, but my body wouldn't let me."

They both sat in silence. Randi closed her eyes and tears rolled down her cheeks.

"I'm sorry, baby," he whispered. He slid over to where she was and pulled her against him. Her head lay on his chest as she wept quietly.

Chapter 20

A couple more days passed before Anthony finally convinced Randi to come home with him. He promised her that he wouldn't bother her. He would move out of their bedroom, she could finish school, and he would be there to help with things for the baby.

Kathy took them to the airport. She knew that Anthony loved Randi, but she hated what he did to her. She held onto her friend when they were ready to board.

"You let me know if you need anything. You hear me?"

Randi nodded. Kathy looked at Anthony.

"Thanks," he said to her. He knew he wouldn't have been able to take his wife home if it weren't for her.

"You take care of her," Kathy said. "Don't let this shit happen again." She hugged him.

Randi didn't say a word on their trip home. He took her bags upstairs to their bedroom. The maid had everything cleaned up, and their wedding pictures were re-framed. No sign remained of the damage that Randi had caused.

After a couple of days, Randi decided to move back out. She couldn't handle the pain of seeing him every day. He tried to convince her to let him be the one to move out, but she wouldn't. He helped her get a place that wasn't too far away from him or her school. At least she was still in L.A.

She refused to take his calls, saying that she wanted to move on with her life, that he was no longer a part of it. Anthony was going crazy without her. He started a routine of sitting outside her apartment, watching her to make sure that she came home alone. He couldn't bear the thought of her being with another man.

One day while he watched her, he sat in his car with a half-full bottle of beer in his hand and two empty bottles in the floor. He looked down at the clock on his stereo system. It was 3:30 in the afternoon. Randi would be home any minute, he thought as he took a swallow of beer.

At 3:35, her Jag pulled into the parking lot. *Right on time,* he said to himself. He took another swallow of beer as he watched her get out of the car. She stood there as if she was waiting on something or someone. He hadn't noticed the Ford Explorer that followed her into the parking lot until a tall, dark, muscular brother got out. She smiled at him as he approached her.

Anthony sat up in his seat to get a better look as his wife talked to this man. They laughed, and she pointed up to her apartment building.

"Damn it, Randi," Anthony growled as he quickly threw his beer bottle down to the floor with the others and got out. He felt himself turning warm. Randi and the stranger started walking toward her building.

"Hey," Anthony yelled as he ran up to them. Randi recognized his voice. They stopped and turned around. She closed her eyes and shook her head when she saw him. She knew that he was going to cause a scene. She opened her eyes and looked up at him as he stood in front of them.

"What the hell's going on?" He stared down at her. His nostrils were flaring and he was breathing hard. She knew she didn't owe him an explanation, but she didn't want to make the situation any worse than it was.

"This is Mark Scales. He's in one of my classes."

"I don't give a shit who he is. What the hell is he doing here?" He was pissed.

Randi was surprised by the way he talked to her. She

had never seen him act like this before. He reminded her of Eric.

"Randi, is everything okay?" Mark finally spoke up. He looked up at Anthony and fixed his jaw as he set his mind for a street fight. He wasn't as tall as Anthony, but he would beat the hell out of him if he had to.

This set Anthony off. "What the fuck—" He growled as he looked down at Mark. "Is everything okay? Nigga, I'm her fucking husband and the father of the child that she's carrying. Hell yeah, everything is okay!" He turned his body as if he was preparing to take a swing at him. "You better get the hell outta here before I beat the shit outta you."

"Anthony!" Randi yelled as she grabbed his arm. "Stop it!"

He ignored her. She looked at Mark.

"I'm sorry," she apologized. "I'll bring it to class tomorrow and give it to you."

"You sure?" He looked concerned. He didn't like the idea of leaving her there with this raging mad man, even if it was her husband.

Anthony was losing his patience. He couldn't believe this guy. "Nigga . . . " He clenched his fists as well as his teeth. "You don't know who you fucking with!"

"Please." Randi touched Mark's arm.

He looked at her a while longer before he finally gave in. "Call me if you need anything," he said just to aggravate Anthony. He knew that she didn't have his number. He looked at Anthony without a word, shook his head and walked away.

"And you stay the hell away from my wife!" Anthony called after him then turned to Randi. "This is bullshit, Randi, and you know it. And you ain't fucking calling him either!" He glared at her as if he wanted to hit her.

She looked up at him in matched anger. She knew he

had been drinking because she could smell the alcohol on his breath. So this was her husband, she thought, the man that she was married to.

"Why are you doing this to me?" she asked. Her lips trembled.

He ignored her question. "What were you gonna do, fuck him just to get back at me?"

She couldn't believe what he was saying. It was all she could do not to reach up and slap him. Her breathing became hard as she fumed over his comment. "I'm going to ignore that remark because I know you're drunk."

"I'm not drunk. I'm just mad as hell. Now, what the fuck was he doing here?" he demanded.

"I'm not dealing with this." Randi breathed out as she turned to walk away.

"Oh, hell no." Anthony grabbed her arm and spun her back around to face him. "You're not walking away from me. You got some swollen-ass nigga over here and then—"

"No!" Randi cut him off. "I think you've got it backwards. I didn't do anything wrong, Anthony. You were the one who screwed up. You were the one who threw our marriage away for a blow-job. Now, let me tell you what isn't going to happen. I am not gonna stand here and let you verbally abuse me like one of your hos. Did you forget who I am? I'm your wife. I don't care how angry you are or how hurt you are or how drunk you are when you see me. You will talk to me like you've got the good sense that God gave you." She snatched her arm away from him. "Now, I've got better things to do than stand here and watch you have a temper tantrum."

Anthony stared down at her small, angry face as it turned red. It had been a while since she had to stand up to him. He had almost forgotten how spirited she could be. He had forgotten that she wasn't a pushover for him and that she would put him in his place if she needed to.

Although she was tiny, smiled all the time, and spoke softly, she was never one to take his bullshit. He may have had a few beers in him, but he still had the good sense to know that she wasn't going to put up with his crap. He decided that it would be best for him to back off. His entire disposition changed.

"I'm sorry, baby," he quickly apologized. "I didn't mean that shit. I'm just going crazy. I just don't know what to do."

Randi blinked. Tears raced down her face. She held her lips tight as she stared up at him for another second or two. Without a word, she turned and walked away.

"I just don't know what to do," he repeated as he watched her disappear into her building.

When Randi got inside her apartment, she quickly locked the door behind her, slid down onto the floor, pulled her knees to her chest and sobbed quietly. How was she ever going to make it through all this? How was she supposed to go on with her life?

Anthony stood in the parking lot looking up at her building. He knew that he had fucked up again, but he couldn't help himself. He couldn't let any other men come into the lives of his wife and unborn baby.

For the next few months, Anthony continued sitting outside her apartment building, watching her. He didn't know if Randi knew that she was being watched, but no more men followed her home.

He refused to work on his music and drank even more. His friends came over to try to cheer him up, but it was useless. Randi was his life, and without her he couldn't survive. He would just sit in a corner and stare at her photo while he attempted to drink his pain away.

He finally told his parents what happened. Sylvia tried to tell her son that it would be all right, but she could tell that he was slowly dying inside. His parents decided to visit him since they couldn't convince him to fly home for a while to get his mind off his problems. When they saw him, he was a wreck. He hadn't bathed or shaven in days, and he reeked of alcohol. Sylvia had never seen her son like this.

"I know you love Randi, but you can't let yourself fall apart like this," his mother said. "If you're going to get your wife back, then you've got to get yourself together."

"But she doesn't want me anymore."

"She caught you with another woman. She has to go through this. You can't expect to say I'm sorry and for her to just say okay. You know all the pain she went through before you. You just compounded that. Give her some time."

"It's been three months, Mom. How long do I have to go through this?"

"Stop being selfish," she snapped. She didn't like her son sounding pitiful, especially since he brought it on himself.

He looked at her with surprise. His mom had never talked to him like that.

"You talk about how long you have to go through this. What about Randi? That poor child is alone, pregnant, and heartbroken. You cheated on her; she didn't cheat on you. You'll go through it for as long as she needs you to."

He knew she was right. He made the mistake of spitting in the air. Now he had to wait for it to fall back in face. He didn't mean to be selfish, but he felt like he was drowning and he couldn't scream for help. Randi wasn't joking. This shit hurt, and it hurt like hell. Then he realized

201

that if he felt this bad, he couldn't imagine what she was going through.

His mother's voice softened. "We've got something for the baby, so we're going to take it over to her. Meanwhile, you get yourself cleaned up and try to figure out what you need to do get this marriage back together."

***

Randi sat at her computer working on a story. Her doorbell rang. When she answered it, she found Sylvia and Paul standing there. She was surprised.

"Hey, baby." Sylvia tried to smile.

"Hi." Randi smiled, though she was puzzled.

"Can we come in?"

"Oh sure," she answered nervously. "I'm sorry."

They stepped into the spacious apartment. "How are you doing, Randi?" Sylvia asked

Randi took a deep breath. "Okay." Seeing them made her want to cry.

Sylvia could see this and she hugged her. It felt good to be held. Randi wiped a tear from her eye when Sylvia released her and then Paul hugged her.

"It's going to be okay, sweetness," he said before he let her go.

She invited them to sit down.

She was starting to show, and Sylvia noticed it. "You mind if I touch your belly?" she asked.

"No." She was the first person to ask. Sylvia put both hands on Randi's swollen belly and grinned with joy. She was going to be a grandma.

"I can remember when I carried those boys. Michael was quiet, didn't move around much, but that Anthony, he

202

was steady kicking trying to get out." They all laughed. "Do you know what it is?"

"Not yet." I'm having a sonogram next Friday. Then I'll find out." She was excited.

"What are you hoping for?"

"Doesn't matter. Just a happy, healthy baby."

"So, how's the morning sickness?"

"It finally went away. Thank goodness. I was so tired of being sick."

Sylvia was happy to see how healthy Randi looked. "You look like you been taking good care of yourself."

"I'm taking my prenatal vitamins and I try to eat healthy."

"And the doctor says everything with the baby is going well?" Paul asked.

"Yeah. He said my weight was good. My blood pressure was perfect. No signs of gestational diabetes, and the baby is growing at a normal rate."

"Anthony misses you a lot, dear," Sylvia said.

"I miss him too." She looked sad.

"But we aren't here to talk about Anthony. We've got something for the baby. It's in the car." She looked at her husband. "Could you go ahead and get it, dear?"

Paul stood up and went outside to the car.

"Is he doing okay?" Randi asked. "Anthony."

Sylvia smiled. "He's miserable. But he deserves it."

Randi smiled. She wondered if he was as miserable as she was.

Shortly, Paul returned, carrying the beginnings of a baby's crib. "I hope you haven't got one already," Sylvia said. "It's Anthony's old crib."

"No." Randi smiled. "I haven't done any shopping for the baby yet."

"If you want me to, I can go ahead and put this in the baby's room and set it up for you," Paul offered.

"You would do that for me?"

"Of course, sweetness. Just show me where the baby's room is."

She showed him to the baby's room then fixed them some refreshments. They all helped in putting the beautiful crib together.

"We couldn't keep Anthony in it," Sylvia said. "As soon as he could stand up, he was crawling out of the bed and climbing in the bed with Mike." They laughed.

"We have the rest of his baby furniture. Once you get the room painted we'll send it to you," Paul said.

"Thanks." Randi smiled. She was grateful that they didn't hate her for leaving their son.

Chapter 21

Randi sat in the waiting room at her gynecologist's office. She was scheduled to have a sonogram and she was excited. Since she was a little early for her appointment, she flipped through a baby magazine to occupy her time. She finished one magazine and reached for another. When she looked up, she saw Anthony walking toward her. She hadn't told him about the appointment, so she was surprised to see him.

A month had gone by since the incident at her apartment building. Surprisingly, it didn't hurt as much to see him as it did last time. He looked handsome, she thought as he sat down in the chair next to her. She waited for an explanation for why he was there.

He was nervous and didn't know what to say to her. She looked increasingly beautiful every day. Pregnancy agreed with her.

"You look great," he finally said to break the silence.

"Thank you." She looked down at the magazine.

"I'm sorry about the way I acted at your apartment," he said. "I was crazy. And that comment I made; I know you wouldn't do anything like that."

"What are you doing here?" Her voice was soft, almost a whisper, but she didn't acknowledge his apology.

He figured she was still pissed. "Mom told me about the sonogram," he said. "I wanted to be here. I would have called and asked, but I was afraid that you would try to talk me out of coming."

"I would have," she admitted.

She wanted to lay her head on his chest. She wanted him to tell her everything was going to be okay. She wanted to be able to believe him, but she knew she couldn't. "So, how are you doing?" she asked.

"Not good." It was hard for him to look at her and not be able to touch her. "How about you?"

"Not good."

"How's the baby?" He looked at her belly. He couldn't tell how big she was since she was sitting down.

"The baby's doing fine." She instinctively rubbed her stomach.

"Can I?" He wanted to feel his baby.

"Yes." She felt she owed him that much.

Gently, he placed his large hand over her small, swollen belly. He smiled as he felt the roundness of his baby. This was really happening, he thought. He was going to be a father.

This was the first time he had touched her in months, but it was still gentle and familiar to her. She looked down at his hand. He still wore his wedding band.

"Is she moving yet?" he asked with hand still on her belly.

"She?" Randi said. "You think it's a girl?"

"It is a girl. I can feel it." He looked in Randi's eyes. "Just like I can feel that you and I are supposed to be together. It's not too late for us, baby."

"Randi Talbert." The nurse called her name.

Randi looked over at her. "That's us," she said, avoided Anthony's eyes. She put her magazine down and they both stood up.

"How are you doing today?" the nursed asked when they reached her.

"Fine." Randi smiled.

They followed the nurse down the hall into the examination room. She instructed Randi to lay down on the table. Anthony set her purse down and helped her up on the table. He felt like they were a team again. He missed having her in his life so much.

"The doctor will be here in a minute," the nurse told them before she left.

Randi stared up at the ceiling while Anthony looked at the posters of the progression of pregnancy. He never thought about the whole process until he found out they were having a baby. Now he wanted to know everything about it. He looked at how the woman's body grew during each trimester. He was fascinated with how much the fetus changed as it matured, and he wondered what his baby looked like.

He glanced over at Randi as she lay looking at the ceiling. How could he fix this? She looked fragile, lonely. He was lonely too. He missed wrapping his arms around her at night while they slept. He missed listening to her light snoring when she was exhausted. He missed the way the soft skin of her legs felt against his when he rubbed up against her. Being without her made the days seem long and the nights even longer. Sleepless nights plagued him. He wondered if she ever rolled over in the middle of the night and reached for him like he reached for her.

Randi twiddled her fingers as she waited. Although it had only been three months, the picture of the woman with her husband had started to fade. It wasn't such a vivid memory anymore, but it was still there every day, reminding her how he betrayed her. Whenever she felt the urge to go back home, to tell her husband how much she still loved him and still ached for his touch in the middle of the night, the events of that night would come rushing back. She remembered how much pain he caused and she knew how much more he could bring. Still, she missed the way he made love to her like she was the only woman in the world. She felt the love in his gentle touch and his soul-drinking kisses.

"Mom said that the baby's room needed painting. I can come over and do that for you." He didn't like the idea of her getting the baby's room ready. It was a sign that she wasn't coming back home. Nevertheless, if painting the baby's room was the only way he could get a chance to be near her, then he would do it.

She looked over at him. "You don't have to do that."

"I want to." He walked over to where she lay. "Please. Let me help."

She stared at him, not knowing what to say.

"I just want to help." He was desperate.

The doctor quietly knocked on the door and walked in with the nurse behind him. "Good morning, Randi." He wore a big smile.

"Morning." She smiled back. She liked Dr. Linville because he was personable.

"And you must be Mr. Randi," he said to Anthony.

They shook hands.

"Yes, but you can call me Anthony."

He turned back to Randi. "How are we doing today?"

"Just fine."

"And baby?"

"Baby's fine."

"You feeling any movements, like fluttering?" He pulled up Randi's maternity top and exposed her belly.

Anthony smiled when he saw her fullness. That was his little girl she was carrying.

"Two days ago I started feeling the fluttering."

Dr. Linville pulled the stethoscope from around his neck and slipped the tips into his ears. He placed the chest piece on her belly as he listened for the heartbeat. When he heard the tiny thumping, he smiled and looked at Anthony. "You want to hear your baby's heartbeat?" he asked.

"Yes," Anthony quickly answered.

Randi watched Anthony's smile broaden when he heard his baby's heartbeat for the first time. She knew how he felt. It was overwhelming.

Anthony started to laugh at the quick little heartbeats that vibrated through his ears. He was happy to be there with his wife and his baby.

Dr. Linville measured Randi's uterus to see how the baby's growth was progressing. Everything looked like it was right on time.

"Are you ready to see what this little booger is?" Dr. Linville asked.

"My husband thinks it's a girl." *My husband*, Randi thought. It had been a long time since she said those words. It sounded good to her ears.

"A girl." The doctor looked at Anthony. "You know something we don't know?"

"I can feel it." He smiled.

"Well, let's see if your feeling is correct."

The nurse pulled the waistband of Randi's pants down even farther.

"This is cold," she told Randi as she placed tissue paper along Randi's waistband and prepared to spread gel on her belly.

Anthony watched as she squirted the greenish-colored gel all over Randi's stomach and smoothed it over with her gloved hand. The doctor pulled the ultrasound machine over to the table where Randi lay. She could hardly wait to see her baby.

The nurse turned on the machine. Dr. Linville sat

down on a stool by Randi's side and Anthony moved over and stood by her head. The doctor turned the monitor so they could see it. He placed the transducer on Randi's belly and moved it around as he tried to get an image on the screen. Randi and Anthony didn't know what they were looking at until Dr. Linville explained it to them.

"This is your baby's head," he said. "I'm going to take a few measurements." He clicked the computer mouse and measured from one side of the head to the other. "These measurements will help pinpoint exactly how old the baby is and when you should deliver."

Anthony stared at the image on the screen. He could see the head. He could see his baby. He was at a loss for words. Randi looked at the screen and then at her husband. The look on his face was something she wanted to remember. He was in total awe.

"Can you see it?" she asked him.

"Yes." He nodded without taking his eyes off the screen.

Randi looked back at the monitor as the doctor moved the transducer over her belly again. "Is that the arm?" she asked.

"Yes," the doctor answered as he took more measurements.

"I can see her." Anthony finally said. "She's beautiful."

The doctor measured the baby's legs and showed them its spine and heart. They saw it beating. It was unreal to both of them. They had created this miracle out of their love for each other.

Anthony looked down at Randi and his hand automatically stroked her hair. She looked up at him. She wanted to go back home with him. She wanted to be his wife again and raise this little baby together.

"So, you think you're having a little girl?" the doctor asked Anthony. "Are you ready to find out?"

Anthony and Randi looked back at the monitor.

"Yes," he said as he squeezed Randi's hand.

The doctor slid the transducer over her belly until both of the baby's legs appeared on the monitor.

"Well, she's not modest. Her legs are opened," he said.

"Her," Randi said. "So, it is a girl."

"It's a girl," Dr. Linville said. "Right here." He pointed to the area between the baby's leg. "If it was a boy, you would see the penis and testicles right here, but there are none." He looked up at Anthony. "You were right. You've got yourself a daughter."

Without thinking, Anthony leaned over and kissed Randi on the lips. Instinctively, she kissed him back. When he raised his head, he stared down at her. Randi avoided his eyes and looked back at the monitor.

The doctor printed out a few pictures of their baby and gave them to Anthony.

"Everything looks good. Baby's growth is consistent with how many months she is, so I guess we'll be having a baby in five months." He looked at Randi. "Have you signed up for your Lamaze classes yet?"

"No." She shook her head.

"The schedule is on the wall in the hallway. You can decide which times are best for you and sign up. Don't wait too late. Eight months is usually a good starting point."

She nodded. "Okay, doctor."

"Do you have any questions?" He looked at Randi then at Anthony.

"No," they said.

"Well, we'll see you next month," he said to Randi and

211

then to Anthony, "Nice meeting you." He shook his hand. "You take care her."

"I will," Anthony promised.

Dr. Linville left the examining room while the nurse gave Anthony some paper towels. "You can help her clean herself up," she said to him. "Randi, stop by the front desk on your way out so we can set up your next appointment."

Randi nodded and with that, the nurse left the room.

"I'm sorry about the kiss," he said as he wiped the gel off of her belly. "I didn't mean to. It was just . . . "

"I know." She watched his face. Although he was more handsome than she remembered, she still saw traces of sleepless nights in his eyes. "Your mom says you haven't been working on your music."

He kept his eyes on her belly as he wiped the last few spots of the gel off her. "I can't think. Can't get you out of my head." He looked at her face. "I can't believe I threw away the best thing I ever had."

She pulled down her blouse and he helped her sit up. "You know you can't throw away your career over this."

"Without you, Randi, I see no point."

"It'll get better," she assured him. She knew from experience.

"Promise," he said.

"I promise." She smiled as she reached up and touched his cheek.

He put his hand over hers, turned his head, and kissed her palm. "I love you so much," he whispered. "Will you ever forgive me?"

She slowly pulled her hand away from him and slid down off the table. She picked up her purse, placed one hand on the doorknob, and looked up at him. "I forgave you a long time ago, baby," she said then opened the door.

He followed her down the hall and they stopped to look at the schedule for Lamaze classes. She found some class dates that she could fit into her routine.

"I'd like to be your coach," he said.

"It's only going to make it harder for you."

"I want to be there for you and the baby. I'm not gonna abandon you just because I screwed up. Whatever you need, I got you."

She agreed that he could be her Lamaze coach. After she set up her next appointment, he walked her to her car. She gave him one of the pictures of the sonogram and allowed him to touch his baby once more before she drove off.

It was hard to let her go. Randi promised him that it would get better, but he couldn't see that happening. He hurt just as much this day as he did when she first walked out of his life. He had to be patient. He had to get her back no matter how long it took. He knew she still loved him as much as he loved her. He just had to wait.

By the end of the week, he had gotten in touch with Randi. She agreed to go with him to purchase the paint for the baby's room. After they settled on a nice shade of pink, they returned to her apartment. He surveyed the apartment to see if there was any sign of him there, maybe a picture or something, but there was none. He was disappointed.

She showed him to the baby's room and told him what she wanted. He set up everything and started painting. After he put on the first coat, she fixed him some lunch. She sat down at the table and ate with him.

He listened as she told him about school and a novel that she was working on. She hoped to finish the novel before their daughter's birth. Although he was happy that she could focus on her writing through all they were going through, he was disappointed that she seemed to be moving on with her life without him.

He watched her closely as he ate. The thought of divorce crept into his head. Randi had never brought it up, and he hoped that she wouldn't. He didn't think he could handle it if she did.

"Baby names." He took a sip of water. "Have you thought of any?"

"Yeah." She smiled. "What do you think of Sidney?"

"Sidney," he repeated to see how it would roll off his tongue. He smiled. "I like it. What about a middle name?"

"I'll let you have that one."

He had already picked a name. "Jordan," he said.

"Sidney Jordan," she said. She liked the sound of it.

"Sidney Jordan Talbert," he corrected.

"I can live with that." She smiled.

"I can too." He walked over to her, kneeled down beside her and placed his hand on her belly. "I love you, Sidney," he whispered then looked up at Randi. "Thank you for this gift," he said. "Thank you for this gift." He looked back down at her belly. "I'm gonna be the best father I can be, Sidney. I promise you that."

Later, when the first coat of paint dried, he applied a second. While he painted, Randi sat at her computer and worked on her novel. She leaned back in her chair and rubbed her belly as she tried to picture the scene she was about to start writing. She could hear Anthony singing. He sang Montell Jordan's "Missing You." It was one of her favorites. She whispered the lyrics along with him.

After he finished the room, he called her to look it over. She was very pleased. They sat around for another hour talking before he decided to leave. He didn't want to, but he didn't want to put too much pressure on her. It was as if they were starting all over again. He would have to earn her trust one more time.

Chapter 22

As the months went by, Randi and Anthony became more comfortable being with each other. They didn't talk about what happened between them. They didn't discuss getting back together. They became friends. He was there whenever she needed something; she was there to talk to him in the middle of the night when he couldn't sleep. He didn't think it was possible, but he fell in love with her even more deeply.

He watched as her body expanded with the growth of his child. She would let him feel the baby kick. It fascinated both of them. Randi couldn't get over the amazing feeling of her baby moving around inside of her, and Anthony couldn't get over how much more beautiful she grew with each passing day.

She watched how her husband's face lit up when they went baby shopping together. He was surprised at how small the clothes were, and couldn't believe that a baby could be so tiny. He was happy. She knew that in his heart he wanted things to work out between them, but she had resolved that it was over for them. She could be his friend again, but she couldn't go back to being his wife.

During her eighth month, she started her Lamaze class. Anthony was her coach. They sat on the floor at the class, Randi between his legs. The instructor told the mothers-to-be to lean back on their coaches and try to relax. Randi closed her eyes and leaned against him as he massaged her belly. It felt good to have his arms around her again. She felt safe. If only she could stay there forever, she thought, but she knew she couldn't. She knew that when class ended, they would go back to their separate lives.

Anthony listened intensely to the instructor as she assigned them exercises to perform. He wanted to get this right. He wanted to show her that he could be there for her, that she could trust him again, that it was all right to love him again. Randi had underestimated his love for her. They had separated over seven months ago and he was still there. He was still trying to fix what he had broken. Most men would have given up by then, but he hadn't.

She watched him as he talked to the instructor after class. He got some extra literature to read. She was impressed. He had changed. He wasn't the boy she met at Deveraux's so long ago. He was a man.

***

Randi's back had been aching for two hours and although she attempted to massage it to make it feel better, it was useless. She looked over at the glowing lights of her alarm clock. It was 3:09 in the morning. She sighed at the thought of her 8:00 class. She only had four more hours to get to sleep. She rolled over on her back and looked up at the ceiling. Her mind slipped to Anthony. She wondered what he was doing. Was he having another one of his sleepless nights, or had they finally left him alone?

She felt the baby kick. Sidney was awake. She placed her hand over her swollen belly to feel her kick against it.

"Hello, Sidney Jordan Talbert," she whispered. "What are you doing up this early in the morning? Can't sleep, huh? Me neither."

Only two more weeks, Randi thought as she rolled back over on her side. The pain was in her lower back. She tried massaging it again to no avail. It was a dull ache. It

217

wasn't enough to call the doctor, but enough to aggravate her the rest of the night.

"Well, no need for us to lie here in the dark since we both can't sleep." She maneuvered her swollen belly around as she sat up on the edge of the bed. She slipped on her housecoat, went into the living room, and over to her computer. This would be the perfect time to work on her novel, she thought. With only a couple more chapters to write, she hoped to finish it before the baby arrived.

After turning on the computer, she wobbled into the kitchen to get a glass of water. In front of the refrigerator with the door open, she felt a lot of pressure on her lower belly. Soon after, a sudden gush of water raced down her legs. She looked down at the kitchen floor and found herself standing in a puddle. It took her a second or two to realize what had happened. Her water had broken. After the initial shock, she called Anthony.

Anthony rolled over and looked at the telephone when he heard it ring. He looked at the clock then back at the telephone. After just falling asleep, the telephone waking him up did not put him in a good mood. It better be an emergency, he thought as he picked up the receiver.

"Hello?" His voice was groggy.

"Anthony, it's me. It's time."

The sound of her voice woke him up fully. He sat up in the bed. "It's time," he repeated.

"It's time." She was calm.

He expected her to be screaming and hysterical. "But she's not due for another two weeks."

"My water broke."

"Your water broke."

"Stop repeating everything I say and get over here."

The pain in her lower back had traveled around to her

entire belly. She felt her stomach become rock hard as she had another contraction.

"Oh God," she moaned.

"Randi, are you okay?" He heard the pain in her voice. She didn't answer. She couldn't.

"Randi, what's going on?"

"Contraction," she said as the pain subsided.

"I'm on my way."

He pulled on his pants and T-shirt and hoped that everything was okay. She was two weeks early. First babies were usually late. He learned that from the literature he got at their Lamaze class. The baby's lungs may not be fully developed yet. He slipped on his shoes and ran out to his car as he prayed that they both would be all right.

Randi cracked the door so she wouldn't have to open it when he got there. She wobbled into the bathroom and put on a sanitary napkin, because with every contraction, a gush of fluid would rush down her legs. Between contractions, she worked. She pulled her packed suitcase into the living room, packed up some last minute toiletries, and called Dr. Linville. He said he would meet them at the hospital.

When she felt a contraction approaching, she braced herself for the pain. They came closer and closer together. She felt the pressure of the baby as it lowered itself down into her birth canal. Where was Anthony? She was afraid that she might give birth alone in her apartment.

The pain became so intense that the only way she could deal with it was to get down her hands and knees. As she watched each contraction pull her belly into a hard knot, she tried to remember her breathing technique.

"He-ha-he-ha-he-ha." She breathed. She assumed that

219

she was doing it wrong because it definitely did nothing for the pain.

When Anthony got there, he found her on her hands and knees. Thinking she had fallen, he ran over to her.

"Randi, are you okay?"

She looked up at him but couldn't speak. He tried to help her up, but she wouldn't let him.

"Contraction," she finally said when it was over. "I can handle them better from down here."

"Let's get you to the hospital." He helped her off the floor, grabbed her bags and they left.

***

"Oh God. Somebody help me!" she cried out as another contraction gripped her. She had been at the hospital for three hours. The contractions came, one on top of the other. Dr. Linville checked her cervix and she was only at six centimeters; she had four more to go. Randi didn't know if she could make it.

Anthony stood by her bed with a worried look on his face. He had never seen anyone in so much pain. She was drenched in sweat as the contractions assaulted her body. He tried to comfort her as he wiped the sweat from her forehead.

"It's going to be okay, baby," he assured her. "Just breathe like the doctor showed you."

"I don't wanna breathe," she whined. "It doesn't work. I wanna go home."

"I wish I could take you, but I can't." He tried to show her the bright side. "In a couple of hours we're gonna have a baby. We're gonna have a little girl."

She tried to smile. She knew he was right. This would all be over in a couple of hours and they would have a beautiful daughter to show for it. They would have a beautiful daughter created when their world was still perfect.

Another contraction charged her. She changed her mind. "I don't want to do this. I can't do this." She gripped his hand. "Please, Anthony. I can't do this." She moaned. "Please make it stop."

"Baby, I can't." He leaned over and kissed her. "I wish I could take the pain for you."

The contractions were so close that she didn't get any down time. She couldn't tell when one stopped and the other one started. She tried to adjust her body, but nothing she did relieved her.

Dr. Linville entered the room. "How are we doing?" He smiled, looking at the readout from the baby's heartbeat monitor. "These look pretty strong."

"She's not doing too good," Anthony said. "The contractions won't let up."

"Now, that's good news." He moved over to the bed where Randi battled another contraction.

"Is there anything you can give her? The epidural isn't working," Anthony asked.

Randi moaned in pain. "Please," she begged. "Please help me."

"From the amount of pain that she's in, it may be time to push. I'll check her cervix again, and then we'll work from there."

After checking her cervix, he informed them of the good news. "Well, you're one hundred percent effaced, the baby's head is at station minus two, and you're ten centimeters dilated, which in layman terms means it's time to push."

"It's time, baby," Anthony said.

She nodded.

"As soon as you get the next contraction, I want you to take a deep breath and push. And for every contraction after that, I want you to push like you're having a bowel movement, okay?" Dr. Linville directed.

She nodded again.

"Anthony, you help her by helping her sit up every time she starts pushing."

Randi felt the next contraction approaching. She took in a deep breath and pushed. Anthony started counting the way they taught him in class. "Seven, eight, nine, ten."

Nurses and doctors hurried in and around the room. Randi continued to push, but nothing appeared to happen. The contractions continued their assault and she became exhausted.

"This is hard." She moaned. "She won't come out."

"You can do it," Anthony encouraged her.

Dr. Linville sat between her opened legs. "Now, Anthony, with the next contraction I want you to help her sit up again and then pull her leg to her chest to help get this baby out."

Anthony and Randi both thought the doctor was crazy, and it showed on their faces.

"Follow the nurse's lead," he said.

The nurse stood on the other side of the bed. Without a word, Randi started pushing again. The nurse put her hand under the bottom of Randi's right thigh and pulled it to her chest. Anthony followed her lead by taking Randi's other leg and doing the same thing. Randi felt her bottom opening up.

"Five, six, seven, eight, nine and ten," Anthony counted. His face was so tense that it looked like he was the one in labor.

"That was a good one," the doctor said. "I can see the baby's head."

222

Randi wanted to laugh from relief.

"A few more good ones like that, and you'll be holding your little girl soon."

Randi pushed a couple more times using the same method.

"Okay, stop." the doctor said. "We've got her head."

Anthony leaned over to look as the doctor rotated the baby's head and cleaned out her mouth. He looked back at Randi.

"I can see her." He smiled joyfully. They were almost there.

"Now, give me one more big push then I can officially declare you Mommy and Daddy." The doctor chuckled.

Randi took in a deep breath and pushed with all her strength. She felt her baby pour out of her body and into the doctor's waiting hands. Her daughter started crying. It was a beautiful sound. Randi fell back exhausted into the bed. She was so happy that she started laughing and crying at the same time. Anthony rained kisses all over her face.

"You were wonderful." Tears of relief streamed down his face onto hers.

Without thinking, Randi looked up at him and whispered, "I love you."

"I love you too," he whispered back before kissing her the way she needed to be kissed. He savored the sweetness of her mouth as if he would never get another chance. She didn't try to stop him. She only wished that this could last forever.

Dr. Linville cleared his throat to get their attention. Anthony raised his head and looked at him. The doctor carefully handed his daughter to him.

"Hello, Sidney Jordan Talbert," Anthony said as he placed her across Randi's chest. "Meet your mommy." The baby continued to cry. She was beautiful and perfect.

"Hello, Sidney," Randi whispered. "It's nice to finally meet the little one that's been kicking my butt these last few months."

Sidney quieted at the sound of her mother's voice. She looked just like a doll baby. Giant, black satin curls covered her tiny head. She had deep brown saucer-shaped eyes that stared up at Randi. Her lips were full and bow-shaped like her father's, and she had round, fat, kissable cheeks. Her miniature hand wrapped around one of Randi's fingers. Randi fell in love with her immediately.

Anthony stroked Randi's hair and kissed her forehead as he stood by the bed and gazed at their daughter. He was in complete awe of this little girl. She was so tiny and fragile. She looked like she would break. This was his daughter. This was their daughter. This was his family. He looked at Randi. Through all that she had just been through, she was still the most beautiful woman he had ever seen. This was a day that he would never forget.

Chapter 23

A year later, Anthony rode through the streets of L.A in his new white diamond Cadillac Escalade. His head bobbed to the music that vibrated from his speakers. It was Sidney's first birthday, and Randi had thrown her a party. She invited her family and friends over to help celebrate.

A lot of things had changed in the past year. Anthony had started working on his music again after Thomas released him from his contract. Randi had graduated and published her first novel. Sales on her novel were so good that some executives were interested in turning it into a movie. Everything was looking up for both of them, but they still were not together.

On the day Sidney was born, Anthony decided to give Randi a year to come back to him. He knew that he would always love her and that she could never be replaced, but he knew that he couldn't wait for her forever.

He had no problem meeting other women, but he could never imagine loving anyone but Randi. He didn't want to love anyone but her. Although they didn't spend a great deal of time together anymore, he considered her his best friend.

He didn't know if she was seeing anybody new. They never discussed it, but he knew that one day she would. The thought of her with another man made his heart sink.

He did everything he possibly could to get her back, but she just couldn't get past his infidelity. He didn't hold it against her. He knew that if the situation were reversed, if he had caught another man going down on her, he would never be able to get over it or let it go. He remembered Mark Scales.

He remembered how he lost it when he saw him at Randi's apartment. The thought of her with someone else drove him crazy. No, he couldn't hold it against her for not coming back to him.

After today, the year would be up. He would have to move on. The thought of that saddened him. He wanted to be with his family, with his wife and his daughter. She just didn't want him anymore.

***

"Sidney Jordan Talbert!" Randi scolded when she walked into the room to find her daughter covered in chocolate cake and ice cream. She shoved another fistful of cake into her tiny mouth. Kathy stood in the living room laughing.

"Why didn't you stop her?" Randi asked.

"I was trying to feed her, but she wanted to do it herself." Kathy tried not to giggle.

"Let her be a baby," Randi's mother said, coming to Kathy's defense. "It's her birthday. Let her have fun."

"But Anthony will be here any minute and she's a mess."

"You do have soap and water in this big fancy house, don't you?" her mother teased.

Randi bought the house six months earlier. Anthony wasn't happy about it. He tried to talk her out of it, seeing it as confirmation that she was over him and she would never come home. Randi saw the house as a symbol of what she had accomplished. After all, her novel was doing great. She could afford it. Furthermore, she needed room for Sidney.

She wanted a place for Sidney to be able to run and play. Besides, her apartment didn't allow puppies and she had

226

purchased one for her daughter. Trouble was his name. Anthony didn't know it, but she named the puppy after him. He once told her that he couldn't avoid trouble; it always followed him around like a shadow.

"Stop giving her a hard time," her father, Randall, said to her mother. "You know how you were when the kids were younger. You wouldn't even let them play in the dirt."

"That was different," her mother said.

"Hold on, hold on. Let me tell you a story about when you were little." He shot a glance at her mother then continued. "When Randi was four, her mother wanted to wash her hair, but Randi wanted to play outside. So, when Sandra called her to come inside to get her hair washed, Randi ran. Sandra had to drag her into the house kicking and screaming. Well, she finally got Randi's hair washed, told Randi that that wasn't so bad, and sent her off to play." Her father looked at her. "You were so mad, Randi, that you ran back outside and threw handfuls of dirt into your hair." The whole room laughed.

Anthony turned onto Randi's street, pulled up in front of her house, and got out of the car. The sun shone brightly in the sky. Its heat felt good against his skin. *Nice day for a party,* he thought as he looked up at the sky. The forecast was calling for thunderstorms, but he could see no sign of any.

He noticed all the cars in the driveway. She had quite a few people there. The ones from out of town didn't just fly over for the birthday party. They also wanted to see Randi's new home. It wasn't a huge house, nothing like his mansion, but it was nice.

She was so excited about buying her first home. He remembered the first time she showed it to him. He was happy for her but sad for himself. She wasn't coming home. *One year,* he had told himself then. *Don't give up yet. You still have six months to bring her home.* But today would be the end of his fight for her.

He looked down at his wedding ring and wondered if he would be able to take it off. Slowly, he walked up to the house and rang the doorbell.

Kathy answered it. "Hey." She smiled when she saw him. She gave him a big hug. She knew he was a good guy even though he had screwed up his marriage. She was just sorry that he and Randi couldn't get it back together.

"You look good," she told him.

"Well, I try." He laughed.

"Come on in." She moved back for him to enter.

He stepped inside and looked around the room. Although he didn't see Randi or Sidney, the rest of her family was there.

"Hey, everybody," he said as he raised his hand and gave a quick wave.

Randi's father stood up and shook his hand. "Hey Anthony. How you doing?"

"Just fine."

Randi's mother walked over and hugged him. Randi never told her family what happened between them to break up their marriage. They just knew that she was heartbroken and figured that he had been unfaithful. Still, they didn't hold any grudges against him. They knew that people make mistakes and they knew that he still loved Randi. He kissed her mother on the cheek.

"So, what's up?" Randi's brother, James, asked as he shook his hand.

"Nothing much. Just here to pick up Sidney."

"Oh, Randi's got her in the bathroom cleaning her up.

She got a little carried away with the ice cream and cake." He smiled. "Sit down."

"So, how's the music business?" her father asked.

"Just fine. Hip-hop is as hot as it can be right now. That's the place to be."

"Still making all the money?" James asked.

"I do all right." He laughed.

"Yeah, I wish I could do all right."

"You rap?"

"I can do a little something-something," he said, nodding his head.

Anthony pulled a business card out of his wallet. He gave it to her brother. "Give me a call sometime. Show me what you got. I'm into some new stuff now, and I need some talent."

James took the card. "Sure thing, man."

"Oh God," her mother said jokingly. "Not another rapper in the family."

Sadly, Anthony didn't feel like he was part of the family anymore.

Randi walked into the room carrying Sidney and her diaper bag. She smiled when she saw Anthony. He looked good as usual, but there was something different about him.

"Hi," she said as she walked over to him.

"Hey." He looked at Sidney. "Hey, sweetie." He smiled as he rubbed his hand through the giant black curls that covered her head. She started trying to jump out of Randi's arms when she saw him.

"She's ready for you." Randi laughed as she handed the baby to him.

He kissed her fat, juicy cheeks. She smelled like chocolate. She looked up at him with her big, brown, saucer-like eyes. She was beautiful, Anthony thought. She looked just like Randi.

"I put three changes of clothes in her bag, four bottles of milk and three jars of baby food. I only put in a few diapers since you already have some at your place. You think that'll be enough?"

"Plenty."

Randi kissed her daughter's cheek.

"Hey, Randi, can I speak with you outside for a minute?"

She looked up at him. "Sure." She followed him to the front door.

"It was good seeing you again," he said as he waved to her family.

"You too." They waved back.

He and Randi stepped outside the house. She closed the door behind them.

"Walk me to the car?" he asked. He looked serious.

"Sure."

"I read your book," he said as they walked side by side to the car. He looked over at her. "*Rap Superstar.*" He laughed.

"What did you think?" She was curious, since the story was about them.

"I thought it was great. I knew you were a great writer." They reached the car and stopped. He turned to face her. Sidney started pulling on his chin.

Anthony studied this beautiful woman. She was back to pre-pregnancy size. It was impossible for anyone to be able to tell that she had a baby. As soon as Sidney was born, she hit the gym hard, and within twelve weeks, she had lost all of the baby weight.

Anthony liked her determination, her drive to succeed at whatever she did. Too bad she didn't have the drive to make their marriage work. "You made me look like a good guy."

"No, I didn't. I made you look like yourself. You are a good guy." She smiled at him.

"So, is it gonna be a movie?"

"It's going to be a movie," she said excitedly.

"Congratulations. I'm proud of you. Everything that you wanted is falling into place."

"It is." She nodded.

"Well, I've made a few changes."

Sidney yawned. She was getting tired. She laid her head on her daddy's chest and tried to fight it, but her eyelids grew so heavy that she couldn't hold them open anymore. She finally submitted to sleep and began to snore lightly. Anthony smiled. It reminded him of Randi's snoring.

"What kind of changes?"

He leaned back against his Escalade. Randi stood directly in front of him.

"Thomas let me out of my contract, and I've stopped rapping. I've bought my own studio. I'm producing now."

She smiled. "That's good. I'm happy for you."

He continued. "I'm off the road. I'm home every night. I can be a full-time father. Most of all, I can be a full-time husband." He reached for her hand and pulled her closer. He looked down and saw she still wore her wedding ring.

Randi looked up at the sky when she felt a drop of rain fall on her. The forecast had called for it. She knew it was going to be a storm. She looked back at him.

"I still love you, Randi. I still need you. I want to be your husband again." Now he felt the rain falling from the sky.

Without a word, she pulled her hand away from him and took a few steps back. The rain started falling a little harder.

"You better get her out of the rain," she said then turned and started walking away. She wanted to be strong. She had been struggling with this for over a year now. She knew that she still loved Anthony and he knew it too, but to go back to him after what he had done was out of the question. Besides, she had just purchased a new home. How would that look to go back to him now?

Anthony sighed and closed his eyes. *Time's up*, he said to himself. He turned and started putting Sidney in her car seat.

Randi stopped and turned around. "Anthony," she called. She was tired of fighting her true feelings. She loved him so much that it was ridiculous. If going back to him was senseless, outrageous or just plain illogical, then she would be those things. She needed him. She wanted him, and she would be a fool for him.

He closed the car door and looked at her. She walked back toward him. The rain streamed down on both of them. He started walking toward her. When they reached each other, she looked up at him. Tears raced down her face, mingling with raindrops. They stood looking at each other without saying a word. He didn't know what to do. He brought one hand up and touched her face. "What?" he whispered.

"I still love you too," she whispered back. "I want to come home."

He couldn't believe his ears. "You want to come home?"

She nodded through her tears. "I want to come home."

These were the words that he had been waiting to hear for nearly two years. Without a sound, he lowered his head and captured her lips with his. Gently, tenderly, he savored her lips. They tasted sweeter than he remembered.

Her arms slipped around his waist as she pushed herself against him. Their kiss deepened as his tongue explored the depths of her soul. His hands slid down her neck and back as he crushed her against him. The rain pounded down on them, but they didn't care.

Anthony finally let her go. He stepped back and without taking his eyes off her, he opened the car door.

"Let's go home," he whispered.

She looked up at him and smiled. "Let's go home," she whispered back before slipping into the Escalade.

He closed the door behind her and looked up at the heavens. "I promise I'm going to get it right this time," he vowed before he ran to his side of the car and got in. He looked in the back seat at his sleeping daughter then at his wife. This time, he had to get it right. He had no more second chances.

Chapter 24

Two years later, Randi sat in front of her computer. She was working on her latest novel, *Platinum Princess.* Her back ached from sitting in the uncomfortable chair for so long. She tried to massage the pain away, but it was useless. Anthony constantly scolded her about sitting at her desk for so long. He had purchased her a laptop so she could write in bed, but she was stubborn and insisted on writing at her desk.

He walked up behind her, pulled her hair to the side, and kissed her neck. She closed her eyes at the touch of his soft lips against her skin. *She smells delicious,* he thought. It was her hair. It always smelled like a floral perfume. He slid one large hand down over her swollen belly.

She was eight months pregnant. The baby kicked against his hand as if it knew that he was there. It was a boy this time. They had already picked out a name for him. Randi wanted to name the baby after Anthony, but Anthony didn't want a junior. They finally settled on Nicholas Emanuel.

Anthony smiled at the thought of having a son. He had always wanted a daughter, but since he already had Sidney, the prospect of having a little boy made him feel good. His son could keep him company when Randi and Sidney were off doing girly things.

Randi anxiously awaited the arrival of their son. Soon after his birth, she would start film school. And while she was excited about having another baby, she didn't know how she would find time to juggle motherhood, school, and her writing.

Anthony was a big help. He would take Sidney to the studio with him to allow Randi some free time to write.

Sidney enjoyed going to the studio with her daddy. She liked the music and the people who came to see him. They were always nice to her, bringing her toys and candy.

After Randi converted *Rap Superstar* from a novel to a screenplay, they started filming. The movie was still in production. Marvin Sadler was handling everything.

Anthony was working with three new acts. He also produced the soundtrack for *Rap Superstar*. Randi's brother James had laid down a few tracks for him. Anthony was impressed and was interested in continuing to work with him.

Thomas finally came around and apologized to Randi and Anthony for what he did to them. Although they accepted his apology, they still kept their distance. They would run into each other at parties in the hip-hop industry and they were civil toward each other, but that was as far as it went.

Sidney was excited about having a little brother. She would rub her mother's stomach and call him Nick because she couldn't say Nicholas yet. She was fascinated by the way he kicked and moved inside her mommy's belly, and she had promised Randi that she would teach Nick how to rap after he was born. Dragging her keyboard and microphone behind her, she walked into the room where Anthony and Randi sat.

Anthony had given her the keyboard and microphone for Christmas. He wanted her to be a rapper. Randi wanted her to become an actress. They had plenty of years to go before they had to worry about her career, though she was growing up so fast.

"Daddy, look," Sidney said as she plopped down on the floor in front of her keyboard. She clicked on the power button and brought the microphone to her tiny lips. They both looked over at her.

Earlier, Randi had brushed Sidney's giant curls up into a ponytail on top of her head, but Sidney had taken it loose.

She always liked to play with her hair. This drove her mother crazy. Her once neat curls now spilled all over her head and almost covered her large, round eyes. Randi wondered how she could see what she was doing.

Sidney pounded on the keyboard and rapped into the microphone as her head bobbed up and down like her daddy's friends did in the studio. Anthony and Randi laughed. They could only understand a few words she said. The rest was unrecognizable.

They moved over to sit beside Sidney. Anthony helped Randi maneuver her swollen belly around as she sat down on the floor. He sat across from them.

"Let me show you how it's done," he said. "You play and I'll rap."

Sidney handed him the microphone as her eyes lit up. She loved to hear her daddy talk real fast to music.

Anthony leaned over and pushed Sidney's curls back away from her eyes. "Go ahead. Start the music."

She pounded on the keyboard but kept her eyes on him. Anthony bobbed his head up and down as he began to rap.

> *Mommy and Daddy and Sidney make three,*
> *In another month, we'll have another baby.*
> *Never in my life did I imagine this could be,*
> *My three babies make me so happy.*
> *And I'm never gonna give 'em up,*
> *Never give 'em up,*
> *Never gonna give up my family.*

Sidney giggled uncontrollably as she clapped her hands together. He leaned over and kissed her fat cheeks. She started pounding on her keyboard again. Anthony slipped his

236

THE PROTESTANT ETHIC AND
THE SPIRIT OF CAPITALISM

MAX WEBER

The Protestant Ethic
and the
Spirit of Capitalism

TRANSLATED BY TALCOTT PARSONS

INTRODUCTION

BY

ANTHONY GIDDENS
Fellow of King's College, Cambridge

CHARLES SCRIBNER'S SONS
NEW YORK

INTRODUCTION

The Protestant Ethic and the Spirit of Capitalism undoubtedly ranks as one of the most renowned, and controversial, works of modern social science. First published as a two-part article in 1904–5, in the *Archiv für Sozialwissenschaft und Sozialpolitik,* of which Weber was one of the editors, it immediately provoked a critical debate, in which Weber participated actively, and which, some seventy years later, has still not gone off the boil. This English translation is in fact taken from the revised version of the work, that first appeared in Weber's *Gesammelte Aufsätze zur Religionssoziologie (Collected Essays on the Sociology of Religion),* published in 1920–1 just after Weber's death, and thus contains comments on the critical literature to which its initial appearance had given rise.

Weber wrote *The Protestant Ethic* at a pivotal period of his intellectual career, shortly after his recovery from a depressive illness that had incapacitated him from serious academic work for a period of some four years. Prior to his sickness, most of Weber's works, although definitely presaging the themes developed in the later phase of his life, were technical researches in economic history, economics and jurisprudence. They include studies of mediaeval trading law (his doctoral dissertation), the development of Roman land-tenure, and the contemporary socio-economic conditions of rural workers in the eastern part of Germany. These writings took their inspiration in some substantial part from the so-called 'historical school' of economics which, in conscious divergence from British political economy, stressed the need to examine economic life within the context of the historical development of culture as a whole. Weber always remained indebted to this standpoint. But the series of works he began on his return to health, and which preoccupied him for the remainder of his career, concern a range of problems much broader in compass than those covered in the earlier period. *The Protestant Ethic* was a first fruit of these new endeavours.

An appreciation of what Weber sought to achieve in the book demands at least an elementary grasp of two aspects of the circumstances in which it was produced: the intellectual climate within which he wrote, and the connections between the work itself and the massive programme of study that he set himself in the second phase of his career.

1. *The background*

German philosophy, political theory and economics in the nineteenth century were very different from their counterparts in Britain. The dominant position of utilitarianism and classical political economy in the latter country was not reproduced in Germany, where these were held at arm's length by the influence of Idealism and, in the closing decades of the nineteenth century, by the growing impact of Marxism. In Britain, J. S. Mill's *System of Logic* (1843) unified the natural and social sciences in a framework that fitted comfortably within existing traditions in that country. Mill was Comte's most distinguished British disciple, if sharply critical of some of his excesses. Comte's positivism never found a ready soil in Germany; and Dilthey's sympathetic but critical reception of Mill's version of the 'moral sciences' gave an added impulse to what came to be known as the *Geisteswissenschaften* (originally coined precisely as a translation of 'moral sciences'). The tradition of the *Geisteswissenschaften*, or the 'hermeneutic' tradition, stretches back well before Dilthey, and from the middle of the eighteenth century onwards was intertwined with, but also partly set off from, the broader stream of Idealistic philosophy. Those associated with the hermeneutic viewpoint insisted upon the differentiation of the sciences of nature from the study of man. While we can 'explain' natural occurrences in terms of the application of causal laws, human conduct is intrinsically meaningful, and has to be 'interpreted' or 'understood' in a way which has no counterpart in nature. Such an emphasis linked closely with a stress upon the centrality of history in the study of human conduct, in economic action as in other areas, because the cultural values that lend meanings to human life, it was held, are created by specific processes of social development.

Just as he accepted the thesis that history is of focal importance to the social sciences, Weber adopted the idea that the 'understanding' (*Verstehen*) of meaning is essential to the explication of human action. But he was critical of the notions of 'intuition', 'empathy', etc. that were regarded by many others as necessarily tied to the interpretative understanding of conduct. Most important, he rejected the view that recognition of the 'meaningful' character of human conduct entails that causal explanation cannot be undertaken in the social sciences. On the level of abstract method, Weber was not able to work out a satisfactory reconciliation of the diverse threads that he tried to knit together; but his effort at synthesis produced a distinctive style of historical study, combining a sensitivity to diverse cultural meanings with an insistence upon the fundamental causal role of 'material' factors in influencing the course of history.

It was from such an intellectual background that Weber approached Marxism, both as a set of doctrines and a political force promoting practical ends. Weber was closely associated with the *Verein für Sozialpolitik* (Association for Social Policy), a group of liberal scholars interested in the promotion of progressive social reform.[1] He was a member of the so-called 'younger generation' associated with the *Verein*, the first group to acquire a sophisticated knowledge of Marxist theory and to attempt to creatively employ elements drawn from Marxism – without ever accepting it as an overall system of thought, and recoiling from its revolutionary politics. While acknowledging the contributions of Marx, Weber held a more reserved attitude towards Marxism (often being bitterly critical of the works and political involvements of some of Marx's professed followers) than did his illustrious contemporary, Sombart. Each shared, however, a concern with the origins and likely course of evolution of industrial capitalism, in Germany specifically and in the West as a whole.[2] Specifically, they saw the economic conditions that Marx believed determined the development and future transformation of capitalism as embedded within a unique cultural totality.[3] Both devoted much of their work to identifying the emergence of this 'ethos' or 'spirit' (*Geist*) of modern Western capitalism.

2. *The themes of* The Protestant Ethic

In seeking to specify the distinctive characteristics of modern capitalism in *The Protestant Ethic*, Weber first of all separates off capitalistic enterprise from the pursuit of gain as such. The desire for wealth has existed in most times and places, and has in itself nothing to do with capitalistic action, which involves a regular orientation to the achievement of profit through (nominally peaceful) economic exchange. 'Capitalism', thus defined, in the shape of mercantile operations, for instance, has existed in various forms of society: in Babylon and Ancient Egypt, China, India and mediaeval Europe. But only in the West, and in relatively recent times, has capitalistic activity become associated with the *rational organisation of formally free labour*.[4] By 'rational organisation' of labour here Weber means its routinised, calculated administration within continuously functioning enterprises.

A rationalised capitalistic enterprise implies two things: a disciplined labour force, and the regularised investment of capital. Each contrasts profoundly with traditional types of economic activity. The significance of the former is readily illustrated by the experience of those who have set up modern productive organisations in communities where they have not previously been known. Let us suppose such employers, in order to raise productivity, introduce piece-rates, whereby workers can improve their wages, in the expectation that this will provide the members of their labour force with an incentive to work harder. The result may be that the latter actually work less than before: because they are interested, not in maximising their daily wage, but only in earning enough to satisfy their traditionally established needs. A parallel phenomenon exists among the wealthy in traditional forms of society, where those who profit from capitalist enterprise do so only in order to acquire money for the uses to which it can be put, in buying material comfort, pleasure or power. The regular reproduction of capital, involving its continual investment and reinvestment for the end of economic efficiency, is foreign to traditional types of enterprise. It is associated with an outlook of a very specific kind: the continual accumulation of wealth for its own sake, rather than for the material rewards that it can serve to bring. 'Man is dominated by the making of money, by acquisition as the ultimate purpose of his life. Economic acquisition is no longer subordinated to man as the means for the satisfaction of his material needs.' (p. 53) This, according to Weber, is the essence of the spirit of modern capitalism.

What explains this historically peculiar circumstance of a drive to the accumulation of wealth conjoined to an absence of interest in the worldly pleasures which it can purchase? It would certainly be mistaken, Weber argues, to suppose that it derives from the relaxation of traditional moralities: this novel outlook is a distinctively *moral* one, demanding in fact unusual self-discipline. The entrepreneurs associated with the development of rational capitalism combine the impulse to accumulation with a positively frugal life-style. Weber finds the answer in the 'this-worldly asceticism' of Puritanism, as focused through the concept of the 'calling'. The notion of the calling, according to Weber, did not exist either in Antiquity or in Catholic theology; it was introduced by the Reformation. It refers basically to the idea that the highest form of moral obligation of the individual is to fulfil his duty in worldly affairs. This projects religious behaviour into the day-to-day world, and stands in contrast to the Catholic ideal of the monastic life, whose object is to transcend the demands of mundane existence. Moreover, the moral responsibility of the Protestant is cumulative: the cycle of sin, repentance and forgiveness, renewed throughout the life of the Catholic, is absent in Protestantism.

Although the idea of the calling was already present in Luther's doctrines, Weber argues, it became more rigorously developed in the various Puritan sects: Calvinism, Methodism, Pietism and Baptism. Much of Weber's discussion is in fact concentrated upon the first of these, although he is interested not just in Calvin's doctrines as such but in their later evolution within the Calvinist movement. Of the elements in Calvinism that Weber singles out for special attention,

4

perhaps the most important, for his thesis, is the doctrine of predestination: that only some human beings are chosen to be saved from damnation, the choice being predetermined by God. Calvin himself may have been sure of his own salvation, as the instrument of Divine prophecy; but none of his followers could be. 'In its extreme inhumanity', Weber comments, 'this doctrine must above all have had one consequence for the life of a generation which surrendered to its magnificent consistency . . . a feeling of unprecedented inner loneliness.' (p. 104) From this torment, Weber holds, the capitalist spirit was born. On the pastoral level, two developments occurred: it became obligatory to regard oneself as chosen, lack of certainty being indicative of insufficient faith; and the performance of 'good works' in worldly activity became accepted as the medium whereby such surety could be demonstrated. Hence success in a calling eventually came to be regarded as a 'sign' – never a means – of being one of the elect. The accumulation of wealth was morally sanctioned in so far as it was combined with a sober, industrious career; wealth was condemned only if employed to support a life of idle luxury or self-indulgence.

Calvinism, according to Weber's argument, supplies the moral energy and drive of the capitalist entrepreneur; Weber speaks of its doctrines as having an 'iron consistency' in the bleak discipline which it demands of its adherents. The element of ascetic self-control in worldly affairs is certainly there in the other Puritan sects also: but they lack the dynamism of Calvinism. Their impact, Weber suggests, is mainly upon the formation of a moral outlook enhancing labour discipline within the lower and middle levels of capitalist economic organisation. 'The virtues favoured by Pietism', for example, were those 'of the faithful official, clerk, labourer, or domestic worker' (p.139).

3. The Protestant Ethic *in the context of Weber's other writings*

For all its fame, *The Protestant Ethic* is a fragment. It is much shorter and less detailed than Weber's studies of the other 'world religions': ancient Judaism, Hinduism and Buddhism, and Confucianism (Weber also planned, but did not complete, a full-scale study of Islam). Together, these form an integrated series of works.[5] Neither *The Protestant Ethic* nor any of the other studies was conceived of by Weber as a descriptive account of types of religion. They were intended as analyses of divergent modes of the rationalisation of culture, and as attempts to trace out the significance of such divergencies for socio-economic development.

In his study of India, Weber placed particular emphasis upon the period when Hinduism became first established (about four or five centuries before the birth of Christ). The beliefs and practices grouped together as 'Hinduism' vary considerably. Weber singles out as especially important for his purposes the doctrines of reincarnation and compensation (*Karma*), each tied in closely to the caste system. The conduct of an individual in any one incarnation, in terms of the enactment of his caste obligations, determines his fate in his next life; the faithful can contemplate the possibility of moving up a hierarchy towards divinity in the course of successive incarnations. There is an important emphasis upon asceticism in Hinduism, but it is, in Weber's term, 'other-worldly': that is to say, it is directed towards escaping the encumbrances of the material world rather than, as in Puritanism, towards the rational mastery of that world itself. During the same period at which Hinduism became systematised, trade and manufacture reached a peak in India. But the influence of Hinduism, and of the emergent caste system which interlaced with it, effectively inhibited any economic development comparable to modern European capitalism. 'A ritual law,' Weber remarks, 'in which every change of occupation, every change in work technique, may result in ritual degradation is certainly not capable of giving birth to economic and technical revolutions from within itself . . .'[6] The phrase 'from within itself' is a vital one: Weber's concerns were with the first origins of modern capitalism in Europe, not with its subsequent adoption elsewhere.

As in India, in China at certain periods trade and manufacture reached a fairly high level of evolution; trade and craft guilds flourished; there was a monetary system; there existed a developed framework of law. All of these elements Weber regards as preconditions for the development of rational capitalism in Europe. While the character of Confucianism, as Weber portrays it, is very different from Hinduism, it no more provided for 'the incorporation of the acquisitive drive in a this-worldly ethic of conduct'[7] than did Hinduism. Confucianism is, in an important sense, a 'this-worldly' religion, but not one which embodies ascetic values. The Calvinist ethic introduced an activism into the believer's approach to worldly affairs, a drive to mastery in a quest for virtue in the eyes of God, that are altogether lacking in Confucianism. Confucian values do not promote such a rational instrumentalism, nor do they sanctify the transcendence of mundane affairs in the manner of Hinduism; instead they set as an ideal the harmonious adjustment of the individual to the established order of things. The religiously cultivated man is one who makes his behaviour coherent with the intrinsic harmony of the cosmos. An ethic which stresses rational adjustment to the world 'as it is' could not have generated a moral dynamism in economic activity comparable to that characteristic of the spirit of European capitalism.

Weber's other completed study of the 'world religions', that of ancient Judaism, is also an important element of his overall project. For the first origins of Judaism in ancient Palestine mark the nexus of circumstances in which certain fundamental differences between the religions of the Near and Far East became elaborated. The distinctive doctrines forged in Judaism were perpetuated in Christianity, and hence incorporated into Western culture as a whole. Judaism introduced a tradition of 'ethical prophecy', involving the active propagation of a Divine mission, that contrasts with the 'exemplary prophecy' more characteristic of India and China. In the latter type, the prophet offers the example of his own life as a model for his followers to strive after: the active missionary zeal characteristic of ethical prophecy is lacking in the teachings of the exemplary prophets. Judaism and Christianity rest on the tension between sin and salvation and that gives them a basic transformative capacity which the Far Eastern religions lack, being more contemplative in orientation. The opposition between the imperfections of the world and the perfection of God, in Christian theodicy, enjoins the believer to achieve his salvation through refashioning the world in accordance with Divine purpose. Calvinism, for Weber, both maximises the moral impulsion deriving from the active commitment to the achievement of salvation and focuses it upon economic activity.

The Protestant Ethic, Weber says, traces 'only one side of the causal chain' connecting Puritanism to modern capitalism (p. 27). He certainly does not claim that differences in the rationalisation of religious ethics he identifies are the only significant influences that separate economic development in the West from that of the Eastern civilisations. On the contrary, he specifies a number of fundamental socio-economic factors which distinguish the European experience from that of India and of China, and which were of crucial importance to the emergence of modern capitalism. These include the following: 1. The separation of the productive enterprise from the household which, prior to the development of industrial capitalism, was much more advanced in the West than it ever became elsewhere. In China, for example, extended kinship units provided the major forms of economic co-operation, thus limiting the influence both of the guilds and of individual entrepreneurial activity. 2. The development of the Western city. In post-mediaeval Europe, urban communities reached a high level of political autonomy, thus setting off 'bourgeois' society from agrarian feudalism. In the Eastern civilisations, however, partly because of the influence of kinship connections that cut across the urban-rural differentiation, cities remained more embedded in the local agrarian economy. 3. The existence, in Europe, of an inherited tradition of Roman law, providing a more integrated and developed rationalisation of juridical practice than came into being elsewhere. 4. This in turn was one factor making possible the development of the nation-state, administered by full-time

7

bureaucratic officials, beyond anything achieved in the Eastern civilisations. The rational-legal system of the Western state was in some degree adapted within business organisations themselves, as well as providing an overall framework for the co-ordination of the capitalist economy. 5. The development of double-entry book-keeping in Europe. In Weber's view, this was a phenomenon of major importance in opening the way for the regularising of capitalistic enterprise. 6. That series of changes which, as Marx emphasised, prepared the way for the formation of a 'free' mass of wage-labourers, whose livelihood depends upon the sale of labour-power in the market. This presupposes the prior erosion of the monopolies over the disposal of labour which existed in the form of feudal obligations (and were maximised in the East in the form of the caste system).

Taken together, these represent a mixture of necessary and precipitating conditions which, in conjunction with the moral energy of the Puritans, brought about the rise of modern Western capitalism. But if Puritanism provided that vital spark igniting the sequence of change creating industrial capitalism, the latter order, once established, eradicates the specifically religious elements in the ethic which helped to produce it:

'When asceticism was carried out of monastic cells into everyday life, and began to dominate worldly morality, it did its part in building the tremendous cosmos of the modern economic order . . . victorious capitalism, since it rests on mechanical foundations, needs its support no longer . . . the idea of duty in one's calling prowls about in our lives like the ghost of dead religious beliefs.' (pp. 181–2)

Here *The Protestant Ethic,* concerned above all with the origins of modern capitalism, connects up with Weber's sombre indictment of the latter-day progression of contemporary industrial culture as a whole. Puritanism has played a part in creating the 'iron cage' in which modern man has to exist – an increasingly bureaucratic order from which the 'spontaneous enjoyment of life' is ruthlessly expunged. 'The Puritan', Weber concludes, 'wanted to work in a calling; we are forced to do so.' (p. 181).

4. The controversy

The Protestant Ethic was written with polemical intent, evident in various references Weber makes to 'Idealism' and 'Materialism'. The study, he says, is 'a contribution to the understanding of the manner in which ideas become effective forces in history', and is directed against economic determinism. The Reformation, and the development of the Puritan sects subsequently, cannot be explained as 'a historically necessary result' of prior economic changes (pp. 90–1). It seems clear that Weber has Marxism in mind here, or at least the cruder forms of Marxist historical analysis which were prominent at the time.[8] But he is emphatic that he does not want to substitute for such a deterministic Materialism an equally monistic Idealist account of history (cf. p. 183). Rather the work expresses his conviction that there are no 'laws of history': the emergence of modern capitalism in the West was an outcome of an historically specific conjunction of events.

The latent passion of Weber's account may be glimpsed in the comments on Puritanism and its residue with which *The Protestant Ethic* concludes. The 'iron cage' is imagery enough to carry Weber's distaste for the celebration of the mundane and the routine he thought central to modern culture. He adds, however, a quotation from Goethe: 'Specialists without spirit, sensualists without heart; this nullity imagines that it has attained a level of civilisation never before achieved.' (p. 182) Such sweeping evaluation contrasts oddly with the cautious way in which Weber surrounds the main theses of the book with a battery of qualifications. Perhaps it is this contrast, unexplicated in the book itself, although clarified when the work is regarded as one element in Weber's project as a whole, that helped to stimulate the controversy to which its publication gave rise. But what explains the intensity of the debate which it has aroused; and why has the controversy been actively carried on for so long?

The most important reason for the emotional intensity provoked by the book is no doubt the fact that the two major terms in Weber's equation, 'religion' and 'capitalism', were each potentially explosive when applied to the interpretation of the origins of the modern Western economy. Weber argued for the transformative force of certain religious ideas, thus earning the opposition of most contemporary Marxists; his characterisation of Catholicism as lacking in mundane discipline, and as a retarding rather than a stimulating influence upon modern economic development, ensured the hostility of many Catholic historians; and his analysis of Protestantism, emphasising the role of the Puritan sects (whose influence is in turn linked to the 'iron cage' of modern culture), was hardly likely to meet a universal welcome from Protestant thinkers. Finally, the use of the term 'capitalism' was controversial in itself: many were, and some still are, inclined to argue that the notion has no useful application in economic history.

The very diversity of responses thus stimulated by *The Protestant Ethic* helps to explain the protracted character of the debate. But there are other significant underlying factors. The intellectual power of Weber's arguments derives in no small part from his disregard of traditional subject-boundaries, made possible by the extraordinary compass of his own scholarship. Consequently, his work can be approached on several levels: as a specific historical thesis, claiming a correlation between Calvinism and entrepreneurial attitudes; as a causal analysis of the influence of Puritanism upon capitalistic activity; as an interpretation of the origins of key components of modern Western society as a whole; and, set in the context of Weber's comparative studies, as part of an attempt to identify divergent courses in the rationalisation of culture in the major civilisations of West and East. The controversy over *The Protestant Ethic* has moved back and forward between these levels, embracing along the way not only such substantive themes, but also most of the methodological issues which Weber wrote the book to help illuminate; and it has drawn in a dazzling variety of contributors from economics, history and economic histroy, comparative religion, anthropology and sociology. Moreover, through the works of others who have accepted some or all of Weber's analysis and tried to extend elements of it, secondary controversies have sprung into being – such as that surrounding R. K. Merton's account of the influence of Protestantism on science in seventeenth-century England.[9]

It would be difficult to deny that some of the critical responses to *The Protestant Ethic,* particularly immediately following its original publication in Germany, and on the first appearance of this translation in 1930, were founded upon either direct misunderstandings of the claims Weber put forward, or upon an inadequate grasp of what he was trying to achieve in the work. Some such misinterpretations by his early critics, such as Fischer and Rachfahl, were accepted by Weber as partly his responsibility.[10] These critics, of course, did not have the possibility of placing *The Protestant Ethic* in the context of Weber's broad range of comparative analyses. They can perhaps be forgiven for not appreciating the partial character of the study, even if Weber did caution his readers as to the limitations on its scope. But it is less easy to excuse the many subsequent critics writing in the 1920s and 1930s (including von Below, R. H. Tawney, F. H. Knight, H. M. Robertson and P. Gordon Walker) who almost completely ignored *Gesammelte Aufsätze zur Religions-soziologie* and *Wirtschaft und Gesellschaft (Economy and Society)*.[11] Some of the literature of this period is quite valueless, at least as relevant to the assessment of Weber's own arguments: as where, for instance, authors took Weber to task for suggesting that Calvinism was 'the' cause of the development of modern capitalism; or where they pointed out that some contemporary countries, such as Japan, have experienced rapid economic development without possessing anything akin to a 'Protestant ethic'.

This nonetheless leaves a considerable variety of potentially justifiable forms of criticism that have been levelled against Weber, incorporated in discussions which stretch from those that dismiss his claims out of hand to those which propose relatively minor modifications to his work. They can perhaps be classified as embodying one or more of the following points of view:[12]

1. Weber's characterisation of Protestantism was faulty. Critiques here have been directed to Weber's treatment of the Reformation, to his interpretation of the Puritan sects in general, and to Calvinism in particular. It has been held that Weber was mistaken in supposing that Luther introduced a concept of 'calling' which differed from anything previously available in scriptural exegesis; and that Calvinist ethics were in fact 'anti-capitalistic' rather than ever sanctioning the accumulation of wealth, even as an indirect end. Others have argued that Weber's exposition of Benjamin Franklin's ideas, which occupies a central place in *The Protestant Ethic,* as well as other aspects of his analysis of American Puritanism, are unacceptable.[13] This is of some significance, if correct, since Weber regarded the influence of Puritanism upon business activity in the United States as being a particularly clear and important exemplification of his thesis.[14]

2. Weber misinterpreted Catholic doctrine. Critics have pointed out that Weber apparently did not study Catholicism in any detail, although his argument is based on the notion that there were basic differences between it and Protestantism in respect of economically relevant values. It has been held that post-mediaeval Catholicism involves elements positively favourable to the 'capitalist spirit'; and that the Reformation is in fact to be seen as a reaction against the latter rather than as clearing the ground for its subsequent emergence.[15]

3. Weber's statement of the connections between Puritanism and modern capitalism is based upon unsatisfactory empirical materials. This was one of the themes of Fischer and Rachfahl, and has been echoed many times since, in various forms. It has been noted that the only numerical analysis Weber refers to is a study of the economic activities of Catholics and Protestants in Baden in 1895 – and the accuracy even of these figures has been questioned.[16] More generally, however, critics have pointed out that Weber's sources are mainly Anglo-Saxon, and have claimed that research into economic development in the Rhineland, the Netherlands and Switzerland, in the sixteenth and seventeenth centuries, does not reveal any close association between Calvinism and capitalistic enterprise.[17]

4. Weber was not justified in drawing as sharp a contrast as he tried to do between modern, or 'rational' capitalism, and preceding types of capitalistic activity. It has been argued, on the one hand, that Weber slanted his concept of 'modern capitalism' in such a way as to make it conform to the elements of Puritanism he fastens upon; and on the other, that much of what Weber calls the 'spirit' of modern capitalism was indeed present in prior periods. Tawney accepts the differentiation between Lutheranism and the later Protestant sects, but argues that it was the prior development of the 'capitalist spirit' that moulded the evolution of Puritanism rather than vice versa.[18]

5. Weber mistakes the nature of the causal relation between Puritanism and modern capitalism. It is, of course, the conclusion of many of the authors taking one or other of the points of view mentioned above that there was no such causal relation. At this point, however, the debate broadens out into one concerned with abstract problems of historical method, and indeed with the very possibility of causal analysis in history at all. Marxist critics have tended to reject Weber's case for a 'pluralistic' view of historical causation, and some have attempted to reinterpret the thesis of *The Protestant Ethic,* treating the Puritan doctrines Weber analyses as epiphenomena of previously established economic changes.[19] Other authors, not necessarily Marxist, have rejected the methodological framework within which Weber worked, and have tried to show that this has consequences for his account of the origins of the capitalist spirit.[20]

How much of Weber's account survives the tremendous critical battering it has received? There are still some who would answer, virtually all of it: either most of the criticisms are mistaken, or they derive from misunderstandings of Weber's position.[21] I do not believe, however, that such a view can be substantiated. It is obvious that at least certain of Weber's critics must be wrong, because the literature is partly self-contradictory: the claims made by some authors in criticism of Weber contradict those made by others. Nonetheless, some of the critiques carry considerable force, and taken together they represent a formidable indictment of Weber's views. The elements of Weber's analysis that are most definitely called into question, I would say, are: the distinctiveness of the notion of the 'calling' in Lutheranism;[22] the supposed lack of 'affinity' between Catholicism and regularised entrepreneurial activity; and, the very centrepoint of the thesis, the degree to which Calvinist ethics actually served to dignify the accumulation of wealth in the manner suggested by Weber. If Weber were wrong on these matters, tracing out the consequences for the broad spectrum of his writings would still remain a complicated matter. To be at all satisfactory, it would involve considering the status of the companion studies of the 'world religions', the general problem of the rationalisation of culture – and the methodological framework within which Weber worked. No author has yet attempted such a task, and perhaps it would need someone with a scholarly range approaching that of Weber himself to undertake it with any hope of success.

ANTHONY GIDDENS
Cambridge, 1976

1. Dieter Lindenlaub: *Richtungskämpfe im Verein für Sozialpolitik*. Wiesbaden, 1967.

2. Talcott Parsons: ' "Capitalism" in recent German literature: Sombart and Weber', Parts 1 and 2, *The Journal of Political Economy*, Vols 36 and 37, 1928 and 1929; Philip Siegelman: 'Introduction' to Werner Sombart: *Luxury and Capitalism*. Ann Arbor, 1967.

3. Anthony Giddens: *Politics and Sociology in the Thought of Max Weber*. London, 1972.

4. See Max Weber: *General Economic History*. New York, 1961.

5. *Ancient Judaism*. Glencoe, 1952; *The Religion of India*. Glencoe, 1958; *The Religion of China*. London, 1964 (all bracketed within the collection *Gesammelte Aufsätze zur Religionssoziologie*); cf. Bryan S. Turner: *Weber and Islam*. London, 1974.

6. *The Religion of India*, p. 112.

7. *The Religion of India*, p. 337.

8. Anthony Giddens: 'Marx, Weber, and the development of capitalism', *Sociology*, Vol 4, 1970.

9. R. K. Merton: 'Science, technology and society in seventeenth century England', *Osiris*, Vol 4, 1938 (reprinted as a single volume, New York, 1970).

10. Max Weber: 'Antikritisches Schlusswort zum "Geist des Kapitalismus" ', *Archiv für Sozialwissenschaft und Sozialpolitik*, Vol 31, 1910. See, for example, the following footnotes in the present work: Chapter 1, footnote, 1; Chapter 2, footnotes 10, 12, 13 and 29; Chapter 3, footnotes 1 and 3 Chapter 4, footnotes 3 and 4; Chapter 5, footnotes 31, 58 and 84.

11. For the best survey of the debate up to the early 1940s, see Ephraim Fischoff: 'The Protestant ethic and the spirit of capitalism: the history of a controversy', *Social Research*, Vol 11, 1944.

12. For a somewhat different classification, see Ehud Sprinzak: 'Weber's thesis as an historical explanation', *History and Theory*, Vol 11, 1972.

13. Brentano was one of the first to criticise Weber's treatment of the 'calling'. See Lujo Brentano: *Die Anfänge des moderne Kapitalismus*. Munich, 1916; also H. M. Robertson: *Aspects of the Rise of Economic Individualism.*. Cambridge, 1933. On Puritanism: Albert Hyma: *Renaissance to Reformation*. Grand Rapids, 1951; Gabriel Kolko: 'Max Weber on America: theory and evidence', *History and Theory*, Vol 1, 1960–61. There are many, many others: as on each of the further points noted below. A partial bibliography appears in S. N. Eisenstadt: *The Protestant Ethic and Modernisation*. New York, 1968; see also David Little: *Religion, Order, and the Law*. Oxford, 1970, pp. 226–37.

14. Cf. Max Weber: 'Die Protestantischen Sekten und der Geist des Kapitalismus' ('The Protestant sects and the spirit of capitalism'), in *Gesammelte Aufsätze zur Religionssoziologie*.

15. W. Sombart: *The Quintessence of Capitalism*. London, 1951; Hyma, *op.cit.*; A. Fanfani: *Catholicism, Protestantism and Capitalism*. London, 1935; R. H. Tawney: *Religion and the Rise of Capitalism*. London, 1926; Herbert Lüthy: 'Once again: Calvinism and capitalism', *Encounter*, Vol 22, 1964.

16. Kurt Samuelsson: *Religion and Economic Action*. London, 1961, pp. 137ff.

17. W. Hudson: 'The Weber thesis re-examined', *Church History*, Vol 30, 1961; Michael Walzer: *The Revolution of the Saints*. London, 1966 (pp. 306ff); and especially Samuelsson, *op.cit.*

18 Sombart, *op.cit.*; H. Sée: 'Dans quelle mesure Puritains et Juifs ont-ils contribué au progrès du capitalisme moderne?', *Revue historique*, Vol 155, 1927; Tawney, *op.cit.*; Christopher Hill: 'Protestantism and the rise of capitalism', in F. J. Fisher: *Essays in the Economic and Social History of Tudor and Stuart England*. Cambridge, 1961.

19 E.g. Karl Kautsky: *Materialistische Geschichtsauffassung*.

20 For a recent version, see Alasdair MacIntyre: 'A mistake about causality in the social sciences', in Peter Laslett and W. G. Runciman: *Philosophy, Politics and Society*, Vol 2, Oxford, 1962. (Certain of the views expressed in the article have however been subsequently abandoned by its author.)

21. See, for instance, Little; *op.cit.*; Sprinzak: *op.cit.*.

22. Weber's detailed reply to Brentano's criticism on this point appears below, in footnotes 1–3, Chapter 3.

NOTE

The Author's Introduction, which is placed before the main essay, was written by Weber in 1920 for the whole series on the Sociology of Religion. It has been included in this translation because it gives some of the general background of ideas and problems into which Weber himself meant this particular study to fit. That has seemed particularly desirable since, in the voluminous discussion which has grown up in Germany around Weber's essay, a great deal of misplaced criticism has been due to the failure properly to appreciate the scope and limitations of the study. While it is impossible to appreciate that fully without a thorough study of Weber's sociological work as a whole, the Author's Introduction should suffice to prevent a great deal of misunderstanding.

Talcott Parsons (1930)

AUTHOR'S INTRODUCTION

A PRODUCT of modern European civilization, studying any problem of universal history, is bound to ask himself to what combination of circumstances the fact should be attributed that in Western civilization, and in Western civilization only, cultural phenomena have appeared which (as we like to think) lie in a line of development having *universal* significance and value.

Only in the West does science exist at a stage of development which we recognize to-day as valid. Empirical knowledge, reflection on problems of the cosmos and of life, philosophical and theological wisdom of the most profound sort, are not confined to it, though in the case of the last the full development of a systematic theology must be credited to Christianity under the influence of Hellenism, since there were only fragments in Islam and in a few Indian sects. In short, knowledge and observation of great refinement have existed elsewhere, above all in India, China, Babylonia, Egypt. But in Babylonia and elsewhere astronomy lacked—which makes its development all the more astounding—the mathematical foundation which it first received from the Greeks. The Indian geometry had no rational proof; that was another product of the Greek intellect, also the creator of mechanics and physics. The Indian natural sciences, though well developed in observation, lacked the method of experiment, which was, apart from beginnings in antiquity, essentially a product of the Renaissance, as was the modern laboratory. Hence medicine, especially in India, though highly developed

13

in empirical technique, lacked a biological and particularly a biochemical foundation. A rational chemistry has been absent from all areas of culture except the West.

The highly developed historical scholarship of China did not have the method of Thucydides. Machiavelli, it is true, had predecessors in India; but all Indian political thought was lacking in a systematic method comparable to that of Aristotle, and, indeed, in the possession of rational concepts. Not all the anticipations in India (School of Mimamsa), nor the extensive codification especially in the Near East, nor all the Indian and other books of law, had the strictly systematic forms of thought, so essential to a rational jurisprudence, of the Roman law and of the Western law under its influence. A structure like the canon law is known only to the West.

A similar statement is true of art. The musical ear of other peoples has probably been even more sensitively developed than our own, certainly not less so. Polyphonic music of various kinds has been widely distributed over the earth. The co-operation of a number of instruments and also the singing of parts have existed elsewhere. All our rational tone intervals have been known and calculated. But rational harmonious music, both counterpoint and harmony, formation of the tone material on the basis of three triads with the harmonic third; our chromatics and enharmonics, not interpreted in terms of space, but, since the Renaissance, of harmony; our orchestra, with its string quartet as a nucleus, and the organization of ensembles of wind instruments; our bass accompani-

14

ment; our system of notation, which has made possible the composition and production of modern musical works, and thus their very survival; our sonatas, symphonies, operas; and finally, as means to all these, our fundamental instruments, the organ, piano, violin, etc.; all these things are known only in the Occident, although programme music, tone poetry, alteration of tones and chromatics, have existed in various musical traditions as means of expression.

In architecture, pointed arches have been used else-where as a means of decoration, in antiquity and in Asia; presumably the combination of pointed arch and cross-arched vault was not unknown in the Orient. But the rational use of the Gothic vault as a means of distributing pressure and of roofing spaces of all forms, and above all as the constructive principle of great monumental buildings and the foundation of a *style* extending to sculpture and painting, such as that created by our Middle Ages, does not occur elsewhere. The technical basis of our architecture came from the Orient. But the Orient lacked that solution of the problem of the dome and that type of classic rational-ization of all art—in painting by the rational utilization of lines and spatial perspective—which the Renaissance created for us. There was printing in China. But a printed literature, designed *only* for print and only possible through it, and, above all, the Press and periodicals, have appeared only in the Occident. Institutions of higher education of all possible types, even some superficially similar to our universities, or at least academies, have existed (China, Islam). But a rational, systematic, and specialized pursuit of science, with trained and specialized personnel, has only existed in the West in a sense at all approaching its present dominant place in our culture. Above all is this true of the trained official, the pillar of both the modern State and of the economic life of the West. He forms a type of which there have heretofore only been suggestions, which have never remotely approached its present importance for the social order. Of course the official, even the specialized official, is a very old constituent of the most various societies. But no country and no age has ever experienced, in the same sense as the modern Occident, the absolute and complete dependence of its whole existence, of the political, technical, and economic conditions of its life, on a specially trained *organization* of officials. The most important functions of the everyday life of society have come to be in the hands of technically, commercially, and above all legally trained government officials.

Organization of political and social groups in feudal classes has been common. But even the feudal[1] state of *rex et regnum* in the Western sense has only been known to our culture. Even more are parliaments of periodically elected representatives, with government by demagogues and party leaders as ministers responsible to the parliaments, peculiar to us, although there have, of course, been parties, in the sense of organizations for exerting influence and gaining control of political power, all over the world. In fact, the State itself, in the sense of a political association with a rational, written constitution, rationally ordained law, and an administration bound to rational rules or laws, administered by trained officials, is known, in this combination of characteristics, only in the Occident, despite all other approaches to it.

And the same is true of the most fateful force in our modern life, capitalism. The impulse to acquisition, pursuit of gain, of money, of the greatest possible amount of money, has in itself nothing to do with capitalism. This impulse exists and has existed among waiters, physicians, coachmen, artists, prostitutes, dishonest officials, soldiers, nobles, crusaders, gamblers, and beggars. One may say that it has been common to all sorts and conditions of men at all times and in all countries of the earth, wherever the objective possibility of it is or has been given. It should be taught in the kindergarten of cultural history that this naïve idea of capitalism must be given up once and for all. Unlimited greed for gain is not in the least identical with capitalism, and is still less its spirit. Capitalism *may* even be identical with the restraint, or at least a rational tempering, of this irrational impulse. But capitalism is identical with the pursuit of profit, and forever *renewed* profit, by means of continuous, rational, capitalistic enterprise. For it must be so: in a wholly capitalistic order of society, an individual capitalistic enterprise which did not take advantage of its opportunities for profit-making would be doomed to extinction.

Let us now define our terms somewhat more carefully than is generally done. We will define a capitalistic economic action as one which rests on the expectation of profit by the utilization of opportunities for exchange, that is on (formally) peaceful chances of profit. Acquisition by force (formally and actually) follows its own particular laws, and it is not expedient, however little one can forbid this, to place it in the same category with action which is, in the last analysis, oriented to profits from exchange.[2] Where capitalistic acquisition is rationally pursued, the corresponding action is adjusted to calculations in terms of capital. This means that the action is adapted to a systematic utilization of goods or personal services as means of acquisition in such a way that, at the close of a business period, the balance of the enterprise in money assets (or, in the case of a continuous enterprise, the periodically estimated money value of assets) exceeds the capital, i.e. the estimated value of the material means of production used for acquisition in exchange. It makes no difference whether it involves a quantity of goods entrusted *in natura* to a travelling merchant, the proceeds of which may consist in other goods *in natura* acquired by trade, or whether it involves a manufacturing enterprise, the assets of which consist of buildings, machinery, cash, raw materials, partly and wholly manufactured goods, which are balanced against liabilities. The important fact is always that a calculation of capital in terms of money is made, whether by modern book-keeping methods or in any other way, however primitive and crude. Everything is done in terms of balances: at the beginning of the enterprise an initial balance, before every individual decision a calculation to ascertain its probable profitableness, and at the end a final balance to ascertain how much profit has been made. For instance, the initial balance of a *commenda*[3] transaction would determine an agreed money value of the assets put into

18

it (so far as they were not in money form already), and a final balance would form the estimate on which to base the distribution of profit and loss at the end. So far as the transactions are rational, calculation underlies every single action of the partners. That a really accurate calculation or estimate may not exist, that the procedure is pure guess-work, or simply traditional and conventional, happens even to-day in every form of capitalistic enterprise where the circumstances do not demand strict accuracy. But these are points affecting only the *degree* of rationality of capitalistic acquisition.

For the purpose of this conception all that matters is that an actual adaptation of economic action to a comparison of money income with money expenses takes place, no matter how primitive the form. Now in this sense capitalism and capitalistic enterprises, even with a considerable rationalization of capitalistic calculation, have existed in all civilized countries of the earth, so far as economic documents permit us to judge. In China, India, Babylon, Egypt, Mediterranean antiquity, and the Middle Ages, as well as in modern times. These were not merely isolated ventures, but economic enterprises which were entirely dependent on the continual renewal of capitalistic undertakings, and even continuous operations. However, trade especially was for a long time not continuous like our own, but consisted essentially in a series of individual undertakings. Only gradually did the activities of even the large merchants acquire an inner cohesion (with branch organizations, etc.). In any case, the capitalistic enterprise and the capitalistic entrepreneur, not only

19

as occasional but as regular entrepreneurs, are very old and were very widespread.

Now, however, the Occident has developed capitalism both to a quantitative extent, and (carrying this quantitative development) in types, forms, and directions which have never existed elsewhere. All over the world there have been merchants, wholesale and retail, local and engaged in foreign trade. Loans of all kinds have been made, and there have been banks with the most various functions, at least comparable to ours of, say, the sixteenth century. Sea loans,[4] *commenda*, and transactions and associations similar to the *Kommanditgesellschaft*,[5] have all been widespread, even as continuous businesses. Whenever money finances of public bodies have existed, money-lenders have appeared, as in Babylon, Hellas, India, China, Rome. They have financed wars and piracy, contracts and building operations of all sorts. In overseas policy they have functioned as colonial entrepreneurs, as planters with slaves, or directly or indirectly forced labour, and have farmed domains, offices, and, above all, taxes. They have financed party leaders in elections and *condottieri* in civil wars. And, finally, they have been speculators in chances for pecuniary gain of all kinds. This kind of entrepreneur, the capitalistic adventurer, has existed everywhere. With the exception of trade and credit and banking transactions, their activities were predominantly of an irrational and speculative character, or directed to acquisition by force, above all the acquisition of booty, whether directly in war or in the form of continuous fiscal booty by exploitation of subjects.

Introduction

The capitalism of promoters, large-scale speculators, concession hunters, and much modern financial capitalism even in peace time, but, above all, the capitalism especially concerned with exploiting wars, bears this stamp even in modern Western countries, and some, but only some, parts of large-scale international trade are closely related to it, to-day as always.

But in modern times the Occident has developed, in addition to this, a very different form of capitalism which has appeared nowhere else: the rational capitalistic organization of (formally) free labour. Only suggestions of it are found elsewhere. Even the organization of unfree labour reached a considerable degree of rationality only on plantations and to a very limited extent in the *Ergasteria* of antiquity. In the manors, manorial workshops, and domestic industries on estates with serf labour it was probably somewhat less developed. Even real domestic industries with free labour have definitely been proved to have existed in only a few isolated cases outside the Occident. The frequent use of day labourers led in a very few cases—especially State monopolies, which are, however, very different from modern industrial organization—to manufacturing organizations, but never to a rational organization of apprenticeship in the handicrafts like that of our Middle Ages.

Rational industrial organization, attuned to a regular market, and neither to political nor irrationally speculative opportunities for profit, is not, however, the only peculiarity of Western capitalism. The modern rational organization of the capitalistic enterprise would not have been possible without two other important factors in its development: the separation of business from the household, which completely dominates modern economic life, and closely connected with it, rational book-keeping. A spatial separation of places of work from those of residence exists elsewhere, as in the Oriental bazaar and in the *ergasteria* of other cultures. The development of capitalistic associations with their own accounts is also found in the Far East, the Near East, and in antiquity. But compared to the modern independence of business enterprises, those are only small beginnings. The reason for this was particularly that the indispensable requisites for this independence, our rational business book-keeping and our legal separation of corporate from personal property, were entirely lacking, or had only begun to develop.[6] The tendency everywhere else was for acquisitive enterprises to arise as parts of a royal or manorial *household* (of the *oikos*), which is, as Rodbertus has perceived, with all its superficial similarity, a fundamentally different, even opposite, development.

However, all these peculiarities of Western capitalism have derived their significance in the last analysis only from their association with the capitalistic organization of labour. Even what is generally called commercialization, the development of negotiable securities and the rationalization of speculation, the exchanges, etc., is connected with it. For without the rational capitalistic organization of labour, all this, so far as it was possible at all, would have nothing like the same significance, above all for the social structure and all the specific problems of the modern Occident connected with it. Exact calculation—the basis of everything else—is only possible on a basis of free labour.[7]

Introduction

And just as, or rather because, the world has known no rational organization of labour outside the modern Occident, it has known no rational socialism. Of course, there has been civic economy, a civic food-supply policy, mercantilism and welfare policies of princes, rationing, regulation of economic life, protectionism, and *laissez-faire* theories (as in China). The world has also known socialistic and communistic experiments of various sorts: family, religious, or military communism, State socialism (in Egypt), monopolistic cartels, and consumers' organizations. But although there have everywhere been civic market privileges, companies, guilds, and all sorts of legal differences between town and country, the concept of the citizen has not existed outside the Occident, and that of the bourgeoisie outside the modern Occident. Similarly, the proletariat as a class could not exist, because there was no rational organization of free labour under regular discipline. Class struggles between creditor and debtor classes; landowners and the landless, serfs, or tenants; trading interests and consumers or landlords, have existed everywhere in various combinations. But even the Western mediæval struggles between putters-out and their workers exist elsewhere only in beginnings. The modern conflict of the large-scale industrial entrepreneur and free-wage labourers was entirely lacking. And thus there could be no such problems as those of socialism.

Hence in a universal history of culture the central problem for us is not, in the last analysis, even from a purely economic view-point, the development of capitalistic activity as such, differing in different cultures only

23

in form: the adventurer type, or capitalism in trade, war, politics, or administration as sources of gain. It is rather the origin of this sober bourgeois capitalism with its rational organization of free labour. Or in terms of cultural history, the problem is that of the origin of the Western bourgeois class and of its peculiarities, a problem which is certainly closely connected with that of the origin of the capitalistic organization of labour, but is not quite the same thing. For the bourgeois as a class existed prior to the development of the peculiar modern form of capitalism, though, it is true, only in the Western hemisphere.

Now the peculiar modern Western form of capitalism has been, at first sight, strongly influenced by the development of technical possibilities. Its rationality is to-day essentially dependent on the calculability of the most important technical factors. But this means fundamentally that it is dependent on the peculiarities of modern science, especially the natural sciences based on mathematics and exact and rational experiment. On the other hand, the development of these sciences and of the technique resting upon them now receives important stimulation from these capitalistic interests in its practical economic application. It is true that the origin of Western science cannot be attributed to such interests. Calculation, even with decimals, and algebra have been carried on in India, where the decimal system was invented. But it was only made use of by developing capitalism in the West, while in India it led to no modern arithmetic or book-keeping. Neither was the origin of mathematics and mechanics determined by capitalistic interests. But the *technical* utilization of scientific knowledge, so important for the living conditions of the mass of people, was certainly encouraged by economic considerations, which were extremely favourable to it in the Occident. But this encouragement was derived from the peculiarities of the social structure of the Occident. We must hence ask, from *what* parts of that structure was it derived, since not all of them have been of equal importance?

Among those of undoubted importance are the rational structures of law and of administration. For modern rational capitalism has need, not only of the technical means of production, but of a calculable legal system and of administration in terms of formal rules. Without it adventurous and speculative trading capitalism and all sorts of politically determined capitalisms are possible, but no rational enterprise under individual initiative, with fixed capital and certainty of calculations. Such a legal system and such administration have been available for economic activity in a comparative state of legal and formalistic perfection only in the Occident. We must hence inquire where that law came from. Among other circumstances, capitalistic interests have in turn undoubtedly also helped, but by no means alone nor even principally, to prepare the way for the predominance in law and administration of a class of jurists specially trained in rational law. But these interests did not themselves create that law. Quite different forces were at work in this development. And why did not the capitalistic interests do the same in China or India? Why did not the scientific, the artistic, the political, or the economic development there enter upon that path of rationalization which is peculiar to the Occident?

For in all the above cases it is a question of the specific and peculiar rationalism of Western culture. Now by this term very different things may be understood, as the following discussion will repeatedly show. There is, for example, rationalization of mystical contemplation, that is of an attitude which, viewed from other departments of life, is specifically irrational, just as much as there are rationalizations of economic life, of technique, of scientific research, of military training, of law and administration. Furthermore, each one of these fields may be rationalized in terms of very different ultimate values and ends, and what is rational from one point of view may well be irrational from another. Hence rationalizations of the most varied character have existed in various departments of life and in all areas of culture. To characterize their differences from the view-point of cultural history it is necessary to know what departments are rationalized, and in what direction. It is hence our first concern to work out and to explain genetically the special peculiarity of Occidental rationalism, and within this field that of the modern Occidental form. Every such attempt at explanation must, recognizing the fundamental importance of the economic factor, above all take account of the economic conditions. But at the same time the opposite correlation must not be left out of consideration. For though the development of economic rationalism is partly dependent on rational technique and law, it is at the same time determined by the ability and disposition of men to adopt certain types of practical rational conduct. When these types have been obstructed by spiritual obstacles, the development of rational economic conduct has also met serious inner resistance. The magical and religious forces, and the ethical ideas of duty based upon them, have in the past always been among the most important formative influences on conduct. In the studies collected here we shall be concerned with these forces.[8]

Two older essays have been placed at the beginning which attempt, at one important point, to approach the side of the problem which is generally most difficult to grasp: the influence of certain religious ideas on the development of an economic spirit, or the *ethos* of an economic system. In this case we are dealing with the connection of the spirit of modern economic life with the rational ethics of ascetic Protestantism. Thus we treat here only one side of the causal chain. The later studies on the Economic Ethics of the World Religions attempt, in the form of a survey of the relations of the most important religions to economic life and to the social stratification of their environment, to follow out both causal relationships, so far as it is necessary in order to find points of comparison with the Occidental development. For only in this way is it possible to attempt a causal evaluation of those elements of the economic ethics of the Western religions which differentiate them from others, with a hope of attaining even a tolerable degree of approximation. Hence these studies do not claim to be complete analyses of cultures, however brief. On the contrary, in every culture they quite deliberately emphasize the elements in which it differs from Western civilization. They are, hence, definitely oriented to the problems which seem important for the understanding of Western culture from *this* view-point. With our object in view, any other procedure did not seem possible. But to avoid misunderstanding we must here lay special emphasis on the limitation of our purpose.

In another respect the uninitiated at least must be warned against exaggerating the importance of these investigations. The Sinologist, the Indologist, the Semitist, or the Egyptologist, will of course find no facts unknown to him. We only hope that he will find nothing definitely wrong in points that are essential. How far it has been possible to come as near this ideal as a non-specialist is able to do, the author cannot know. It is quite evident that anyone who is forced to rely on translations, and furthermore on the use and evaluation of monumental, documentary, or literary sources, has to rely himself on a specialist literature which is often highly controversial, and the merits of which he is unable to judge accurately. Such a writer must make modest claims for the value of his work. All the more so since the number of available translations of real sources (that is, inscriptions and documents) is, especially for China, still very small in comparison with what exists and is important. From all this follows the definitely provisional character of these studies, and especially of the parts dealing with Asia.[9] Only the specialist is entitled to a final judgment. And, naturally, it is only because expert studies with this special purpose and from this particular view-point have not hitherto been made, that the present ones have been written at all. They are destined to be superseded in a much more important sense than this can be said, as it can be, of all scientific work. But however objectionable it may be, such trespassing on other special fields cannot be avoided in comparative work. But one must take the consequences by resigning oneself to considerable doubts regarding the degree of one's success.

Fashion and the zeal of the *literati* would have us think that the specialist can to-day be spared, or degraded to a position subordinate to that of the seer. Almost all sciences owe something to dilettantes, often very valuable view-points. But dilettantism as a leading principle would be the end of science. He who yearns for seeing should go to the cinema, though it will be offered to him copiously to-day in literary form in the present field of investigation also.[10] Nothing is farther from the intent of these thoroughly serious studies than such an attitude. And, I might add, whoever wants a sermon should go to a conventicle. The question of the relative value of the cultures which are compared here will not receive a single word. It is true that the path of human destiny cannot but appall him who surveys a section of it. But he will do well to keep his small personal commentaries to himself, as one does at the sight of the sea or of majestic mountains, unless he knows himself to be called and gifted to give them expression in artistic or prophetic form. In most other cases the voluminous talk about intuition does nothing but conceal a lack of perspective toward the object, which merits the same judgment as a similar lack of perspective toward men.

Some justification is needed for the fact that ethnographical material has not been utilized to anything like the extent which the value of its contributions naturally demands in any really thorough investigation, especially of Asiatic religions. This limitation has not only been imposed because human powers of work are restricted. This omission has also seemed to be permissible because we are here necessarily dealing with the religious ethics of the classes which were the culture-bearers of their respective countries. We are concerned with the influence which *their* conduct has had. Now it is quite true that this can only be completely known in all its details when the facts from ethnography and folk-lore have been compared with it. Hence we must expressly admit and emphasize that this is a gap to which the ethnographer will legitimately object. I hope to contribute something to the closing of this gap in a systematic study of the Sociology of Religion.[11] But such an undertaking would have transcended the limits of this investigation with its closely circumscribed purpose. It has been necessary to be content with bringing out the points of comparison with our Occidental religions as well as possible.

Finally, we may make a reference to the *anthropological* side of the problem. When we find again and again that, even in departments of life apparently mutually independent, certain types of rationalization have developed in the Occident, and only there, it would be natural to suspect that the most important reason lay in differences of heredity. The author admits that he is inclined to think the importance of biological heredity very great. But in spite of the notable achievements of anthropological research, I see up to the present no way of exactly or even approximately measuring either the extent or, above all, the form of its influence on the development investigated here.

It must be one of the tasks of sociological and historical investigation first to analyse all the influences and causal relationships which can satisfactorily be explained in terms of reactions to environmental conditions. Only then, and when comparative racial neurology and psychology shall have progressed beyond their present and in many ways very promising beginnings, can we hope for even the probability of a satisfactory answer to that problem.[12] In the meantime that condition seems to me not to exist, and an appeal to heredity would therefore involve a premature renunciation of the possibility of knowledge attainable now, and would shift the problem to factors (at present) still unknown.

PART I

THE PROBLEM

CHAPTER I

RELIGIOUS AFFILIATION AND SOCIAL STRATIFICATION[1]

A GLANCE at the occupational statistics of any country of mixed religious composition brings to light with remarkable frequency[2] a situation which has several times provoked discussion in the Catholic press and literature,[3] and in Catholic congresses in Germany, namely, the fact that business leaders and owners of capital, as well as the higher grades of skilled labour, and even more the higher technically and commercially trained personnel of modern enterprises, are overwhelmingly Protestant.[4] This is true not only in cases where the difference in religion coincides with one of nationality, and thus of cultural development, as in Eastern Germany between Germans and Poles. The same thing is shown in the figures of religious affiliation almost wherever capitalism, at the time of its great expansion, has had a free hand to alter the social distribution of the population in accordance with its needs, and to determine its occupational structure. The more freedom it has had, the more clearly is the effect shown. It is true that the greater relative participation of Protestants in the ownership of capital,[5] in management, and the upper ranks of labour in great modern industrial and commercial enterprises,[6] may in part be explained in terms of historical circumstances[7] which extend far back into the past, and in which religious affiliation is not a cause of the economic conditions, but to a certain extent appears to be a result

35

of them. Participation in the above economic functions usually involves some previous ownership of capital, and generally an expensive education; often both. These are to-day largely dependent on the possession of inherited wealth, or at least on a certain degree of material well-being. A number of those sections of the old Empire which were most highly developed economically and most favoured by natural resources and situation, in particular a majority of the wealthy towns, went over to Protestantism in the sixteenth century. The results of that circumstance favour the Protestants even to-day in their struggle for economic existence. There arises thus the historical question: why were the districts of highest economic development at the same time particularly favourable to a revolution in the Church? The answer is by no means so simple as one might think.

The emancipation from economic traditionalism appears, no doubt, to be a factor which would greatly strengthen the tendency to doubt the sanctity of the religious tradition, as of all traditional authorities. But it is necessary to note, what has often been forgotten, that the Reformation meant not the elimination of the Church's control over everyday life, but rather the substitution of a new form of control for the previous one. It meant the repudiation of a control which was very lax, at that time scarcely perceptible in practice, and hardly more than formal, in favour of a regulation of the whole of conduct which, penetrating to all departments of private and public life, was infinitely burdensome and earnestly enforced. The rule of the Catholic Church, "punishing the heretic, but indulgent

36

to the sinner", as it was in the past even more than to-day, is now tolerated by peoples of thoroughly modern economic character, and was borne by the richest and economically most advanced peoples on earth at about the turn of the fifteenth century. The rule of Calvinism, on the other hand, as it was enforced in the sixteenth century in Geneva and in Scotland, at the turn of the sixteenth and seventeenth centuries in large parts of the Netherlands, in the seventeenth in New England, and for a time in England itself, would be for us the most absolutely unbearable form of ecclesiastical control of the individual which could possibly exist. That was exactly what large numbers of the old commercial aristocracy of those times, in Geneva as well as in Holland and England, felt about it. And what the reformers complained of in those areas of high economic development was not too much supervision of life on the part of the Church, but too little. Now how does it happen that at that time those countries which were most advanced economically, and within them the rising bourgeois middle classes, not only failed to resist this unexampled tyranny of Puritanism, but even developed a heroism in its defence? For bourgeois classes as such have seldom before and never since displayed heroism. It was "the last of our heroisms", as Carlyle, not without reason, has said.

But further, and especially important: it may be, as has been claimed, that the greater participation of Protestants in the positions of ownership and management in modern economic life may to-day be understood, in part at least, simply as a result of the greater material wealth they have inherited. But there are

37

certain other phenomena which cannot be explained in the same way. Thus, to mention only a few facts: there is a great difference discoverable in Baden, in Bavaria, in Hungary, in the type of higher education which Catholic parents, as opposed to Protestant, give their children. That the percentage of Catholics among the students and graduates of higher educational institutions in general lags behind their proportion of the total population,[8] may, to be sure, be largely explicable in terms of inherited differences of wealth. But among the Catholic graduates themselves the percentage of those graduating from the institutions preparing, in particular, for technical studies and industrial and commercial occupations, but in general from those preparing for middle-class business life, lags still farther behind the percentage of Protestants.[9] On the other hand, Catholics prefer the sort of training which the humanistic Gymnasium affords. That is a circumstance to which the above explanation does not apply, but which, on the contrary, is one reason why so few Catholics are engaged in capitalistic enterprise.

Even more striking is a fact which partly explains the smaller proportion of Catholics among the skilled labourers of modern industry. It is well known that the factory has taken its skilled labour to a large extent from young men in the handicrafts; but this is much more true of Protestant than of Catholic journeymen. Among journeymen, in other words, the Catholics show a stronger propensity to remain in their crafts, that is they more often become master craftsmen, whereas the Protestants are attracted to a larger extent into the factories in order to fill the upper ranks of skilled labour and administrative positions.[10] The explanation of these cases is undoubtedly that the mental and spiritual peculiarities acquired from the environment, here the type of education favoured by the religious atmosphere of the home community and the parental home, have determined the choice of occupation, and through it the professional career.

The smaller participation of Catholics in the modern business life of Germany is all the more striking because it runs counter to a tendency which has been observed at all times [11] including the present. National or religious minorities which are in a position of subordination to a group of rulers are likely, through their voluntary or involuntary exclusion from positions of political influence, to be driven with peculiar force into economic activity. Their ablest members seek to satisfy the desire for recognition of their abilities in this field, since there is no opportunity in the service of the State. This has undoubtedly been true of the Poles in Russia and Eastern Prussia, who have without question been undergoing a more rapid economic advance than in Galicia, where they have been in the ascendant. It has in earlier times been true of the Huguenots in France under Louis XIV, the Nonconformists and Quakers in England, and, last but not least, the Jew for two thousand years. But the Catholics in Germany have shown no striking evidence of such a result of their position. In the past they have, unlike the Protestants, undergone no particularly prominent economic development in the times when they were persecuted or only tolerated, either in Holland or in England. On the other hand, it is a fact that the Protestants (especi-

39

ally certain branches of the movement to be fully discussed later) both as ruling classes and as ruled, both as majority and as minority, have shown a special tendency to develop economic rationalism which cannot be observed to the same extent among Catholics either in the one situation or in the other.[12] Thus the principal explanation of this difference must be sought in the permanent intrinsic character of their religious beliefs, and not only in their temporary external historico-political situations.[13]

It will be our task to investigate these religions with a view to finding out what peculiarities they have or have had which might have resulted in the behaviour we have described. On superficial analysis, and on the basis of certain current impressions, one might be tempted to express the difference by saying that the greater other-worldliness of Catholicism, the ascetic character of its highest ideals, must have brought up its adherents to a greater indifference toward the good things of this world. Such an explanation fits the popular tendency in the judgment of both religions. On the Protestant side it is used as a basis of criticism of those (real or imagined) ascetic ideals of the Catholic way of life, while the Catholics answer with the accusation that materialism results from the seculariza- tion of all ideals through Protestantism. One recent writer has attempted to formulate the difference of their attitudes toward economic life in the following manner: "The Catholic is quieter, having less of the acquisitive impulse; he prefers a life of the greatest possible security, even with a smaller income, to a life of risk and excitement, even though it may bring the chance of gaining honour and riches. The proverb says jokingly, 'either eat well or sleep well'. In the present case the Protestant prefers to eat well, the Catholic to sleep undisturbed.''[14]

In fact, this desire to eat well may be a correct though incomplete characterization of the motives of many nominal Protestants in Germany at the present time. But things were very different in the past: the English, Dutch, and American Puritans were characterized by the exact opposite of the joy of living, a fact which is indeed, as we shall see, most important for our present study. Moreover, the French Protestants, among others, long retained, and retain to a certain extent up to the present, the characteristics which were impressed upon the Calvinistic Churches everywhere, especially under the cross in the time of the religious struggles. Nevertheless (or was it, perhaps, as we shall ask later, precisely on that account?) it is well known that these characteristics were one of the most important factors in the industrial and capitalistic development of France, and on the small scale permitted them by their persecution remained so. If we may call this seriousness and the strong predominance of religious interests in the whole conduct of life otherworldliness, then the French Calvinists were and still are at least as otherworldly as, for instance, the North German Catholics, to whom their Catholicism is undoubtedly as vital a matter as religion is to any other people in the world. Both differ from the predominant religious trends in their respective countries in much the same way. The Catholics of France are, in their lower ranks, greatly interested in the enjoyment of life,

41

in the upper directly hostile to religion. Similarly, the Protestants of Germany are to-day absorbed in worldly economic life, and their upper ranks are most indifferent to religion.[15] Hardly anything shows so clearly as this parallel that, with such vague ideas as that of the alleged otherworldliness of Catholicism, and the alleged materialistic joy of living of Protestantism, and others like them, nothing can be accomplished for our purpose. In such general terms the distinction does not even adequately fit the facts of to-day, and certainly not of the past. If, however, one wishes to make use of it at all, several other observations present themselves at once which, combined with the above remarks, suggest that the supposed conflict between other-worldliness, asceticism, and ecclesiastical piety on the one side, and participation in capitalistic acquisition on the other, might actually turn out to be an intimate relationship.

As a matter of fact it is surely remarkable, to begin with quite a superficial observation, how large is the number of representatives of the most spiritual forms of Christian piety who have sprung from commercial circles. In particular, very many of the most zealous adherents of Pietism are of this origin. It might be explained as a sort of reaction against mammonism on the part of sensitive natures not adapted to commercial life, and, as in the case of Francis of Assisi, many Pietists have themselves interpreted the process of their conversion in these terms. Similarly, the remarkable circumstance that so many of the greatest capitalistic entrepreneurs—down to Cecil Rhodes—have come from clergymen's families might be explained as a reaction against their ascetic upbringing. But this form of explanation fails where an extraordinary capitalistic business sense is combined in the same persons and groups with the most intensive forms of a piety which penetrates and dominates their whole lives. Such cases are not isolated, but these traits are charac-teristic of many of the most important Churches and sects in the history of Protestantism. Especially Calvinism, wherever it has appeared,[16] has shown this combination. However little, in the time of the expansion of the Reformation, it (or any other Protest-ant belief) was bound up with any particular social class, it is characteristic and in a certain sense typical that in French Huguenot Churches monks and business men (merchants, craftsmen) were particularly numer-ous among the proselytes, especially at the time of the persecution.[17] Even the Spaniards knew that heresy (i.e. the Calvinism of the Dutch) promoted trade, and this coincides with the opinions which Sir William Petty expressed in his discussion of the reasons for the capitalistic development of the Netherlands. Gothein [18] rightly calls the Calvinistic diaspora the seed-bed of capitalistic economy.[19] Even in this case one might consider the decisive factor to be the superiority of the French and Dutch economic cultures from which these communities sprang, or perhaps the immense influence of exile in the breakdown of traditional relationships.[20] But in France the situation was, as we know from Colbert's struggles, the same even in the seventeenth century. Even Austria, not to speak of other countries, directly imported Protestant craftsmen.

But not all the Protestant denominations seem to have had an equally strong influence in this direction.

43

That of Calvinism, even in Germany, was among the strongest, it seems, and the reformed faith[21] more than the others seems to have promoted the development of the spirit of capitalism, in the Wupperthal as well as elsewhere. Much more so than Lutheranism, as comparison both in general and in particular instances, especially in the Wupperthal, seems to prove.[22] For Scotland, Buckle, and among English poets, Keats, have emphasized these same relationships.[23] Even more striking, as it is only necessary to mention, is the connection of a religious way of life with the most intensive development of business acumen among those sects whose otherworldliness is as proverbial as their wealth, especially the Quakers and the Mennonites. The part which the former have played in England and North America fell to the latter in Germany and the Netherlands. That in East Prussia Frederick William I tolerated the Mennonites as indispensable to industry, in spite of their absolute refusal to perform military service, is only one of the numerous well-known cases which illustrates the fact, though, considering the character of that monarch, it is one of the most striking. Finally, that this combination of intense piety with just as strong a development of business acumen, was also characteristic of the Pietists, is common knowledge.[24]

It is only necessary to think of the Rhine country and of Calw. In this purely introductory discussion it is unnecessary to pile up more examples. For these few already all show one thing: that the spirit of hard work, of progress, or whatever else it may be called, the awakening of which one is inclined to ascribe to

Protestantism, must not be understood, as there is a tendency to do, as joy of living nor in any other sense as connected with the Enlightenment. The old Protestantism of Luther, Calvin, Knox, Voet, had precious little to do with what to-day is called progress. To whole aspects of modern life which the most extreme religionist would not wish to suppress to-day, it was directly hostile. If any inner relationship between certain expressions of the old Protestant spirit and modern capitalistic culture is to be found, we must attempt to find it, for better or worse, not in its alleged more or less materialistic or at least anti-ascetic joy of living, but in its purely religious characteristics. Montesquieu says (*Esprit des Lois*, Book XX, chap. 7) of the English that they "had progressed the farthest of all peoples of the world in three important things: in piety, in commerce, and in freedom". Is it not possible that their commercial superiority and their adaptation to free political institutions are connected in some way with that record of piety which Montesquieu ascribes to them?

A large number of possible relationships, vaguely perceived, occur to us when we put the question in this way. It will now be our task to formulate what occurs to us confusedly as clearly as is possible, considering the inexhaustible diversity to be found in all historical material. But in order to do this it is necessary to leave behind the vague and general concepts with which we have dealt up to this point, and attempt to penetrate into the peculiar characteristics of and the differences between those great worlds of religious thought which have existed historically in the various branches of Christianity.

Before we can proceed to that, however, a few remarks are necessary, first on the peculiarities of the phenomenon of which we are seeking an historical explanation, then concerning the sense in which such an explanation is possible at all within the limits of these investigations.

CHAPTER II

THE SPIRIT OF CAPITALISM

In the title of this study is used the somewhat pretentious phrase, the *spirit* of capitalism. What is to be understood by it? The attempt to give anything like a definition of it brings out certain difficulties which are in the very nature of this type of investigation.

If any object can be found to which this term can be applied with any understandable meaning, it can only be an historical individual, i.e. a complex of elements associated in historical reality which we unite into a conceptual whole from the standpoint of their cultural significance.

Such an historical concept, however, since it refers in its content to a phenomenon significant for its unique individuality, cannot be defined according to the formula *genus proximum, differentia specifica*, but it must be gradually put together out of the individual parts which are taken from historical reality to make it up. Thus the final and definitive concept cannot stand at the beginning of the investigation, but must come at the end. We must, in other words, work out in the course of the discussion, as its most important result, the best conceptual formulation of what we here understand by the spirit of capitalism, that is the best from the point of view which interests us here. This point of view (the one of which we shall speak later) is, further, by no means the only possible one from which the historical phenomena we are investigating can be analysed. Other standpoints would, for this as for every

47

historical phenomenon, yield other characteristics as the essential ones. The result is that it is by no means necessary to understand by the spirit of capitalism only what it will come to mean to *us* for the purposes of our analysis. This is a necessary result of the nature of historical concepts which attempt for their methodological purposes not to grasp historical reality in abstract general formulæ, but in concrete genetic sets of relations which are inevitably of a specifically unique and individual character.[1]

Thus, if we try to determine the object, the analysis and historical explanation of which we are attempting, it cannot be in the form of a conceptual definition, but at least in the beginning only a provisional description of what is here meant by the spirit of capitalism. Such a description is, however, indispensable in order clearly to understand the object of the investigation. For this purpose we turn to a document of that spirit which contains what we are looking for in almost classical purity, and at the same time has the advantage of being free from all direct relationship to religion, being thus, for our purposes, free of preconceptions.

"Remember, that *time* is money. He that can earn ten shillings a day by his labour, and goes abroad, or sits idle, one half of that day, though he spends but sixpence during his diversion or idleness, ought not to reckon *that* the only expense; he has really spent, or rather thrown away, five shillings besides.

"Remember, that *credit* is money. If a man lets his money lie in my hands after it is due, he gives me the interest, or so much as I can make of it during that time. This amounts to a considerable sum where a man has good and large credit, and makes good use of it.

"Remember, that money is of the prolific, generating nature. Money can beget money, and its offspring can beget more, and so on. Five shillings turned is six, turned again it is seven and threepence, and so on, till it becomes a hundred pounds. The more there is of it, the more it produces every turning, so that the profits rise quicker and quicker. He that kills a breeding-sow, destroys all her offspring to the thousandth generation. He that murders a crown, destroys all that it might have produced, even scores of pounds."

"Remember this saying, *The good paymaster is lord of another man's purse*. He that is known to pay punctually and exactly to the time he promises, may at any time, and on any occasion, raise all the money his friends can spare. This is sometimes of great use. After industry and frugality, nothing contributes more to the raising of a young man in the world than punctuality and justice in all his dealings; therefore never keep borrowed money an hour beyond the time you promised, lest a disappointment shut up your friend's purse for ever.

"The most trifling actions that affect a man's credit are to be regarded. The sound of your hammer at five in the morning, or eight at night, heard by a creditor, makes him easy six months longer; but if he sees you at a billiard-table, or hears your voice at a tavern, when you should be at work, he sends for his money the next day; demands it, before he can receive it, in a lump.

"It shows, besides, that you are mindful of what you

owe; it makes you appear a careful as well as an honest man, and that still increases your credit.

"Beware of thinking all your own that you possess, and of living accordingly. It is a mistake that many people who have credit fall into. To prevent this, keep an exact account for some time both of your expenses and your income. If you take the pains at first to mention particulars, it will have this good effect: you will discover how wonderfully small, trifling expenses mount up to large sums, and will discern what might have been, and may for the future be saved, without occasioning any great inconvenience."

"For six pounds a year you may have the use of one hundred pounds, provided you are a man of known prudence and honesty.

"He that spends a groat a day idly, spends idly above six pounds a year, which is the price for the use of one hundred pounds.

"He that wastes idly a groat's worth of his time per day, one day with another, wastes the privilege of using one hundred pounds each day.

"He that idly loses five shillings' worth of time, loses five shillings, and might as prudently throw five shillings into the sea.

"He that loses five shillings, not only loses that sum, but all the advantage that might be made by turning it in dealing, which by the time that a young man becomes old, will amount to a considerable sum of money."[2]

It is Benjamin Franklin who preaches to us in these sentences, the same which Ferdinand Kürnberger satirizes in his clever and malicious *Picture of American Culture*[3] as the supposed confession of faith of the Yankee. That it is the spirit of capitalism which here speaks in characteristic fashion, no one will doubt, however little we may wish to claim that everything which could be understood as pertaining to that spirit is contained in it. Let us pause a moment to consider this passage, the philosophy of which Kürnberger sums up in the words, "They make tallow out of cattle and money out of men". The peculiarity of this philosophy of avarice appears to be the ideal of the honest man of recognized credit, and above all the idea of a duty of the individual toward the increase of his capital, which is assumed as an end in itself. Truly what is here preached is not simply a means of making one's way in the world, but a peculiar ethic. The infraction of its rules is treated not as foolishness but as forgetfulness of duty. That is the essence of the matter. It is not mere business astuteness, that sort of thing is common enough, it is an ethos. *This* is the quality which interests us.

When Jacob Fugger, in speaking to a business associate who had retired and who wanted to persuade him to do the same, since he had made enough money and should let others have a chance, rejected that as pusillanimity and answered that "he (Fugger) thought otherwise, he wanted to make money as long as he could",[4] the spirit of his statement is evidently quite different from that of Franklin. What in the former case was an expression of commercial daring and a personal inclination morally neutral,[5] in the latter takes on the character of an ethically coloured maxim

51

for the conduct of life. The concept spirit of capitalism is here used in this specific sense,[6] it is the spirit of modern capitalism. For that we are here dealing only with Western European and American capitalism is obvious from the way in which the problem was stated. Capitalism existed in China, India, Babylon, in the classic world, and in the Middle Ages. But in all these cases, as we shall see, this particular ethos was lacking.

Now, all Franklin's moral attitudes are coloured with utilitarianism. Honesty is useful, because it assures credit; so are punctuality, industry, frugality, and that is the reason they are virtues. A logical deduction from this would be that where, for instance, the appearance of honesty serves the same purpose, that would suffice, and an unnecessary surplus of this virtue would evidently appear to Franklin's eyes as unproductive waste. And as a matter of fact, the story in his autobiography of his conversion to those virtues,[7] or the discussion of the value of a strict maintenance of the appearance of modesty, the assiduous belittlement of one's own deserts in order to gain general recognition later,[8] confirms this impression. According to Franklin, those virtues, like all others, are only in so far virtues as they are actually useful to the individual, and the surrogate of mere appearance is always sufficient when it accomplishes the end in view. It is a conclusion which is inevitable for strict utilitarianism. The impression of many Germans that the virtues professed by Americanism are pure hypocrisy seems to have been confirmed by this striking case. But in fact the matter is not by any means so simple. Benjamin Franklin's own character, as it appears in the really unusual candidness of his autobiography, belies that suspicion. The circumstance that he ascribes his recognition of the utility of virtue to a divine revelation which was intended to lead him in the path of righteousness, shows that something more than mere garnishing for purely egocentric motives is involved.

In fact, the *summum bonum* of this ethic, the earning of more and more money, combined with the strict avoidance of all spontaneous enjoyment of life, is above all completely devoid of any eudæmonistic, not to say hedonistic, admixture. It is thought of so purely as an end in itself, that from the point of view of the happiness of, or utility to, the single individual, it appears entirely transcendental and absolutely irrational.[9] Man is dominated by the making of money, by acquisition as the ultimate purpose of his life. Economic acquisition is no longer subordinated to man as the means for the satisfaction of his material needs. This reversal of what we should call the natural relationship, so irrational from a naïve point of view, is evidently as definitely a leading principle of capitalism as it is foreign to all peoples not under capitalistic influence. At the same time it expresses a type of feeling which is closely connected with certain religious ideas. If we thus ask, *why* should "money be made out of men", Benjamin Franklin himself, although he was a colourless deist, answers in his autobiography with a quotation from the Bible, which his strict Calvinistic father drummed into him again and again in his youth: "Seest thou a man diligent in his business? He shall stand before kings" (Prov. xxii. 29). The earning of money within the modern economic order is, so long as it is done legally, the result and the expression of virtue and proficiency in a calling; and this virtue and proficiency are, as it is now not difficult to see, the real Alpha and Omega of Franklin's ethic, as expressed in the passages we have quoted, as well as in all his works without exception.[10]

And in truth this peculiar idea, so familiar to us to-day, but in reality so little a matter of course, of one's duty in a calling, is what is most characteristic of the social ethic of capitalistic culture, and is in a sense the fundamental basis of it. It is an obligation which the individual is supposed to feel and does feel towards the content of his professional[11] activity, no matter in what it consists, in particular no matter whether it appears on the surface as a utilization of his personal powers, or only of his material possessions (as capital).

Of course, this conception has not appeared only under capitalistic conditions. On the contrary, we shall later trace its origins back to a time previous to the advent of capitalism. Still less, naturally, do we maintain that a conscious acceptance of these ethical maxims on the part of the individuals, entrepreneurs or labourers, in modern capitalistic enterprises, is a condition of the further existence of present-day capitalism. The capitalistic economy of the present day is an immense cosmos into which the individual is born, and which presents itself to him, at least as an individual, as an unalterable order of things in which he must live. It forces the individual, in so far as he is involved in the system of market relationships, to conform to capitalistic rules of action. The manufacturer who in the long run acts counter to these norms, will just as inevitably be eliminated from the economic scene as the worker who cannot or will not adapt himself to them will be thrown into the streets without a job.

Thus the capitalism of to-day, which has come to dominate economic life, educates and selects the economic subjects which it needs through a process of economic survival of the fittest. But here one can easily see the limits of the concept of selection as a means of historical explanation. In order that a manner of life so well adapted to the peculiarities of capitalism could be selected at all, i.e. should come to dominate others, it had to originate somewhere, and not in isolated individuals alone, but as a way of life common to whole groups of men. This origin is what really needs explanation. Concerning the doctrine of the more naïve historical materialism, that such ideas originate as a reflection or superstructure of economic situations, we shall speak more in detail below. At this point it will suffice for our purpose to call attention to the fact that without doubt, in the country of Benjamin Franklin's birth (Massachusetts), the spirit of capitalism (in the sense we have attached to it) was present before the capitalistic order. There were complaints of a peculiarly calculating sort of profit-seeking in New England, as distinguished from other parts of America, as early as 1632. It is further undoubted that capitalism remained far less developed in some of the neighbouring colonies, the later Southern States of the United States of America, in spite of the fact that these latter were founded by large capitalists for business motives, while the New England colonies were founded by preachers and seminary graduates with the help of small bourgeois, craftsmen and yoemen, for religious reasons. In this case the causal relation is certainly the reverse of that suggested by the materialistic standpoint.

But the origin and history of such ideas is much more complex than the theorists of the superstructure suppose. The spirit of capitalism, in the sense in which we are using the term, had to fight its way to supremacy against a whole world of hostile forces. A state of mind such as that expressed in the passages we have quoted from Franklin, and which called forth the applause of a whole people, would both in ancient times and in the Middle Ages [12] have been proscribed as the lowest sort of avarice and as an attitude entirely lacking in self-respect. It is, in fact, still regularly thus looked upon by all those social groups which are least involved in or adapted to modern capitalistic conditions. This is not wholly because the instinct of acquisition was in those times unknown or undeveloped, as has often been said. Nor because the *auri sacra fames*, the greed for gold, was then, or now, less powerful outside of bourgeois capitalism than within its peculiar sphere, as the illusions of modern romanticists are wont to believe. The difference between the capitalistic and pre-capitalistic spirits is not to be found at this point. The greed of the Chinese Mandarin, the old Roman aristocrat, or the modern peasant, can stand up to any comparison. And the *auri sacra fames* of a Neapolitan cab-driver or *barcaiuolo*, and certainly of Asiatic representatives of similar trades, as well as of the craftsmen of southern European or Asiatic countries, is, as anyone can find out for himself, very much more intense, and especially more unscrupulous than that of, say, an Englishman in similar circumstances.[13]

The universal reign of absolute unscrupulousness in the pursuit of selfish interests by the making of money has been a specific characteristic of precisely those countries whose bourgeois-capitalistic development, measured according to Occidental standards, has remained backward. As every employer knows, the lack of *coscienziosità* of the labourers[14] of such countries, for instance Italy as compared with Germany, has been, and to a certain extent still is, one of the principal obstacles to their capitalistic development. Capitalism cannot make use of the labour of those who practise the doctrine of undisciplined *liberum arbitrium*, any more than it can make use of the business man who seems absolutely unscrupulous in his dealings with others, as we can learn from Franklin. Hence the difference does not lie in the degree of development of any impulse to make money. The *auri sacra fames* is as old as the history of man. But we shall see that those who submitted to it without reserve as an uncontrolled impulse, such as the Dutch sea-captain who "would go through hell for gain, even though he scorched his sails", were by no means the representatives of that attitude of mind from which the specifically modern capitalistic spirit as a mass phenomenon is derived, and that is what matters. At all periods of history, wherever it was possible, there has been ruthless acquisition, bound to no ethical norms whatever. Like war and piracy, trade has often been unrestrained in its relations with foreigners and those outside the group. The double ethic has permitted here what was forbidden in dealings among brothers.

Capitalistic acquisition as an adventure has been at home in all types of economic society which have known trade with the use of money and which have offered it opportunities, through *commenda*, farming of taxes, State loans, financing of wars, ducal courts and office-holders. Likewise the inner attitude of the adventurer, which laughs at all ethical limitations, has been universal. Absolute and conscious ruthlessness in acquisition has often stood in the closest connection with the strictest conformity to tradition. Moreover, with the breakdown of tradition and the more or less complete extension of free economic enterprise, even to within the social group, the new thing has not generally been ethically justified and encouraged, but only tolerated as a fact. And this fact has been treated either as ethically indifferent or as reprehensible, but unfortunately unavoidable. This has not only been the normal attitude of all ethical teachings, but, what is more important, also that expressed in the practical action of the average man of pre-capitalistic times, pre-capitalistic in the sense that the rational utilization of capital in a permanent enterprise and the rational capitalistic organization of labour had not yet become dominant forces in the determination of economic activity. Now just this attitude was one of the strongest inner obstacles which the adaptation of men to the conditions of an ordered bourgeois-capitalistic economy has encountered everywhere.

The most important opponent with which the spirit of capitalism, in the sense of a definite standard of life claiming ethical sanction, has had to struggle, was that type of attitude and reaction to new situations which we may designate as traditionalism. In this case also every attempt at a final definition must be held in abeyance. On the other hand, we must try to make the provisional meaning clear by citing a few cases. We will begin from below, with the labourers.

One of the technical means which the modern employer uses in order to secure the greatest possible amount of work from his men is the device of piece-rates. In agriculture, for instance, the gathering of the harvest is a case where the greatest possible intensity of labour is called for, since, the weather being uncertain, the difference between high profit and heavy loss may depend on the speed with which the harvesting can be done. Hence a system of piece-rates is almost universal in this case. And since the interest of the employer in a speeding-up of harvesting increases with the increase of the results and the intensity of the work, the attempt has again and again been made, by increasing the piece-rates of the workmen, thereby giving them an opportunity to earn what is for them a very high wage, to interest them in increasing their own efficiency. But a peculiar difficulty has been met with surprising frequency: raising the piece-rates has often had the result that not more but less has been accomplished in the same time, because the worker reacted to the increase not by increasing but by decreasing the amount of his work. A man, for instance, who at the rate of 1 mark per acre mowed $2\frac{1}{2}$ acres per day and earned $2\frac{1}{2}$ marks, when the rate was raised to 1·25 marks per acre mowed, not 3 acres, as he might easily have done, thus earning 3·75 marks, but only 2 acres, so that he could still earn the $2\frac{1}{2}$ marks to which he was accustomed. The opportunity of earning more was less attractive than that of working less. He did not ask: how much can I earn in a day if I do as much work as possible? but: how much must I work in order to earn the wage, $2\frac{1}{2}$ marks, which I earned before and which takes care of my traditional needs? This is an example of what is here meant by traditionalism. A man does not "by nature" wish to earn more and more money, but simply to live as he is accustomed to live and to earn as much as is necessary for that purpose. Wherever modern capitalism has begun its work of increasing the productivity of human labour by increasing its intensity, it has encountered the immensely stubborn resistance of this leading trait of pre-capitalistic labour. And to-day it encounters it the more, the more backward (from a capitalistic point of view) the labouring forces are with which it has to deal.

Another obvious possibility, to return to our example, since the appeal to the acquisitive instinct through higher wage-rates failed, would have been to try the opposite policy, to force the worker by reduction of his wage-rates to work harder to earn the same amount than he did before. Low wages and high profits seem even to-day to a superficial observer to stand in correlation; everything which is paid out in wages seems to involve a corresponding reduction of profits. That road capitalism has taken again and again since its beginning. For centuries it was an article of faith, that low wages were productive, i.e. that they increased the material results of labour so that, as Pieter de la Cour, on this point, as we shall see, quite in the spirit of the old

Calvinism, said long ago, the people only work because and so long as they are poor.

But the effectiveness of this apparently so efficient method has its limits.[15] Of course the presence of a surplus population which it can hire cheaply in the labour market is a necessity for the development of capitalism. But though too large a reserve army may in certain cases favour its quantitative expansion, it checks its qualitative development, especially the transition to types of enterprise which make more intensive use of labour. Low wages are by no means identical with cheap labour.[16] From a purely quantitative point of view the efficiency of labour decreases with a wage which is physiologically insufficient, which may in the long run even mean a survival of the unfit. The present-day average Silesian mows, when he exerts himself to the full, little more than two-thirds as much land as the better paid and nourished Pomeranian or Mecklenburger, and the Pole, the further East he comes from, accomplishes progressively less than the German. Low wages fail even from a purely business point of view wherever it is a question of producing goods which require any sort of skilled labour, or the use of expensive machinery which is easily damaged, or in general wherever any great amount of sharp attention or of initiative is required. Here low wages do not pay, and their effect is the opposite of what was intended. For not only is a developed sense of responsibility absolutely indispensable, but in general also an attitude which, at least during working hours, is freed from continual calculations of how the customary wage may be earned with a maximum of comfort and a minimum of exertion. Labour must, on the contrary, be performed as if it were an absolute end in itself, a calling. But such an attitude is by no means a product of nature. It cannot be evoked by low wages or high ones alone, but can only be the product of a long and arduous process of education. To-day, capitalism, once in the saddle, can recruit its labouring force in all industrial countries with comparative ease. In the past this was in every case an extremely difficult problem.[17] And even to-day it could probably not get along without the support of a powerful ally along the way, which, as we shall see below, was at hand at the time of its development.

What is meant can again best be explained by means of an example. The type of backward traditional form of labour is to-day very often exemplified by women workers, especially unmarried ones. An almost universal complaint of employers of girls, for instance German girls, is that they are almost entirely unable and unwilling to give up methods of work inherited or once learned in favour of more efficient ones, to adapt themselves to new methods, to learn and to concentrate their intelligence, or even to use it at all. Explanations of the possibility of making work easier, above all more profitable to themselves, generally encounter a complete lack of understanding. Increases of piece-rates are without avail against the stone wall of habit. In general it is otherwise, and that is a point of no little importance from our view-point, only with girls having a specifically religious, especially a Pietistic, background. One often hears, and statistical investigation confirms it,[18] that by far the best chances of economic education are found among this group. The ability of mental concentration, as well as the absolutely essential feeling of obligation to one's job, are here most often combined with a strict economy which calculates the possibility of high earnings, and a cool self-control and frugality which enormously increase performance. This provides the most favourable foundation for the conception of labour as an end in itself, as a calling which is necessary to capitalism: the chances of overcoming traditionalism are greatest on account of the religious upbringing. This observation of present-day capitalism [19] in itself suggests that it is worth while to ask how this connection of adaptability to capitalism with religious factors may have come about in the days of the early development of capitalism. For that they were even then present in much the same form can be inferred from numerous facts. For instance, the dislike and the persecution which Methodist workmen in the eighteenth century met at the hands of their comrades were not solely nor even principally the result of their religious eccentricities, England had seen many of those and more striking ones. It rested rather, as the destruction of their tools, repeatedly mentioned in the reports, suggests, upon their specific willingness to work as we should say to-day.

However, let us again return to the present, and this time to the entrepreneur, in order to clarify the meaning of traditionalism in his case.

Sombart, in his discussions of the genesis of capitalism,[20] has distinguished between the satisfaction of needs and acquisition as the two great leading principles in economic history. In the former case the

63

attainment of the goods necessary to meet personal needs, in the latter a struggle for profit free from the limits set by needs, have been the ends controlling the form and direction of economic activity. What he calls the economy of needs seems at first glance to be identical with what is here described as economic traditionalism. That may be the case if the concept of needs is limited to traditional needs. But if that is not done, a number of economic types which must be considered capitalistic according to the definition of capital which Sombart gives in another part of his work,[21] would be excluded from the category of acquisitive economy and put into that of needs economy. Enterprises, namely, which are carried on by private entrepreneurs by utilizing capital (money or goods with a money value) to make a profit, purchasing the means of production and selling the product, i.e. undoubted capitalistic enterprises, may at the same time have a traditionalistic character. This has, in the course even of modern economic history, not been merely an occasional case, but rather the rule, with continual interruptions from repeated and increasingly powerful conquests of the capitalistic spirit. To be sure the capitalistic form of an enterprise and the spirit in which it is run generally stand in some sort of adequate relationship to each other, but not in one of necessary interdependence. Nevertheless, we provisionally use the expression spirit of (modern) capitalism[22] to describe that attitude which seeks profit rationally and systematically in the manner which we have illustrated by the example of Benjamin Franklin. This, however, is justified by the historical fact that that attitude of

64

mind has on the one hand found its most suitable expression in capitalistic enterprise, while on the other the enterprise has derived its most suitable motive force from the spirit of capitalism.

But the two may very well occur separately. Benjamin Franklin was filled with the spirit of capitalism at a time when his printing business did not differ in form from any handicraft enterprise. And we shall see that at the beginning of modern times it was by no means the capitalistic entrepreneurs of the commercial aristocracy, who were either the sole or the predominant bearers of the attitude we have here called the spirit of capitalism.[23] It was much more the rising strata of the lower industrial middle classes. Even in the nineteenth century its classical representatives were not the elegant gentlemen of Liverpool and Hamburg, with their commercial fortunes handed down for generations, but the self-made parvenus of Manchester and Westphalia, who often rose from very modest circumstances. As early as the sixteenth century the situation was similar; the industries which arose at that time were mostly created by parvenus.[24]

The management, for instance, of a bank, a wholesale export business, a large retail establishment, or of a large putting-out enterprise dealing with goods produced in homes, is certainly only possible in the form of a capitalistic enterprise. Nevertheless, they may all be carried on in a traditionalistic spirit. In fact, the business of a large bank of issue cannot be carried on in any other way. The foreign trade of whole epochs has rested on the basis of monopolies and legal privileges of strictly traditional character. In retail trade—and we are not here talking of the small men without capital who are continually crying out for Government aid— the revolution which is making an end of the old traditionalism is still in full swing. It is the same development which broke up the old putting-out system, to which modern domestic labour is related only in form. How. this revolution takes place and what is its significance may, in spite of the fact these things are so familiar, be again brought out by a concrete example.

Until about the middle of the past century the life of a putter-out was, at least in many of the branches of the Continental textile industry,[25] what we should to-day consider very comfortable. We may imagine its routine somewhat as follows: The peasants came with their cloth, often (in the case of linen) principally or entirely made from raw material which the peasant himself had produced, to the town in which the putter-out lived, and after a careful, often official, appraisal of the quality, received the customary price for it. The putter-out's customers, for markets any appreciable distance away, were middlemen, who also came to him, generally not yet following samples, but seeking traditional qualities, and bought from his warehouse, or, long before delivery, placed orders which were probably in turn passed on to the peasants. Personal canvassing of customers took place, if at all, only at long intervals. Otherwise correspondence sufficed, though the sending of samples slowly gained ground. The number of business hours was very moderate, perhaps five to six a day, sometimes considerably less; in the rush season, where there was one, more. Earnings were moderate; enough to lead a respectable life and in good times to put away a little. On the whole, relations among competitors were relatively good, with a large degree of agreement on the fundamentals of business. A long daily visit to the tavern, with often plenty to drink, and a congenial circle of friends, made life comfortable and leisurely.

The form of organization was in every respect capitalistic; the entrepreneur's activity was of a purely business character; the use of capital, turned over in the business, was indispensable; and finally, the objective aspect of the economic process, the book-keeping, was rational. But it was traditionalistic business, if one considers the spirit which animated the entrepreneur: the traditional manner of life, the traditional rate of profit, the traditional amount of work, the traditional manner of regulating the relationships with labour, and the essentially traditional circle of customers and the manner of attracting new ones. All these dominated the conduct of the business, were at the basis, one may say, of the *ethos* of this group of business men.

Now at some time this leisureliness was suddenly destroyed, and often entirely without any essential change in the form of organization, such as the transition to a unified factory, to mechanical weaving, etc. What happened was, on the contrary, often no more than this: some young man from one of the putting-out families went out into the country, carefully chose weavers for his employ, greatly increased the rigour of his supervision of their work, and thus turned them from peasants into labourers. On the other hand, he would begin to change his marketing methods by so far as possible going directly to the final consumer, would take the details into his own hands, would personally solicit customers, visiting them every year, and above all would adapt the quality of the product directly to their needs and wishes. At the same time he began to introduce the principle of low prices and large turnover. There was repeated what everywhere and always is the result of such a process of rationalization: those who would not follow suit had to go out of business. The idyllic state collapsed under the pressure of a bitter competitive struggle, respectable fortunes were made, and not lent out at interest, but always reinvested in the business. The old leisurely and comfortable attitude toward life gave way to a hard frugality in which some participated and came to the top, because they did not wish to consume but to earn, while others who wished to keep on with the old ways were forced to curtail their consumption.[26]

And, what is most important in this connection, it was not generally in such cases a stream of new money invested in the industry which brought about this revolution—in several cases known to me the whole revolutionary process was set in motion with a few thousands of capital borrowed from relations—but the new spirit, the spirit of modern capitalism, had set to work. The question of the motive forces in the expansion of modern capitalism is not in the first instance a question of the origin of the capital sums which were available for capitalistic uses, but, above all, of the development of the spirit of capitalism. Where it appears and is able to work itself out, it produces its own capital and monetary supplies as the means to its ends, but the reverse is not true.[27] Its entry on the scene was not generally peaceful. A flood of mistrust, sometimes of hatred, above all of moral indignation, regularly opposed itself to the first innovator. Often—I know of several cases of the sort—regular legends of mysterious shady spots in his previous life have been produced. It is very easy not to recognize that only an unusually strong character could save an entrepreneur of this new type from the loss of his temperate self-control and from both moral and economic shipwreck. Furthermore, along with clarity of vision and ability to act, it is only by virtue of very definite and highly developed ethical qualities that it has been possible for him to command the absolutely indispensable confidence of his customers and workmen. Nothing else could have given him the strength to overcome the innumerable obstacles, above all the infinitely more intensive work which is demanded of the modern entrepreneur. But these are ethical qualities of quite a different sort from those adapted to the traditionalism of the past.

And, as a rule, it has been neither dare-devil and unscrupulous speculators, economic adventurers such as we meet at all periods of economic history, nor simply great financiers who have carried through this change, outwardly so inconspicuous, but nevertheless so decisive for the penetration of economic life with the new spirit. On the contrary, they were men who had grown up in the hard school of life, calculating and daring at the same time, above all temperate and reliable, shrewd and completely devoted to their business, with strictly bourgeois opinions and principles.

One is tempted to think that these personal moral qualities have not the slightest relation to any ethical maxims, to say nothing of religious ideas, but that the essential relation between them is negative. The ability to free oneself from the common tradition, a sort of liberal enlightenment, seems likely to be the most suitable basis for such a business man's success. And to-day that is generally precisely the case. Any relationship between religious beliefs and conduct is generally absent, and where any exists, at least in Germany, it tends to be of the negative sort. The people filled with the spirit of capitalism to-day tend to be indifferent, if not hostile, to the Church. The thought of the pious boredom of paradise has little attraction for their active natures; religion appears to them as a means of drawing people away from labour in this world. If you ask them what is the meaning of their restless activity, why they are never satisfied with what they have, thus appearing so senseless to any purely worldly view of life, they would perhaps give the answer, if they know any at all: "to provide for my children and grandchildren". But more often and, since that motive is not peculiar to them, but was just as effective for the traditionalist, more correctly, simply: that business with its continuous work has become a necessary part of their lives. That is in fact the only possible motivation, but it at the same time expresses what is, seen from the view-point of personal happiness, so irrational about this sort of life, where a man exists for the sake of his business, instead of the reverse.

Of course, the desire for the power and recognition which the mere fact of wealth brings plays its part.

When the imagination of a whole people has once been turned toward purely quantitative bigness, as in the United States, this romanticism of numbers exercises an irresistible appeal to the poets among business men. Otherwise it is in general not the real leaders, and especially not the permanently successful entrepreneurs, who are taken in by it. In particular, the resort to entailed estates and the nobility, with sons whose conduct at the university and in the officers' corps tries to cover up their social origin, as has been the typical history of German capitalistic parvenu families, is a product of later decadence. The ideal type [28] of the capitalistic entrepreneur, as it has been represented even in Germany by occasional outstanding examples, has no relation to such more or less refined climbers. He avoids ostentation and unnecessary expenditure, as well as conscious enjoyment of his power, and is embarrassed by the outward signs of the social recognition which he receives. His manner of life is, in other words, often, and we shall have to investigate the historical significance of just this important fact, distinguished by a certain ascetic tendency, as appears clearly enough in the sermon of Franklin which we have quoted. It is, namely, by no means exceptional, but rather the rule, for him to have a sort of modesty which is essentially more honest than the reserve which Franklin so shrewdly recommends. He gets nothing out of his wealth for himself, except the irrational sense of having done his job well.

But it is just that which seems to the pre-capitalistic man so incomprehensible and mysterious, so unworthy and contemptible. That anyone should be able to make it the sole purpose of his life-work, to sink into the grave weighed down with a great material load of money and goods, seems to him explicable only as the product of a perverse instinct, the *auri sacra fames*.

At present under our individualistic political, legal, and economic institutions, with the forms of organization and general structure which are peculiar to our economic order, this spirit of capitalism might be understandable, as has been said, purely as a result of adaptation. The capitalistic system so needs this devotion to the calling of making money, it is an attitude toward material goods which is so well suited to that system, so intimately bound up with the conditions of survival in the economic struggle for existence, that there can to-day no longer be any question of a necessary connection of that acquisitive manner of life with any single *Weltanschauung*. In fact, it no longer needs the support of any religious forces, and feels the attempts of religion to influence economic life, in so far as they can still be felt at all, to be as much an unjustified interference as its regulation by the State. In such circumstances men's commercial and social interests do tend to determine their opinions and attitudes. Whoever does not adapt his manner of life to the conditions of capitalistic success must go under, or at least cannot rise. But these are phenomena of a time in which modern capitalism has become dominant and has become emancipated from its old supports. But as it could at one time destroy the old forms of mediæval regulation of economic life only in alliance with the growing power of the modern State, the same, we may say provisionally, may have been the case in its relations with religious forces. Whether and in what sense that was the case, it is our task to investigate. For that the conception of money-making as an end in itself to which people were bound, as a calling, was contrary to the ethical feelings of whole epochs, it is hardly necessary to prove. The dogma *Deo placere vix potest* which was incorporated into the canon law and applied to the activities of the merchant, and which at that time (like the passage in the gospel about interest) [29] was considered genuine, as well as St. Thomas's characterization of the desire for gain as *turpitudo* (which term even included unavoidable and hence ethically justified profit-making), already contained a high degree of concession on the part of the Catholic doctrine to the financial powers with which the Church had such intimate political relations in the Italian cities, [30] as compared with the much more radically anti-chrematistic views of comparatively wide circles. But even where the doctrine was still better accommodated to the facts, as for instance with Anthony of Florence, the feeling was never quite overcome, that activity directed to acquisition for its own sake was at bottom a *pudendum* which was to be tolerated only because of the unalterable necessities of life in this world.

Some moralists of that time, especially of the nominalistic school, accepted developed capitalistic business forms as inevitable, and attempted to justify them, especially commerce, as necessary. The *industria* developed in it they were able to regard, though not without contradictions, as a legitimate source of profit, and hence ethically unobjectionable. But the dominant

73

doctrine rejected the spirit of capitalistic acquisition as *turpitudo*, or at least could not give it a positive ethical sanction. An ethical attitude like that of Benjamin Franklin would have been simply unthinkable. This was, above all, the attitude of capitalistic circles themselves. Their life-work was, so long as they clung to the tradition of the Church, at best something morally indifferent. It was tolerated, but was still, even if only on account of the continual danger of collision with the Church's doctrine on usury, somewhat dangerous to salvation. Quite considerable sums, as the sources show, went at the death of rich people to religious institutions as conscience money, at times even back to former debtors as *usura* which had been unjustly taken from them. It was otherwise, along with heretical and other tendencies looked upon with disapproval, only in those parts of the commercial aristocracy which were already emancipated from the tradition. But even sceptics and people indifferent to the Church often reconciled themselves with it by gifts, because it was a sort of insurance against the uncertainties of what might come after death, or because (at least according to the very widely held latter view) an external obedience to the commands of the Church was sufficient to insure salvation.[31] Here the either non-moral or immoral character of their action in the opinion of the participants themselves comes clearly to light.

Now, how could activity, which was at best ethically tolerated, turn into a calling in the sense of Benjamin Franklin? The fact to be explained historically is that in the most highly capitalistic centre of that time, in

Florence of the fourteenth and fifteenth centuries, the money and capital market of all the great political Powers, this attitude was considered ethically unjustifiable, or at best to be tolerated. But in the backwoods small bourgeois circumstances of Pennsylvania in the eighteenth century, where business threatened for simple lack of money to fall back into barter, where there was hardly a sign of large enterprise, where only the earliest beginnings of banking were to be found, the same thing was considered the essence of moral conduct, even commanded in the name of duty. To speak here of a reflection of material conditions in the ideal superstructure would be patent nonsense. What was the background of ideas which could account for the sort of activity apparently directed toward profit alone as a calling toward which the individual feels himself to have an ethical obligation? For it was this idea which gave the way of life of the new entrepreneur its ethical foundation and justification.

The attempt has been made, particularly by Sombart, in what are often judicious and effective observations, to depict economic rationalism as the salient feature of modern economic life as a whole. Undoubtedly with justification, if by that is meant the extension of the productivity of labour which has, through the subordination of the process of production to scientific points of view, relieved it from its dependence upon the natural organic limitations of the human individual. Now this process of rationalization in the field of technique and economic organization undoubtedly determines an important part of the ideals of life of modern bourgeois society. Labour in the service of a rational organization for the provision of humanity with material goods has without doubt always appeared to representatives of the capitalistic spirit as one of the most important purposes of their life-work. It is only necessary, for instance, to read Franklin's account of his efforts in the service of civic improvements in Philadelphia clearly to apprehend this obvious truth. And the joy and pride of having given employment to numerous people, of having had a part in the economic progress of his home town in the sense referring to figures of population and volume of trade which capitalism associated with the word, all these things obviously are part of the specific and undoubtedly idealistic satisfactions in life to modern men of business. Similarly it is one of the fundamental characteristics of an individualistic capitalistic economy that it is rationalized on the basis of rigorous calculation, directed with foresight and caution toward the economic success which is sought in sharp contrast to the hand-to-mouth existence of the peasant, and to the privileged traditionalism of the guild craftsman and of the adventurers' capitalism, oriented to the exploitation of political opportunities and irrational speculation.

It might thus seem that the development of the spirit of capitalism is best understood as part of the development of rationalism as a whole, and could be deduced from the fundamental position of rationalism on the basic problems of life. In the process Protestantism would only have to be considered in so far as it had formed a stage prior to the development of a purely rationalistic philosophy. But any serious attempt to carry this thesis through makes it evident that such a simple way of putting the question will not work, simply because of the fact that the history of rationalism shows a development which by no means follows parallel lines in the various departments of life. The rationalization of private law, for instance, if it is thought of as a logical simplification and rearrangement of the content of the law, was achieved in the highest hitherto known degree in the Roman law of late antiquity. But it remained most backward in some of the countries with the highest degree of economic rationalization, notably in England, where the Renaissance of Roman Law was overcome by the power of the great legal corporations, while it has always retained its supremacy in the Catholic countries of Southern Europe. The worldly rational philosophy of the eighteenth century did not find favour alone or even principally in the countries of highest capitalistic development. The doctrines of Voltaire are even to-day the common property of broad upper, and what is practically more important, middle-class groups in the Romance Catholic countries. Finally, if under practical rationalism is understood the type of attitude which sees and judges the world consciously in terms of the worldly interests of the individual ego, then this view of life was and is the special peculiarity of the peoples of the *liberum arbitrium*, such as the Italians and the French are in very flesh and blood. But we have already convinced ourselves that this is by no means the soil in which that relationship of a man to his calling as a task, which is necessary to capitalism, has pre-eminently grown. In fact, one may—this simple proposition, which is often forgotten, should be placed at the beginning of every study which essays to deal with rationalism—rationalize life from fundamentally different basic points of view and in very different directions. Rationalism is an historical concept which covers a whole world of different things. It will be our task to find out whose intellectual child the particular concrete form of rational thought was, from which the idea of a calling and the devotion to labour in the calling has grown, which is, as we have seen, so irrational from the standpoint of purely eudæmonistic self-interest, but which has been and still is one of the most characteristic elements of our capitalistic culture. We are here particularly interested in the origin of precisely the irrational element which lies in this, as in every conception of a calling.

CHAPTER III

LUTHER'S CONCEPTION OF THE CALLING

TASK OF THE INVESTIGATION

Now it is unmistakable that even in the German word *Beruf*, and perhaps still more clearly in the English *calling*, a religious conception, that of a task set by God, is at least suggested. The more emphasis is put upon the word in a concrete case, the more evident is the connotation. And if we trace the history of the word through the civilized languages, it appears that neither the predominantly Catholic peoples nor those of classical antiquity[1] have possessed any expression of similar connotation for what we know as a calling (in the sense of a life-task, a definite field in which to work), while one has existed for all predominantly Protestant peoples. It may be further shown that this is not due to any ethnical peculiarity of the languages concerned. It is not, for instance, the product of a Germanic spirit, but in its modern meaning the word comes from the Bible translations, through the spirit of the translator, not that of the original.[2] In Luther's translation of the Bible it appears to have first been used at a point in Jesus Sirach (xi. 20 and 21) precisely in our modern sense.[3] After that it speedily took on its present meaning in the everyday speech of all Protestant peoples, while earlier not even a suggestion of such a meaning could be found in the secular literature of any of them, and even, in religious writings, so far as I can ascertain, it is only found in one of the German

79

mystics whose influence on Luther is well known.

Like the meaning of the word, the idea is new, a product of the Reformation. This may be assumed as generally known. It is true that certain suggestions of the positive valuation of routine activity in the world, which is contained in this conception of the calling, had already existed in the Middle Ages, and even in late Hellenistic antiquity. We shall speak of that later. But at least one thing was unquestionably new: the valuation of the fulfilment of duty in worldly affairs as the highest form which the moral activity of the individual could assume. This it was which inevitably gave every-day worldly activity a religious significance, and which first created the conception of a calling in this sense. The conception of the calling thus brings out that central dogma of all Protestant denominations which the Catholic division of ethical precepts into *præcepta* and *consilia* discards. The only way of living acceptably to God was not to surpass worldly morality in monastic asceticism, but solely through the fulfilment of the obligations imposed upon the individual by his position in the world. That was his calling.

Luther[4] developed the conception in the course of the first decade of his activity as a reformer. At first, quite in harmony with the prevailing tradition of the Middle Ages, as represented, for example, by Thomas Aquinas,[5] he thought of activity in the world as a thing of the flesh, even though willed by God. It is the indispensable natural condition of a life of faith, but in itself, like eating and drinking, morally neutral.[6] But with the development of the conception of *sola fide* in all its consequences, and its logical result, the increasingly sharp emphasis against the Catholic *consilia evangelica* of the monks as dictates of the devil, the calling grew in importance. The monastic life is not only quite devoid of value as a means of justification before God, but he also looks upon its renunciation of the duties of this world as the product of selfishness, withdrawing from temporal obligations. In contrast, labour in a calling appears to him as the outward expression of brotherly love. This he proves by the observation that the division of labour forces every individual to work for others, but his view-point is highly naïve, forming an almost grotesque contrast to Adam Smith's well-known statements on the same subject.[7] However, this justification, which is evidently essentially scholastic, soon disappears again, and there remains, more and more strongly emphasized, the statement that the fulfilment of worldly duties is under all circumstances the only way to live acceptably to God. It and it alone is the will of God, and hence every legitimate calling has exactly the same worth in the sight of God.[8]

That this moral justification of worldly activity was one of the most important results of the Reformation, especially of Luther's part in it, is beyond doubt, and may even be considered a platitude.[9] This attitude is worlds removed from the deep hatred of Pascal, in his contemplative moods, for all worldly activity, which he was deeply convinced could only be understood in terms of vanity or low cunning.[10] And it differs even more from the liberal utilitarian compromise with the world at which the Jesuits arrived. But just what the practical significance of this achievement of Protestantism was in detail is dimly felt rather than clearly perceived.

In the first place it is hardly necessary to point out that Luther cannot be claimed for the spirit of capitalism in the sense in which we have used that term above, or for that matter in any sense whatever. The religious circles which to-day most enthusiastically celebrate that great achievement of the Reformation are by no means friendly to capitalism in any sense. And Luther himself would, without doubt, have sharply repudiated any connection with a point of view like that of Franklin. Of course, one cannot consider his complaints against the great merchants of his time, such as the Fuggers,[11] as evidence in this case. For the struggle against the privileged position, legal or actual, of single great trading companies in the sixteenth and seventeenth centuries may best be compared with the modern campaign against the trusts, and can no more justly be considered in itself an expression of a traditionalistic point of view. Against these people, against the Lombards, the monopolists, speculators, and bankers patronized by the Anglican Church and the kings and parliaments of England and France, both the Puritans and the Huguenots carried on a bitter struggle.[12] Cromwell, after the battle of Dunbar (September 1650), wrote to the Long Parliament: "Be pleased to reform the abuses of all professions: and if there be any one that makes many poor to make a few rich, that suits not a Commonwealth." But, nevertheless, we will find Cromwell following a quite specifically capitalistic line of thought.[13] On the other hand, Luther's numerous statements against usury or interest in any form reveal a conception of the nature of capitalistic acquisition which, compared with that of late Scholasticism, is, from a capitalistic view-point, definitely backward.[14] Especially, of course, the doctrine of the sterility of money which Anthony of Florence had already refuted.

But it is unnecessary to go into detail. For, above all, the consequences of the conception of the calling in the religious sense for worldly conduct were susceptible to quite different interpretations. The effect of the Reformation as such was only that, as compared with the Catholic attitude, the moral emphasis on and the religious sanction of, organized worldly labour in a calling was mightily increased. The way in which the concept of the calling, which expressed this change, should develop further depended upon the religious evolution which now took place in the different Protestant Churches. The authority of the Bible, from which Luther thought he had derived his idea of the calling, on the whole favoured a traditionalistic interpretation. The old Testament, in particular, though in the genuine prophets it showed no sign of a tendency to excel worldly morality, and elsewhere only in quite isolated rudiments and suggestions, contained a similar religious idea entirely in this traditionalistic sense. Everyone should abide by his living and let the godless run after gain. That is the sense of all the statements which bear directly on worldly activities. Not until the Talmud is a partially, but not even then fundamentally, different attitude to be found. The personal attitude of Jesus is characterized in classical purity by the typical antique-Oriental plea: "Give us this day our daily bread." The element of radical repudiation of the world, as expressed in the μαμωνᾶς τῆς ἀδικίας,

83

excluded the possibility that the modern idea of a calling should be based on his personal authority.[15] In the apostolic era as expressed in the New Testament, especially in St. Paul, the Christian looked upon worldly activity either with indifference, or at least essentially traditionalistically; for those first generations were filled with eschatological hopes. Since everyone was simply waiting for the coming of the Lord, there was nothing to do but remain in the station and in the worldly occupation in which the call of the Lord had found him, and labour as before. Thus he would not burden his brothers as an object of charity, and it would only be for a little while. Luther read the Bible through the spectacles of his whole attitude; at the time and in the course of his development from about 1518 to 1530 this not only remained traditionalistic but became ever more so.[16]

In the first years of his activity as a reformer he was, since he thought of the calling as primarily of the flesh, dominated by an attitude closely related, in so far as the form of world[17] activity was concerned, to the Pauline eschatological indifference as expressed in 1 Cor. vii.[17] One may attain salvation in any walk of life; on the short pilgrimage of life there is no use in laying weight on the form of occupation. The pursuit of material gain beyond personal needs must thus appear as a symptom of lack of grace, and since it can apparently only be attained at the expense of others, directly reprehensible.[18] As he became increasingly involved in the affairs of the world, he came to value work in the world more highly. But in the concrete calling an individual pursued he saw more and more a special command of God to

84

fulfil these particular duties which the Divine Will had imposed upon him. And after the conflict with the Fanatics and the peasant disturbances, the objective historical order of things in which the individual has been placed by God becomes for Luther more and more a direct manifestation of divine will.[19] The stronger and stronger emphasis on the providential element, even in particular events of life, led more and more to a traditionalistic interpretation based on the idea of Providence. The individual should remain once and for all in the station and calling in which God had placed him, and should restrain his worldly activity within the limits imposed by his established station in life. While his economic traditionalism was originally the result of Pauline indifference, it later became that of a more and more intense belief in divine providence,[20] which identified absolute obedience to God's will,[21] with absolute acceptance of things as they were. Starting from this background, it was impossible for Luther to establish a new or in any way fundamental connection between worldly activity and religious principles.[22] His acceptance of purity of doctrine as the one infallible criterion of the Church, which became more and more irrevocable after the struggles of the 'twenties, was in itself sufficient to check the development of new points of view in ethical matters.

Thus for Luther the concept of the calling remained traditionalistic.[23] His calling is something which man has to accept as a divine ordinance, to which he must adapt himself. This aspect outweighed the other idea which was also present, that work in the calling was a, or rather *the*, task set by God.[24] And in its further development, orthodox Lutheranism emphasized this aspect still more. Thus, for the time being, the only ethical result was negative; worldly duties were no longer subordinated to ascetic ones; obedience to authority and the acceptance of things as they were, were preached.[25] In this Lutheran form the idea of a calling had, as will be shown in our discussion of mediæval religious ethics, to a considerable extent been anticipated by the German mystics. Especially in Tauler's equalization of the values of religious and worldly occupations, and the decline in valuation of the traditional forms of ascetic practices [26] on account of the decisive significance of the ecstatic-contemplative absorption of the divine spirit by the soul. To a certain extent Lutheranism means a step backward from the mystics, in so far as Luther, and still more his Church, had, as compared with the mystics, partly undermined the psychological foundations for a rational ethics. (The mystic attitude on this point is reminiscent partly of the Pietest and partly of the Quaker psychology of faith.[27]) That was precisely because he could not but suspect the tendency to ascetic self-discipline of leading to salvation by works, and hence he and his Church were forced to keep it more and more in the background.

Thus the mere idea of the calling in the Lutheran sense is at best of questionable importance for the problems in which we are interested. This was all that was meant to be determined here.[28] But this is not in the least to say that even the Lutheran form of the renewal of the religious life may not have had some practical significance for the objects of our investigation; quite the contrary. Only that significance evidently

86

cannot be derived directly from the attitude of Luther and his Church to worldly activity, and is perhaps not altogether so easily grasped as the connection with other branches of Protestantism. It is thus well for us next to look into those forms in which a relation between practical life and a religious motivation can be more easily perceived than in Lutheranism. We have already called attention to the conspicuous part played by Calvinism and the Protestant sects in the history of capitalistic development. As Luther found a different spirit at work in Zwingli than in himself, so did his spiritual successors in Calvinism. And Catholicism has to the present day looked upon Calvinism as its real opponent.

Now that may be partly explained on purely political grounds. Although the Reformation is unthinkable without Luther's own personal religious development, and was spiritually long influenced by his personality, without Calvinism his work could not have had permanent concrete success. Nevertheless, the reason for this common repugnance of Catholics and Lutherans lies, at least partly, in the ethical peculiarities of Calvinism. A purely superficial glance shows that there is here quite a different relationship between the religious life and earthly activity than in either Catholicism or Lutheranism. Even in literature motivated purely by religious factors that is evident. Take for instance the end of the *Divine Comedy*, where the poet in Paradise stands speechless in his passive contemplation of the secrets of God, and compare it with the poem which has come to be called the *Divine Comedy of Puritanism*. Milton closes the last song of *Paradise*

87

Lost after describing the *expulsion* from paradise as follows:—

> "They, looking back, all the eastern side beheld
> Of paradise, so late their happy seat,
> Waved over by that flaming brand; the gate
> With dreadful faces thronged and fiery arms.
> Some natural tears they dropped, but wiped them soon:
> The world was all before them, there to choose
> Their place of rest, and Providence their guide."

And only a little before Michael had said to Adam:

>   . . . "Only add
> Deeds to thy knowledge answerable; add faith;
> Add virtue, patience, temperance; add love,
> By name to come called Charity, the soul
> Of all the rest: then wilt thou not be loth
> To leave this Paradise, but shall possess
> A Paradise within thee, happier far."

One feels at once that this powerful expression of the Puritan's serious attention to this world, his acceptance of his life in the world as a task, could not possibly have come from the pen of a mediæval writer. But it is just as uncongenial to Lutheranism, as expressed for instance in Luther's and Paul Gerhard's chorales. It is now our task to replace this vague feeling by a somewhat more precise logical formulation, and to investigate the fundamental basis of these differences. The appeal to national character is generally a mere confession of ignorance, and in this case it is entirely untenable. To ascribe a unified national character to the Englishmen of the seventeenth century would be simply to falsify history. Cavaliers and Roundheads did not appeal to each other simply as two parties, but as radically distinct species of men, and whoever looks into the matter carefully must agree with them.[29] On the other hand, a difference of character between the English merchant adventurers and the old Hanseatic merchants is not to be found; nor can any other fundamental difference between the English and German characters at the end of the Middle Ages, which cannot easily be explained by the differences of their political history.[30] It was the power of religious influence, not alone, but more than anything else, which created the differences of which we are conscious to-day.[31]

We thus take as our starting-point in the investigation of the relationship between the old Protestant ethic and the spirit of capitalism the works of Calvin, of Calvinism, and the other Puritan sects. But it is not to be understood that we expect to find any of the founders or representatives of these religious movements considering the promotion of what we have called the spirit of capitalism as in any sense the end of his life-work. We cannot well maintain that the pursuit of worldly goods, conceived as an end in itself, was to any of them of positive ethical value. Once and for all it must be remembered that programmes of ethical reform never were at the centre of interest for any of the religious reformers (among whom, for our purposes, we must include men like Menno, George Fox, and Wesley). They were not the founders of societies for ethical culture nor the proponents of humanitarian projects for social reform or cultural ideals. The salvation of the soul and that alone was the centre of their

89

life and work. Their ethical ideals and the practical results of their doctrines were all based on that alone, and were the consequences of purely religious motives. We shall thus have to admit that the cultural consequences of the Reformation were to a great extent, perhaps in the particular aspects with which we are dealing predominantly, unforeseen and even unwished-for results of the labours of the reformers. They were often far removed from or even in contradiction to all that they themselves thought to attain.

The following study may thus perhaps in a modest way form a contribution to the understanding of the manner in which ideas become effective forces in history. In order, however, to avoid any misunderstanding of the sense in which any such effectiveness of purely ideal motives is claimed at all, I may perhaps be permitted a few remarks in conclusion to this introductory discussion.

In such a study, it may at once be definitely stated, no attempt is made to evaluate the ideas of the Reformation in any sense, whether it concern their social or their religious worth. We have continually to deal with aspects of the Reformation which must appear to the truly religious consciousness as incidental and even superficial. For we are merely attempting to clarify the part which religious forces have played in forming the developing web of our specifically worldly modern culture, in the complex interaction of innumerable different historical factors. We are thus inquiring only to what extent certain characteristic features of this culture can be imputed to the influence of the Reformation. At the same time we must free ourselves from the idea that it is possible to deduce the Reformation, as a historically necessary result, from certain economic changes. Countless historical circumstances, which cannot be reduced to any economic law, and are not susceptible of economic explanation of any sort, especially purely political processes, had to concur in order that the newly created Churches should survive at all.

On the other hand, however, we have no intention whatever of maintaining such a foolish and doctrinaire thesis[32] as that the spirit of capitalism (in the provisional sense of the term explained above) could only have arisen as the result of certain effects of the Reformation, or even that capitalism as an economic system is a creation of the Reformation. In itself, the fact that certain important forms of capitalistic business organization are known to be considerably older than the Reformation is a sufficient refutation of such a claim. On the contrary, we only wish to ascertain whether and to what extent religious forces have taken part in the qualitative formation and the quantitative expansion of that spirit over the world. Furthermore, what concrete aspects of our capitalistic culture can be traced to them, In view of the tremendous confusion of interdependent influences between the material basis, the forms of social and political organization, and the ideas current in the time of the Reformation, we can only proceed by investigating whether and at what points certain correlations between forms of religious belief and practical ethics can be worked out. At the same time we shall as far as possible clarify the manner and the general *direction* in which, by virtue of those relationships, the religious movements have influenced the development of material culture. Only when this has been determined with reasonable accuracy can the attempt be made to estimate to what extent the historical development of modern culture can be attributed to those religious forces and to what extent to others.

PART II

THE PRACTICAL ETHICS OF THE ASCETIC BRANCHES OF PROTESTANTISM

CHAPTER IV

THE RELIGIOUS FOUNDATIONS OF WORLDLY ASCETICISM

IN history there have been four principal forms of ascetic Protestantism (in the sense of word here used): (1) Calvinism in the form which it assumed in the main area of its influence in Western Europe, especially in the seventeenth century; (2) Pietism; (3) Methodism; (4) the sects growing out of the Baptist movement.[1] None of these movements was completely separated from the others, and even the distinction from the non-ascetic Churches of the Reformation is never perfectly clear. Methodism, which first arose in the middle of the eighteenth century within the Established Church of England, was not, in the minds of its founders, intended to form a new Church, but only a new awakening of the ascetic spirit within the old. Only in the course of its development, especially in its extension to America, did it become separate from the Anglican Church.

Pietism first split off from the Calvinistic movement in England, and especially in Holland. It remained loosely connected with orthodoxy, shading off from it by imperceptible gradations, until at the end of the seventeenth century it was absorbed into Lutheranism under Spener's leadership. Though the dogmatic adjustment was not entirely satisfactory, it remained a movement within the Lutheran Church. Only the faction dominated by Zinzendorf, and affected by lingering Hussite and Calvinistic influences within the

Moravian brotherhood, was forced, like Methodism against its will, to form a peculiar sort of sect. Calvinism and Baptism were at the beginning of their development sharply opposed to each other. But in the Baptism of the latter part of the seventeenth century they were in close contact. And even in the Independent sects of England and Holland at the beginning of the seventeenth century the transition was not abrupt. As Pietism shows, the transition to Lutheranism is also gradual, and the same is true of Calvinism and the Anglican Church, though both in external character and in the spirit of its most logical adherents the latter is more closely related to Catholicism. It is true that both the mass of the adherents and especially the staunchest champions of that ascetic movement which, in the broadest sense of a highly ambiguous word, has been called Puritanism,[2] did attack the foundations of Anglicanism; but even here the differences were only gradually worked out in the course of the struggle. Even if for the present we quite ignore the questions of government and organization which do not interest us here, the facts are just the same. The dogmatic differences, even the most important, such as those over the doctrines of predestination and justification, were combined in the most complex ways, and even at the beginning of the seventeenth century regularly, though not without exception, prevented the maintenance of unity in the Church. Above all, the types of moral conduct in which we are interested may be found in a similar manner among the adherents of the most various denominations, derived from any one of the four sources mentioned above, or a combination of several

of them. We shall see that similar ethical maxims may
be correlated with very different dogmatic foundations.
Also the important literary tools for the saving of
souls, above all the casuistic compendia of the various
denominations, influenced each other in the course of
time; one finds great similarities in them, in spite of
very great differences in actual conduct.

It would almost seem as though we had best completely ignore both the dogmatic foundations and the
ethical theory and confine our attention to the moral
practice so far as it can be determined. That, however,
is not true. The various different dogmatic roots of
ascetic morality did no doubt die out after terrible
struggles. But the original connection with those
dogmas has left behind important traces in the later
undogmatic ethics; moreover, only the knowledge of the
original body of ideas can help us to understand the
connection of that morality with the idea of the after-
life which absolutely dominated the most spiritual
men of that time. Without its power, overshadowing
everything else, no moral awakening which seriously
influenced practical life came into being in that period.

We are naturally not concerned with the question of
what was theoretically and officially taught in the
ethical compendia of the time, however much practical
significance this may have had through the influence
of Church discipline, pastoral work, and preaching.[3]
We are interested rather in something entirely different:
the influence of those psychological sanctions which,
originating in religious belief and the practice of religion, gave a direction to practical conduct and held
the individual to it. Now these sanctions were to a large

extent derived from the peculiarities of the religious ideas behind them. The men of that day were occupied with abstract dogmas to an extent which itself can only be understood when we perceive the connection of these dogmas with practical religious interests. A few observations on dogma,[4] which will seem to the non-theological reader as dull as they will hasty and superficial to the theologian, are indispensable. We can of course only proceed by presenting these religious ideas in the artificial simplicity of ideal types, as they could at best but seldom be found in history. For just because of the impossibility of drawing sharp boundaries in historical reality we can only hope to understand their specific importance from an investigation of them in their most consistent and logical forms.

A. CALVINISM

Now Calvinism[5] was the faith[6] over which the great political and cultural struggles of the sixteenth and seventeenth centuries were fought in the most highly developed countries, the Netherlands, England, and France. To it we shall hence turn first. At that time, and in general even to-day, the doctrine of predestination was considered its most characteristic dogma. It is true that there has been controversy as to whether it is the most essential dogma of the Reformed Church or only an appendage. Judgments of the importance of a historical phenomenon may be judgments of value or faith, namely, when they refer to what is alone interesting, or alone in the long run valuable in it. Or, on the other hand, they may refer to its influence on other historical processes as a causal factor. Then we are concerned with judgments of historical imputation. If now we start, as we must do here, from the latter standpoint and inquire into the significance which is to be attributed to that dogma by virtue of its cultural and historical consequences, it must certainly be rated very highly.[7] The movement which Oldenbarneveld led was shattered by it. The schism in the English Church became irrevocable under James I after the Crown and the Puritans came to differ dogmatically over just this doctrine. Again and again it was looked upon as the real element of political danger in Calvinism and attacked as such by those in authority.[8] The great synods of the seventeenth century, above all those of Dordrecht and Westminster, besides numerous smaller ones, made its elevation to canonical authority the central purpose of their work. It served as a rallying-point to countless heroes of the Church militant, and in both the eighteenth and the nineteenth centuries it caused schisms in the Church and formed the battle-cry of great new awakenings. We cannot pass it by, and since to-day it can no longer be assumed as known to all educated men, we can best learn its content from the authoritative words of the Westminster Confession of 1647, which in this regard is simply repeated by both Independent and Baptist creeds.

"Chapter IX (of Free Will), No. 3. Man, by his fall into a state of sin, hath wholly lost all ability of will to any spiritual good accompanying salvation. So that a natural man, being altogether averse from that Good, and dead in sin, is not able, by his own strength, to convert himself, or to prepare himself thereunto.

"Chapter III (of God's Eternal Decree), No. 3. By the decree of God, for the manifestation of His glory, some men and angels are predestinated unto everlasting life, and others foreordained to everlasting death.

"No. 5. Those of mankind that are predestinated unto life, God before the foundation of the world was laid, according to His eternal and immutable purpose, and the secret counsel and good pleasure of His will, hath chosen in Christ unto everlasting glory, out of His mere free grace and love, without any foresight of faith or good works, or perseverance in either of them, or any other thing in the creature as conditions, or causes moving Him thereunto, and all to the praise of His glorious grace.

"No. 7. The rest of mankind God was pleased, according to the unsearchable counsel of His own will, whereby He extendeth, or with-holdeth mercy, as He pleaseth, for the glory of His sovereign power over His creatures, to pass by, and to ordain them to dishonour and wrath for their sin, to the praise of His glorious justice.

"Chapter X (of Effectual Calling), No. 1. All those whom God hath predestinated unto life, and those only, He is pleased in His appointed and accepted time effectually to call, by His word and spirit (out of that state of sin and death, in which they are by nature) . . . taking away their heart of stone, and giving unto them an heart of flesh; renewing their wills, and by His almighty power determining them to that which is good. . . .

"Chapter V (of Providence), No. 6. As for those wicked and ungodly men, whom God as a righteous judge, for former sins doth blind and harden, from them He not only with-holdeth His grace, whereby they might have been enlightened in their understandings and wrought upon in their hearts, but sometimes also withdraweth the gifts which they had and exposeth them to such objects as their corruption makes occasion of sin: and withal, gives them over to their own lusts, the temptations of the world, and the power of Satan: whereby it comes to pass that they harden themselves, even under those means, which God useth for the softening of others."[9]

"Though I may be sent to Hell for it, such a God will never command my respect", was Milton's well-known opinion of the doctrine.[10] But we are here concerned not with the evaluation, but the historical significance of the dogma. We can only briefly sketch the question of how the doctrine originated and how it fitted into the framework of Calvinistic theology.

Two paths leading to it were possible. The phenomenon of the religious sense of grace is combined, in the most active and passionate of those great worshippers which Christianity has produced again and again since Augustine, with the feeling of certainty that that grace is the sole product of an objective power, and not in the least to be attributed to personal worth. The powerful feeling of light-hearted assurance, in which the tremendous pressure of their sense of sin is released, apparently breaks over them with elemental force and destroys every possibility of the belief that this over-powering gift of grace could owe anything to their own co-operation or could be connected with achievements or qualities of their own faith and will. At the time of Luther's greatest religious creativeness, when he was capable of writing his *Freiheit eines Christenmenschen*, God's secret decree was also to him most definitely the sole and ultimate source of his state of religious grace.[11] Even later he did not formally abandon it. But not only did the idea not assume a central position for him, but it receded more and more into the background, the more his position as responsible head of his Church forced him into practical politics. Melancthon quite deliberately avoided adopting the dark and dangerous teaching in the Augsburg Confession, and for the Church fathers of Lutheranism it was an article of faith that grace was revocable (*amissibilis*), and could be won again by penitent humility and faithful trust in the word of God and in the sacraments.

With Calvin the process was just the opposite; the significance of the doctrine for him increased,[12] perceptibly in the course of his polemical controversies with theological opponents. It is not fully developed until the third edition of his *Institutes*, and only gained its position of central prominence after his death in the great struggles which the Synods of Dordrecht and Westminster sought to put an end to. With Calvin the *decretum horribile* is derived not, as with Luther, from religious experience, but from the logical necessity of his thought; therefore its importance increases with every increase in the logical consistency of that religious thought. The interest of it is solely in God, not in man; God does not exist for men, but men for the sake of

God.[13] All creation, including of course the fact, as it undoubtedly was for Calvin, that only a small proportion of men are chosen for eternal grace, can have any meaning only as means to the glory and majesty of God. To apply earthly standards of justice to His sovereign decrees is meaningless and an insult to His Majesty,[14] since He and He alone is free, i.e. is subject to no law. His decrees can only be understood by or even known to us in so far as it has been His pleasure to reveal them. We can only hold to these fragments of eternal truth. Everything else, including the meaning of our individual destiny, is hidden in dark mystery which it would be both impossible to pierce and presumptuous to question.

For the damned to complain of their lot would be much the same as for animals to bemoan the fact they were not born as men. For everything of the flesh is separated from God by an unbridgeable gulf and deserves of Him only eternal death, in so far as He has not decreed otherwise for the glorification of His Majesty. We know only that a part of humanity is saved, the rest damned. To assume that human merit or guilt play a part in determining this destiny would be to think of God's absolutely free decrees, which have been settled from eternity, as subject to change by human influence, an impossible contradiction. The Father in heaven of the New Testament, so human and understanding, who rejoices over the repentance of a sinner as a woman over the lost piece of silver she has found, is gone. His place has been taken by a transcendental being, beyond the reach of human understanding, who with His quite incomprehensible decrees has decided the fate of every individual and regulated the tiniest details of the cosmos from eternity.[15] God's grace is, since His decrees cannot change, as impossible for those to whom He has granted it to lose as it is unattainable for those to whom He has denied it.

In its extreme inhumanity this doctrine must above all have had one consequence for the life of a generation which surrendered to its magnificent consistency. That was a feeling of unprecedented inner loneliness of the single individual.[16] In what was for the man of the age of the Reformation the most important thing in life, his eternal salvation, he was forced to follow his path alone to meet a destiny which had been decreed for him from eternity. No one could help him. No priest, for the chosen one can understand the word of God only in his own heart. No sacraments, for though the sacraments had been ordained by God for the increase of His glory, and must hence be scrupulously observed, they are not a means to the attainment of grace, but only the subjective *externa subsidia* of faith. No Church, for though it was held that *extra ecclesiam nulla salus* in the sense that whoever kept away from the true Church could never belong to God's chosen band,[17] nevertheless the membership of the external Church included the doomed. They should belong to it and be subjected to its discipline, not in order thus to attain salvation, that is impossible, but because, for the glory of God, they too must be forced to obey His commandments. Finally, even no God. For even Christ had died only for the elect,[18] for whose benefit God had decreed His martyrdom from eternity. This, the complete elimination of salvation through the

Church and the sacraments (which was in Lutheranism by no means developed to its final conclusions), was what formed the absolutely decisive difference from Catholicism.

That great historic process in the development of religions, the elimination of magic from the world[19] which had begun with the old Hebrew prophets and, in conjunction with Hellenistic scientific thought, had repudiated all magical means to salvation as superstition and sin, came here to its logical conclusion. The genuine Puritan even rejected all signs of religious ceremony at the grave and buried his nearest and dearest without song or ritual in order that no superstition, no trust in the effects of magical and sacramental forces on salvation, should creep in.[20]

There was not only no magical means of attaining the grace of God for those to whom God had decided to deny it, but no means whatever. Combined with the harsh doctrines of the absolute transcendentality of God and the corruption of everything pertaining to the flesh, this inner isolation of the individual contains, on the one hand, the reason for the entirely negative attitude of Puritanism to all the sensuous and emotional elements in culture and in religion, because they are of no use toward salvation and promote sentimental illusions and idolatrous superstitions. Thus it provides a basis for a fundamental antagonism to sensuous culture of all kinds.[21] On the other hand, it forms one of the roots of that disillusioned and pessimistically inclined individualism[22] which can even to-day be identified in the national characters and the institutions of the peoples with a Puritan past, in such a striking contrast to the quite different spectacles through which the Enlightenment later looked upon men.[23] We can clearly identify the traces of the influence of the doctrine of predestination in the elementary forms of conduct and attitude toward life in the era with which we are concerned, even where its authority as a dogma was on the decline. It was in fact only the most extreme form of that exclusive trust in God in which we are here interested. It comes out for instance in the strikingly frequent repetition, especially in the English Puritan literature, of warnings against any trust in the aid of friendship of men.[24] Even the amiable Baxter counsels deep distrust of even one's closest friend, and Bailey directly exhorts to trust no one and to say nothing compromising to anyone. Only God should be your confidant.[25] In striking contrast to Lutheranism, this attitude toward life was also connected with the quiet disappearance of the private confession, of which Calvin was suspicious only on account of its possible sacramental misinterpretation, from all the regions of fully developed Calvinism. That was an occurrence of the greatest importance. In the first place it is a symptom of the type of influence this religion exercised. Further, however, it was a psychological stimulus to the development of their ethical attitude. The means to a periodical discharge of the emotional sense of sin [26] was done away with.

Of the consequences for the ethical conduct of everyday life we speak later. But for the general religious situation of a man the consequences are evident. In spite of the necessity of membership in the true Church [27] for salvation, the Calvinist's intercourse with his God was carried on in deep spiritual isolation. To see the specific results [28] of this peculiar atmosphere, it is only necessary to read Bunyan's *Pilgrim's Progress*,[29] by far the most widely read book of the whole Puritan literature. In the description of Christian's attitude after he had realized that he was living in the City of Destruction and he had received the call to take up his pilgrimage to the celestial city, wife and children cling to him, but stopping his ears with his fingers and crying, "life, eternal life", he staggers forth across the fields. No refinement could surpass the naive feeling of the tinker who, writing in his prison cell, earned the applause of a believing world, in expressing the emotions of the faithful Puritan, thinking only of his own salvation. It is expressed in the unctuous conversations which he holds with fellow-seekers on the way, in a manner somewhat reminiscent of Gottfried Keller's *Gerechte Kammacher*. Only when he himself is safe does it occur to him that it would be nice to have his family with him. It is the same anxious fear of death and the beyond which we feel so vividly in Alfonso of Liguori, as Döllinger has described him to us. It is worlds removed from that spirit of proud worldliness which Machiavelli expresses in relating the fame of those Florentine citizens who, in their struggle against the Pope and his excommunication, had held "Love of their native city higher than the fear for the salvation of their souls". And it is of course even farther from the feelings which Richard Wagner puts into the mouth of Siegmund before his fatal combat, "Grüsse mir Wotan, grüsse mir Wallhall—Doch von Wallhall's spröden Wonnen sprich du wahrlich mir nicht". But the effects of this fear on Bunyan and Liguori are characteristically different. The same fear which drives the latter to every conceivable self-humiliation spurs the former on to a restless and systematic struggle with life. Whence comes this difference?

It seems at first a mystery how the undoubted superiority of Calvinism in social organization can be connected with this tendency to tear the individual away from the closed ties with which he is bound to this world.[30] But, however strange it may seem, it follows from the peculiar form which the Christian brotherly love was forced to take under the pressure of the inner isolation of the individual through the Calvinistic faith. In the first place it follows dogmatically.[31] The world exists to serve the glorification of God and for that purpose alone. The elected Christian is in the world only to increase this glory of God by fulfilling His commandments to the best of his ability. But God requires social achievement of the Christian because He wills that social life shall be organized according to His commandments, in accordance with that purpose. The social[32] activity of the Christian in the world is solely activity *in majorem gloriam Dei*. This character is hence shared by labour in a calling which serves the mundane life of the community. Even in Luther we found specialized labour in callings justified in terms of brotherly love. But what for him remained an uncertain, purely intellectual suggestion became for the Calvinists a characteristic element in their ethical system. Brotherly love, since it may only be practised for the glory of God[33] and not in .the service of the flesh,[34] is expressed in the first place in the fulfilment of the daily tasks given by the *lex naturæ*; and in the process this fulfilment assumes a peculiarly objective and impersonal character, that of service in the interest of the rational organization of our social environment. For the wonderfully purposeful organization and arrangement of this cosmos is, according both to the revelation of the Bible and to natural intuition, evidently designed by God to serve the utility of the human race. This makes labour in the service of impersonal social usefulness appear to promote the glory of God and hence to be willed by Him. The complete elimination of the theodicy problem and of all those questions about the meaning of the world and of life, which have tortured others, was as self-evident to the Puritan as, for quite different reasons, to the Jew, and even in a certain sense to all the non-mystical types of Christian religion.

To this economy of forces Calvinism added another tendency which worked in the same direction. The conflict between the individual and the ethic (in Sören Kierkegaard's sense) did not exist for Calvinism, although it placed the individual entirely on his own responsibility in religious matters. This is not the place to analyse the reasons for this fact, or its significance for the political and economic rationalism of Calvinism. The source of the utilitarian character of Calvinistic ethics lies here, and important peculiarities of the Calvinistic idea of the calling were derived from the same source as well.[35] But for the moment we must return to the special consideration of the doctrine of predestination.

For us the decisive problem is: How was this doctrine borne[36] in an age to which the after-life was not only more important, but in many ways also more certain, than all the interests of life in this world?[37] The question, Am I one of the elect? must sooner or later have arisen for every believer and have forced all other interests into the background. And how can I be sure of this state of grace?[38] For Calvin himself this was not a problem. He felt himself to be a chosen agent of the Lord, and was certain of his own salvation. Accordingly, to the question of how the individual can be certain of his own election, he has at bottom only the answer that we should be content with the knowledge that God has chosen and depend further only on that implicit trust in Christ which is the result of true faith. He rejects in principle the assumption that one can learn from the conduct of others whether they are chosen or damned. It is an unjustifiable attempt to force God's secrets. The elect differ externally in this life in no way from the damned[39]; and even all the subjective experiences of the chosen are, as *ludibria spiritus sancti*, possible for the damned with the single exception of that *finaliter* expectant, trusting faith. The elect thus are and remain God's invisible Church.

Quite naturally this attitude was impossible for his followers as early as Beza, and, above all, for the broad mass of ordinary men. For them the *certitudo salutis* in the sense of the recognizability of the state of grace necessarily became of absolutely dominant importance.[40] So, wherever the doctrine of predestination was held, the question could not be suppressed whether there were any infallible criteria by which membership in the *electi* could be known. Not only has this question continually had a central importance in the development of the Pietism which first arose on the basis of the Reformed Church; it has in fact in a certain sense at times been fundamental to it. But when we consider the great political and social importance of the Reformed doctrine and practice of the Communion, we shall see how great a part was played during the whole seventeenth century outside of Pietism by the possibility of ascertaining the state of grace of the individual. On it depended, for instance, his admission to Communion, i.e. to the central religious ceremony which determined the social standing of the participants.

It was impossible, at least so far as the question of a man's own state of grace arose, to be satisfied[41] with Calvin's trust in the testimony of the expectant faith resulting from grace, even though the orthodox doctrine had never formally abandoned that criterion.[42] Above all, practical pastoral work, which had immediately to deal with all the suffering caused by the doctrine, could not be satisfied. It met these difficulties in various ways.[43] So far as predestination was not reinterpreted, toned down, or fundamentally abandoned,[44] two principal, mutually connected, types of pastoral advice appear. On the one hand it is held to be an absolute duty to consider oneself chosen, and to combat all doubts as temptations of the devil,[45] since lack of self-confidence is the result of insufficient faith, hence of imperfect grace. The exhortation of the apostle to make fast one's own call is here interpreted as a duty to attain certainty of one's own election and justification in the daily struggle of life. In the place of the humble sinners to whom Luther promises grace if they trust themselves to God in penitent faith are bred those self-confident saints[46] whom we can rediscover in the hard Puritan merchants of the heroic age of capitalism and in isolated instances down to the present. On the other hand, in order to attain that self-confidence intense worldly activity is recommended as the most suitable means.[47] It and it alone disperses religious doubts and gives the certainty of grace.

That worldly activity should be considered capable of this achievement, that it could, so to speak, be considered the most suitable means of counteracting feelings of religious anxiety, finds its explanation in the fundamental peculiarities of religious feeling in the Reformed Church, which come most clearly to light in its differences from Lutheranism in the doctrine of justification by faith. These differences are analysed so subtly and with such objectivity and avoidance of value-judgments in Schneckenburger's excellent lectures,[48] that the following brief observations can for the most part simply rest upon his discussion.

The highest religious experience which the Lutheran faith strives to attain, especially as it developed in the course of the seventeenth century, is the *unio mystica* with the deity.[49] As the name itself, which is unknown to the Reformed faith in this form, suggests, it is a feeling of actual absorption in the deity, that of a real entrance of the divine into the soul of the believer. It is qualitatively similar to the aim of the contemplation of the German mystics and is characterized by its passive search for the fulfilment of the yearning for rest in God.

Now the history of philosophy shows that religious belief which is primarily mystical may very well be compatible with a pronounced sense of reality in the field of empirical fact; it may even support it directly on account of the repudiation of dialectic doctrines. Furthermore, mysticism may indirectly even further the interests of rational conduct. Nevertheless, the positive valuation of external activity is lacking in its relation to the world. In addition to this, Lutheranism combines the *unio mystica* with that deep feeling of sin-stained unworthiness which is essential to preserve the *pœnitentia quotidiana* of the faithful Lutheran, thereby maintaining the humility and simplicity indispensable for the forgiveness of sins. The typical religion of the Reformed Church, on the other hand, has from the beginning repudiated both this purely inward emotional piety of Lutheranism and the Quietist escape from everything of Pascal. A real penetration of the human soul by the divine was made impossible by the absolute transcendentality of God compared to the flesh: *finitum non est capax infiniti.* The community of the elect with their God could only take place and be perceptible to them in that God worked (*operatur*) through them and that they were conscious of it. That is, their action originated from the faith caused by God's grace, and this faith in turn justified itself by the quality of that action. Deep-lying differences of the most important conditions of salvation[50] which apply to the classification of all practical religious activity appear here. The religious believer can make himself sure of his state of grace either in that he feels himself to be the vessel of the Holy Spirit or the tool of the divine will. In the former case his religious life tends to mysticism and emotionalism, in the latter to ascetic action; Luther stood close to the former type, Calvinism belonged definitely to the latter. The Calvinist also wanted to be saved *sola fide*. But since Calvin viewed all pure feelings and emotions, no matter how exalted they might seem to be, with suspicion,[51] faith had to be proved by its objective results in order to provide a firm foundation for the *certitudo salutis*. It must be a *fides efficax*,[52] the call to salvation an effectual calling (expression used in Savoy Declaration).

If we now ask further, by what fruits the Calvinist thought himself able to identify true faith? the answer is: by a type of Christian conduct which served to increase the glory of God. Just what does so serve is to be seen in his own will as revealed either directly through the Bible or indirectly through the purposeful order of the world which he has created (*lex naturæ*).[53] Especially by comparing the condition of one's own soul with that of the elect, for instance the patriarchs, according to the Bible, could the state of one's own grace be known.[54] Only one of the elect really has the *fides efficax*,[55] only he is able by virtue of his rebirth (*regeneratio*) and the resulting sanctification (*sanctificatio*) of his whole life, to augment the glory of God by real, and not merely apparent, good works. It was through the consciousness that his conduct, at least in its fundamental character and constant ideal (*propositum obœdientiæ*), rested on a power[56] within himself working for the glory of God; that it is not only willed of God but rather done by God[57] that he attained the highest good towards which this religion strove, the certainty of salvation.[58] That it was attainable was proved by 2 Cor. xiii. 5.[59] Thus, however useless good works might be as a means of attaining salvation, for even the elect remain beings of the flesh, and everything they do falls infinitely short of divine standards, nevertheless, they are indispensable as a sign of election.[60] They are the technical means, not of purchasing salvation, but of getting rid of the fear of damnation. In this sense they are occasionally referred to as directly necessary for salvation[61] or the *possessio salutis* is made conditional on them.[62]

In practice this means that God helps those who help themselves.[63] Thus the Calvinist, as it is sometimes put, himself creates[64] his own salvation, or, as would be more correct, the conviction of it. But this creation cannot, as in Catholicism, consist in a gradual accumulation of individual good works to one's credit, but rather in a systematic self-control which at every moment stands before the inexorable alternative, chosen or damned. This brings us to a very important point in our investigation.

It is common knowledge that Lutherans have again and again accused this line of thought, which was worked out in the Reformed Churches and sects with increasing clarity,[65] of reversion to the doctrine of salvation by works.[66] And however justified the protest of the accused against identification of their dogmatic position with the Catholic doctrine, this accusation has surely been made with reason if by it is meant the practical consequences for the everyday life of the average Christian of the Reformed Church.[67] For a more intensive form of the religious valuation of moral action than that to which Calvinism led its adherents has perhaps never existed. But what is important for the practical significance of this sort of salvation by works must be sought in a knowledge of the particular qualities which characterized their type of ethical conduct and distinguished it from the everyday life of an average Christian of the Middle Ages. The difference may well be formulated as follows: the normal mediæval Catholic layman [68] lived ethically, so to speak, from hand to mouth. In the first place he conscientiously fulfilled his traditional duties. But beyond that minimum his good works did not necessarily form a connected, or at least not a rationalized, system of life, but rather remained a succession of individual acts. He could use them as occasion demanded, to atone for particular sins, to better his chances for salvation, or, toward the end of his life, as a sort of insurance premium. Of course the Catholic ethic was an ethic of intentions. But the concrete *intentio* of the single act determined its value. And the single good or bad action was credited to the doer determining his temporal and eternal fate. Quite realistically the Church recognized that man was not an absolutely clearly defined unity to be judged one way or the other, but that his moral life was normally subject to conflicting motives and his action contradictory. Of course, it required as an ideal a change of life in principle. But it weakened just this requirement (for the average) by one of its most important means of power and education, the sacrament of absolution, the function of which was connected with the deepest roots of the peculiarly Catholic religion.

The rationalization of the world, the elimination of magic as a means to salvation,[69] the Catholics had not carried nearly so far as the Puritans (and before them the Jews) had done. To the Catholic[70] the absolution of his Church was a compensation for his own imperfection. The priest was a magician who performed the miracle of transubstantiation, and who held the key to eternal life in his hand. One could turn to him in grief and penitence. He dispensed atonement, hope of grace, certainty of forgiveness, and thereby granted release from that tremendous tension to which the Calvinist was doomed by an inexorable fate, admitting of no mitigation. For him such friendly and human comforts did not exist. He could not hope to atone for hours of weakness or of thoughtlessness by increased good will at other times, as the Catholic or even the Lutheran could. The God of Calvinism demanded of his believers not single good works, but a life of good works combined into a unified system.[71] There was no place for the very human Catholic cycle of sin, repentance, atonement, release, followed by renewed sin. Nor was there any balance of merit for a life as a whole which could be adjusted by temporal punishments or the Churches' means of grace.

The moral conduct of the average man was thus deprived of its planless and unsystematic character and subjected to a consistent method for conduct as a whole. It is no accident that the name of Methodists stuck to the participants in the last great revival of Puritan ideas in the eighteenth century just as the term Precisians, which has the same meaning, was applied to their spiritual ancestors in the seventeenth century.[72]

For only by a fundamental change in the whole meaning of life at every moment and in every action[73] could the effects of grace transforming a man from the *status naturæ* to the *status gratiæ* be proved.

The life of the saint was directed solely toward a transcendental end, salvation. But precisely for that reason it was thoroughly rationalized in this world and dominated entirely by the aim to add to the glory of God on earth. Never has the precept *omnia in majorem dei gloriam* been taken with more bitter seriousness.[74] Only a life guided by constant thought could achieve conquest over the state of nature. Descartes's *cogito ergo sum* was taken over by the contemporary Puritans with this ethical reinterpretation.[75] It was this rationalization which gave the Reformed faith its peculiar ascetic tendency, and is the basis both of its relationship[76] to and its conflict with Catholicism. For naturally similar things were not unknown to Catholicism.

Without doubt Christian asceticism, both outwardly and in its inner meaning, contains many different things. But it has had a definitely rational character in its highest Occidental forms as early as the Middle Ages, and in several forms even in antiquity. The great historical significance of Western monasticism, as contrasted with that of the Orient, is based on this fact, not in all cases, but in its general type. In the rules of St. Benedict, still more with the monks of Cluny, again with the Cistercians, and most strongly the Jesuits, it has become emancipated from planless otherworldliness and irrational self-torture. It had developed a systematic method of rational conduct with the purpose of overcoming the *status naturæ*, to free man from the power of irrational impulses and his dependence on the world and on nature. It attempted to subject man to the supremacy of a purposeful will,[77] to bring his actions under constant self-control with a careful consideration of their ethical consequences. Thus it trained the monk, objectively, as a worker in the service of the kingdom of God, and thereby further, subjectively, assured the salvation of his soul. This active self-control, which formed the end of the *exercitia* of St. Ignatius and of the rational monastic virtues everywhere,[78] was also the most important practical ideal of Puritanism.[79] In the deep contempt with which the cool reserve of its adherents is contrasted, in the reports of the trials of its martyrs, with the undisciplined blustering of the noble prelates and officials[80] can be seen that respect for quiet self-control which still distinguishes the best type of English or American gentleman to-day.[81] To put it in our terms[82]: The Puritan, like every rational type of asceticism, tried to enable a man to maintain and act upon his constant motives, especially those which it taught him itself, against the emotions. In this formal psychological sense of the term it tried to make him into a personality. Contrary to many popular ideas, the end of this asceticism was to be able to lead an alert, intelligent life: the most urgent task the destruction of spontaneous, impulsive enjoyment, the most important means was to bring order into the conduct of its adherents. All these important points are emphasized in the rules of Catholic monasticism as strongly[83] as in the principles of conduct of the Calvinists.[84] On this methodical control over the whole man rests the enormous expansive power of both, especially the ability of Calvinism as against Lutheranism to defend the cause of Protestantism as the Church militant.

On the other hand, the difference of the Calvinistic from the mediæval asceticism is evident. It consisted in the disappearance of the *consilia evangelica* and the accompanying transformation of asceticism to activity within the world. It is not as though Catholicism had restricted the methodical life to monastic cells. This was by no means the case either in theory or in practice. On the contrary, it has already been pointed out that, in spite of the greater ethical moderation of Catholicism, an ethically unsystematic life did not satisfy the highest ideals which it had set up even for the life of the layman.[85] The tertiary order of St. Francis was, for instance, a powerful attempt in the direction of an ascetic penetration of everyday life, and, as we know, by no means the only one. But, in fact, works like the *Nachfolge Christi* show, through the manner in which their strong influence was exerted, that the way of life preached in them was felt to be something higher than the everyday morality which sufficed as a minimum, and that this latter was not measured by such standards as Puritanism demanded. Moreover, the practical use made of certain institutions of the Church, above all of indulgences inevitably counteracted the tendencies toward systematic worldly asceticism. For that reason it was not felt at the time of the Reformation to be merely an unessential abuse, but one of the most fundamental evils of the Church.

But the most important thing was the fact that the man who, *par excellence*, lived a rational life in the religious sense was, and remained, alone the monk. Thus asceticism, the more strongly it gripped an individual, simply served to drive him farther away from everyday life, because the holiest task was definitely to surpass all worldly morality.[86] Luther, who was not in any sense fulfilling any law of development, but acting upon his quite personal experience, which was, though at first somewhat uncertain in its practical consequences, later pushed farther by the political situation, had repudiated that tendency, and Calvinism simply took this over from him.[87] Sebastian Franck struck the central characteristic of this type of religion when he saw the significance of the Reformation in the fact that now every Christian had to be a monk all his life. The drain of asceticism from everyday worldly life had been stopped by a dam, and those passionately spiritual natures which had formerly supplied the highest type of monk were now forced to pursue their ascetic ideals within mundane occupations.

But in the course of its development Calvinism added something positive to this, the idea of the necessity of proving one's faith in worldly activity.[88] Therein it gave the broader groups of religiously inclined people a positive incentive to asceticism. By founding its ethic in the doctrine of predestination, it substituted for the spiritual aristocracy of monks outside of and above the world the spiritual aristocracy of the predestined saints of God within the world.[89] It was an aristocracy which, with its *character indelebilis*, was divided from the eternally damned remainder of humanity by a more impassable and in its invisibility more terrifying gulf,[90] than separated the monk of the

Middle Ages from the rest of the world about him, a gulf which penetrated all social relations with its sharp brutality. This consciousness of divine grace of the elect and holy was accompanied by an attitude toward the sin of one's neighbour, not of sympathetic understanding based on consciousness of one's own weakness, but of hatred and contempt for him as an enemy of God bearing the signs of eternal damnation.[91] This sort of feeling was capable of such intensity that it sometimes resulted in the formation of sects. This was the case when, as in the Independent movement of the seventeenth century, the genuine Calvinist doctrine that the glory of God required the Church to bring the damned under the law, was outweighed by the conviction that it was an insult to God if an unregenerate soul should be admitted to His house and partake in the sacraments, or even, as a minister, administer them.[92] Thus, as a consequence of the doctrine of proof, the Donatist idea of the Church appeared, as in the case of the Calvinistic Baptists. The full logical consequence of the demand for a pure Church, a community of those proved to be in a state of grace, was not often drawn by forming sects. Modifications in the constitution of the Church resulted from the attempt to separate regenerate from unregenerate Christians, those who were from those who were not prepared for the sacrament, to keep the government of the Church or some other privilege in the hands of the former, and only to ordain ministers of whom there was no question.[93]

The norm by which it could always measure itself, of which it was evidently in need, this asceticism naturally found in the Bible. It is important to note that the well-known bibliocracy of the Calvinists held the moral precepts of the Old Testament, since it was fully as authentically revealed, on the same level of esteem as those of the New. It wàs only necessary that they should not obviously be applicable only to the historical circumstances of the Hebrews, or have been specifically denied by Christ. For the believer, the law was an ideal though never quite attainable norm[94] while Luther, on the other hand, originally had prized freedom from subjugation to the law as a divine privilege of the believer.[95] The influence of the God-fearing but perfectly unemotional wisdom of the Hebrews, which is expressed in the books most read by the Puritans, the Proverbs and the Psalms, can be felt in their whole attitude toward life. In particular, its rational suppression of the mystical, in fact the whole emotional side of religion, has rightly been attributed by Sanford[96] to the influence of the Old Testament. But this Old Testament rationalism was as such essentially of a small bourgeois, traditionalistic type, and was mixed not only with the powerful pathos of the prophets, but also with elements which encouraged the development of a peculiarly emotional type of religion even in the Middle Ages.[97] It was thus in the last analysis the peculiar, fundamentally ascetic, character of Calvinism itself which made it select and assimilate those elements of Old Testament religion which suited it best.

Now that systematization of ethical conduct which the asceticism of Calvinistic Protestantism had in common with the rational forms of life in the Catholic orders is expressed quite superficially in the way in which the conscientious Puritan continually supervised[98] his own state of grace. To be sure, the religious account-books in which sins, temptations, and progress made in grace were entered or tabulated were common to both the most enthusiastic Reformed circles[99] and some parts of modern Catholicism (especially in France), above all under the influence of the Jesuits. But in Catholicism it served the purpose of completeness of the confession, or gave the *directeur de l'âme* a basis for his authoritarian guidance of the Christian (mostly female). The Reformed Christian, however, felt his own pulse with its aid. It is mentioned by all the moralists and theologians, while Benjamin Franklin's tabulated statistical book-keeping on his progress in the different virtues is a classic example.[100] On the other hand, the old mediæval (even ancient) idea of God's book-keeping is carried by Bunyan to the characteristically tasteless extreme of comparing the relation of a sinner to his God with that of customer and shopkeeper. One who has once got into debt may well, by the product of all his virtuous acts, succeed in paying off the accumulated interest but never the principal.[101]

As he observed his own conduct, the later Puritan also observed that of God and saw His finger in all the details of life. And, contrary to the strict doctrine of Calvin, he always knew why God took this or that measure. The process of sanctifying life could thus almost take on the character of a business enterprise.[102] A thoroughgoing Christianization of the whole of life was the consequence of this methodical quality of ethical conduct into which Calvinism as distinct from Lutheranism forced men. That this rationality was decisive in its influence on practical life must always be borne in mind in order rightly to understand the influence of Calvinism. On the one hand we can see that it took this element to exercise such an influence at all. But other faiths as well necessarily had a similar influence when their ethical motives were the same in this decisive point, the doctrine of proof.

So far we have considered only Calvinism, and have thus assumed the doctrine of predestination as the dogmatic background of the Puritan morality in the sense of methodically rationalized ethical conduct. This could be done because the influence of that dogma in fact extended far beyond the single religious group which held in all respects strictly to Calvinistic principles, the Presbyterians. Not only the Independent Savoy Declaration of 1658, but also the Baptist Confession of Hanserd Knolly of 1689 contained it, and it had a place within Methodism. Although John Wesley, the great organizing genius of the movement, was a believer in the universality of Grace, one of the great agitators of the first generation of Methodists and their most consistent thinker, Whitefield, was an adherent of the doctrine. The same was true of the circle around Lady Huntingdon, which for a time had considerable influence. It was this doctrine in its magnificent consistency which, in the fateful epoch of the seventeenth century, upheld the belief of the militant defenders of the holy life that they were weapons in the hand of God, and executors of His providential will.[103] Moreover, it prevented a premature collapse into a purely utilitarian doctrine of good works in this world which would never have been capable of motivating such tremendous sacrifices for non-rational ideal ends.

The combination of faith in absolutely valid norms with absolute determinism and the complete transcendentality of God was in its way a product of great genius. At the same time it was, in principle, very much more modern than the milder doctrine, making greater concessions to the feelings which subjected God to the moral law. Above all, we shall see again and again how fundamental is the idea of proof for our problem. Since its practical significance as a psychological basis for rational morality could be studied in such purity in the doctrine of predestination, it was best to start there with the doctrine in its most consistent form. But it forms a recurring framework for the connection between faith and conduct in the denominations to be studied below. Within the Protestant movement the consequences which it inevitably had for the ascetic tendencies of the conduct of its first adherents form in principle the strongest antithesis to the relative moral helplessness of Lutheranism. The Lutheran *gratia amissibilis*, which could always be regained through penitent contrition evidently, in itself, contained no sanction for what is for us the most important result of ascetic Protestantism, a systematic rational ordering of the moral life as a whole.[104] The Lutheran faith thus left the spontaneous vitality of impulsive action and naïve emotion more nearly unchanged. The motive to constant self-control and thus to a deliberate regulation of one's own life, which the gloomy doctrine of Calvinism gave, was lacking. A religious genius like Luther could live in this atmosphere of openness and freedom without difficulty and, so long as his enthusiasm was powerful enough, without danger of falling back into the *status naturalis*. That simple, sensitive, and peculiarly emotional form of piety, which is the ornament of many of the highest types of Lutherans, like their free and spontaneous morality, finds few parallels in genuine Puritanism, but many more in the mild Anglicanism of such men as Hooker, Chillingsworth, etc. But for the everyday Lutheran, even the able one, nothing was more certain than that he was only temporarily, as long as the single confession or sermon affected him, raised above the *status naturalis*.

There was a great difference which was very striking to contemporaries between the moral standards of the courts of Reformed and of Lutheran princes, the latter often being degraded by drunkenness and vulgarity.[105] Moreover, the helplessness of the Lutheran clergy, with their emphasis on faith alone, against the ascetic Baptist movement, is well known. The typical German quality often called good nature (*Gemütlichkeit*) or naturalness contrasts strongly, even in the facial expressions of people, with the effects of that thorough destruction of the spontaneity of the *status naturalis* in the Anglo-American atmosphere, which Germans are accustomed to judge unfavourably as narrowness, unfreeness, and inner constraint. But the differences of conduct, which are very striking, have clearly originated in the lesser degree of ascetic penetration of life in Lutheranism as distinguished from Calvinism. The antipathy of every spontaneous child of nature to everything ascetic is expressed in those feelings. The fact is that Lutheranism, on account of its doctrine of grace, lacked a psychological sanction of systematic conduct to compel the methodical rationalization of life.

This sanction, which conditions the ascetic character of religion, could doubtless in itself have been furnished by various different religious motives, as we shall soon see. The Calvinistic doctrine of predestination was only one of several possibilities. But nevertheless we have become convinced that in its way it had not only a quite unique consistency, but that its psychological effect was extraordinarily powerful.[106] In comparison with it the non-Calvinistic ascetic movements, considered purely from the view-point of the religious motivation of asceticism, form an attenuation of the inner consistency and power of Calvinism.

But even in the actual historical development the situation was, for the most part, such that the Calvinistic form of asceticism was either imitated by the other ascetic movements or used as a source of inspiration or of comparison in the development of their divergent principles. Where, in spite of a different doctrinal basis, similar ascetic features have appeared, this has generally been the result of Church organization. Of this we shall come to speak in another connection.[107]

B. Pietism

Historically the doctrine of predestination is also the starting-point of the ascetic movement usually known as Pietism. In so far as the movement remained within the Reformed Church, it is almost impossible to draw the line between Pietistic and non-Pietistic Calvinists.[108] Almost all the leading representatives of Puritanism are sometimes classed among the Pietists. It is even quite legitimate to look upon the whole connection between predestination and the doctrine of proof, with its fundamental interest in the attainment of the *certitudo salutis* as discussed above, as in itself a Pietistic development of Calvin's original doctrines. The occurrence of ascetic revivals within the Reformed Church was, especially in Holland, regularly accompanied by a regeneration of the doctrine of predestination which had been temporarily forgotten or not strictly held to. Hence for England it is not customary to use the term Pietism at all.[109]

But even the Continental (Dutch and Lower Rhenish) Pietism in the Reformed Church was, at least fundamentally, just as much a simple intensification of the Reformed asceticism as, for instance, the doctrines of Bailey. The emphasis was placed so strongly on the *praxis pietatis* that doctrinal orthodoxy was pushed into the background; at times, in fact, it seemed quite a matter of indifference. Those predestined for grace could occasionally be subject to dogmatic error as well as to other sins and experience showed that often those Christians who were quite uninstructed in the theology of the schools exhibited the fruits of faith most clearly, while on the other hand it became evident that mere knowledge of theology by no means guaranteed the proof of faith through conduct.[110]

Thus election could not be proved by theological learning at all.[111] Hence Pietism, with a deep distrust of the Church of the theologians,[112] to which—this is characteristic of it—it still belonged officially, began to gather the adherents of the *praxis pietatis* in conventicles removed from the world.[113] It wished to make the invisible Church of the elect visible on this earth. Without going so far as to form a separate sect, its members attempted to live, in this community, a life freed from all the temptations of the world and in all its details dictated by God's will, and thus to be made certain of their own rebirth by external signs manifested in their daily conduct. Thus the *ecclesiola* of the true converts— this was common to all genuinely Pietistic groups— wished, by means of intensified asceticism, to enjoy the blissfulness of community with God in this life.

Now this latter tendency had something closely related to the Lutheran *unio mystica*, and very often led to a greater emphasis on the emotional side of religion than was acceptable to orthodox Calvinism. In fact this may, from our view-point, be said to be the decisive characteristic of the Pietism which developed within the Reformed Church. For this element of emotion, which was originally quite foreign to Calvinism, but on the other hand related to certain mediæval forms of religion, led religion in practice to strive for the enjoyment of salvation in this world rather than to engage in the ascetic struggle for certainty about the future world. Moreover, the emotion was capable of such intensity, that religion took on a positively hysterical character, resulting in the alternation which is familiar from examples without number and neuropathologically understandable, of half-conscious states of religious ecstasy with periods of nervous exhaustion, which were felt as abandonment by God. The effect was the direct opposite of the strict and temperate discipline under which men were placed by the systematic life of holiness of the Puritan. It meant a weakening of the inhibitions which protected the rational personality of the Calvinist from his passions.[114] Similarly it was possible for the Calvinistic idea of the depravity of the flesh, taken emotionally, for instance in the form of the so-called worm-feeling, to lead to a deadening of enterprise in worldly activity.[115] Even the doctrine of predestination could lead to fatalism if, contrary to the predominant tendencies of rational Calvinism, it were made the object of emotional contemplation.[116] Finally, the desire to separate the elect from the world could, with a strong emotional intensity, lead to a sort of monastic community life of half-communistic character, as the history of Pietism, even within the Reformed Church, has shown again and again.[117]

But so long as this extreme effect, conditioned by this emphasis on emotion, did not appear, as long as Reformed Pietism strove to make sure of salvation within the everyday routine of life in a worldly calling, the practical effect of Pietistic principles was an even stricter ascetic control of conduct in the calling, which provided a still more solid religious basis for the ethic of the calling, than the mere worldly respectability of the normal Reformed Christian, which was felt by the superior Pietist to be a second-rate Christianity. The religious aristocracy of the elect, which developed in every form of Calvinistic asceticism, the more seriously it was taken, the more surely, was then organized, in Holland, on a voluntary basis in the form of conventicles within the Church. In English Puritanism, on the other hand, it led partly to a virtual differentiation between active and passive Christians within the Church organization, and partly, as has been shown above, to the formation of sects.

On the other hand, the development of German Pietism from a Lutheran basis, with which the names of Spener, Francke, and Zinzendorf are connected, led away from the doctrine of predestination. But at the same time it was by no means outside the body of ideas of which that dogma formed the logical climax, as is especially attested by Spener's own account of the influence which English and Dutch Pietism had upon him, and is shown by the fact that Bailey was read in his first conventicles.[118]

From our special point of view, at any rate, Pietism meant simply the penetration of methodically controlled and supervised, thus of ascetic, conduct into the non-Calvinistic denominations.[119] But Lutheranism necessarily felt this rational asceticism to be a foreign element, and the lack of consistency in German Pietistic doctrines was the result of the difficulties growing out of that fact. As a dogmatic basis of systematic religious conduct Spener combines Lutheran ideas with the specifically Calvinistic doctrine of good works as such which are undertaken with the "intention of doing honour to God".[120] He also has a faith, suggestive of Calvinism, in the possibility of the elect attaining a relative degree of Christian perfection.[121] But the theory lacked consistency. Spener, who was strongly influenced by the mystics,[122] attempted, in a rather uncertain but essentially Lutheran manner, rather to describe the systematic type of Christian conduct which was essential to even his form of Pietism than to justify it. He did not derive the *certitudo salutis* from sanctification; instead of the idea of proof, he adopted Luther's somewhat loose connection between faith and works, which has been discussed above.[123]

But again and again, in so far as the rational and ascetic element of Pietism outweighed the emotional, the ideas essential to our thesis maintained their place. These were: (1) that the methodical development of one's own state of grace to a higher and higher degree of certainty and perfection in terms of the law was a sign of grace [124]; and (2) that "God's Providence works through those in such a state of perfection", i.e. in that He gives them His signs if they wait patiently and deliberate methodically.[125] Labour in a calling was also the ascetic activity *par excellence* for A. H. Francke [126]; that God Himself blessed His chosen ones through the success of their labours was as undeniable to him as we shall find it to have been to the Puritans.

And as a substitute for the double decree Pietism worked out ideas which, in a way essentially similar to Calvinism, though milder, established an aristocracy of the elect[127] resting on God's especial grace, with all the psychological results pointed out above. Among them belongs, for instance, the so-called doctrine of Terminism,[128] which was generally (though unjustly) attributed to Pietism by its opponents. It assumes that grace is offered to all men, but for everyone either once at a definite moment in his life or at some moment for the last time.[129] Anyone who let that moment pass was beyond the help of the universality of grace; he was in the same situation as those neglected by God in the Calvinistic doctrine. Quite close to this theory was the idea which Francke took from his personal experience, and which was very widespread in Pietism, one may even say predominant, that grace could only become effective under certain unique and peculiar circumstances, namely, after previous repentance.[130] Since, according to Pietist doctrine, not everyone was capable of such experiences, those who, in spite of the use of the ascetic methods recommended by the Pietists to bring it about, did not attain it, remained in the eyes of the regenerate a sort of passive Christian. On the other hand, by the creation of a method to induce repentance even the attainment of divine grace became in effect an object of rational human activity.

Moreover, the antagonism to the private confessional, which, though not shared by all—for instance, not by Francke—was characteristic of many Pietists, especially, as the repeated questions in Spener show, of Pietist pastors, resulted from this aristocracy of grace. This antagonism helped to weaken its ties with Lutheranism. The visible effects on conduct of grace gained through repentance formed a necessary criterion for admission to absolution; hence it was impossible to let *contritio* alone suffice.[131]

Zinzendorf's conception of his own religious position, even though it vacillated in the face of attacks from orthodoxy, tended generally toward the instrumental idea. Beyond that, however, the doctrinal standpoint of this remarkable religious dilettante, as Ritschl calls him, is scarcely capable of clear formula-

tion in the points of importance for us.[132] He repeatedly
designated himself a representative of Pauline-Lutheran
Christianity; hence he opposed the Pietistic type
associated with Jansen with its adherence to the law.
But the Brotherhood itself in practice upheld, as early
as its Protocol of August 12, 1729, a standpoint which
in many respects closely resembled that of the Calvinistic aristocracy of the elect.[133] And in spite of his
repeated avowals of Lutheranism,[134] he permitted and
encouraged it. The famous stand of attributing the Old
Testament to Christ, taken on November 12, 1741, was
the outward expression of somewhat the same attitude.
However, of the three branches of the Brotherhood,
both the Calvinistic and the Moravian accepted the
Reformed ethics in essentials from the beginning.
And even Zinzendorf followed the Puritans in expressing to John Wesley the opinion that even though
a man himself could not, others could know his state
of grace by his conduct.[135]

But on the other hand, in the peculiar piety of
Herrnhut, the emotional element held a very prominent
place. In particular Zinzendorf himself continually
attempted to counteract the tendency to ascetic
sanctification in the Puritan sense [136] and to turn the
interpretation of good works in a Lutheran direction.[137]
Also under the influence of the repudiation of conventicles and the retention of the confession, there
developed an essentially Lutheran dependence on the
sacraments. Moreover, Zinzendorf's peculiar principle
that the childlikeness of religious feeling was a sign of
its genuineness, as well as the use of the lot as a means
of revealing God's will, strongly counteracted the

influence of rationality in conduct. On the whole,
within the sphere of influence of the Count,[138] the
anti-rational, emotional elements predominated much
more in the religion of the Herrnhuters than elsewhere
in Pietism.[139] The connection between morality and
the forgiveness of sins in Spangenberg's *Idea fides
fratrum* is as loose [140] as in Lutheranism generally.
Zinzendorf's repudiation of the Methodist pursuit of
perfection is part, here as everywhere, of his fundamentally eudæmonistic ideal of having men experience
eternal bliss (he calls it happiness) emotionally in the
present,[141] instead of encouraging them by rational
labour to make sure of it in the next world.[142]

Nevertheless, the idea that the most important value
of the Brotherhood as contrasted with other Churches
lay in an active Christian life, in missionary, and, which
was brought into connection with it, in professional
work in a calling,[143] remained a vital force with them.
In addition, the practical rationalization of life from
the standpoint of utility was very essential to Zinzendorf's philosophy.[144] It was derived for him, as for
other Pietists, on the one hand from his decided dislike
of philosophical speculation as dangerous to faith,
and his corresponding preference for empirical knowledge [145]; on the other hand, from the shrewd common
sense of the professional missionary. The Brotherhood
was, as a great mission centre, at the same time a
business enterprise. Thus it led its members into the
paths of worldly asceticism, which everywhere first
seeks for tasks and then carries them out carefully and
systematically. However, the glorification of the apostolic poverty, of the disciples[146] chosen by God

136

through predestination, which was derived from the example of the apostles as missionaries, formed another obstacle. It meant in effect a partial revival of the *consilia evangelica*. The development of a rational economic ethic similar to the Calvinistic was certainly retarded by these factors, even though, as the development of the Baptist movement shows, it was not impossible, but on the contrary subjectively strongly encouraged by the idea of work solely for the sake of the calling.

All in all, when we consider German Pietism from the point of view important for us, we must admit a vacillation and uncertainty in the religious basis of its asceticism which makes it definitely weaker than the iron consistency of Calvinism, and which is partly the result of Lutheran influences and partly of its emotional character. To be sure, it is very one-sided to make this emotional element the distinguishing characteristic of Pietism as opposed to Lutheranism.[147] But compared to Calvinism, the rationalization of life was necessarily less intense because the pressure of occupation with a state of grace which had continually to be proved, and which was concerned for the future in eternity, was diverted to the present emotional state. The place of the self-confidence which the elect sought to attain, and continually to renew in restless and successful work at his calling, was taken by an attitude of humility and abnegation.[148] This in turn was partly the result of emotional stimulus directed solely toward spiritual experience; partly of the Lutheran institution of the confession, which, though it was often looked upon with serious doubts by Pietism, was still generally tolerated.[149] All this shows the influence of the peculiarly Lutheran conception of salvation by the forgiveness of sins and not by practical sanctification. In place of the systematic rational struggle to attain and retain certain knowledge of future (otherworldly) salvation comes here the need to feel reconciliation and community with God now. Thus the tendency of the pursuit of present enjoyment to hinder the rational organization of economic life, depending as it does on provision for the future, has in a certain sense a parallel in the field of religious life.

Evidently, then, the orientation of religious needs to present emotional satisfaction could not develop so powerful a motive to rationalize worldly activity, as the need of the Calvinistic elect for proof with their exclusive preoccupation with the beyond. On the other hand, it was considerably more favourable to the methodical penetration of conduct with religion than the traditionalistic faith of the orthodox Lutheran, bound as it was to the Word and the sacraments. On the whole Pietism from Francke and Spener to Zinzendorf tended toward increasing emphasis on the emotional side. But this was not in any sense the expression of an immanent law of development. The differences resulted from differences of the religious (and social) environments from which the leaders came. We cannot enter into that here, nor can we discuss how the peculiarities of German Pietism have affected its social and geographical extension.[150] We must again remind ourselves that this emotional Pietism of course shades off into the way of life of the Puritan elect by quite gradual stages. If we can, at least provisionally, point out any practical consequence of the difference, we may say that the virtues favoured by Pietism were more those on the one hand of the faithful official, clerk, labourer, or domestic worker,[151] and on the other of the predominantly patriarchal employer with a pious condescension (in Zinzendorf's manner). Calvinism, in comparison, appears to be more closely related to the hard legalism and the active enterprise of bourgeois-capitalistic entrepreneurs.[152] Finally, the purely emotional form of Pietism is, as Ritschl[153] has pointed out, a religious dilettantism for the leisure classes. However far this characterization falls short of being exhaustive, it helps to explain certain differences in the character (including the economic character) of peoples which have been under the influence of one or the other of these two ascetic movements.

C. Methodism

The combination of an emotional but still ascetic type of religion with increasing indifference to or repudiation of the dogmatic basis of Calvinistic asceticism is characteristic also of the Anglo-American movement corresponding to Continental Pietism, namely Methodism.[154] The name in itself shows what impressed contemporaries as characteristic of its adherents: the methodical, systematic nature of conduct for the purpose of attaining the *certitudo salutis*. This was from the beginning the centre of religious aspiration for this movement also, and remained so. In spite of all the differences, the undoubted relationship to certain branches of German Pietism[155] is shown above all by the fact that the method was used primarily to bring about the emotional act of conversion. And the emphasis on feeling, in John Wesley awakened by Moravian and Lutheran influences, led Methodism, which from the beginning saw its mission among the masses, to take on a strongly emotional character, especially in America. The attainment of repentance under certain circumstances involved an emotional struggle of such intensity as to lead to the most terrible ecstasies, which in America often took place in a public meeting. This formed the basis of a belief in the undeserved possession of divine grace and at the same time of an immediate consciousness of justification and forgiveness.

Now this emotional religion entered into a peculiar alliance, containing no small inherent difficulties, with the ascetic ethics which had for good and all been stamped with rationality by Puritanism. For one thing, unlike Calvinism, which held everything emotional to be illusory, the only sure basis for the *certitudo salutis* was in principle held to be a pure feeling of absolute certainty of forgiveness, derived immediately from the testimony of the spirit, the coming of which could be definitely placed to the hour. Added to this is Wesley's doctrine of sanctification which, though a decided departure from the orthodox doctrine, is a logical development of it. According to it, one reborn in this manner can, by virtue of the divine grace already working in him, even in this life attain sanctification, the consciousness of perfection in the sense of freedom from sin, by a second, generally separate and often sudden spiritual transformation. However difficult of attainment this end is, generally not till toward the end of one's life, it must inevitably be sought, because it finally guarantees the *certitudo salutis* and substitutes a serene confidence for the sullen worry of the Calvinist.[156] And it distinguishes the true convert in his own eyes and those of others by the fact that sin at least no longer has power over him.

In spite of the great significance of self-evident feeling, righteous conduct according to the law was thus naturally also adhered to. Whenever Wesley attacked the emphasis on works of his time, it was only to revive the old Puritan doctrine that works are not the cause, but only the means of knowing one's state of grace, and even this only when they are performed solely for the glory of God. Righteous conduct alone did not suffice, as he had found out for himself. The feeling of grace was necessary in addition. He himself sometimes described works as a condition of grace, and in the Declaration of August 9, 1771,[157] he emphasized that he who performed no good works was not a true believer. In fact, the Methodists have always maintained that they did not differ from the Established Church in doctrine, but only in religious practice. This emphasis on the fruits of belief was mostly justified by 1 John iii, 9; conduct is taken as a clear sign of rebirth.

But in spite of all that there were difficulties.[158] For those Methodists who were adherents of the doctrine of predestination, to think of the *certitudo salutis* as appearing in the immediate feeling[159] of grace and perfection instead of the consciousness of grace which grew out of ascetic conduct in continual proof of faith—

since then the certainty of the *perservantia* depended only on the single act of repentance—meant one of two things. For weak natures there was a fatalistic interpretation of Christian freedom, and with it the breakdown of methodical conduct; or, where this path was rejected, the self-confidence of the righteous man[160] reached untold heights, an emotional intensification of the Puritan type. In the face of the attacks of opponents, the attempt was made to meet these consequences. On the one hand by increased emphasis on the normative authority of the Bible and the indispensability of proof [161]; on the other by, in effect, strengthening Wesley's anti-Calvinistic faction within the movement with its doctrine that grace could be lost. The strong Lutheran influences to which Wesley was exposed[162] through the Moravians strengthened this tendency and increased the uncertainty of the religious basis of the Methodist ethics.[163] In the end only the concept of regeneration, an emotional certainty of salvation as the immediate result of faith, was definitely maintained as the indispensable foundation of grace; and with it sanctification, resulting in (at least virtual) freedom from the power of sin, as the consequent proof of grace. The significance of external means of grace, especially the sacraments, was correspondingly diminished. In any case, the general awakening which followed Methodism everywhere, for example in New England, meant a victory for the doctrine of grace and election.[164]

Thus from our view-point the Methodist ethic appears to rest on a foundation of uncertainty similar to Pietism. But the aspiration to the higher life, the second blessedness, served it as a sort of makeshift for the doctrine of predestination. Moreover, being English in origin, its ethical practice was closely related to that of English Puritanism, the revival of which it aspired to be.

The emotional act of conversion was methodically induced. And after it was attained there did not follow a pious enjoyment of community with God, after the manner of the emotional Pietism of Zinzendorf, but the emotion, once awakened, was directed into a rational struggle for perfection. Hence the emotional character of its faith did not lead to a spiritualized religion of feeling like German Pietism. It has already been shown by Schneckenburger that this fact was connected with the less intensive development of the sense of sin (partly directly on account of the emotional experience of conversion), and this has remained an accepted point in the discussion of Methodism. The fundamentally Calvinistic character of its religious feeling here remained decisive. The emotional excitement took the form of enthusiasm which was only occasionally, but then powerfully stirred, but which by no means destroyed the otherwise rational character of conduct.[165] The regeneration of Methodism thus created only a supplement to the pure doctrine of works, a religious basis for ascetic conduct after the doctrine of predestination had been given up. The signs given by conduct which formed an indispensable means of ascertaining true conversion, even its condition as Wesley occasionally says, were in fact just the same as those of Calvinism. As a late product [166] we can, in the following discussion, generally neglect Methodism, as it added nothing new to the development [167] of the idea of calling.

143

D. THE BAPTIST SECTS

The Pietism of the Continent of Europe and the Methodism of the Anglo-Saxon peoples are, considered both in their content of ideas and their historical significance, secondary movements.[168] On the other hand, we find a second independent source of Protestant asceticism besides Calvinism in the Baptist movement and the sects[169] which, in the course of the sixteenth and seventeenth centuries, came directly from it or adopted its forms of religious thought, the Baptists, Mennonites, and, above all, the Quakers.[170] With them we approach religious groups whose ethics rest upon a basis differing in principle from the Calvinistic doctrine. The following sketch, which only emphasizes what is important for us, can give no true impression of the diversity of this movement. Again we lay the principal emphasis on the development in the older capitalistic countries.

The feature of all these communities, which is both historically and in principle most important, but whose influence on the development of culture can only be made quite clear in a somewhat different connection, is something with which we are already familiar, the believer's Church.[171] This means that the religious community, the visible Church in the language of the Reformation Churches,[172] was no longer looked upon as a sort of trust foundation for supernatural ends, an institution, necessarily including both the just and the unjust, whether for increasing the glory of God (Calvinistic) or as a medium for bringing the means of salvation to men (Catholic and Lutheran), but

144

solely as a community of personal believers of the reborn, and only these. In other words, not as a Church but as a sect.[173] This is all that the principle, in itself purely external, that only adults who have personally gained their own faith should be baptized, is meant to symbolize.[174] The justification through this faith was for the Baptists, as they have insistently repeated in all religious discussions, radically different from the idea of work in the world in the service of Christ, such as dominated the orthodox dogma of the older Protestantism.[175] It consisted rather in taking spiritual possession of His gift of salvation. But this occurred through individual revelation, by the working of the Divine Spirit in the individual, and only in that way. It was offered to everyone, and it sufficed to wait for the Spirit, and not to resist its coming by a sinful attachment to the world. The significance of faith in the sense of knowledge of the doctrines of the Church, but also in that of a repentant search for divine grace, was consequently quite minimized, and there took place, naturally with great modifications, a renaissance of Early Christian pneumatic doctrines. For instance, the sect to which Menno Simons in his *Fondamentboek* (1539) gave the first reasonably consistent doctrine, wished, like the other Baptist sects, to be the true blameless Church of Christ; like the apostolic community, consisting entirely of those personally awakened and called by God. Those who have been born again, and they alone, are brethren of Christ, because they, like Him, have been created in spirit directly by God.[176] A strict avoidance of the world, in the sense of all not strictly necessary intercourse with worldly people, together with the strictest bibliocracy in the sense of taking the life of the first generations of Christians as a model, were the results for the first Baptist communities, and this principle of avoidance of the world never quite disappeared so long as the old spirit remained alive.[177]

As a permanent possession, the Baptist sects retained from these dominating motives of their early period a principle with which, on a somewhat different foundation, we have already become acquainted in Calvinism, and the fundamental importance of which will again and again come out. They absolutely repudiated all idolatry of the flesh, as a detraction from the reverence due to God alone.[178] The Biblical way of life was conceived by the first Swiss and South German Baptists with a radicalism similar to that of the young St. Francis, as a sharp break with all the enjoyment of life, a life modelled directly on that of the Apostles. And, in truth, the life of many of the earlier Baptists is reminiscent of that of St. Giles. But this strict observation of Biblical precepts[179] was not on very secure foundations in its connection with the pneumatic character of the faith. What God had revealed to the prophets and apostles was not all that He could and would reveal. On the contrary, the continued life of the Word, not as a written document, but as the force of the Holy Spirit working in daily life, which speaks directly to any individual who is willing to hear, was the sole characteristic of the true Church. That, as Schwenkfeld taught as against Luther and later Fox against the Presbyterians, was the testimony of the early Christian communities. From this idea of the continuance of revelation developed the well-known doctrine, later consistently worked out by the Quakers, of the (in the last analysis decisive) significance of the inner testimony of the Spirit in reason and conscience. This did away, not with the authority, but with the sole authority, of the Bible, and started a development which in the end radically eliminated all that remained of the doctrine of salvation through the Church; for the Quakers even with Baptism and the Communion.[180]

The Baptist denominations along with the pre-destinationists, especially the strict Calvinists, carried out the most radical devaluation of all sacraments as means to salvation, and thus accomplished the religious rationalization of the world in its most extreme form. Only the inner light of continual revelation could enable one truly to understand even the Biblical revelations of God.[181] On the other hand, at least according to the Quaker doctrine which here drew the logical conclusion, its effects could be extended to people who had never known revelation in its Biblical form. The proposition *extra ecclesiam nulla salus* held only for this *in*visible Church of those illuminated by the Spirit. Without the inner light, the natural man, even the man guided by natural reason,[182] remained purely a creature of the flesh, whose godlessness was condemned by the Baptists, including the Quakers, almost even more harshly than by the Calvinists. On the other hand, the new birth caused by the Spirit, if we wait for it and open our hearts to it, may, since it is divinely caused, lead to a state of such complete conquest of the power of sin,[183] that relapses, to say nothing of the loss of the state of grace, become practically impossible. However, as in Methodism at a later time, the attainment of that state was not thought of as the rule, but rather the degree of perfection of the individual was subject to development.

But all Baptist communities desired to be pure Churches in the sense of the blameless conduct of their members. A sincere repudiation of the world and its interests, and unconditional submission to God as speaking through the conscience, were the only unchallengeable signs of true rebirth, and a corresponding type of conduct was thus indispensable to salvation. And hence the gift of God's grace could not be earned, but only one who followed the dictates of his conscience could be justified in considering himself reborn. Good works in this sense were a *causa sine qua non*. As we see, this last reasoning of Barclay, to whose exposition we have adhered, was again the equivalent in practice of the Calvinistic doctrine, and was certainly developed under the influence of the Calvinistic asceticism, which surrounded the Baptist sects in England and the Netherlands. George Fox devoted the whole of his early missionary activity to the preaching of its earnest and sincere adoption.

But, since predestination was rejected, the peculiarly rational character of Baptist morality rested psychologically above all on the idea of expectant waiting for the Spirit to descend, which even to-day is characteristic of the Quaker meeting, and is well analysed by Barclay. The purpose of this silent waiting is to overcome everything impulsive and irrational, the passions and subjective interests of the natural man. He must be stilled in order to create that deep repose of the

148

soul in which alone the word of God can be heard. Of course, this waiting might result in hysterical conditions, prophecy, and, as long as eschatological hopes survived, under certain circumstances even in an outbreak of chiliastic enthusiasm, as is possible in all similar types of religion. That actually happened in the movement which went to pieces in Münster.

But in so far as Baptism affected the normal workaday world, the idea that God only speaks when the flesh is silent evidently meant an incentive to the deliberate weighing of courses of action and their careful justification in terms of the individual conscience.[184] The later Baptist communities, most particularly the Quakers, adopted this quiet, moderate, eminently conscientious character of conduct. The radical elimination of magic from the world allowed no other psychological course than the practice of worldly asceticism. Since these communities would have nothing to do with the political powers and their doings, the external result also was the penetration of life in the calling with these ascetic virtues. The leaders of the earliest Baptist movement were ruthlessly radical in their rejection of worldliness. But naturally, even in the first generation, the strictly apostolic way of life was not maintained as absolutely essential to the proof of rebirth for everyone. Well-to-do bourgeois there were, even in this generation and even before Menno, who definitely defended the practical worldly virtues and the system of private property; the strict morality of the Baptists had turned in practice into the path prepared by the Calvinistic ethic.[185] This was simply because the road to the otherworldly monastic form of asceticism had been closed as unbiblical and savouring of salvation by works since Luther, whom the Baptists also followed in this respect.

Nevertheless, apart from the half-communistic communities of the early period, one Baptist sect, the so-called Dunckards (*Tunker, dompelaers*), has to this day maintained its condemnation of education and of every form of possession beyond that indispensable to life. And even Barclay looks upon the obligation to one's calling not in Calvinistic or even Lutheran terms, but rather Thomistically, as *naturali ratione*, the necessary consequence of the believers having to live in the world.[186]

This attitude meant a weakening of the Calvinistic conception of the calling similar to those of Spener and the German Pietists. But, on the other hand, the intensity of interest in economic occupations was considerably increased by various factors at work in the Baptist sects. In the first place, by the refusal to accept office in the service of the State, which originated as a religious duty following from the repudiation of everything worldly. After its abandonment in principle it still remained, at least for the Mennonites and Quakers, effective in practice, because the strict refusal to bear arms or to take oaths formed a sufficient disqualification for office. Hand in hand with it in all Baptists' denominations went an invincible antagonism to any sort of aristocratic way of life. Partly, as with the Calvinists, it was a consequence of the prohibition of all idolatry of the flesh, partly a result of the aforementioned unpolitical or even anti-political principles. The whole shrewd and conscientious rationality of

Baptist conduct was thus forced into non-political callings.

At the same time, the immense importance which was attributed by the Baptist doctrine of salvation to the rôle of the conscience as the revelation of God to the individual gave their conduct in worldly callings a character which was of the greatest significance for the development of the spirit of capitalism. We shall have to postpone its consideration until later, and it can then be studied only in so far as this is possible without entering into the whole political and social ethics of Protestant asceticism. But, to anticipate this much, we have already called attention to that most important principle of the capitalistic ethic which is generally formulated "honesty is the best policy".[187] Its classical document is the tract of Franklin quoted above. And even in the judgment of the seventeenth century the specific form of the worldly asceticism of the Baptists, especially the Quakers, lay in the practical adoption of this maxim.[188] On the other hand, we shall expect to find that the influence of Calvinism was exerted more in the direction of the liberation of energy for private acquisition. For in spite of all the formal legalism of the elect, Goethe's remark in fact applied often enough to the Calvinist: "The man of action is always ruthless; no one has a conscience but an observer."[189]

A further important element which promoted the intensity of the worldly asceticism of the Baptist denominations can in its full significance also be considered only in another connection. Nevertheless, we may anticipate a few remarks on it to justify the order of presentation we have chosen. We have quite deliberately not taken as a starting-point the objective social institutions of the older Protestant Churches, and their ethical influences, especially not the very important Church discipline. We have preferred rather to take the results which subjective adoption of an ascetic faith might have had in the conduct of the individual. This was not only because this side of the thing has previously received far less attention than the other, but also because the effect of Church discipline was by no means always a similar one. On the contrary, the ecclesiastical supervision of the life of the individual, which, as it was practised in the Calvinistic State Churches, almost amounted to an inquisition, might even retard that liberation of individual powers which was conditioned by the rational ascetic pursuit of salvation, and in some cases actually did so.

The mercantilistic regulations of the State might develop industries, but not, or certainly not alone, the spirit of capitalism; where they assumed a despotic, authoritarian character, they to a large extent directly hindered it. Thus a similar effect might well have resulted from ecclesiastical regimentation when it became excessively despotic. It enforced a particular type of external conformity, but in some cases weakened the subjective motives of rational conduct. Any discussion of this point[190] must take account of the great difference between the results of the authoritarian moral discipline of the Established Churches and the corresponding discipline in the sects which rested on voluntary submission. That the Baptist movement everywhere and in principle founded sects and not Churches was certainly as favourable to the intensity of their asceticism as was the case, to differing degrees, with those Calvinistic, Methodist, and Pietist communities which were driven by their situations into the formation of voluntary groups.[191]

It is our next task to follow out the results of the Puritan idea of the calling in the business world, now that the above sketch has attempted to show its religious foundations. With all the differences of detail and emphasis which these different ascetic movements show in the aspects with which we have been concerned, much the same characteristics are present and important in all of them.[192] But for our purposes the decisive point was, to recapitulate, the conception of the state of religious grace, common to all the denominations, as a status which marks off its possessor from the degradation of the flesh, from the world.[193]

On the other hand, though the means by which it was attained differed for different doctrines, it could not be guaranteed by any magical sacraments, by relief in the confession, nor by individual good works. That was only possible by proof in a specific type of conduct unmistakably different from the way of life of the natural man. From that followed for the individual an incentive methodically to supervise his own state of grace in his own conduct, and thus to penetrate it with asceticism. But, as we have seen, this ascetic conduct meant a rational planning of the whole of one's life in accordance with God's will. And this asceticism was no longer an *opus supererogationis*, but something which could be required of everyone who would be certain of salvation. The religious life of the saints, as distinguished from the natural life, was—the most important point—no longer lived outside the world in monastic communities, but within the world and its institutions. This rationalization of conduct within this world, but for the sake of the world beyond, was the consequence of the concept of calling of ascetic Protestantism.

Christian asceticism, at first fleeing from the world into solitude, had already ruled the world which it had renounced from the monastery and through the Church. But it had, on the whole, left the naturally spontaneous character of daily life in the world untouched. Now it strode into the market-place of life, slammed the door of the monastery behind it, and undertook to penetrate just that daily routine of life with its methodicalness, to fashion it into a life in the world, but neither of nor for this world. With what result, we shall try to make clear in the following discussion.

CHAPTER V

ASCETICISM AND THE SPIRIT OF CAPITALISM

In order to understand the connection between the fundamental religious ideas of ascetic Protestantism and its maxims for everyday economic conduct, it is necessary to examine with especial care such writings as have evidently been derived from ministerial practice. For in a time in which the beyond meant everything, when the social position of the Christian depended upon his admission to the communion, the clergyman, through his ministry, Church discipline, and preaching, exercised an influence (as a glance at collections of *consilia*, *casus conscientiæ*, etc., shows) which we modern men are entirely unable to picture. In such a time the religious forces which express themselves through such channels are the decisive influences in the formation of national character.

For the purposes of this chapter, though by no means for all purposes, we can treat ascetic Protestantism as a single whole. But since that side of English Puritanism which was derived from Calvinism gives the most consistent religious basis for the idea of the calling, we shall, following our previous method, place one of its representatives at the centre of the discussion. Richard Baxter stands out above many other writers on Puritan ethics, both because of his eminently practical and realistic attitude, and, at the same time, because of the universal recognition accorded to his works, which have gone through many

155

new editions and translations. He was a Presbyterian and an apologist of the Westminster Synod, but at the same time, like so many of the best spirits of his time, gradually grew away from the dogmas of pure Calvinism. At heart he opposed Cromwell's usurpation as he would any revolution. He was unfavourable to the sects and the fanatical enthusiasm of the saints, but was very broad-minded about external peculiarities and objective towards his opponents. He sought his field of labour most especially in the practical promotion of the moral life through the Church. In the pursuit of this end, as one of the most successful ministers known to history, he placed his services at the disposal of the Parliamentary Government, of Cromwell, and of the Restoration,[1] until he retired from office under the last, before St. Bartholomew's day. His *Christian Directory* is the most complete compendium of Puritan ethics, and is continually adjusted to the practical experiences of his own ministerial activity. In comparison we shall make use of Spener's *Theologische Bedenken*, as representative of German Pietism, Barclay's *Apology* for the Quakers, and some other representatives of ascetic ethics,[2] which, however, in the interest of space, will be limited as far as possible.[3]

Now, in glancing at Baxter's *Saints' Everlasting Rest*, or his *Christian Directory*, or similar works of others,[4] one is struck at first glance by the emphasis placed, in the discussion of wealth[5] and its acquisition, on the ebionitic elements of the New Testament.[6] Wealth as such is a great danger; its temptations never end, and its pursuit[7] is not only senseless as compared with the dominating importance of the Kingdom of God, but it is morally suspect. Here asceticism seems to have turned much more sharply against the acquisition of earthly goods than it did in Calvin, who saw no hindrance to the effectiveness of the clergy in their wealth, but rather a thoroughly desirable enhancement of their prestige. Hence he permitted them to employ their means profitably. Examples of the condemnation of the pursuit of money and goods may be gathered without end from Puritan writings, and may be contrasted with the late mediæval ethical literature, which was much more open-minded on this point.

Moreover, these doubts were meant with perfect seriousness; only it is necessary to examine them somewhat more closely in order to understand their true ethical significance and implications. The real moral objection is to relaxation in the security of possession,[8] the enjoyment of wealth with the consequence of idleness and the temptations of the flesh, above all of distraction from the pursuit of a righteous life. In fact, it is only because possession involves this danger of relaxation that it is objectionable at all. For the saints' everlasting rest is in the next world; on earth man must, to be certain of his state of grace, "do the works of him who sent him, as long as it is yet day". Not leisure and enjoyment, but only activity serves to increase the glory of God, according to the definite manifestations of His will.[9]

Waste of time is thus the first and in principle the deadliest of sins. The span of human life is infinitely short and precious to make sure of one's own election. Loss of time through sociability, idle talk,[10] luxury,[11] even more sleep than is necessary for health,[12] six to at most eight hours, is worthy of absolute moral condemnation.[13] It does not yet hold, with Franklin, that time is money, but the proposition is true in a certain spiritual sense. It is infinitely valuable because every hour lost is lost to labour for the glory of God.[14] Thus inactive contemplation is also valueless, or even directly reprehensible if it is at the expense of one's daily work.[15] For it is less pleasing to God than the active performance of His will in a calling.[16] Besides, Sunday is provided for that, and, according to Baxter, it is always those who are not diligent in their callings who have no time for God when the occasion demands it.[17]

Accordingly, Baxter's principal work is dominated by the continually repeated, often almost passionate preaching of hard, continuous bodily or mental labour.[18] It is due to a combination of two different motives.[19] Labour is, on the one hand, an approved ascetic technique, as it always has been[20] in the Western Church, in sharp contrast not only to the Orient but to almost all monastic rules the world over.[21] It is in particular the specific defence against all those temptations which Puritanism united under the name of the unclean life, whose rôle for it was by no means small. The sexual asceticism of Puritanism differs only in degree, not in fundamental principle, from that of monasticism; and on account of the Puritan conception of marriage, its practical influence is more far-reaching than that of the latter. For sexual intercourse is permitted, even within marriage, only as the means willed by God for the increase of His glory according to the commandment, "Be fruitful and multiply." [22] Along with a moderate vegetable diet and cold baths, the same prescription is given for all sexual temptations as is used against religious doubts and a sense of moral unworthiness: "Work hard in your calling." [23] But the most important thing was that even beyond that labour came to be considered in itself [24] the end of life, ordained as such by God. St. Paul's "He who will not work shall not eat" holds unconditionally for everyone.[25] Unwillingness to work is symptomatic of the lack of grace.[26]

Here the difference from the mediæval view-point becomes quite evident. Thomas Aquinas also gave an interpretation of that statement of St. Paul. But for him[27] labour is only necessary *naturali ratione* for the maintenance of individual and community. Where this end is achieved, the precept ceases to have any meaning. Moreover, it holds only for the race, not for every individual. It does not apply to anyone who can live without labour on his possessions, and of course contemplation, as a spiritual form of action in the Kingdom of God, takes precedence over the commandment in its literal sense. Moreover, for the popular theology of the time, the highest form of monastic productivity lay in the increase of the *Thesaurus ecclesiæ* through prayer and chant.

Now only do these exceptions to the duty to labour naturally no longer hold for Baxter, but he holds most emphatically that wealth does not exempt anyone from the unconditional command.[28] Even the wealthy shall not eat without working, for even though they do not need to labour to support their own needs, there is God's commandment which they, like the poor, must obey.[29] For everyone without exception God's Providence has prepared a calling, which he should profess and in which he should labour. And this calling is not, as it was for the Lutheran,[30] a fate to which he must submit and which he must make the best of, but God's commandment to the individual to work for the divine glory. This seemingly subtle difference had far-reaching psychological consequences, and became connected with a further development of the providential interpretation of the economic order which had begun in scholasticism.

The phenomenon of the division of labour and occupations in society had, among others, been interpreted by Thomas Aquinas, to whom we may most conveniently refer, as a direct consequence of the divine scheme of things. But the places assigned to each man in this cosmos follow *ex causis naturalibus* and are fortuitous (contingent in the Scholastic terminology). The differentiation of men into the classes and occupations established through historical development became for Luther, as we have seen, a direct result of the divine will. The perseverance of the individual in the place and within the limits which God had assigned to him was a religious duty.[31] This was the more certainly the consequence since the relations of Lutheranism to the world were in general uncertain from the beginning and remained so. Ethical principles for the reform of the world could not be found in Luther's realm of ideas; in fact it never quite freed itself from Pauline indifference. Hence the world had to be accepted as it was, and this alone could be made a religious duty.

But in the Puritan view, the providential character of the play of private economic interests takes on a somewhat different emphasis. True to the Puritan tendency to pragmatic interpretations, the providential purpose of the division of labour is to be known by its fruits. On this point Baxter expresses himself in terms which more than once directly recall Adam Smith's well-known apotheosis of the division of labour.[32] The specialization of occupations leads, since it makes the development of skill possible, to a quantitative and qualitative improvement in production, and thus serves the common good, which is identical with the good of the greatest possible number. So far, the motivation is purely utilitarian, and is closely related to the customary view-point of much of the secular literature of the time.[33]

But the characteristic Puritan element appears when Baxter sets at the head of his discussion the statement that "outside of a well-marked calling the accomplishments of a man are only casual and irregular, and he spends more time in idleness than at work", and when he concludes it as follows: "and he [the specialized worker] will carry out his work in order while another remains in constant confusion, and his business knows neither time nor place [34] . . . therefore is a certain calling the best for everyone". Irregular work, which the ordinary labourer is often forced to accept, is often unavoidable, but always an unwelcome state of transition. A man without a calling thus lacks the systematic, methodical character which is, as we have seen, demanded by worldly asceticism.

The Quaker ethic also holds that a man's life in his calling is an exercise in ascetic virtue, a proof of his state of grace through his conscientiousness, which is expressed in the care [35] and method with which he pursues his calling. What God demands is not labour in itself, but rational labour in a calling. In the Puritan concept of the calling the emphasis is always placed on this methodical character of worldly asceticism, not, as with Luther, on the acceptance of the lot which God has irretrievably assigned to man.[36]

Hence the question whether anyone may combine several callings is answered in the affirmative, if it is useful for the common good or one's own,[37] and not injurious to anyone, and if it does not lead to unfaithfulness in one of the callings. Even a change of calling is by no means regarded as objectionable, if it is not thoughtless and is made for the purpose of pursuing a calling more pleasing to God,[38] which means, on general principles, one more useful.

It is true that the usefulness of a calling, and thus its favour in the sight of God, is measured primarily in moral terms, and thus in terms of the importance of the goods produced in it for the community. But a further, and, above all, in practice the most important, criterion is found in private profitableness.[39] For if that God, whose hand the Puritan sees in all the occurrences of life, shows one of His elect a chance of profit, he must do it with a purpose. Hence the faithful Christian must follow the call by taking advantage of the opportunity.[40] "If God show you a way in which you may lawfully get more than in another way (without wrong to your soul or to any other), if you refuse this, and choose the less gainful way, you cross one of the ends of your calling, and you refuse to be God's steward, and to accept His gifts and use them for Him when He requireth it: you may labour to be rich for God, though not for the flesh and sin."[41]

162

Wealth is thus bad ethically only in so far as it is a temptation to idleness and sinful enjoyment of life, and its acquisition is bad only when it is with the purpose of later living merrily and without care. But as a performance of duty in a calling it is not only morally permissible, but actually enjoined.[42] The parable of the servant who was rejected because he did not increase the talent which was entrusted to him seemed to say so directly.[43] To wish to be poor was, it was often argued, the same as wishing to be unhealthy [44]; it is objectionable as a glorification of works and derogatory to the glory of God. Especially begging, on the part of one able to work, is not only the sin of slothfulness, but a violation of the duty of brotherly love according to the Apostle's own word.[45]

The emphasis on the ascetic importance of a fixed calling provided an ethical justification of the modern specialized division of labour. In a similar way the providential interpretation of profit-making justified the activities of the business man.[46] The superior indulgence of the *seigneur* and the parvenu ostentation of the *nouveau riche* are equally detestable to asceticism. But, on the other hand, it has the highest ethical appreciation of the sober, middle-class, self-made man.[47] "God blesseth His trade" is a stock remark about those good men[48] who had successfully followed the divine hints. The whole power of the God of the Old Testament, who rewards His people for their obedience in this life,[49] necessarily exercised a similar influence on the Puritan who, following Baxter's advice, compared his own state of grace with that of the heroes of the Bible,[50] and in the process interpreted

163

the statements of the Scriptures as the articles of a book of statutes.

Of course, the words of the Old Testament were not entirely without ambiguity. We have seen that Luther first used the concept of the calling in the secular sense in translating a passage from Jesus Sirach. But the book of Jesus Sirach belongs, with the whole atmosphere expressed in it, to those parts of the broadened Old Testament with a distinctly traditionalistic tendency, in spite of Hellenistic influences. It is characteristic that down to the present day this book seems to enjoy a special favour among Lutheran German peasants,[51] just as the Lutheran influence in large sections of German Pietism has been expressed by a preference for Jesus Sirach.[52]

The Puritans repudiated the Apocrypha as not inspired, consistently with their sharp distinction between things divine and things of the flesh.[53] But among the canonical books that of Job had all the more influence. On the one hand it contained a grand conception of the absolute sovereign majesty of God, beyond all human comprehension, which was closely related to that of Calvinism. With that, on the other hand, it combined the certainty which, though incidental for Calvin, came to be of great importance for Puritanism, that God would bless His own in this life—in the book of Job only—and also in the material sense.[54] The Oriental quietism, which appears in several of the finest verses of the Psalms and in the Proverbs, was interpreted away, just as Baxter did with the traditionalistic tinge of the passage in the 1st Epistle to the Corinthians, so important for the idea of the calling.

164

But all the more emphasis was placed on those parts of the Old Testament which praise formal legality as a sign of conduct pleasing to God. They held the theory that the Mosaic Law had only lost its validity through Christ in so far as it contained ceremonial or purely historical precepts applying only to the Jewish people, but that otherwise it had always been valid as an expression of the natural law, and must hence be retained.[55] This made it possible, on the one hand, to eliminate elements which could not be reconciled with modern life. But still, through its numerous related features, Old Testament morality was able to give a powerful impetus to that spirit of self-righteous and sober legality which was so characteristic of the worldly asceticism of this form of Protestantism.[56]

Thus when authors, as was the case with several contemporaries as well as later writers, characterize the basic ethical tendency of Puritanism, especially in England, as English Hebraism[57] they are, correctly understood, not wrong. It is necessary, however, not to think of Palestinian Judaism at the time of the writing of the Scriptures, but of Judaism as it became under the influence of many centuries of formalistic, legalistic, and Talmudic education. Even then one must be very careful in drawing parallels. The general tendency of the older Judaism toward a naïve acceptance of life as such was far removed from the special characteristics of Puritanism. It was, however, just as far—and this ought not to be overlooked—from the economic ethics of mediæval and modern Judaism, in the traits which determined the positions of both in the development of the capitalistic ethos. The Jews stood on the side of the politically and speculatively oriented adventurous capitalism; their ethos was, in a word, that of pariah-capitalism. But Puritanism carried the ethos of the rational organization of capital and labour. It took over from the Jewish ethic only what was adapted to this purpose.

To analyse the effects on the character of peoples of the penetration of life with Old Testament norms—a tempting task which, however, has not yet satisfactorily been done even for Judaism [58]—would be impossible within the limits of this sketch. In addition to the relationships already pointed out, it is important for the general inner attitude of the Puritans, above all, that the belief that they were God's chosen people saw in them a great renaissance.[59] Even the kindly Baxter thanked God that he was born in England, and thus in the true Church, and nowhere else. This thankfulness for one's own perfection by the grace of God penetrated the attitude toward life [60] of the Puritan middle class, and played its part in developing that formalistic, hard, correct character which was peculiar to the men of that heroic age of capitalism.

Let us now try to clarify the points in which the Puritan idea of the calling and the premium it placed upon ascetic conduct was bound directly to influence the development of a capitalistic way of life. As we have seen, this asceticism turned with all its force against one thing: the spontaneous enjoyment of life and all it had to offer. This is perhaps most characteristically brought out in the struggle over the *Book of Sports* [61] which James I and Charles I made into law expressly as a means of counteracting Puritanism, and which

166

the latter ordered to be read from all the pulpits. The fanatical opposition of the Puritans to the ordinances of the King, permitting certain popular amusements on Sunday outside of Church hours by law, was not only explained by the disturbance of the Sabbath rest, but also by resentment against the intentional diversion from the ordered life of the saint, which it caused. And, on his side, the King's threats of severe punishment for every attack on the legality of those sports were motivated by his purpose of breaking the anti-authoritarian ascetic tendency of Puritanism, which was so dangerous to the State. The feudal and monarchical forces protected the pleasure seekers against the rising middle-class morality and the anti-authoritarian ascetic conventicles, just as to-day capitalistic society tends to protect those willing to work against the class morality of the proletariat and the anti-authoritarian trade union.

As against this the Puritans upheld their decisive characteristic, the principle of ascetic conduct. For otherwise the Puritan aversion to sport, even for the Quakers, was by no means simply one of principle. Sport was accepted if it served a rational purpose, that of recreation necessary for physical efficiency. But as a means for the spontaneous expression of undisciplined impulses, it was under suspicion; and in so far as it became purely a means of enjoyment, or awakened pride, raw instincts or the irrational gambling instinct, it was of course strictly condemned. Impulsive enjoyment of life, which leads away both from work in a calling and from religion, was as such the enemy of rational asceticism, whether in the form of seigneurial

167

sports, or the enjoyment of the dance-hall or the public-house of the common man.[62]

Its attitude was thus suspicious and often hostile to the aspects of culture without any immediate religious value. It is not, however, true that the ideals of Puritanism implied a solemn, narrow-minded contempt of culture. Quite the contrary is the case at least for science, with the exception of the hatred of Scholasticism. Moreover, the great men of the Puritan movement were thoroughly steeped in the culture of the Renaissance. The sermons of the Presbyterian divines abound with classical allusions,[63] and even the Radicals, although they objected to it, were not ashamed to display that kind of learning in theological polemics. Perhaps no country was ever so full of graduates as New England in the first generation of its existence. The satire of their opponents, such as, for instance, Butler's *Hudibras*, also attacks primarily the pedantry and highly trained dialectics of the Puritans. This is partially due to the religious valuation of knowledge which followed from their attitude to the Catholic *fides implicita*.

But the situation is quite different when one looks at non-scientific literature,[64] and especially the fine arts. Here asceticism descended like a frost on the life of "Merrie old England." And not only worldly merriment felt its effect. The Puritan's ferocious hatred of everything which smacked of superstition, of all survivals of magical or sacramental salvation, applied to the Christmas festivities and the May Pole [65] and all spontaneous religious art. That there was room in Holland for a great, often uncouthly realistic art[66] proves only how far from completely the authoritarian moral discipline of that country was able to counteract the influence of the court and the regents (a class of *rentiers*), and also the joy in life of the parvenu bourgeoisie, after the short supremacy of the Calvinistic theocracy had been transformed into a moderate national Church, and with it Calvinism had perceptibly lost in its power of ascetic influence.[67]

The theatre was obnoxious to the Puritans,[68] and with the strict exclusion of the erotic and of nudity from the realm of toleration, a radical view of either literature or art could not exist. The conceptions of idle talk, of superfluities,[69] and of vain ostentation, all designations of an irrational attitude without objective purpose, thus not ascetic, and especially not serving the glory of God, but of man, were always at hand to serve in deciding in favour of sober utility as against any artistic tendencies. This was especially true in the case of decoration of the person, for instance clothing.[70] That powerful tendency toward uniformity of life, which to-day so immensely aids the capitalistic interest in the standardization of production,[71] had its ideal foundations in the repudiation of all idolatry of the flesh.[72]

Of course we must not forget that Puritanism included a world of contradictions, and that the instinctive sense of eternal greatness in art was certainly stronger among its leaders than in the atmosphere of the Cavaliers.[73] Moreover, a unique genius like Rembrandt, however little his conduct may have been acceptable to God in the eyes of the Puritans, was very strongly influenced in the character of his work by his religious environment.[74] But that does not alter the picture as a whole. In so far as the development of

169

the Puritan tradition could, and in part did, lead to a powerful spiritualization of personality, it was a decided benefit to literature. But for the most part that benefit only accrued to later generations.

Although we cannot here enter upon a discussion of the influence of Puritanism in all these directions, we should call attention to the fact that the toleration of pleasure in cultural goods, which contributed to purely æsthetic or athletic enjoyment, certainly always ran up against one characteristic limitation: they must not cost anything. Man is only a trustee of the goods which have come to him through God's grace. He must, like the servant in the parable, give an account of every penny entrusted to him,[75] and it is at least hazardous to spend any of it for a purpose which does not serve the glory of God but only one's own enjoyment.[76] What person, who keeps his eyes open, has not met representatives of this view-point even in the present?[77] The idea of a man's duty to his possessions, to which he subordinates himself as an obedient steward, or even as an acquisitive machine, bears with chilling weight on his life. The greater the possessions the heavier, if the ascetic attitude toward life stands the test, the feeling of responsibility for them, for holding them undiminished for the glory of God and increasing them by restless effort. The origin of this type of life also extends in certain roots, like so many aspects of the spirit of capitalism, back into the Middle Ages.[78] But it was in the ethic of ascetic Protestantism that it first found a consistent ethical foundation. Its significance for the development of capitalism is obvious.[79]

This worldly Protestant asceticism, as we may

recapitulate up to this point, acted powerfully against the spontaneous enjoyment of possessions; it restricted consumption, especially of luxuries. On the other hand, it had the psychological effect of freeing the acquisition of goods from the inhibitions of traditionalistic ethics. It broke the bonds of the impulse of acquisition in that it not only legalized it, but (in the sense discussed) looked upon it as directly willed by God. The campaign against the temptations of the flesh, and the dependence on external things, was, as besides the Puritans the great Quaker apologist Barclay expressly says, not a struggle against the rational acquisition, but against the irrational use of wealth.

But this irrational use was exemplified in the outward forms of luxury which their code condemned as idolatry of the flesh,[80] however natural they had appeared to the feudal mind. On the other hand, they approved the rational and utilitarian uses of wealth which were willed by God for the needs of the individual and the community. They did not wish to impose mortification[81] on the man of wealth, but the use of his means for necessary and practical things. The idea of comfort characteristically limits the extent of ethically permissible expenditures. It is naturally no accident that the development of a manner of living consistent with that idea may be observed earliest and most clearly among the most consistent representatives of this whole attitude toward life. Over against the glitter and ostentation of feudal magnificence which, resting on an unsound economic basis, prefers a sordid elegance to a sober simplicity, they set the clean and solid comfort of the middle-class home as an ideal.[82]

On the side of the production of private wealth, asceticism condemned both dishonesty and impulsive avarice. What was condemned as covetousness, Mammonism, etc., was the pursuit of riches for their own sake. For wealth in itself was a temptation. But here asceticism was the power "which ever seeks the good but ever creates evil" [83]; what was evil in its sense was possession and its temptations. For, in conformity with the Old Testament and in analogy to the ethical valuation of good works, asceticism looked upon the pursuit of wealth as an end in itself as highly reprehensible; but the attainment of it as a fruit of labour in a calling was a sign of God's blessing. And even more important: the religious valuation of restless, continuous, systematic work in a worldly calling, as the highest means to asceticism, and at the same time the surest and most evident proof of rebirth and genuine faith, must have been the most powerful conceivable lever for the expansion of that attitude toward life which we have here called the spirit of capitalism. [84]

When the limitation of consumption is combined with this release of acquisitive activity, the inevitable practical result is obvious: accumulation of capital through ascetic compulsion to save. [85] The restraints which were imposed upon the consumption of wealth naturally served to increase it by making possible the productive investment of capital. How strong this influence was is not, unfortunately, susceptible of exact statistical demonstration. In New England the connection is so evident that it did not escape the eye of so discerning a historian as Doyle. [86] But also in Holland, which was really only dominated by strict

Calvinism for seven years, the greater simplicity of life in the more seriously religious circles, in combination with great wealth, led to an excessive propensity to accumulation.[87]

That, furthermore, the tendency which has existed everywhere and at all times, being quite strong in Germany to-day, for middle-class fortunes to be absorbed into the nobility, was necessarily checked by the Puritan antipathy to the feudal way of life, is evident. English Mercantilist writers of the seventeenth century attributed the superiority of Dutch capital to English to the circumstance that newly acquired wealth there did not regularly seek investment in land. Also, since it is not simply a question of the purchase of land, it did not there seek to transfer itself to feudal habits of life, and thereby to remove itself from the possibility of capitalistic investment.[88] The high esteem for agriculture as a peculiarly important branch of activity, also especially consistent with piety, which the Puritans shared, applied (for instance in Baxter) not to the landlord, but to the yeoman and farmer, in the eighteenth century not to the squire, but the rational cultivator.[89] Through the whole of English society in the time since the seventeenth century goes the conflict between the squirearchy, the representatives of "merrie old England", and the Puritan circles of widely varying social influence.[90] Both elements, that of an unspoiled naïve joy of life, and of a strictly regulated, reserved self-control, and conventional ethical conduct are even to-day combined to form the English national character.[91] Similarly, the early history of the North American Colonies is dominated by the sharp contrast of the adventurers, who wanted to set up plantations with the labour of indentured servants, and live as feudal lords, and the specifically middle-class outlook of the Puritans.[92]

As far as the influence of the Puritan outlook extended, under all circumstances—and this is, of course, much more important than the mere encouragement of capital accumulation—it favoured the development of a rational bourgeois economic life; it was the most important, and above all the only consistent influence in the development of that life. It stood at the cradle of the modern economic man.

To be sure, these Puritanical ideals tended to give way under excessive pressure from the temptations of wealth, as the Puritans themselves knew very well. With great regularity we find the most genuine adherents of Puritanism among the classes which were rising from a lowly status,[93] the small bourgeois and farmers, while the *beati possidentes*, even among Quakers, are often found tending to repudiate the old ideals.[94] It was the same fate which again and again befell the predecessor of this worldly asceticism, the monastic asceticism of the Middle Ages. In the latter case, when rational economic activity had worked out its full effects by strict regulation of conduct and limitation of consumption, the wealth accumulated either succumbed directly to the nobility, as in the time before the Reformation, or monastic discipline threatened to break down, and one of the numerous reformations became necessary.

In fact the whole history of monasticism is in a certain sense the history of a continual struggle with the problem of the secularizing influence of wealth. The same is true on a grand scale of the worldly asceticism of Puritanism. The great revival of Method-ism, which preceded the expansion of English industry toward the end of the eighteenth century, may well be compared with such a monastic reform. We may hence quote here a passage[95] from John Wesley himself which might well serve as a motto for everything which has been said above. For it shows that the leaders of these ascetic movements understood the seemingly paradoxical rela-tionships which we have here analysed perfectly well, and in the same sense that we have given them.[96] He wrote:

"I fear, wherever riches have increased, the essence of religion has decreased in the same proportion. Therefore I do not see how it is possible, in the nature of things, for any revival of true religion to continue long. For religion must necessarily produce both industry and frugality, and these cannot but produce riches. But as riches increase, so will pride, anger, and love of the world in all its branches. How then is it possible that Methodism, that is, a religion of the heart, though it flourishes now as a green bay tree, should continue in this state? For the Methodists in every place grow diligent and frugal; consequently they increase in goods. Hence they proportionately increase in pride, in anger, in the desire of the flesh, the desire of the eyes, and the pride of life. So, although the form of religion remains, the spirit is swiftly vanishing away. Is there no way to prevent this—this continual decay of pure religion? We ought not to prevent people from being diligent and frugal; *we must exhort all Christians to gain all they can, and to save all they can*; *that is, in effect, to grow rich.*" [97]

175

There follows the advice that those who gain all they can and save all they can should also give all they can, so that they will grow in grace and lay up a treasure in heaven. It is clear that Wesley here expresses, even in detail, just what we have been trying to point out.[98]

As Wesley here says, the full economic effect of those great religious movements, whose significance for economic development lay above all in their ascetic educative influence, generally came only after the peak of the purely religious enthusiasm was past. Then the intensity of the search for the Kingdom of God commenced gradually to pass over into sober economic virtue; the religious roots died out slowly, giving way to utilitarian worldliness. Then, as Dowden puts it, as in *Robinson Crusoe*, the isolated economic man who carries on missionary activities on the side [99] takes the place of the lonely spiritual search for the Kingdom of Heaven of Bunyan's pilgrim, hurrying through the market-place of Vanity.

When later the principle "to make the most of both worlds" became dominant in the end, as Dowden has remarked, a good conscience simply became one of the means of enjoying a comfortable bourgeois life, as is well expressed in the German proverb about the soft pillow. What the great religious epoch of the seventeenth century bequeathed to its utilitarian successor was, however, above all an amazingly good, we may even say a pharisaically good, conscience in the acquisition of money, so long as it took place legally. Every trace of the *deplacere vix potest* has disappeared.[100]

A specifically bourgeois economic ethic had grown up. With the consciousness of standing in the fullness of God's grace and being visibly blessed by Him, the bourgeois business man, as long as he remained within the bounds of formal correctness, as long as his moral conduct was spotless and the use to which he put his wealth was not objectionable, could follow his pecuniary interests as he would and feel that he was fulfilling a duty in doing so. The power of religious asceticism provided him in addition with sober, conscientious, and unusually industrious workmen, who clung to their work as to a life purpose willed by God.[101]

Finally, it gave him the comforting assurance that the unequal distribution of the goods of this world was a special dispensation of Divine Providence, which in these differences, as in particular grace, pursued secret ends unknown to men.[102] Calvin himself had made the much-quoted statement that only when the people, i.e. the mass of labourers and craftsmen, were poor did they remain obedient to God.[103] In the Netherlands (Pieter de la Court and others), that had been secularized to the effect that the mass of men only labour when necessity forces them to do so. This formulation of a leading idea of capitalistic economy later entered into the current theories of the productivity of low wages. Here also, with the dying out of the religious root, the utilitarian interpretation crept in unnoticed, in the line of development which we have again and again observed.

Mediæval ethics not only tolerated begging but actually glorified it in the mendicant orders. Even secular beggars, since they gave the person of means opportunity for good works through giving alms, were sometimes considered an estate and treated as such. Even the Anglican social ethic of the Stuarts was very close to this attitude. It remained for Puritan Asceticism to take part in the severe English Poor Relief Legislation which fundamentally changed the situation. And it could do that, because the Protestant sects and the strict Puritan communities actually did not know any begging in their own midst.[104]

On the other hand, seen from the side of the workers, the Zinzendorf branch of Pietism, for instance, glorified the loyal worker who did not seek acquisition, but lived according to the apostolic model, and was thus endowed with the *charisma*[105] of the disciples.[106] Similar ideas had originally been prevalent among the Baptists in an even more radical form.

Now naturally the whole ascetic literature of almost all denominations is saturated with the idea that faithful labour, even at low wages, on the part of those whom life offers no other opportunities, is highly pleasing to God. In this respect Protestant Asceticism added in itself nothing new. But it not only deepened this idea most powerfully, it also created the force which was alone decisive for its effectiveness: the psychological sanction of it through the conception of this labour as a calling, as the best, often in the last analysis the only means of attaining certainty of grace.[107] And on the other hand it legalized the exploitation of this specific willingness to work, in that it also interpreted the employer's business activity as a calling.[108] It is obvious how powerfully the exclusive search for the Kingdom of God only through the fulfilment of duty in the calling, and the strict asceticism which Church discipline naturally imposed, especially on the propertyless classes, was bound to affect the productivity of labour in the capitalistic sense of the word. The treatment of labour as a calling became as characteristic of the modern worker as the corresponding attitude toward acquisition of the business man. It was a perception of this situation, new at his time, which caused so able an observer as Sir William Petty to attribute the economic power of Holland in the seventeenth century to the fact that the very numerous dissenters in that country (Calvinists and Baptists) "are for the most part thinking, sober men, and such as believe that Labour and Industry is their duty towards God".[109]

Calvinism opposed organic social organization in the fiscal-monopolistic form which it assumed in Anglicanism under the Stuarts, especially in the conceptions of Laud, this alliance of Church and State with the monopolists on the basis of a Christian-social ethical foundation. Its leaders were universally among the most passionate opponents of this type of politically privileged commercial, putting-out, and colonial capitalism. Over against it they placed the individualistic motives of rational legal acquisition by virtue of one's own ability and initiative. And, while the politically privileged monopoly industries in England all disappeared in short order, this attitude played a large and decisive part in the development of the industries which grew up in spite of and against the authority of the State.[110] The Puritans (Prynne, Parker) repudiated all connection with the large-scale capitalistic courtiers and projectors as an ethically suspicious class. On the other hand, they took pride in their own superior middle-class business morality, which formed the true reason for the persecutions to which they were subjected on the part of those circles. Defoe proposed to win the battle against dissent by boycotting bank credit and withdrawing deposits. The difference of the two types of capitalistic attitude went to a very large extent hand in hand with religious differences. The opponents of the Nonconformists, even in the eighteenth century, again and again ridiculed them for personifying the spirit of shopkeepers, and for having ruined the ideals of old England. Here also lay the difference of the Puritan economic ethic from the Jewish; and contemporaries (Prynne) knew well that the former and not the latter was the bourgeois capitalistic ethic.[111]

One of the fundamental elements of the spirit of modern capitalism, and not only of that but of all modern culture: rational conduct on the basis of the idea of the calling, was born—that is what this discussion has sought to demonstrate—from the spirit of Christian asceticism. One has only to re-read the passage from Franklin, quoted at the beginning of this essay, in order to see that the essential elements of the attitude which was there called the spirit of capitalism are the same as what we have just shown to be the content of the Puritan worldly asceticism,[112] only without the religious basis, which by Franklin's time had died away. The idea that modern labour has an ascetic character is of course not new. Limitation to specialized work, with a renunciation of the Faustian universality of man which it involves, is a condition of any valuable work in the modern world; hence deeds and renunciation inevitably condition each other today. This fundamentally ascetic trait of middle-class life, if it attempts to be a way of life at all, and not simply the absence of any, was what Goethe wanted to teach, at the height of his wisdom, in the *Wanderjahren*, and in the end which he gave to the life of his *Faust*.[113] For him the realization meant a renunciation, a departure from an age of full and beautiful humanity, which can no more be repeated in the course of our cultural development than can the flower of the Athenian culture of antiquity.

The Puritan wanted to work in a calling; we are forced to do so. For when asceticism was carried out of monastic cells into everyday life, and began to dominate worldly morality, it did its part in building the tremendous cosmos of the modern economic order. This order is now bound to the technical and economic conditions of machine production which to-day determine the lives of all the individuals who are born into this mechanism, not only those directly concerned with economic acquisition, with irresistible force. Perhaps it will so determine them until the last ton of fossilized coal is burnt. In Baxter's view the care for external goods should only lie on the shoulders of the "saint like a light cloak, which can be thrown aside at any moment".[114] But fate decreed that the cloak should become an iron cage.

Since asceticism undertook to remodel the world and to work out its ideals in the world, material goods have gained an increasing and finally an inexorable power over the lives of men as at no previous period in history. To-day the spirit of religious asceticism—whether finally, who knows?—has escaped from the cage. But victorious capitalism, since it rests on mechanical foundations, needs its support no longer. The rosy blush of its laughing heir, the Enlightenment, seems also to be irretrievably fading, and the idea of duty in one's calling prowls about in our lives like the ghost of dead religious beliefs. Where the fulfilment of the calling cannot directly be related to the highest spiritual and cultural values, or when, on the other hand, it need not be felt simply as economic compulsion, the individual generally abandons the attempt to justify it at all. In the field of its highest development, in the United States, the pursuit of wealth, stripped of its religious and ethical meaning, tends to become associated with purely mundane passions, which often actually give it the character of sport.[115]

No one knows who will live in this cage in the future, or whether at the end of this tremendous development entirely new prophets will arise, or there will be a great rebirth of old ideas and ideals, or, if neither, mechanized petrification, embellished with a sort of convulsive self-importance. For of the last stage of this cultural development, it might well be truly said: "Specialists without spirit, sensualists without heart; this nullity imagines that it has attained a level of civilization never before achieved."

But this brings us to the world of judgments of value and of faith, with which this purely historical discussion need not be burdened. The next task would be rather to show the significance of ascetic rationalism, which has only been touched in the foregoing sketch, for the content of practical social ethics, thus for the types of organization and the functions of social groups from the conventicle to the State. Then its relations to humanistic rationalism,[116] its ideals of life and cultural influence; further to the development of philosophical and scientific empiricism, to technical development and to spiritual ideals would have to be analysed. Then its historical development from the mediæval beginnings of worldly asceticism to its dissolution into pure utilitarianism would have to be traced out through all the areas of ascetic religion. Only then could the quantitative cultural significance of ascetic Protestantism in its relation to the other plastic elements of modern culture be estimated.

Here we have only attempted to trace the fact and the direction of its influence to their motives in one, though a very important point. But it would also further be necessary to investigate how Protestant Asceticism was in turn influenced in its development and its character by the totality of social conditions, especially economic.[117] The modern man is in general, even with the best will, unable to give religious ideas a significance for culture and national character which they deserve. But it is, of course, not my aim to substitute for a one-sided materialistic an equally one-sided spiritualistic causal interpretation of culture and of history. Each is equally possible,[118] but each, if it does not serve as the preparation, but as the conclusion of an investigation, accomplishes equally little in the interest of historical truth.[119]

NOTES

INTRODUCTION

1. *Ständestaat*. The term refers to the late form taken by feudalism in Europe in its transition to absolute monarchy.—TRANSLATOR'S NOTE.

2. Here, as on some other points, I differ from our honoured master, Lujo Brentano (in his work to be cited later). Chiefly in regard to terminology, but also on questions of fact. It does not seem to me expedient to bring such different things as acquisition of booty and acquisition by management of a factory together under the same category; still less to designate every tendency to the acquisition of money as the spirit of capitalism as against other types of acquisition. The second sacrifices all precision of concepts, and the first the possibility of clarifying the specific difference between Occidental capitalism and other forms. Also in Simmel's *Philosophie des Geldes* money economy and capitalism are too closely identified, to the detriment of his concrete analysis. In the writings of Werner Sombart, above all in the second edition of his most important work, *Der moderne Kapitalismus*, the *differentia specifica* of Occidental capitalism —at least from the view-point of my problem—the rational organization of labour, is strongly overshadowed by genetic factors which have been operative everywhere in the world.

3. *Commenda* was a form of mediæval trading association, entered into *ad hoc* for carrying out one sea voyage. A producer or exporter of goods turned them over to another who took them abroad (on a ship provided sometimes by one party, sometimes by the other) and sold them, receiving a share in the profits. The expenses of the voyage were divided between the two in agreed proportion, while the original shipper bore the risk. See Weber, "Handelsgesellschaften im Mittelalter", *Gesammelte Aufsätze zur Sozial- und Wirtschaftsgeschichte*, pp. 323–8.—TRANSLATOR'S NOTE.

4. The sea loan, used in maritime commerce in the Middle Ages, was "a method of insuring against the risks of the sea without violating the prohibitions against usury. . . . When certain risky maritime ventures were to be undertaken, a certain sum . . . was obtained for the cargo belonging to such and such a person or capitalist. If the ship was lost, no repayment was exacted by the lender; if it reached port safely, the borrower paid a considerable premium, sometimes 50 per cent." Henri Sée, *Modern Capitalism*, p. 189.—TRANSLATOR'S NOTE.

5. A form of company between the partnership and the limited liability corporation. At least one of the participants is made liable without limit, while the others enjoy limitation of liability to the amount of their investment.—TRANSLATOR'S NOTE.

185

6. Naturally the difference cannot be conceived in absolute terms. The politically oriented capitalism (above all tax-farming) of Mediterranean and Oriental antiquity, and even of China and India, gave rise to rational, continuous enterprises whose book-keeping—though known to us only in pitiful fragments—probably had a rational character. Furthermore, the politically oriented adventurers' capitalism has been closely associated with rational bourgeois capitalism in the development of modern banks, which, including the Bank of England, have for the most part originated in transactions of a political nature, often connected with war. The difference between the characters of Paterson, for instance—a typical promoter—and of the members of the directorate of the Bank who gave the keynote to its permanent policy, and very soon came to be known as the "Puritan usurers of Grocers' Hall", is characteristic of it. Similarly, we have the aberration of the policy of this most solid bank at the time of the South Sea Bubble. Thus the two naturally shade off into each other. But the difference is there. The great promoters and financiers have no more created the rational organization of labour than—again in general and with individual exceptions—those other typical representatives of financial and political capitalism, the Jews. That was done, typically, by quite a different set of people.

7. For Weber's discussion of the ineffectiveness of slave labour, especially so far as calculation is concerned, see his essay, "Agrarverhältnisse im Altertum", in the volume *Gesammelte Aufsätze zur Sozial- und Wirtschaftsgeschichte.*—TRANSLATOR'S NOTE.

8. That is, in the whole series of *Aufsätze zur Religionssoziologie*, not only in the essay here translated.. See translator's preface.—TRANSLATOR'S NOTE.

9. The remains of my knowledge of Hebrew are also quite inadequate.

10. I need hardly point out that this does not apply to attempts like that of Karl Jasper's (in his book *Psychologie der Weltanschauungen*, 1919), nor to Klages's *Charakterologie*, and similar studies which differ from our own in their point of departure. There is no space here for a criticism of them.

11. The only thing of this kind which Weber ever wrote is the section on "Religionssoziologie" in his large work *Wirtschaft und Gesellschaft*. It was left unfinished by him and does not really close the gap satisfactorily.—TRANSLATOR'S NOTE.

12. Some years ago an eminent psychiatrist expressed the same opinion to me.

CHAPTER I

1. From the voluminous literature which has grown up around this essay I cite only the most comprehensive criticisms. (1) F. Rachfahl, "Kalvinismus und Kapitalismus", *Internationale Wochenschrift für Wissenschaft, Kunst und Technik* (1909), Nos. 39–43. In

reply, my article: "Antikritisches zum Geist des Kapitalismus," *Archiv für Sozialwissenschaft und Sozialpolitik* (Tübingen), XX, 1910. Then Rachfahl's reply to that: "Nochmals Kalvinismus und Kapitalismus", 1910, Nos. 22–25, of the *Internationale Wochenschrift*. Finally my "Antikritisches Schlusswort", *Archiv*, XXXI. (Brentano, in the criticism presently to be referred to, evidently did not know of this last phase of the discussion, as he does not refer to it.) I have not incorporated anything in this edition from the somewhat unfruitful polemics against Rachfahl. He is an author whom I otherwise admire, but who has in this instance ventured into a field which he has not thoroughly mastered. I have only added a few supplementary references from my anti-critique, and have attempted, in new passages and footnotes, to make impossible any future misunderstanding. (2) W. Sombart, in his book *Der Bourgeois* (Munich and Leipzig, 1913, also translated into English under the title *The Quintessence of Capitalism*, London, 1915), to which I shall return in footnotes below. Finally (3) Lujo Brentano in Part II of the Appendix to his Munich address (in the Academy of Sciences, 1913) on *Die Anfänge des modernen Kapitalismus*, which was published in 1916. (Since Weber's death Brentano has somewhat expanded these essays and incorporated them into his recent book *Der wirtschaftende Mensch in der Geschichte.* —TRANSLATOR'S NOTE.) I shall also refer to this criticism in special footnotes in the proper places. I invite anyone who may be interested to convince himself by comparison that I have not in revision left out, changed the meaning of, weakened, or added materially different statements to, a single sentence of my essay which contained any essential point. There was no occasion to do so, and the development of my exposition will convince anyone who still doubts. The two latter writers engaged in a more bitter quarrel with each other than with me. Brentano's criticism of Sombart's book, *Die Juden und das Wirtschaftsleben*, I consider in many points well founded, but often very unjust, even apart from the fact that Brentano does not himself seem to understand the real essence of the problem of the Jews (which is entirely omitted from this essay, but will be dealt with later [in a later section of the *Religionssoziologie.*—TRANSLATOR'S NOTE]).

From theologians I have received numerous valuable suggestions in connection with this study. Its reception on their part has been in general friendly and impersonal, in spite of wide differences of opinion on particular points. This is the more welcome to me since I should not have wondered at a certain antipathy to the manner in which these matters must necessarily be treated here. What to a theologian is valuable in his religion cannot play a very large part in this study. We are concerned with what, from a religious point of view, are often quite superficial and unrefined aspects of relligious life, but which, and precisely because they were superficial and unrefined, have often influenced outward behaviour most profoundy.

Another book which, besides containing many other things, is a very welcome confirmation of and supplement to this essay in so far as it deals with our problem, is the important work of E. Troeltsch, *Die Soziallehren der christlichen Kirchen und Gruppen* (Tübingen, 1912). It deals with the history of the ethics of Western Christianity from a very comprehensive point of view of its own. I here refer the reader to it for general comparison instead of making repeated references to special points. The author is principally concerned with the doctrines of religion, while I am interested rather in their practical results.

2. The exceptions are explained, not always, but frequently, by the fact that the religious leanings of the labouring force of an industry are naturally, in the first instance, determined by those of the locality in which the industry is situated, or from which its labour is drawn. This circumstance often alters the impression given at first glance by some statistics of religious adherence, for instance in the Rhine provinces. Furthermore, figures can naturally only be conclusive if individual specialized occupations are carefully distinguished in them. Otherwise very large employers may sometimes be grouped together with master craftsmen who work alone, under the category of "proprietors of enterprises". Above all, the fully developed capitalism of the present day, especially so far as the great unskilled lower strata of labour are concerned, has become independent of any influence which religion may have had in the past. I shall return to this point.

3. Compare, for instance, Schell, *Der Katholizismus als Prinzip des Fortschrittes* (Würzburg, 1897), p. 31, and V. Hertling, *Das Prinzip des Katholizismus und die Wissenschaft* (Freiburg, 1899), p. 58.

4. One of my pupils has gone through what is at this time the most complete statistical material we possess on this subject: the religious statistics of Baden. See Martin Offenbacher, "Konfession und soziale Schichtung", *Eine Studie über die wirtschaftliche Lage der Katholiken und Protestanten in Baden* (Tübingen und Leipzig, 1901), Vol. IV, part v, of the *Volkswirtschaftliche Abhandlungen der badischen Hochschulen*. The facts and figures which are used for illustration below are all drawn from this study.

5. For instance, in 1895 in Baden there was taxable capital available for the tax on returns from capital:

> Per 1,000 Protestants .. .. .. 954,000 marks
> Per 1,000 Catholics .. .. .. 589,000 marks

It is true that the Jews, with over four millions per 1,000, were far ahead of the rest. (For details see Offenbacher, *op. cit.*, p. 21.)

6. On this point compare the whole discussion in Offenbacher's study.

7. On this point also Offenbacher brings forward more detailed evidence for Baden in his first two chapters.

8. The population of Baden was composed in 1895 as follows:

Protestants, 37·0 per cent.; Catholics, 61·3 per cent.; Jewish, 1·5 per cent. The students of schools beyond the compulsory public school stage were, however, divided as follows (Offenbacher, p. 16):

	Protestant.	Catholic.	Jews.
	Per Cent.	Per Cent.	Per Cent.
Gymnasien..	43	46	9.5
Realgymnasien	69	31	9
Oberrealschulen	52	41	7
Realschulen	49	40	11
Höhere Bürgerschulen	51	37	12
Average	48	42	10

(In the *Gymnasium* the main emphasis is on the classics. In the *Realgymnasium* Greek is dropped and Latin reduced in favour of modern languages, mathematics and science. The *Realschule* and *Oberrealschule* are similar to the latter except that Latin is dropped entirely in favour of modern languages. See G. E. Bolton, *The Secondary School System in Germany*, New York, 1900.—Translator's Note.)

The same thing may be observed in Prussia, Bavaria, Würtemberg, Alsace-Lorraine, and Hungary (see figures in Offenbacher, pp. 16 ff.).

9. See the figures in the preceding note, which show that the Catholic attendance at secondary schools, which is regularly less than the Catholic share of the total population by a third, only exceeds this by a few per cent. in the case of the grammar schools (mainly in preparation for theological studies). With reference to the subsequent discussion it may further be noted as characteristic that in Hungary those affiliated with the Reformed Church exceed even the average Protestant record of attendance at secondary schools. (See Offenbacher, p. 19, note.)

10. For the proofs see Offenbacher, p. 54, and the tables at the end of his study.

11. Especially well illustrated by passages in the works of Sir William Petty, to be referred to later.

12. Petty's reference to the case of Ireland is very simply explained by the fact that the Protestants were only involved in the capacity of absentee landlords. If he had meant to maintain more he would have been wrong, as the situation of the Scotch-Irish shows. The typical relationship between Protestantism and capitalism existed in Ireland as well as elsewhere. (On the Scotch-Irish see C. A. Hanna, *The Scotch-Irish*, two vols., Putnam, New York.)

13. This is not, of course, to deny that the latter facts have had exceedingly important consequences. As I shall show later, the fact

that many Protestant sects were small and hence homogeneous minorities, as were all the strict Calvinists outside of Geneva and New England, even where they were in possession of political power, was of fundamental significance for the development of their whole character, including their manner of participation in economic life. The migration of exiles of all the religions of the earth, Indian, Arabian, Chinese, Syrian, Phœnician, Greek, Lombard, to other countries as bearers of the commercial lore of highly developed areas, has been of universal occurrence and has nothing to do with our problem. Brentano, in the essay to which I shall often refer, *Die Anfänge des modernen Kapitalismus*, calls to witness his own family. But bankers of foreign extraction have existed at all times and in all countries as the representatives of commercial experience and connections. They are not peculiar to modern capitalism, and were looked upon with ethical mistrust by the Protestants (see below). The case of the Protestant families, such as the Muralts, Pestalozzi, etc., who migrated to Zurich from Locarno, was different. They very soon became identified with a specifically modern (industrial) type of capitalistic development.

14. Offenbacher, *op. cit.*, p. 58.

15. Unusually good observations on the characteristic peculiarities of the different religions in Germany and France, and the relation of these differences to other cultural elements in the conflict of nationalities in Alsace are to be found in the fine study of W. Wittich, "Deutsche und französische Kultur im Elsass", *Illustrierte Elsässische Rundschau* (1900, also published separately).

16. This, of course, was true only when some possibility of capitalistic development in the area in question was present.

17. On this point see, for instance, Dupin de St. André, "L'ancienne église réformée de Tours. Les membres de l'église", *Bull. de la soc. de l'hist. du Protest.*, 4, p. 10. Here again one might, especially from the Catholic point of view, look upon the desire for emancipation from monastic or ecclesiastical control as the dominant motive. But against that view stands not only the judgment of contemporaries (including Rabelais), but also, for instance, the qualms of conscience of the first national synods of the Huguenots (for instance 1st Synod, C. partic. qu. 10 in Aymon, *Synod. Nat.*, p. 10), as to whether a banker might become an elder of the Church; and in spite of Calvin's own definite stand, the repeated discussions in the same bodies of the permissibility of taking interest occasioned by the questions of ultra-scrupulous members. It is partly explained by the number of persons having a direct interest in the question, but at the same time the wish to practise *usuraria pravitas* without the necessity of confession could not have been alone decisive. The same, see below, is true of Holland. Let it be said explicitly that the prohibition of interest in the canon law will play no part in this investigation.

Notes

18. Gothein, *Wirtschaftsgeschichte des Schwarzwaldes*, I, p. 67.

19. In connection with this see Sombart's brief comments (*Der moderne Kapitalismus*, first edition, p. 380). Later, under the influence of a study of F. Keller (*Unternehmung und Mehrwert*, Publications of the Goerres-Gesellschaft, XII), which, in spite of many good observations (which in this connection, however, are not new), falls below the standard of other recent works of Catholic apologetics, Sombart, in what is in these parts in my opinion by far the weakest of his larger works (*Der Bourgeois*), has unfortunately maintained a completely untenable thesis, to which I shall refer in the proper place.

20. That the simple fact of a change of residence is among the most effective means of intensifying labour is thoroughly established (compare note 13 above). The same Polish girl who at home was not to be shaken loose from her traditional laziness by any chance of earning money, however tempting, seems to change her entire nature and become capable of unlimited accomplishment when she is a migratory worker in a foreign country. The same is true of migratory Italian labourers. That this is by no means entirely explicable in terms of the educative influence of the entrance into a higher cultural environment, although this naturally plays a part, is shown by the fact that the same thing happens where the type of occupation, as in agricultural labour, is exactly the same as at home. Furthermore, accommodation in labour barracks, etc., may involve a degradation to a standard of living which would never be tolerated at home. The simple fact of working in quite different surroundings from those to which one is accustomed breaks through the tradition and is the educative force. It is hardly necessary to remark how much of American economic development is the result of such factors. In ancient times the similar significance of the Babylonian exile for the Jews is very striking, and the same is true of the Parsees. But for the Protestants, as is indicated by the undeniable difference in the economic characteristics of the Puritan New England colonies from Catholic Maryland, the Episcopal South, and mixed Rhode Island, the influence of their religious belief quite evidently plays a part as an independent factor. Similarly in India, for instance, with the Jains.

21. It is well known in most of its forms to be a more or less moderated Calvinism or Zwinglianism.

22. In Hamburg, which is almost entirely Lutheran, the only fortune going back to the seventeenth century is that of a well-known Reformed family (kindly called to my attention by Professor A. Wahl).

23. It is thus not new that the existence of this relationship is maintained here. Lavelye, Matthew Arnold, and others already perceived it. What is new, on the contrary, is the quite unfounded denial of it. Our task here is to explain the relation.

24. Naturally this does not mean that official Pietism, like other religious tendencies, did not at a later date, from a patriarchal point

of view, oppose certain progressive features of capitalistic development, for instance, the transition from domestic industry to the factory system. What a religion has sought after as an ideal, and what the actual result of its influence on the lives of its adherents has been, must be sharply distinguished, as we shall often see in the course of our discussion. On the specific adaptation of Pietists to industrial labour, I have given examples from a Westphalian factory in my article, "Zur Psychophysik der gewerblichen Arbeit", *Archiv für Sozialwissenschaft und Sozialpolitik*, XXVIII, and at various other times.

CHAPTER II

1. These passages represent a very brief summary of some aspects of Weber's methodological views. At about the same time that he wrote this essay he was engaged in a thorough criticism and re-valuation of the methods of the Social Sciences, the result of which was a point of view in many ways different from the prevailing one, especially outside of Germany. In order thoroughly to understand the significance of this essay in its wider bearings on Weber's sociological work as a whole it is necessary to know what his methodological aims were. Most of his writings on this subject have been assembled since his death (in 1920) in the volume *Gesammelte Aufsätze zur Wissenschaftslehre*. A shorter exposition of the main position is contained in the opening chapters of *Wirtschaft und Gesellschaft, Grundriss der Sozialökonomik*, III.—TRANSLATOR'S NOTE.

2. The final passage is from *Necessary Hints to Those That Would Be Rich* (written 1736, Works, Sparks edition, II, p. 80), the rest from *Advice to a Young Tradesman* (written 1748, Sparks edition, II, pp. 87 ff.). The italics in the text are Franklin's.

3. *Der Amerikamüde* (Frankfurt, 1855), well known to be an imaginative paraphrase of Lenau's impressions of America. As a work of art the book would to-day be somewhat difficult to enjoy, but it is incomparable as a document of the (now long since blurred-over) differences between the German and the American outlook, one may even say of the type of spiritual life which, in spite of everything, has remained common to all Germans, Catholic and Protestant alike, since the German mysticism of the Middle Ages, as against the Puritan capitalistic valuation of action.

4. Sombart has used this quotation as a motto for his section dealing with the genesis of capitalism (*Der moderne Kapitalismus*, first edition, I, p. 193. See also p. 390).

5. Which quite obviously does not mean either that Jacob Fugger was a morally indifferent or an irreligious man, or that Benjamin Franklin's ethic is completely covered by the above quotations. It scarcely required Brentano's quotations (*Die Anfänge des modernen Kapitalismus*, pp. 150 ff.) to protect this well-known philanthropist

from the misunderstanding which Brentano seems to attribute to me. The problem is just the reverse: how could such a philanthropist come to write these particular sentences (the especially characteristic form of which Brentano has neglected to reproduce) in the manner of a moralist?

6. This is the basis of our difference from Sombart in stating the problem. Its very considerable practical significance will become clear later. In anticipation, however, let it be remarked that Sombart has by no means neglected this ethical aspect of the capitalistic entrepreneur. But in his view of the problem it appears as a result of capitalism, whereas for our purposes we must assume the opposite as an hypothesis. A final position can only ʋe taken up at the end of the investigation. For Sombart's view see *op. cit.*, pp. 357, 380, etc. His reasoning here connects with the brilliant analysis given in Simmel's *Philosophie des Geldes* (final chapter). Of the polemics which he has brought forward against me in his *Bourgeois* I shall come to speak later. At this point any thorough discussion must be postponed.

7. "I grew convinced that truth, sincerity, and integrity in dealings between man and man were of the utmost importance to the felicity of life; and I formed written resolutions, which still remain in my journal book to practise them ever while I lived. Revelation had indeed no weight with me as such; but I entertained an opinion that, though certain actions might not be bad because they were forbidden by it, or good because it commanded them, yet probably these actions might be forbidden because they were bad for us, or commanded because they were beneficial to us in their own nature, all the circumstances of things considered." *Autobiography* (ed. F. W. Pine, Henry Holt, New York, 1916), p. 112.

8. "I therefore put myself as much as I could out of sight and started it"—that is the project of a library which he had initiated— "as a scheme of a *number of friends,* who had requested me to go about and propose it to such as they thought lovers of reading. In this way my affair went on smoothly, and I ever after practised it on such occasions; and from my frequent successes, can heartily recommend it. The present little sacrifice of your vanity will afterwards be amply repaid. If it remains awhile uncertain to whom the merit belongs, someone more vain than yourself will be encouraged to claim it, and then even envy will be disposed to do you justice by plucking those assumed feathers and restoring them to their right owner." *Autobiography,* p. 140.

9. Brentano (*op. cit.,* pp. 125, 127, note 1) takes this remark as an occasion to criticize the later discussion of "that rationalization and discipline" to which worldly asceticism[1] has subjected men. That,

---

[1] This seemingly paradoxical term has been the best translation I could find for Weber's *innerweltliche Askese,* which means asceticism

he says, is a rationalization toward an irrational mode of life. He is, in fact, quite correct. A thing is never irrational in itself, but only from a particular rational point of view. For the unbeliever every religious way of life is irrational, for the hedonist every ascetic standard, no matter whether, measured with respect to its particular basic values, that opposing asceticism is a rationalization. If this essay makes any contribution at all, may it be to bring out the complexity of the only superficially simple concept of the rational.

10. In reply to Brentano's (*Die Anfänge des modernen Kapitalismus*, pp. 150 ff.) long and somewhat inaccurate apologia for Franklin, whose ethical qualities I am supposed to have misunderstood, I refer only to this statement, which should, in my opinion, have been sufficient to make that apologia superfluous.

11. The two terms profession and calling I have used in translation of the German *Beruf*, whichever seemed best to fit the particular context. Vocation does not carry the ethical connotation in which Weber is interested. It is especially to be remembered that profession in this sense is not contrasted with business, but it refers to a particular attitude toward one's occupation, no matter what that occupation may be. This should become abundantly clear from the whole of Weber's argument.—TRANSLATOR'S NOTE.

12. I make use of this opportunity to insert a few anti-critical remarks in advance of the main argument. Sombart (*Bourgeois*) makes the untenable statement that this ethic of Franklin is a word-for-word repetition of some writings of that great and versatile genius of the Renaissance, Leon Battista Alberti, who besides theoretical treatises on Mathematics, Sculpture, Painting, Architecture, and Love (he was personally a woman-hater), wrote a work in four books on household management (*Della Famiglia*). (Unfortunately, I have not at the time of writing been able to procure the edition of Mancini, but only the older one of Bonucci.) The passage from Franklin is printed above word for word. Where then are corresponding passages to be found in Alberti's work, especially the maxim "time is money", which stands at the head, and the exhortations which follow it? The only passage which, so far as I know, bears the slightest resemblance to it is found towards the end of the first book of *Della Famiglia* (ed. Bonucci, II, p. 353), where Alberti speaks in very general terms of money as the *nervus rerum* of the household, which must hence

---

practised within the world as contrasted with *ausserweltliche Askese,* which withdraws from the world (for instance into a monastery). Their precise meaning will appear in the course of Weber's discussion. It is one of the prime points of his essay that asceticism does not need to flee from the world to be ascetic. I shall consistently employ the terms worldly and otherworldly to denote the contrast between the two kinds of asceticism.—TRANSLATOR'S NOTE.

Notes

be handled with special care, just as Cato spoke in *De Re Rustica*. To treat Alberti, who was very proud of his descent from one of the most distinguished cavalier families of Florence (*Nobilissimi Cavalieri, op. cit.*, pp. 213, 228, 247, etc.), as a man of mongrel blood who was filled with envy for the noble families because his illegitimate birth, which was not in the least socially disqualifying, excluded him as a bourgeois from association with the nobility, is quite incorrect. It is true that the recommendation of large enterprises as alone worthy of a *nobile è onesta famiglia* and a *libero è nobile animo*, and as costing less labour is characteristic of Alberti (p. 209; compare *Del governo della Famiglia*, IV, p. 55, as well as p. 116 in the edition for the Pandolfini). Hence the best thing is a putting-out business for wool and silk. Also an ordered and painstaking regulation of his household, i.e. the limiting of expenditure to income. This is the *santa masserizia*, which is thus primarily a principle of maintenance, a given standard of life, and not of acquisition (as no one should have understood better than Sombart). Similarly, in the discussion of the nature of money, his concern is with the management of consumption funds (money or *possessioni*), not with that of capital; all that is clear from the expression of it which is put into the mouth of Gianozzo. He recommends, as protection against the uncertainty of *fortuna*, early habituation to continuous activity, which is also (pp. 73–4) alone healthy in the long run, *in cose magnifiche è ample*, and avoidance of laziness, which always endangers the maintenance of one's position in the world. Hence a careful study of a suitable trade in case of a change of fortune, but every *opera mercenaria* is unsuitable (*op. cit.*, I, p. 209). His idea of *tranquillita dell' animo* and his strong tendency toward the Epicurean λάθε βιώσας (*vivere a sè stesso*, p. 262); especially his dislike of any office (p. 258) as a source of unrest, of making enemies, and of becoming involved in dishonourable dealings; the ideal of life in a country villa; his nourishment of vanity through the thought of his ancestors; and his treatment of the honour of the family (which on that account should keep its fortune together in the Florentine manner and not divide it up) as a decisive standard and ideal—all these things would in the eyes of every Puritan have been sinful idolatry of the flesh, and in those of Benjamin Franklin the expression of incomprehensible aristocratic nonsense. Note, further, the very high opinion of literary things (for the *industria* is applied principally to literary and scientific work), which is really most worthy of a man's efforts. And the expression of the *masserizia*, in the sense of "rational conduct of the household" as the means of living independently of others and avoiding destitution, is in general put only in the mouth of the illiterate Gianozzo as of equal value. Thus the origin of this concept, which comes (see below) from monastic ethics, is traced back to an old priest (p. 249).

Now compare all this with the ethic and manner of life of Benjamin

195

Franklin, and especially of his Puritan ancestors; the works of the Renaissance *littérateur* addressing himself to the humanistic aristocracy, with Franklin's works addressed to the masses of the lower middle class (he especially mentions clerks) and with the tracts and sermons of the Puritans, in order to comprehend the depth of the difference. The economic rationalism of Alberti, everywhere supported by references to ancient authors, is most clearly related to the treatment of economic problems in the works of Xenophon (whom he did not know), of Cato, Varro, and Columella (all of whom he quotes), except that especially in Cato and Varro, *acquisition* as such stands in the foreground in a different way from that to be found in Alberti. Furthermore, the very occasional comments of Alberti on the use of the *fattori*, their division of labour and discipline, on the unreliability of the peasants, etc., really sound as if Cato's homely wisdom were taken from the field of the ancient slave-using household and applied to that of free labour in domestic industry and the metayer system. When Sombart (whose reference to the Stoic ethic is quite misleading) sees economic rationalism as "developed to its farthest conclusions" as early as Cato, he is, with a correct interpretation, not entirely wrong. It is possible to unite the *diligens pater familias* of the Romans with the ideal of the *massajo* of Alberti under the same category. It is above all characteristic for Cato that a landed estate is valued and judged as an object for the investment of consumption funds. The concept of *industria*, on the other hand, is differently coloured on account of Christian influence. And there is just the difference. In the conception of *industria*, which comes from monastic asceticism and which was developed by monastic writers, lies the seed of an *ethos* which was fully developed later in the Protestant worldly asceticism. Hence, as we shall often point out, the relationship of the two, which, however, is less close to the official Church doctrine of St. Thomas than to the Florentine and Siennese mendicant-moralists. In Cato and also in Alberti's own writings this *ethos* is lacking; for both it is a matter of worldly wisdom, not of ethic. In Franklin there is also a utilitarian strain. But the ethical quality of the sermon to young business men is impossible to mistake, and that is the characteristic thing. A lack of care in the handling of money means to him that one so to speak murders capital embryos, and hence it is an ethical defect.

An inner relationship of the two (Alberti and Franklin) exists in fact only in so far as Alberti, whom Sombart calls pious, but who actually, although he took the sacraments and held a Roman benefice, like so many humanists, did not himself (except for two quite colourless passages) in any way make use of religious motives as a justification of the manner of life he recommended, had not yet, Franklin on the other hand no longer, related his recommendation of economy to religious conceptions. Utilitarianism, in Alberti's preference for wool and silk manufacture, also the mercantilist social utilitarianism "that many people should be given employment" (see Alberti, *op. cit.*, p. 292), is in this field at least formally the sole justification for the one as for the other. Alberti's discussions of this subject form an excellent example of the sort of economic rationalism which really existed as a reflection of economic conditions, in the work of authors interested purely in "the thing for its own sake" everywhere and at all times; in the Chinese classicism and in Greece and Rome no less than in the Renaissance and the age of the Enlightenment. There is no doubt that just as in ancient times with Cato, Varro, and Columella, also here with Alberti and others of the same type, especially in the doctrine of *industria*, a sort of economic rationality is highly developed. But how can anyone believe that such a literary *theory* could develop into a revolutionary force at all comparable to the way in which a religious belief was able to set the sanctions of salvation and damnation on the fulfillment of a particular (in this case methodically rationalized) manner of life? What, as compared with it, a really religiously oriented rationalization of conduct looks like, may be seen, outside of the Puritans of all denominations, in the cases of the Jains, the Jews, certain ascetic sects of the Middle Ages, the Bohemian Brothers (an offshoot of the Hussite movement), the Skoptsi and Stundists in Russia, and numerous monastic orders, however much all these may differ from each other.

The essential point of the difference is (to anticipate) that an ethic based on religion places certain psychological sanctions (not of an economic character) on the maintenance of the attitude prescribed by it, sanctions which, so long as the religious belief remains alive, are highly effective, and which mere worldly wisdom like that of Alberti does not have at its disposal. Only in so far as these sanctions work, and, above all, in the direction in which they work, which is often very different from the doctrine of the theologians, does such an ethic gain an independent influence on the conduct of life and thus on the economic order. This is, to speak frankly, the point of this whole essay, which I had not expected to find so completely overlooked.

Later on I shall come to speak of the theological moralists of the late Middle Ages, who were relatively friendly to capital (especially Anthony of Florence and Bernhard of Siena), and whom Sombart has also seriously misinterpreted. In any case Alberti did not belong to that group. Only the concept of *industria* did he take from monastic lines of thought, no matter through what intermediate links. Alberti, Pandolfini, and their kind are representatives of that attitude which, in spite of all its outward obedience, was inwardly already emancipated from the tradition of the Church. With all its resemblance to the current Christian ethic, it was to a large extent of the antique pagan character, which Brentano thinks I have ignored in its significance for the development of modern economic thought (and also modern economic policy). That I do not deal with its influence here is quite true. It would be out of place in a study of the Protestant ethic and the spirit of capitalism. But, as will appear in a different connection, far from denying its significance, I have been and am for good reasons of the opinion that its sphere and direction of influence were entirely different from those of the Protestant ethic (of which the spiritual ancestry, of no small practical importance, lies in the sects and in the ethics of Wyclif and Hus). It was not the mode of life of the rising bourgeoisie which was influenced by this other attitude, but the policy of statesmen and princes; and these two partly, but by no means always, convergent lines of development should for purposes of analysis be kept perfectly distinct. So far as Franklin is concerned, his tracts of advice to business men, at present used for school reading in America, belong in fact to a category of works which have influenced practical life, far more than Alberti's large book, which hardly became known outside of learned circles. But I have expressly denoted him as a man who stood beyond the direct influence of the Puritan view of life, which had paled considerably in the meantime, just as the whole English enlightenment, the relations of which to Puritanism have often been set forth.

13. Unfortunately Brentano (*op. cit.*) has thrown every kind of struggle for gain, whether peaceful or warlike, into one pot, and has then set up as the specific criterion of capitalistic (as contrasted, for instance, with feudal) profit-seeking, its acquisitiveness of *money* (instead of land). Any further differentiation, which alone could lead to a clear conception, he has not only refused to make, but has made against the concept of the spirit of (modern) capitalism which we have formed for our purposes, the (to me) incomprehensible objection that it already includes in its assumptions what is supposed to be proved.

14. Compare the, in every respect, excellent observations of Sombart, *Die deutsche Volkswirtschaft im 19ten Jahrhundert*, p. 123. In general I do not need specially to point out, although the following studies go back in their most important points of view to much older work, how much they owe in their development to the mere existence of Sombart's important works, with their pointed formulations and this even, perhaps especially, where they take a different road. Even those who feel themselves continually and decisively disagreeing with Sombart's views, and who reject many of his theses, have the duty to do so only after a thorough study of his work.

15. Of course we cannot here enter into the question of where these limits lie, nor can we evaluate the familiar theory of the relation between high wages and the high productivity of labour which was first suggested by Brassey, formulated and maintained theoretically by Brentano, and both historically and theoretically by Schulze-Gaevernitz. The discussion was again opened by Hasbach's penetrating studies (*Schmollers Jahrbuch*, 1903, pp. 385–91 and 417 ff.),

and is not yet finally settled. For us it is here sufficient to assent to the fact which is not, and cannot be, doubted by anyone, that low wages and high profits, low wages and favourable opportunities for industrial development, are at least not simply identical, that generally speaking training for capitalistic culture, and with it the possibility of capitalism as an economic system, are not brought about simply through mechanical financial operations. All examples are purely illustrative.

16. It must be remembered that this was written twenty-five years ago, when the above statement was by no means the commonplace that it is now, even among economists, to say nothing of business men.—TRANSLATOR'S NOTE.

17. The establishment even of capitalistic industries has hence often not been possible without large migratory movements from areas of older culture. However correct Sombart's remarks on the difference between the personal skill and trade secrets of the handicraftsman and the scientific, objective modern technique may be, at the time of the rise of capitalism the difference hardly existed. In fact the, so to speak, ethical qualities of the capitalistic workman (and to a certain extent also of the entrepreneur) often had a higher scarcity value than the skill of the craftsman, crystallized in traditions hundreds of years old. And even present-day industry is not yet by any means entirely independent in its choice of location of such qualities of the population, acquired by long-standing tradition and education in intensive labour. It is congenial to the scientific prejudices of to-day, when such a dependence is observed to ascribe it to congenital racial qualities rather than to tradition and education, in my opinion with very doubtful validity.

18. See my "Zur Psychophysik der gewerblichen Arbeit", *Archiv für Sozialwissenschaft und Sozialpolitik*, XXVIII.

19. The foregoing observations might be misunderstood. The tendency of a well-known type of business man to use the belief that "religion must be maintained for the people" for his own purpose, and the earlier not uncommon willingness of large numbers, especially of the Lutheran clergy, from a general sympathy with authority, to offer themselves as black police when they wished to brand the strike as sin and trade unions as furtherers of cupidity, all these are things with which our present problem has nothing to do. The factors discussed in the text do not concern occasional but very common facts, which, as we shall see, continually recur in a typical manner.

20. *Der moderne Kapitalismus*, first edition, I, p. 62.

21. *Ibid.*, p. 195.

22. Naturally that of the modern rational enterprise peculiar to the Occident, not of the sort of capitalism spread over the world for three thousand years, from China, India, Babylon, Greece, Rome, Florence, to the present, carried on by usurers, military contractors,

traders in offices, tax-farmers, large merchants, and financial magnates. See the Introduction.

23. The assumption is thus by no means justified *a priori*, that is all I wish to bring out here, that on the one hand the technique of the capitalistic enterprise, and on the other the spirit of professional work which gives to capitalism its expansive energy, must have had their original roots in the same social classes. Similarly with the social relationships of religious beliefs. Calvinism was historically one of the agents of education in the spirit of capitalism. But in the Netherlands, the large moneyed interests were, for reasons which will be discussed later, not predominately adherents of strict Calvinism, but Arminians. The rising middle and small bourgeoisie, from which entrepreneurs were principally recruited, were for the most part here and elsewhere typical representatives both of capitalistic ethics and of Calvinistic religion. But that fits in very well with our present thesis: there were at all times large bankers and merchants. But a rational capitalistic organization of industrial labour was never known until the transition from the Middle Ages to modern times took place.

24. On this point see the good Zurich dissertation of J. Maliniak (1913).

25. The following picture has been put together as an ideal type from conditions found in different industrial branches and at different places. For the purposes of illustration which it here serves, it is of course of no consequence that the process has not in any one of the examples we have in mind taken place in precisely the manner we have described.

26. For this reason, among others, it is not by chance that this first period of incipient (economic) rationalism in German industry was accompanied by certain other phenomena, for instance the catastrophic degradation of taste in the style of articles of everyday use.

27. This is not to be understood as a claim that changes in the supply of the precious metals are of no economic importance.

28. This is only meant to refer to the type of entrepreneur (business man) whom we are making the object of our study, not any empirical average type. On the concept of the ideal type see my discussion in the *Archiv für Sozialwissenschaft und Sozialpolitik*, XIX, No. 1. (Republished since Weber's death in the *Gesammelte Aufsätze zur Wissenschaftslehre*. The concept was first thoroughly developed by Weber himself in these essays, and is likely to be unfamiliar to non-German readers. It is one of the most important aspects of Weber's methodological work, referred to in a note above.—TRANSLATOR'S NOTE.)

29. This is perhaps the most appropriate place to make a few remarks concerning the essay of F. Keller, already referred to (volume 12 of the publications of the Görres-Gesellschaft), and Sombart's observations (*Der Bourgeois*) in following it up, so far as they are relevant in the present context. That an author should

Notes

criticize a study in which the canonical prohibition of interest (except in one incidental remark which has no connection with the general argument) is not even mentioned, on the assumption that this prohibition of interest, which has a parallel in almost every religious ethic in the world, is taken to be the decisive criterion of the difference between the Catholic and Protestant ethics, is almost inconceivable. One should really only criticize things which one has read, or the argument of which, if read, one has not already forgotten. The campaign against *usuraria pravitas* runs through both the Huguenot and the Dutch Church history of the sixteenth century; Lombards, i.e. bankers, were by virtue of that fact alone often excluded from communion (see Chap. I, note 17). The more liberal attitude of Calvin (which did not, however, prevent the inclusion of regulations against usury in the first plan of the ordinances) did not gain a definite victory until Salmasius. Hence the difference did not lie at this point; quite the contrary. But still worse are the author's own arguments on this point. Compared to the works of Funck and other Catholic scholars (which he has not, in my opinion, taken as fully into consideration as they deserve), and the investigations of Endemann, which, however obsolete in certain points to-day, are still fundamental, they make a painful impression of superficiality. To be sure, Keller has abstained from such excesses as the remarks of Sombart (*Der Bourgeois*, p. 321) that one noticed how the "pious gentlemen" (Bernard of Siena and Anthony of Florence) "wished to excite the spirit of enterprise by every possible means", that is, since they, just like nearly everyone else concerned with the prohibition of interest, interpreted it in such a way as to exempt what we should call the productive investment of capital. That Sombart, on the one hand, places the Romans among the heroic peoples, and on the other, what is for his work as a whole an impossible contradiction, considers economic rationalism to have been developed to its final consequences in Cato (p. 267), may be mentioned by the way as a symptom that this is a book with a thesis in the worst sense.

He has also completely misrepresented the significance of the prohibition of interest. This cannot be set forth here in detail. At one time it was often exaggerated, then strongly underestimated, and now, in an era which produces Catholic millionaires as well as Protestant, has been turned upside down for apologetic purposes. As is well known, it was not, in spite of Biblical authority, abolished until the last century by order of the *Congregatio S. Officii*, and then only *temporum ratione habita* and indirectly, namely, by forbidding confessors to worry their charges by questions about *usuraria pravitas*, even though no claim to obedience was given up in case it should be restored. Anyone who has made a thorough study of the extremely complicated history of the doctrine cannot claim, considering the endless controversies over, for instance, the justification of the purchase of bonds, the discounting of notes and various other contracts (and above all considering the order of the *Congregatio S. Officii*, mentioned above, concerning a municipal loan), that the prohibition of interest was only intended to apply to emergency loans, nor that it had the intention of preserving capital, or that it was even an aid to capitalistic enterprise (p. 25). The truth is that the Church came to reconsider the prohibition of interest comparatively late. At the time when this happened the forms of purely business investment were not loans at fixed interest rate, but the *fœnus nauticum, commenda, societas maris*, and the *dare ad proficuum de mari* (a loan in which the shares of gain and loss were adjusted according to degrees of risk), and were, considering the character of the return on loans to productive enterprise, necessarily of that sort. These were not (or only according to a few rigorous canonists) held to fall under the ban, but when investment at a definite rate of interest and discounting became possible and customary, the first sort of loans also encountered very troublesome difficulties from the prohibition, which led to various drastic measures of the merchant guilds (black lists). But the treatment of usury on the part of the canonists was generally purely legal and formal, and was certainly free from any such tendency to protect capital as Keller ascribes to it. Finally, in so far as any attitude towards capitalism as such can be ascertained, the decisive factors were: on the one hand, a traditional, mostly inarticulate hostility towards the growing power of capital which was impersonal, and hence not readily amenable to ethical control (as it is still reflected in Luther's pronouncements about the Fuggers and about the banking business); on the other hand, the necessity of accommodation to practical needs. But we cannot discuss this, for, as has been said, the prohibition of usury and its fate can have at most a symptomatic significance for us, and that only to a limited degree.

The economic ethic of the Scotists, and especially of certain mendicant theologians of the fourteenth century, above all Bernhard of Siena and Anthony of Florence, that is monks with a specifically rational type of asceticism, undoubtedly deserves a separate treatment, and cannot be disposed of incidentally in our discussion. Otherwise I should be forced here, in reply to criticism, to anticipate what I have to say in my discussion of the economic ethics of Catholicism in its positive relations to capitalism. These authors attempt, and in that anticipate some of the Jesuits, to present the profit of the merchant as a reward for his *industria*, and thus ethically to justify it. (Of course, even Keller cannot claim more.)

The concept and the approval of *industria* come, of course, in the last analysis from monastic asceticism, probably also from the idea of *masserizia*, which Alberti, as he himself says through the mouth of Gianozzo, takes over from clerical sources. We shall later speak more fully of the sense in which the monastic ethics is a forerunner

Notes

of the worldly ascetic denominations of Protestantism. In Greece, among the Cynics, as shown by late-Hellenic tombstone inscriptions, and, with an entirely different background, in Egypt, there were suggestions of similar ideas. But what is for us the most important thing is entirely lacking both here and in the case of Alberti. As we shall see later, the characteristic Protestant conception of the proof of one's own salvation, the *certitudo salutis* in a calling, provided the psychological sanctions which this religious belief put behind the *industria*. But that Catholicism could not supply, because its means to salvation were different. In effect these authors are concerned with an ethical doctrine, not with motives to practical action, dependent on the desire for salvation. Furthermore, they are, as is very easy to see, concerned with concessions to practical necessity, not, as was worldly asceticism, with deductions from fundamental religious postulates. (Incidentally, Anthony and Bernhard have long ago been better dealt with than by Keller.) And even these concessions have remained an object of controversy down to the present. Nevertheless the significance of these monastic ethical conceptions as symptoms is by no means small.

But the real roots of the religious ethics which led the way to the modern conception of a calling lay in the sects and the heterodox movements, above all in Wyclif; although Brodnitz (*Englische Wirtschaftsgeschichte*), who thinks his influence was so great that Puritanism found nothing left for it to do, greatly overestimates his significance. All that cannot be gone into here. For here we can only discuss incidentally whether and to what extent the Christian ethic of the Middle Ages had in fact already prepared the way for the spirit of capitalism.

30. The words μηδὲν ἀπελπίζοντες (Luke vi. 35) and the translation of the Vulgate, *nihil inde sperantes*, are thought (according to A. Merx) to be a corruption of μηδένα ἀπελπίζοντες (or *meminem desperantes*), and thus to command the granting of loans to all brothers, including the poor, without saying anything at all about interest. The passage *Deo placere vix potest* is now thought to be of Arian origin (which, if true, makes no difference to our contentions).

31. How a compromise with the prohibition of usury was achieved is shown, for example, in Book I, chapter 65, of the statutes of the *Arte di Calimala* (at present I have only the Italian edition in Emiliani-Guidici, *Stor. dei Com. Ital.*, III, p. 246). "Procurino i consoli con quelli frate, che parrà loro, che perdono si faccia e come fare si possa il meglio per l'amore di ciascuno, del dono, merito o guiderdono, ovvero interesse per l'anno presente e secondo che altra volta fatto fue." It is thus a way for the guild to secure exemption for its members on account of their official positions, without defiance of authority. The suggestions immediately following, as well as the immediately preceding idea to book all interest and profits as gifts, are very characteristic of the amoral attitude towards profits on

capital. To the present stock exchange black list against brokers who hold back the difference between top price and actual selling price, often corresponded the outcry against those who pleaded before the ecclesiastical court with the *exceptio usurariæ pravitatis*.

CHAPTER III

1. Of the ancient languages, only Hebrew has any similar concept. Most of all in the word מְלָאכָה. It is used for sacerdotal funntions (Exod. xxxv. 21; Neh. xi. 22; 1 Chron. ix. 13; xxiii. 4; xxvi. 30), for business in the service of the king (especially 1 Sam. viii. 16; 1 Chron. iv. 23; xxix. 6), for the service of a royal official (Esther iii. 9; ix. 3), of a superintendant of labour (2 Kings xii. 12), of a slave (Gen. xxxix. 11), of labour in the fields (1 Chron. xxvii. 26), of craftsmen (Exod. xxxi. 5; xxxv. 21; Kings vii. 14), for traders (Psa. cvii. 23), and for worldly activity of any kind in the passage, Sirach xi. 20, to be discussed later. The word is derived from the root לאָךְ, to send, thus meaning originally a task. That it originated in the ideas current in Solomon's bureaucratic kingdom of serfs (*Fronstaat*), built up as it was according to the Egyptian model, seems evident from the above references. In meaning, however, as I learn from A. Merx, this root concept had become lost even in antiquity. The word came to be used for any sort of labour, and in fact became fully as colourless as the German *Beruf*, with which it shared the fate of being used primarily for mental and not manual functions. The expression (חֹק), assignment, task, lesson, which also occurs in Sirach xi. 20, and is translated in the Septuagint with διαθήκη, is also derived from the terminology of the servile bureaucratic regime of the time, as is דִּבְרִיוֹם (Exod. v. 13, cf. Exod. v. 14), where the Septuagint also uses διαθήκη for task. In Sirach xliii. 10 it is rendered in the Septuagint with κρίμα. In Sirach xi. 20 it is evidently used to signify the fulfillment of God's commandments, being thus related to our calling. On this passage in Jesus Sirach reference may here be made to Smend's well-known book on Jesus Sirach, and for the words διαθήκη, ἔργον, πόνος, to his *Index zur Weisheit des Jesus Sirach* (Berlin, 1907). As is well known, the Hebrew text of the Book of Sirach was lost, but has been rediscovered by Schechter, and in part supplemented by quotations from the Talmud. Luther did not possess it, and these two Hebrew concepts could not have had any influence on his use of language. (See below on Prov. xxii. 29.)

In Greek there is no term corresponding in ethical connotation to the German or English words at all. Where Luther, quite in the spirit of the modern usage (see below), translates Jesus Sirach xi. 20 and 21, *bleibe in deinem Beruf*, the Septuagint has at one point ἔργον, at the other, which however seems to be an entirely corrupt passage, πόνος (the Hebrew original speaks of the shining of divine help!). Otherwise in antiquity τὰ προσήκοντο is used in the general sense of duties. In the works of the Stoics κάματος occasionally carries similar connotations, though its linguistic source is indifferent (called to my attention by A. Dieterich). All other expressions (such as τάξις, etc.) have no ethical implications.

In Latin what we translate as calling, a man's sustained activity under the division of labour, which is thus (normally) his source of income and in the long run the economic basis of his existence, is, aside from the colourless *opus*, expressed with an ethical content, at least similar to that of the German word, either by *officium* (from *opificium*, which was originally ethically colourless, but later, as especially in Seneca *de benef*, IV, p. 18, came to mean *Beruf*); or by *munus*, derived from the compulsory obligations of the old civic community; or finally by *professio*. This last word was also characteristically used in this sense for public obligations, probably being derived from the old tax declarations of the citizens. But later it came to be applied in the special modern sense of the liberal professions (as in *professio bene dicendi*), and in this narrower meaning had a significance in every way similar to the German *Beruf*, even in the more spiritual sense of the word, as when Cicero says of someone "non intelligit quid profiteatur", in the sense of "he does not know his real profession". The only difference is that it is, of course, definitely secular without any religious connotation. That is even more true of *ars*, which in Imperial times was used for handicraft. The Vulgate translates the above passages from Jesus Sirach, at one point with *opus*, the other (verse 21) with *locus*, which in this case means something like social station. The addition of *mandaturam tuorum* comes from the ascetic Jerome, as Brentano quite rightly remarks, without, however, here or elsewhere, calling attention to the fact that this was characteristic of precisely the ascetic use of the term, before the Reformation in an otherworldly, afterwards in a worldly, sense. It is furthermore uncertain from what text Jerome's translation was made. An influence of the old liturgical meaning of מְלָאכָה does not seem to be impossible.

In the Romance languages only the Spanish *vocacion* in the sense of an inner call to something, from the analogy of a clerical office, has a connotation partly corresponding to that of the German word, but it is never used to mean calling in the external sense. In the Romance Bible translations the Spanish *vocacion*, the Italian *vocazione* and *chiamamento*, which otherwise have a meaning partly corresponding to the Lutheran and Calvinistic usage to be discussed presently, are used only to translate the κλῆσις of the New Testament, the call of the Gospel to eternal salvation, which in the Vulgate is *vocatio*. Strange to say, Brentano, *op. cit.*, maintains that this fact, which I have myself adduced to defend my view, is evidenced for the existence of the concept of the calling in the sense which it had later, before the Reformation. But it is nothing of the kind. κλῆσις had to be translated by *vocatio*. But where and when in the Middle Ages was it used in our sense? The fact of this translation, and in spite of it, the lack of any application of the word to worldly callings is what is decisive. *Chiamamento* is used in this manner along with *vocazione* in the Italian Bible translation of the fifteenth century, which is printed in the *Collezione di opere inedite e rare* (Bologna, 1887), while the modern Italian translations use the latter alone. On the other hand, the words used in the Romance languages for calling in the external worldly sense of regular acquisitive activity carry, as appears from all the dictionaries and from a report of my friend Professor Baist (of Freiburg), no religious connotation whatever. This is so no matter whether they are derived from *ministerium* or *officium*, which originally had a certain religious colouring, or from *ars, professio*, and *implicare* (*impeigo*), from which it has been entirely absent from the beginning. The passages in Jesus Sirach mentioned above, where Luther used *Beruf*, are translated: in French, v. 20, *office*; v. 21, *labeur* (Calvinistic translation); Spanish, v. 20, *obra*; v. 21, *lugar* (following the Vulgate); recent translations, *posto* (Protestant). The Protestants of the Latin countries, since they were minorities, did not exercise, possibly without even making the attempt, such a creative influence over their respective languages as Luther did over the still less highly rationalized (in an academic sense) German official language.

2. On the other hand, the *Augsburg Confession* only contains the idea implicitly and but partially developed. Article XVI (ed. by Kolde, p. 43) teaches: "Meanwhile it (the Gospel) does not dissolve the ties of civil or domestic economy, but strongly enjoins us to maintain them as ordinances of God and in such ordinances (*ein jeder nach seinem Beruf*) to exercise charity." (Translated by Rev. W. H. Teale, Leeds, 1842.)

(In Latin it is only "et in talibus ordinationibus exercere caritatem". The English is evidently translated directly from the Latin, and does not contain the idea which came into the German version.—TRANSLATOR'S NOTE.)

The conclusion drawn, that one must obey authority, shows that here *Beruf* is thought of, at least primarily, as an objective order in the sense of the passage in 1 Cor. vii. 20.

And Article XXVII (Kolde, p. 83) speaks of *Beruf* (Latin *in vocatione sua*) only in connection with estates ordained by God: clergy, magistrates, princes, lords, etc. But even this is true only of the German version of the *Konkordienbuch*, while in the German *Ed. princeps* the sentence is left out.

Only in Article XXVI (Kolde, p. 81) is the word used in a sense which at least includes our present meaning: "that he did chastise his body, not to deserve by that discipline remission of sin, but to

Notes

have his body in bondage and apt to spiritual things, and to do his calling". Translated by Richard Taverner, Philadelphia Publications Society, 1888. (Latin *juxta vocationem suam*.)

3. According to the lexicons, kindly confirmed by my colleagues Professors Braune and Hoops, the word *Beruf* (Dutch *beroep*, English *calling*, Danish *kald*, Swedish *kallelse*) does not occur in any of the languages which now contain it in its present worldly (secular) sense before Luther's translation of the Bible. The Middle High German, Middle Low German, and Middle Dutch words, which sound like it, all mean the same as *Ruf* in modern German, especially inclusive, in late mediæval times, of the calling (vocation) of a candidate to a clerical benefice by those with the power of appointment. It is a special case which is also often mentioned in the dictionaries of the Scandinavian languages. The word is also occasionally used by Luther in the same sense. However, even though this special use of the word may have promoted its change of meaning, the modern conception of *Beruf* undoubtedly goes linguistically back to the Bible translations by Protestants, and any anticipation of it is only to be found, as we shall see later, in Tauler (died 1361). All the languages which were fundamentally influenced by the Protestant Bible translations have the word, all of which this was not true (like the Romance languages) do not, or at least not in its modern meaning.

Luther renders two quite different concepts with *Beruf*. First the Pauline κλῆσις in the sense of the call to eternal salvation through God. Thus: 1 Cor. i. 26; Eph. i. 18; iv. 1, 4; 2 Thess. i. 11; Heb. iii. 1; 2 Peter i. 10. All these cases concern the purely religious idea of the call through the Gospel taught by the apostle; the word κλῆσις has nothing to do with worldly callings in the modern sense. The German Bibles before Luther use in this case *ruffunge* (so in all those in the Heidelberg Library), and sometimes instead of "von Gott geruffet" say "von Gott gefordert". Secondly, however, he, as we have already seen, translates the words in Jesus Sirach discussed in the previous note (in the Septuagint ἐν τῷ ἔργῳ σου παλαιώθητι and καὶ ἔμμενε τῷ πόνῳ σου), with "beharre in deinem Beruf" and "bliebe in deinem Beruf", instead of "bliebe bei deiner Arbeit". The later (authorized) Catholic translations (for instance that of Fleischütz, Fulda, 1781) have (as in the New Testament passages) simply followed him. Luther's translation of the passage in the Book of Sirach is, so far as I know, the first case in which the German word *Beruf* appears in its present purely secular sense. The preceding exhortation, verse 20, στῆθι εν διαθήκῃ σου, he translates "bliebe in Gottes Wort", although Sirach xiv. 1 and xliii. 10 show that, corresponding to the Hebrew חק, which (according to quotations in the Talmud) Sirach used, διαθήκη really did mean something similar to our calling, namely one's fate or assigned task. In its later and present sense the word *Beruf* did not exist in the German language, nor, so far as I can learn, in the works of the older Bible translators or preachers. The German Bibles before Luther rendered the passage from Sirach with *Werk*. Berthold of Regensburg, at the points in his sermons where the modern would say *Beruf*, uses the word *Arbeit*. The usage was thus the same as in antiquity. The first passage I know, in which not *Beruf* but *Ruf* (as a translation of κλῆσις) is applied to purely worldly labour, is in the fine sermon of Tauler on Ephesians iv (Works, Basle edition, f. 117.v), of peasants who *misten* go: they often fare better "so sie folgen einfeltiglich irem Ruff denn die geistlichen Menschen, die auf ihren Ruf nicht Acht haben". The word in this sense did not find its way into everyday speech. Although Luther's usage at first vacillates between *Ruf* and *Beruf* (see *Werke*, Erlangen edition, p. 51.), that he was directly influenced by Tauler is by no means certain, although the *Freiheit eines Christenmenschen* is in many respects similar to this sermon of Tauler. But in the purely worldly sense of Tauler, Luther did not use the word *Ruf*. (This against Denifle, *Luther*, p. 163.)

Now evidently Sirach's advice in the version of the Septuagint contains, apart from the general exhortation to trust in God, no suggestion of a specifically religious valuation of secular labour in a calling. The term πόνος, toil, in the corrupt second passage would be rather the opposite, if it were not corrupted. What Jesus Sirach says simply corresponds to the exhortation of the psalmist (Psa. xxxvii. 3), "Dwell in the land, and feed on his faithfulness", as also comes out clearly in the connection with the warning not to let oneself be blinded with the works of the godless, since it is easy for God to make a poor man rich. Only the opening exhortation to remain in the פֿן (verse 20) has a certain resemblance to the κλῆσις of the Gospel, but here Luther did not use the word *Beruf* for the Greek διαθήκη. The connection between Luther's two seemingly quite unrelated uses of the word *Beruf* is found in the first letter to the Corinthians and its translation.

In the usual modern editions, the whole context in which the passage stands is as follows, 1 Cor. vii. 17 (English, King James version [American revision, 1901]): "(17) Only as the Lord hath distributed to each man, as God hath called each, so let him walk. And so ordain I in all churches. (18) Was any man called being circumcised? let him not become uncircumcised. Hath any man been called in uncircumcision? let him not be circumcised. (19) Circumcision is nothing and uncircumcision is nothing; but the keeping of the commandments of God. (20) Let each man abide in that calling wherein he was called (ἐν τῇ κλήσει ᾗ ἐκλήθη; an undoubted Hebraism, as Professor Merx tells me). (21) Wast thou called being a bondservant? care not for it; nay even if thou canst become free use it rather. (22) For he that was called in the Lord being a bondservant is the Lord's freedman; likewise he that was called being free is

Christ's bondservant. (23) Ye were bought with a price; become not bondservants of men. (24) Brethren, let each man, wherein he was called, therein abide with God."

In verse 29 follows the remark that time is shortened, followed by the well-known commandments motivated by eschatological expectations: (31) to possess women as though one did not have them, to buy as though one did not have what one had bought, etc. In verse 20 Luther, following the older German translations, even in 1523 in his exigesis of this chapter, renders κλῆσις with *Beruf*, and interprets it with *Stand*. (Erlangen ed., LI, p. 51.)

In fact it is evident that the word κλῆσις at this point, and only at this, corresponds approximately to the Latin *status* and the German *Stand* (status of marriage, status of a servant, etc.). But of course not as Brentano, *op. cit.*, p. 137, assumes, in the modern sense of *Beruf*. Brentano can hardly have read this passage, or what I have said about it, very carefully. In a sense at least suggesting it this word, which is etymologically related to ἐκκλησία, an assembly which has been called, occurs in Greek literature, so far as the lexicons tell, only once in a passage from Dionysius of Halicarnassus, where it corresponds to the Latin *classis*, a word borrowed from the Greek, meaning that part of the citizenry which has been called to the colours. Theophylaktos (eleventh-twelfth century) interprets 1 Cor. vii. 20: ἐν οἶῳ βίῳ καὶ ἐν οἶῳ τάγματι καὶ πολιτεύματι ὢν ἐπίστευσεν. (My colleague Professor Deissmann called my attention to this passage.) Now, even in our passage, κλῆσις does not correspond to the modern *Beruf*. But having translated κλῆσις with *Beruf* in the eschatologically motivated exhortation, that everyone should remain in his present status, Luther, when he later came to translate the Apocrypha, would naturally, on account of the similar content of the exhortations alone, also use *Beruf* for πόνος in the traditionalistic and anti-chrematistic commandment of Jesus Sirach, that everyone should remain in the same business. This is what is important and characteristic. The passage in 1 Cor. vii. 17 does not, as has been pointed out, use κλῆσις at all in the sense of *Beruf*, a definite field of activity.

In the meantime (or about the same time), in the *Augsburg Confession*, the Protestant dogma of the uselessness of the Catholic attempt to excel worldly morality was established, and in it the expression "einem jeglichen nach seinem Beruf" was used (see previous note). In Luther's translation, both this and the positive valuation of the order in which the individual was placed, as holy, which was gaining ground just about the beginning of the 1530's, stand out. It was a result of his more and more sharply defined belief in special Divine Providence, even in the details of life, and at the same time of his increasing inclination to accept the existing order of things in the world as immutably willed by God. *Vocatio*, in the traditional Latin, meant the divine call to a life of holiness, especially in a monastery or as a priest. But now, under the influence of this dogma, life in a worldly calling came for Luther to have the same connotation. For he now translated πόνος and ἔργον in Jesus Sirach with *Beruf*, for which, up to that time, there had been only the (Latin) analogy, coming from the monastic translation. But a few years earlier, in Prov. xxii. 29, he had still translated the Hebrew מְלָאכָה, which was the original of ἔργον in the Greek text of Jesus Sirach, and which, like the German *Beruf* and the Scandinavian *kald, kallelse*, originally related to a *spiritual* call (*Beruf*), as in other passages (Gen. xxxix. 11), with *Geschäft* (Septuagint ἔργον, Vulgate *opus*, English Bibles *business*, and correspondingly in the Scandinavian and all the other translations before me).

The word *Beruf*, in the modern sense which he had finally created, remained for the time being entirely Lutheran. To the Calvinists the Apocrypha are entirely uncanonical. It was only as a result of the development which brought the interest in proof of salvation to the fore that Luther's concept was taken over, and then strongly emphasized by them. But in their first (Romance) translations they had no such word available, and no power to create one in the usage of a language already so stereotyped.

As early as the sixteenth century the concept of *Beruf* in its present sense became established in secular literature. The Bible translators before Luther had used the word *Berufung* for κλῆσις (as for instance in the Heidelberg versions of 1462–66 and 1485), and the Eck translation of 1537 says "in dem Ruf, worin er beruft ist". Most of the later Catholic translators directly follow Luther. In England, the first of all, Wyclif's translation (1382), used *cleping* (the Old English word which was later replaced by the borrowed *calling*). It is quite characteristic of the Lollard ethics to use a word which already corresponded to the later usage of the Reformation. Tyndale's translation of 1534, on the other hand, interprets the idea in terms of *status*: "in the same state wherein he was called", as also does the Geneva Bible of 1557. Cranmer's official translation of 1539 substituted *calling* for *state*, while the (Catholic) Bible of Rheims (1582), as well as the Anglican Court Bibles of the Elizabethan era, characteristically return to vocation, following the Vulgate.

That for England, Cranmer's Bible translation is the source of the Puritan conception of calling in the sense of *Beruf*, trade, has already, quite correctly, been pointed out by Murray. As early as the middle of the sixteenth century calling is used in that sense. In 1588 unlawful callings are referred to, and in 1603 greater callings in the sense of higher occupations, etc. (see Murray). Quite remarkable is Brentano's idea (*op. cit.*, p. 139), that in the Middle Ages *vocatio* was not translated with *Beruf*, and that this concept was not known, because only a free man could engage in a *Beruf*, and freemen, in the middle-class professions, did not exist at that time. Since the

Notes

whole social structure of the mediæval crafts, as opposed to those of antiquity, rested upon free labour, and, above all, almost all the merchants were freemen, I do not clearly understand this thesis.

4. Compare with the following the instructive discussion in K. Eger, *Die Anschauung Luthers vom Beruf* (Giessen, 1900). Perhaps its only serious fault, which is shared by almost all other theological writers, is his insufficiently clear analysis of the concept of *lex naturæ*. On this see E. Troeltsch in his review of Seeberg's *Dogmengeschichte*, and now above all in the relevant parts of his *Soziallehren der christlichen Kirchen*.

5. For when Thomas Aquinas represents the division of men into estates and occupational groups as the work of divine providence, by that he means the objective cosmos of society. But that the individual should take up a particular calling (as we should say; Thomas, however, says *ministerium* or *officium*) is due to *causæ naturales*. *Quæst. quodlibetal*, VII, Art. 17c: "Hæc autem diversificatio hominum in diversis officiis contingit primo ex divina providentia, quæ ita hominum status distribuit . . . secundo etiam ex causis naturalibus, ex quibus contingit, quod in diversis hominibus sunt diversæ inclinationes ad diversa officia. . . ."

Quite similar is Pascal's view when he says that it is chance which determines the choice of a calling. See on Pascal, A. Koester, *Die Ethik Pascals* (1907). Of the organic systems of religious ethics, only the most complete of them, the Indian, is different in this respect. The difference between the Thomistic and the Protestant ideas of the calling is so evident that we may dismiss it for the present with the above quotation. This is true even as between the Thomistic and the later Lutheran ethics, which are very similar in many other respects, especially in their emphasis on Providence. We shall return later to a discussion of the Catholic view-point. On Thomas Aquinas, see Maurenbrecher, *Thomas von Aquino's Stellung zum Wirtschaftsleben seiner Zeit*, 1888. Otherwise, where Luther agrees with Thomas in details, he has probably been influenced rather by the general doctrines of Scholasticism than by Thomas in particular. For, according to Denifle's investigations, he seems really not to have known Thomas very well. See Denifle, *Luther und Luthertum* (1903), p. 501, and on it, Koehler, *Ein Wort zu Denifles Luther* (1904), p. 25.

6. In *Von der Freiheit eines Christenmenschen*, (1) the double nature of man is used for the justification of worldly duties in the sense of the *lex naturæ* (here the natural order of the world). From that it follows (Erlangen edition, 27, p. 188) that man is inevitably bound to his body and to the social community. (2) In this situation he will (p. 196: this is a second justification), if he is a believing Christian, decide to repay God's act of grace, which was done for pure love, by love of his neighbour. With this very loose connection between faith and love is combined (3) (p. 190) the old ascetic justification

of labour as a means of securing to the inner man mastery over the body. (4) Labour is hence, as the reasoning is continued with another appearance of the idea of *lex naturæ* in another sense (here, natural morality), an original instinct given by God to Adam (before the fall), which he has obeyed "solely to please God". Finally (5) (pp. 161 and 199), there appears, in connection with Matt. vii. 18 f., the idea that good work in one's ordinary calling is and must be the result of the renewal of life, caused by faith, without, however, developing the most important Calvinistic idea of proof. The powerful emotion which dominates the work explains the presence of such contradictory ideas.

7. "It is not from the benevolence of the butcher, the brewer, or the baker, that we expect our dinner, but from their regard to their own interest. We address ourselves, not to their humanity, but to their self-love; and never talk to them of our own necessities, but of their advantages" (*Wealth of Nations*, Book I, chap. ii).

8. "Omnia enim per te operabitur (Deus), mulgebit per te vaccam et servilissima quæque opera faciet, ac maxima pariter et minima ipsi grata erunt" (*Exigesis of Genesis, Opera lat. exeget.*, ed. Elsperger, VII, p. 213). The idea is found before Luther in Tauler, who holds the spiritual and the worldly *Ruf* to be in principle of equal value. The difference from the Thomistic view is common to the German mystics and Luther. It may be said that Thomas, principally to retain the moral value of contemplation, but also from the view-point of the mendicant friar, is forced to interpret Paul's doctrine that "if a man will not work he shall not eat" in the sense that labour, which is of course necessary *lege naturæ*, is imposed upon the human race as a whole, but not on all individuals. The gradation in the value of forms of labour, from the *opera servilia* of the peasants upwards, is connected with the specific character of the mendicant friars, who were for material reasons bound to the town as a place of domicile. It was equally foreign to the German mystics and to Luther, the peasant's son; both of them, while valuing all occupations equally, looked upon their order of rank as willed by God. For the relevant passages in Thomas see Maurenbrecher, *op. cit.*, pp. 65 ff.

9. It is astonishing that some investigators can maintain that such a change could have been without effect upon the actions of men. I confess my inability to understand such a view.

10. "Vanity is so firmly imbedded in the human heart that a camp-follower, a kitchen-helper, or a porter, boast and seek admirers. . . ." (Faugeres edition, I, p. 208. Compare Koester, *op. cit.*, pp. 17, 136 ff.). On the attitude of Port Royal and the Jansenists to the calling, to which we shall return, see now the excellent study of Dr. Paul Honigsheim, *Die Staats- und Soziallehren der französischen Jansenisten im 17ten Jahrhundert* (Heidelberg Historical Dissertation, 1914. It is a separately printed part of a more comprehensive work on the *Vorgeschichte der französischen Aufklärung*. Compare especially pp. 138 ff.).

Notes

11. Apropos of the Fuggers, he thinks that it "cannot be right and godly for such a great and regal fortune to be piled up in the lifetime of one man". That is evidently the peasant's mistrust of capital. Similarly (*Grosser Sermon vom Wucher*, Erlangen edition, XX, p. 109) investment in securities he considers ethically undesirable, because it is "ein neues behendes erfunden Ding"—i.e. because it is to him economically incomprehensible; somewhat like margin trading to the modern clergyman.

12. The difference is well worked out by H. Levy (in his study, *Die Grundlagen des ökonomischen Liberalismus in der Geschichte der englischen Volkswirtschaft*, Jena, 1912). Compare also, for instance, the petition of the Levellers in Cromwell's army of 1653 against monopolies and companies, given in Gardiner, *Commonwealth*, II, p. 179. Laud's regime, on the other hand, worked for a Christian, social, economic organization under the joint leadership of Crown and Church, from which the King hoped for political and fiscal-monopolistic advantages. It was against just this that the Puritans were struggling.

13. What I understand by this may be shown by the example of the proclamation addressed by Cromwell to the Irish in 1650, with which he opened his war against them and which formed his reply to the manifestos of the Irish (Catholic) clergy of Clonmacnoise of December 4 and 13, 1649. The most important sentences follow: "Englishmen had good inheritances (namely in Ireland) which many of them purchased with their money . . . they had good leases from Irishmen for long time to come, great stocks thereupon, houses and plantations erected at their cost and charge. . . . You broke the union . . . at a time when Ireland was in perfect peace and when, through the example of English industry, through commerce and traffic, that which was in the nation's hands was better to them than if all Ireland had been in their possession. . . . Is God, will God be with you? I am confident He will not."

This proclamation, which is suggestive of articles in the English Press at the time of the Boer War, is not characteristic, because the capitalistic interests of Englishmen are held to be the justification of the war. That argument could, of course, have just as well been made use of, for instance, in a quarrel between Venice and Genoa over their respective spheres of influence in the Orient (which, in spite of my pointing it out here, Brentano, *op. cit.*, p. 142, strangely enough holds against me). On the contrary, what is interesting in the document is that Cromwell, with the deepest personal conviction, as everyone who knows his character will agree, bases the moral justification of the subjection of the Irish, in calling God to witness, on the fact that English capital has taught the Irish to work. (The proclamation is in Carlyle, and is also reprinted and analysed in Gardiner, *History of the Commonwealth*, I, pp. 163 f.)

14. This is not the place to follow the subject farther. Compare the authors cited in Note 16 below.

15. Compare the remarks in Jülicher's fine book, *Die Gleichnisreden Jesu*, II, pp. 108, 636 f.

16. With what follows, compare above all the discussion in Eger, *op. cit.* Also Schneckenburger's fine work, which is even to-day not yet out of date (*Vergleichende Darstellung der lutherischen und reformierten Lehrbegriffe*, Grüder, Stuttgart, 1855). Luthardt's *Ethik Luthers*, p. 84 of the first edition, the only one to which I have had access, gives no real picture of the development. Further compare Seeberg, *Dogmengeschichte*, II, pp. 262 ff. The article on *Beruf* in the *Realenzyklopädie für protestantische Theologie und Kirche* is valueless. Instead of a scientific analysis of the conception and its origin, it contains all sorts of rather sentimental observations on all possible subjects, such as the position of women, etc. Of the economic literature on Luther, I refer here only to Schmoller's studies ("Geschichte der Nationalökonomischen Ansichten in Deutschland während der Reformationszeit", *Zeitschrift f. Staatswiss.*, XVI, 1860); Wiskemann's prize essay (1861); and the study of Frank G. Ward ("Darstellung und Würdigung von Luthers Ansichten vom Staat und seinen wirtschaftlichen Aufgaben", *Conrads Abhandlungen*, XXI, Jena, 1898). The literature on Luther in commemoration of the anniversary of the Reformation, part of which is excellent, has, so far as I can see, made no definite contribution to this particular problem. On the social ethics of Luther (and the Lutherans) compare, of course, the relevant parts of Troeltsch's *Soziallehren*.

17. *Analysis of the Seventh Chapter of the First Epistle to the Corinthians*, 1523, Erlangen edition, LI, p. 1. Here Luther still interprets the idea of the freedom of every calling before God in the sense of this passage, so as to emphasize (1) that certain human institutions should be repudiated (monastic vows, the prohibition of mixed marriages, etc.), (2) that the fulfillment of traditional worldly duties to one's neighbour (in itself indifferent before God) is turned into a commandment of brotherly love. In fact this characteristic reasoning (for instance pp. 55, 56) fundamentally concerns the question of the dualism of the *lex naturæ* in its relations with divine justice.

18. Compare the passage from *Von Kaufhandlung und Wucher*, which Sombart rightly uses as a motto for his treatment of the handicraft spirit (= traditionalism): "Darum musst du dir fürsetzen, nichts denn deine ziemliche Nahrung zu suchen in solchem Handel, danach Kost, Mühe, Arbeit und Gefahr rechnen und überschlagen und also dann die Ware selbst setzen, steigern oder niedern, dass du solcher Arbeit und Mühe Lohn davon hasst." The principle is formulated in a thoroughly Thomistic spirit.

19. As early as the letter to H. von Sternberg of 1530, in which he dedicates the Exigesis of the 117th Psalm to him, the estate of the

Notes

lower nobility appears to him, in spite of its moral degradation, as ordained of God (Erlangen edition, XL, pp. 282 ff.). The decisive influence of the Münzer disturbances in developing this view-point can clearly be seen in the letter (p. 282). Compare also Eger, *op. cit.*, p. 150.

20. Also in the analysis of the 111th Psalm, verses 5 and 6 (Erlangen edition, XL, pp. 215–16), written in 1530, the starting-point is the polemics against withdrawal from the world into monasteries. But in this case the *lex naturæ* (as distinct from positive law made by the Emperor and the Jurists) is directly identical with divine justice. It is God's ordinance, and includes especially the division of the people into classes (p. 215). The equal value of the classes is emphasized, but only in the sight of God.

21. As taught especially in the works *Von Konzilien und Kirchen* (1539) and *Kurzer Bekenntnis vom heiligen Sakrament* (1545).

22. How far in the background of Luther's thought was the most important idea of proof of the Christian in his calling and his worldly conduct, which dominated Calvinism, is shown by this passage from *Von Konzilien und Kirchen* (1539, Erlangen edition, XXV, p. 376): "Besides these seven principal signs there are more superficial ones by which the holy Christian Church can be known. If we are not unchaste nor drunkards, proud, insolent, nor extravagant, but chaste, modest, and temperate." According to Luther these signs are not so infallible as the others (purity of doctrine, prayer, etc.). "Because certain of the heathen have borne themselves so and sometimes even appeared holier than Christians." Calvin's personal position was, as we shall see, not very different, but that was not true of Puritanism. In any case, for Luther the Christian serves God only *in vocatione*, not *per vocationem* (Eger, pp. 117 ff.). Of the idea of proof, on the other hand (more, however, in its Pietistic than its Calvinistic form), there are at least isolated suggestions in the German mystics (see for instance in Seeberg, *Dogmengeschichte*, p. 195, the passage from Suso, as well as those from Tauler quoted above), even though it was understood only in a psychological sense.

23. His final position is well expressed in some parts of the exegesis of Genesis (in the *op. lat. exeget.* edited by Elsperger).

Vol. IV, p. 109: "Neque hæc fuit levis tentatio, intentum esse suæ vocationi et de aliis non esse curiosum. . . . Paucissimi sunt, qui sua sorte vivant contenti . . . (p. 111). Nostrum autem est, ut vocanti Deo pareamus . . . (p. 112). Regula igitur hæc servanda est, ut unusquisque maneat in sua vocatione et suo dono contentus vivat, de aliis autem non sit curiosus." In effect that is thoroughly in accordance with Thomas Aquinas's formulation of traditionalism (*Secunda secundæ*, Quest. 118, Art. 1): "Unde necesse est, quod bonum hominis circa ea consistat in quadam mensura, dum scilicet homo . . . quærit habere exteriores divitias, prout sunt necessariæ ad vitam ejus secundum suam conditionem. Et ideo in excessu hujus mensuræ consistit peccatum, dum scilicet aliquis supra debitum modum vult eas vel acquirere vel retinere, quod pertinet ad avaritiam." The sinfulness of the pursuit of acquisition beyond the point set by the needs of one's station in life is based by Thomas on the *lex naturæ* as revealed by the purpose (ratio) of external goods; by Luther, on the other hand, on God's will. On the relation of faith and the calling in Luther see also Vol. VII, p. 225: " . . . quando es fidelis, tum placent Deo etiam physica, carnalia, animalia, officia, sive edas, sive bibas, sive vigiles, sive dormias, quæ mere corporalia et animalia sunt. Tanta res est fides. . . . Verum est quidem, placere Deo etiam in impiis sedulitatem et industriam in officio [This activity in practical life is a virtue *lege naturæ*] sed obstat incredulitas et vana gloria, ne possint opera sua referre ad gloriam Dei [reminiscent of Calvinistic ways of speaking]. . . . Merentur igitur etiam impiorum bona opera in hac quidem vita præmia sua [as distinct from Augustine's 'vitia specie virtutum palliata'] sed non numerantur, non colliguntur in altero."

24. In the *Kirchenpostille* it runs (Erlangen edition, X, pp. 233, 235–6): "Everyone is called to some calling." He should wait for this call (on p. 236 it even becomes command) and serve God in it. God takes pleasure not in man's achievements but in his obedience in this respect.

25. This explains why, in contrast to what has been said above about the effects of Pietism on women workers, modern business men sometimes maintain that strict Lutheran domestic workers to-day often, for instance in Westphalia, think very largely in traditional terms. Even without going over to the factory system, and in spite of the temptation of higher earnings, they resist changes in methods of work, and in explanation maintain that in the next world such trifles won't matter anyway. It is evident that the mere fact of Church membership and belief is not in itself of essential significance for conduct as a whole. It has been much more concrete religious values and ideals which have influenced the development of capitalism in its early stages and, to a lesser extent, still do.

26. Compare Tauler, Basle edition, *Bl.*, pp. 161 ff.

27. Compare the peculiarly emotional sermon of Tauler referred to above, and the following one, 17, 18, verse 20.

28. Since this is the sole purpose of these present remarks on Luther, I have limited them to a brief preliminary sketch, which would, of course, be wholly inadequate as an appraisal of Luther's influence as a whole.

29. One who shared the philosophy of history of the Levellers would be in the fortunate position of being able to attribute this in turn to racial differences. They believed themselves to be the defenders of the Anglo-Saxon birthright, against the descendants of William the Conqueror and the Normans. It is astonishing enough that it

has not yet occurred to anyone to maintain that the plebeian Round-heads were round-headed in the anthropometric sense!

30. Especially the English national pride, a result of Magna Charta and the great wars. The saying, so typical to-day, "She looks like an English girl" on seeing any pretty foreign girl, is reported as early as the fifteenth century.

31. These differences have, of course, persisted in England as well. Especially the Squirearchy has remained the centre of "merrie old England" down to the present day, and the whole period since the Reformation may be looked upon as a struggle of the two elements in English society. In this point I agree with M. J. Bonn's remarks (in the *Frankfurter Zeitung*) on the excellent study of v. Schulze-Gaevernitz on British Imperialism. Compare H. Levy in the *Archiv für Sozialwissenschaft und Sozialpolitik*, 46, 3.

32. In spite of this and the following remarks, which in my opinion are clear enough, and have never been changed, I have again and again been accused of this.

CHAPTER IV

1. Zwinglianism we do not discuss separately, since after a short lease of power it rapidly lost in importance. Arminianism, the dog-matic peculiarity of which consisted in the repudiation of the doctrine of predestination in its strict form, and which also repudiated worldly asceticism, was organized as a sect only in Holland (and the United States). In this chapter it is without interest to us, or has only the negative interest of having been the religion of the merchant patricians in Holland (see below). In dogma it resembled the Anglican Church and most of the Methodist denominations. Its Erastian position (i.e. upholding the sovereignty of the State even in Church matters) was, however, common to all the authorities with purely political interests: the Long Parliament in England, Elizabeth, the Dutch States-General, and, above all, Oldenbarnereldt.

2. On the development of the concept of Puritanism see, above all, Sanford, *Studies and Reflections of the Great Rebellion*, p. 65 f. When we use the expression it is always in the sense which it took on in the popular speech of the seventeenth century, to mean the ascetically inclined religious movements in Holland and England without distinction of Church organization or dogma, thus including Inde-pendents, Congregationalists, Baptists, Mennonites, and Quakers.

3. This has been badly misunderstood in the discussion of these questions. Especially Sombart, but also Brentano, continually cite the ethical writers (mostly those of whom they have heard through me) as codifications of rules of conduct without ever asking which of them were supported by psychologically effective religious sanctions.

4. I hardly need to emphasize that this sketch, so far as it is concerned solely with the field of dogma, falls back everywhere on the formulations of the literature of the history of the Church and of doctrine. It makes no claim whatever to originality. Naturally I have attempted, so far as possible, to acquaint myself with the sources for the history of the Reformation. But to ignore in the process the intensive and acute theological research of many decades, instead of, as is quite indispensable, allowing oneself to be led from it to the sources, would have been presumption indeed. I must hope that the necessary brevity of the sketch has not led to incorrect formulations, and that I have at least avoided important misunderstandings of fact. The discussion contributes something new for those familiar with theological literature only in the sense that the whole is, of course, considered from the point of view of our problem. For that reason many of the most important points, for instance the rational character of this asceticism and its significance for modern life, have naturally not been emphasized by theological writers.

This aspect, and in general the sociological side, has, since the appearance of this study, been systematically studied in the work of E. Troeltsch, mentioned above, whose *Gerhard und Melancthon*, as well as numerous reviews in the *Gött. Gel. Anz.*, contained several preliminary studies to his great work. For reasons of space the references have not included everything which has been used, but for the most part only those works which that part of the text follows, or which are directly relevant to it. These are often older authors, where our problems have seemed closer to them. The insufficient pecuniary resources of German libraries have meant that in the provinces the most important source materials or studies could only be had from Berlin or other large libraries on loan for very short periods. This is the case with Voët, Baxter, Tyermans, Wesley, all the Methodist, Baptist, and Quaker authors, and many others of the earlier writers not contained in the *Corpus Reformatorum*. For any thorough study the use of English and American libraries is almost indispensable. But for the following sketch it was necessary (and possible) to be content with material available in Germany. In America recently the characteristic tendency to deny their own sectarian origins has led many university libraries to provide little or nothing new of that sort of literature. It is an aspect of the general tendency to the secularization of American life which will in a short time have dissolved the traditional national character and changed the significance of many of the fundamental institutions of the country completely and finally. It is now necessary to fall back on the small orthodox sectarian colleges.

5. On Calvin and Calvinism, besides the fundamental work of Kampschulte, the best source of information is the discussion of Erick Marcks (in his *Coligny*). Campbell, *The Puritans in Holland*,

Notes

England, and America (2 vols.), is not always critical and unprejudiced.
A strongly partisan anti-Calvinistic study is Pierson, *Studien over
Johan Calvijn*. For the development in Holland compare, besides
Motley, the Dutch classics, especially Groen van Prinsterer, *Geschie-
denis v.h. Vaderland; La Hollande et l'influence de Calvin* (1864); *Le
parti anti-révolutionnaire et confessionnel dans l'église des P.B.* (1860)
(for modern Holland); further, above all, Fruin's *Tien jaren mit den
tachtigjarigen oorlog*, and especially Naber, *Calvinist of Libertijnsch*.
Also W. J. F. Nuyens, *Gesch. der kerkel. an pol. geschillen in de Rep.
d. Ver. Prov.* (Amsterdam, 1886); A. Köhler, *Die Niederl. ref. Kirche*
(Erlangen, 1856), for the nineteenth century. For France, besides
Polenz, now Baird, *Rise of the Huguenots*. For England, besides
Carlyle, Macaulay, Masson, and, last but not least, Ranke, above all,
now the various works of Gardiner and Firth. Further, Taylor,
A Retrospect of the Religious Life in England (1854), and the excellent
book of Weingarten, *Die englischen Revolutionskirchen*. Then the
article on the English Moralists by E. Troeltsch in the *Realenzyklopädie für protestantische Theologie und Kirche*, third edition, and
of course his *Soziallehren*. Also E. Bernstein's excellent essay in
the *Geschichte des Sozialismus* (Stuttgart, 1895, I, p. 50 ff.). The best
bibliography (over seven thousand titles) is in Dexter, *Congregationalism of the Last Three Hundred Years* (principally, though not exclusively, questions of Church organization). The book is very much
better than Price (*History of Nonconformism*), Skeats, and others.
For Scotland see, among others, Sack, *Die Kirche von Schottland*
(1844), and the literature on John Knox. For the American colonies
the outstanding work is Doyle, *The English in America*. Further,
Daniel Wait Howe, *The Puritan Republic*; J. Brown, *The Pilgrim
Fathers of New England and their Puritan Successors* (third edition,
Revell). Further references will be given later.

For the differences of doctrine the following presentation is
especially indebted to Schneckenburger's lectures cited above. Ritschl's
fundamental work, *Die christliche Lehre von der Rechtfertigung und
Versöhnung* (references to Vol. III of third edition), in its mixture of
historical method with judgments of value, shows the marked peculiarities of the author, who with all his fine acuteness of logic does
not always give the reader the certainty of objectivity. Where, for
instance, he differs from Schneckenburger's interpretation I am often
doubtful of his correctness, however little I presume to have an
opinion of my own. Further, what he selects out of the great variety
of religious ideas and feelings as the Lutheran doctrine often seems
to be determined by his own preconceptions. It is what Ritschl
himself conceives to be of permanent value in Lutheranism. It is
Lutheranism as Ritschl would have had it, not always as it was.
That the works of Karl Müller, Seeberg, and others have everywhere
been made use of it is unnecessary to mention particularly. If in

the following I have condemned the reader as well as myself to the penitence of a malignant growth of footnotes, it has been done in order to give especially the non-theological reader an opportunity to check up the validity of this sketch by the suggestion of related lines of thought.

6. In the following discussion we are not primarily interested in the origin, antecedents, or history of these ascetic movements, but take their doctrines as given in a state of full development.

7. For the following discussion I may here say definitely that we are not studying the personal views of Calvin, but Calvinism, and that in the form to which it had evolved by the end of the sixteenth and in the seventeenth centuries in the great areas where it had a decisive influence and which were at the same time the home of capitalistic culture. For the present, Germany is neglected entirely, since pure Calvinism never dominated large areas here. Reformed is, of course, by no means identical with Calvinistic.

8. Even the Declaration agreed upon between the University of Cambridge and the Archbishop of Canterbury on the 17th Article of the Anglican Confession, the so-called Lambeth Article of 1595, which (contrary to the official version) expressly held that there was also predestination to eternal death, was not ratified by the Queen. The Radicals (as in *Hanserd Knolly's Confession*) laid special emphasis on the express predestination to death (not only the admission of damnation, as the milder doctrine would have it).

9. *Westminster Confession*, fifth official edition, London, 1717. Compare the Savoy and the (American) *Hanserd Knolly's Declarations*. On predestination and the Huguenots see, among others, Polenz, I, pp. 545 ff.

10. On Milton's theology see the essay of Eibach in the *Theol. Studien und Kritiken*, 1879. Macaulay's essay on it, on the occasion of Sumner's translation of the *Doctrina Christiana*, rediscovered in 1823 (Tauchnitz edition, 185, pp. 1 ff.), is superficial. For more detail see the somewhat too schematic six-volume English work of Masson, and the German biography of Milton by Stern which rests upon it. Milton early began to grow away from the doctrine of predestination in the form of the double decree, and reached a wholly free Christianity in his old age. In his freedom from the tendencies of his own time he may in a certain sense be compared to Sebastian Franck. Only Milton was a practical and positive person, Franck predominantly critical. Milton is a Puritan only in the broader sense of the rational organization of his life in the world in accordance with the divine will, which formed the permanent inheritance of later times from Calvinism. Franck could be called a Puritan in much the same sense. Both, as isolated figures, must remain outside our investigation.

11. "Hic est fides summus gradus; credere Deum esse clementum,

Notes

qui tam paucos salvat, justum, qui sua voluntate nos damnabiles facit", is the text of the famous passage in *De servo arbitrio*.

12 The truth is that both Luther and Calvin believed fundamentally in a double God (see Ritschl's remarks in *Geschichte des Pietismus* and Kostlin, *Gott* in *Realenzyklopädie für protestantische Theologie und Kirche*, third edition), the gracious and kindly Father of the New Testament, who dominates the first books of the *Institutio Christiana*, and behind him the *Deus absconditus* as an arbitrary despot. For Luther, the God of the New Testament kept the upper hand, because he avoided reflection on metaphysical questions as useless and dangerous, while for Calvin the idea of a transcendental God won out. In the popular development of Calvinism, it is true, this idea could not be maintained, but what took his place was not the Heavenly Father of the New Testament but the Jehovah of the Old.

13. Compare on the following: Scheibe, *Calvins Prädestinationslehre* (Halle, 1897). On Calvinistic theology in general, Heppe, *Dogmatik der evangelisch-reformierten Kirche* (Elberfeld, 1861).

14. *Corpus Reformatorum*, LXXVII, pp. 186 ff.

15. The preceding exposition of the Calvinistic doctrine can be found in much the same form as here given, for instance in Hoornbeek's *Theologia practica* (Utrecht, 1663), L. II, c. 1; *de predestinatione*, the section stands characteristically directly under the heading *De Deo*. The Biblical foundation for it is principally the first chapter of the Epistle to the Ephesians. It is unnecessary for us here to analyse the various inconsistent attempts to combine with the predestination and providence of God the responsibility and free will of the individual. They began as early as in Augustine's first attempt to develop the doctrine.

16. "The deepest community (with God) is found not in institutions or corporations or churches, but in the secrets of a solitary heart", as Dowden puts the essential point in his fine book *Puritan and Anglican* (p. 234). This deep spiritual loneliness of the individual applied as well to the Jansenists of Port Royal, who were also predestinationists.

17. "Contra qui huiusmodi cœtum [namely a Church which maintains a pure doctrine, sacraments, and Church discipline] contemnunt . . . salutis suæ certi esse non possunt; et qui in illo contemtu perseverat electus non est." Olevian, *De subst. fœd.*, p. 222.

18. "It is said that God sent His Son to save the human race, but that was not His purpose, He only wished to help a few out of their degradation—and I say unto you that God died only for the elect" (sermon held in 1609 at Broek, near Rogge, Wtenbogaert, II, p. 9. Compare Nuyens, *op. cit.*, II, p. 232). The explanation of the rôle of Christ is also confused in *Hanserd Knolly's Confession*. It is everywhere assumed that God did not need His instrumentality.

19. *Entzauberung der Welt*. On this process see the other essays in my *Wirtschaftsethik der Weltreligionen*. The peculiar position of

the old Hebrew ethic, as compared with the closely related ethics of Egypt and Babylon, and its development after the time of the prophets, rested, as is shown there, entirely on this fundamental fact, the rejection of sacramental magic as a road to salvation. (This process is for Weber one of the most important aspects of the broader process of rationalization, in which he sums up his philosophy of history. See various parts of *Wirtschaft und Gesellschaft* and H. Grab, *Der Begriff des Rationalen bei Max Weber.*—TRANSLATOR'S NOTE.)

20. Similarly the most consistent doctrine held that baptism was required by positive ordinance, but was not necessary to salvation. For that reason the strictly Puritan Scotch and English Independents were able to maintain the principle that children of obvious reprobates should not be baptized (for instance, children of drunkards). An adult who desired to be baptized, but was not yet ripe for the communion, the Synod of Edam of 1586 (Art. 32, 1) recommended should be baptized only if his conduct were blameless, and he should have placed his desires *sonder superstitie*.

21. This negative attitude toward all sensuous culture is, as Dowden, *op. cit.*, shows, a very fundamental element of Puritanism.

22. The expression individualism includes the most heterogeneous things imaginable. What is here understood by it will, I hope, be clear from the following discussion. In another sense of the word, Lutheranism has been called individualistic, because it does not attempt any ascetic regulation of life. In yet another quite different sense the word is used, for example, by Dietrich Schafer when in his study, "Zur Beurteilung des Wormser Konkordats", *Abh. d. Berl. Akad.* (1905), he calls the Middle Ages the era of pronounced individuality because, for the events relevant for the historian, irrational factors then had a significance which they do not possess to-day. He is right, but so perhaps are also those whom he attacks in his remarks, for they mean something quite different, when they speak of individuality and individualism. Jacob Burchhardt's brilliant ideas are to-day at least partly out of date, and a thorough analysis of these concepts in historical terms would at the present time be highly valuable to science. Quite the opposite is, of course, true when the play impulse causes certain historians to define the concept in such a way as to enable them to use it as a label for any epoch of history they please.

23. And in a similar, though naturally less sharp, contrast to the later Catholic doctrine. The deep pessimism of Pascal, which also rests on the doctrine of predestination, is, on the other hand, of Jansenist origin, and the resulting individualism of renunciation by no means agrees with the official Catholic position. See the study by Honigsheim on the French Jansenists, referred to in Chap. III, note 10.

24. The same holds for the Jansenists.

25. Bailey, *Praxis pietatis* (German edition, Leipzig, 1724), p. 187. Also P. J. Spener in his *Theologische Bedenken* (according to third

edition, Halle, 1712) adopts a similar standpoint. A friend seldom gives advice for the glory of God, but generally for mundane (though not necessarily egotistical) reasons. "He [the knowing man] is blind in no man's cause, but best sighted in his own. He confines himself to the circle of his own affairs and thrusts not his fingers into needless fires. He sees the falseness of it [the world] and therefore learns to trust himself ever, others so far as not to be damaged by their disappointment", is the philosophy of Thomas Adams (*Works of the Puritan Divines*, p. 11). Bailey (*Praxis pietatis*, p. 176) further recommends every morning before going out among people to imagine oneself going into a wild forest full of dangers, and to pray God for the "cloak of foresight and righteousness". This feeling is characteristic of all the ascetic denominations without exception, and in the case of many Pietists led directly to a sort of hermit's life within the world. Even Spangenberg in the (Moravian) *Idea fides fratum*, p. 382, calls attention with emphasis to Jer. xvii. 5: "Cursed is the man who trusteth in man." To grasp the peculiar misanthropy of this attitude, note also Hoornbeek's remarks (*Theologia practica*, I, p. 882) on the duty to love one's enemy: "Denique hoc magis nos ulcisimur, quo proximum, inultum nobis, tradimus ultori Deo—Quo quis plus se ulscitur, eo minus id pro ipso agit Deus." It is the same transfer of vengeance that is found in the parts of the Old Testament written after the exile; a subtle intensification and refinement of the spirit of revenge compared to the older "eye for an eye". On brotherly love, see below, note 34.

26. Of course the confessional did not have only that effect. The explanations, for instance, of Muthmann, *Z. f. Rel. Psych.*, I, Heft 2, p. 65, are too simple for such a highly complex psychological problem as the confessional.

27. This is a fact which is of especial importance for the interpretation of the psychological basis of Calvinistic social organizations. They all rest on spiritually individualistic, rational motives. The individual never enters emotionally into them. The glory of God and one's own salvation always remain above the threshold of consciousness. This accounts for certain characteristic features of the social organization of peoples with a Puritan past even to-day.

28. The fundamentally anti-authoritarian tendency of the doctrine, which at bottom undermined every responsibility for ethical conduct or spiritual salvation on the part of Church or State as useless, led again and again to its proscription, as, for instance, by the States-General of the Netherlands. The result was always the formation of conventicles (as after 1614).

29. On Bunyan compare the biography of Froude in the *English Men of Letters* series, also Macaulay's superficial sketch (*Miscel. Works*, II, p. 227). Bunyan was indifferent to the denominational distinctions within Calvinism, but was himself a strict Calvinistic Baptist.

30. It is tempting to refer to the undoubted importance for the social character of Reformed Christianity of the necessity for salvation, following from the Calvinistic idea of "incorporation into the body of Christ" (Calvin, *Instit. Christ*, III, 11, 10), of reception into a community conforming to the divine prescriptions. From our point of view, however, the centre of the problem is somewhat different. That doctrinal tenet could have been developed in a Church of purely institutional character (*anstaltsmässig*), and, as is well known, this did happen. But in itself it did not possess the psychological force to awaken the initiative to form such communities nor to imbue them with the power which Calvinism possessed. Its tendency to form a community worked itself out very largely in the world outside the Church organizations ordained by God. Here the belief that the Christian proved (see below) his state of grace by action *in majorem Dei gloriam* was decisive, and the sharp condemnation of idolatry of the flesh and of all dependence on personal relations to other men was bound unperceived to direct this energy into the field of objective (impersonal) activity. The Christian who took the proof of his state of grace seriously acted in the service of God's ends, and these could only be impersonal. Every purely emotional, that is not rationally motivated, personal relation of man to man easily fell in the Puritan, as in every ascetic ethic, under the suspicion of idolatry of the flesh. In addition to what has already been said, this is clearly enough shown for the case of friendship by the following warning: "It is an irrational act and not fit for a rational creature to love any one farther than reason will allow us. . . . It very often taketh up men's minds so as to hinder their love of God" (Baxter, *Christian Directory*, IV, p. 253). We shall meet such arguments again and again.

The Calvinist was fascinated by the idea that God in creating the world, including the order of society, must have willed things to be objectively purposeful as a means of adding to His glory; not the flesh for its own sake, but the organization of the things of the flesh under His will. The active energies of the elect, liberated by the doctrine of predestination, thus flowed into the struggle to rationalize the world. Especially the idea that the public welfare, or as Baxter (*Christian Directory*, IV, p. 262) puts it, quite in the sense of later liberal rationalism, "The good of the many" (with a somewhat forced reference to Rom. ix. 3), was to be preferred to any personal or private good of the individual, followed, although not in itself new, for Puritanism from the repudiation of idolatry of the flesh. The traditional American objection to performing personal service is probably connected, besides the other important causes resulting from democratic feelings, at least indirectly with that tradition. Similarly, the relative immunity of formerly Puritan peoples to Cæsarism, and, in general, the subjectively free attitude of the English to their great statesmen as compared with many things which we have experienced since 1878 in Germany positively and negatively. On the one hand, there is a greater willingness to give the great man his due, but, on the other, a repudiation of all hysterical idolization of him and of the naïve idea that political obedience could be due anyone from thankfulness. On the sinfulness of the belief in authority, which is only permissible in the form of an impersonal authority, the Scriptures, as well as of an excessive devotion to even the most holy and virtuous of men, since that might interfere with obedience to God, see Baxter, *Christian Directory* (second edition, 1678), I, p. 56. The political consequences of the renunciation of idolatry of the flesh and the principle which was first applied only to the Church but later to life in general, that God alone should rule, do not belong in this investigation.

31. Of the relation between dogmatic and practical psychological consequence we shall often have to speak. That the two are not identical it is hardly necessary to remark.

32. Social, used of course without any of the implications attached to the modern sense of the word, meaning simply activity within the Church, politics, or any other social organization.

33. "Good works performed for any other purpose than the glory of God are sinful" (*Hanserd Knolly's Confession*, chap. xvi).

34. What such an impersonality of brotherly love, resulting from the orientation of life solely to God's will, means in the field of religious group life itself may be well illustrated by the attitude of the China Inland Mission and the International Missionaries Alliance (see Warneck, *Gesch. d. prot. Missionären*, pp. 99, 111). At tremendous expense an army of missionaries was fitted out, for instance one thousand for China alone, in order by itinerant preaching to offer the Gospel to all the heathen in a strictly literal sense, since Christ had commanded it and made His second coming dependent on it. Whether these heathen should be converted to Christianity and thus attain salvation, even whether they could understand the language in which the missionary preached, was a matter of small importance and could be left to God, Who alone could control such things. According to Hudson Taylor (see Warneck, *op. cit.*), China has about fifty million families; one thousand missionaries could each reach fifty families per day (!) or the Gospel could be presented to all the Chinese in less than three years. It is precisely the same manner in which, for instance, Calvinism carried out its Church discipline. The end was not the salvation of those subject to it, which was the affair of God alone (in practice their own) and could not be in any way influenced by the means at the disposal of the Church, but simply the increase of God's glory. Calvinism as such is not responsible for those feats of missionary zeal, since they rest on an interdenominational basis. Calvin himself denied the duty of sending missions to the heathen since a further expansion of the

Church is *unius Dei opus*. Nevertheless, they obviously originate in the ideas, running through the whole Puritan ethic, according to which the duty to love one's neighbour is satisfied by fulfilling God's commandments to increase His glory. The neighbour thereby receives all that is due him, and anything further is God's affair. Humanity in relation to one's neighbour has, so to speak, died out. That is indicated by the most various circumstances.

Thus, to mention a remnant of that atmosphere, in the field of charity of the Reformed Church, which in certain respects is justly famous, the Amsterdam orphans, with (in the twentieth century!) their coats and trousers divided vertically into a black and a red, or a red and a green half, a sort of fool's costume, and brought in parade formation to church, formed, for the feelings of the past, a highly uplifting spectacle. It served the glory of God precisely to the extent that all personal and human feelings were necessarily insulted by it. And so, as we shall see later, even in all the details of private life. Naturally all that signified only a tendency and we shall later ourselves have to make certain qualifications. But as one very important tendency of this ascetic faith, it was necessary to point it out here.

35. In all these respects the ethic of Port Royal, although predestinationist, takes quite a different standpoint on account of its mystical and otherworldly orientation, which is in so far Catholic (see Honigsheim, *op. cit.*).

36. Hundeshagen (*Beitr. z. Kirchenverfassungsgesch. u. Kirchenpolitik*, 1864, I, p. 37) takes the view, since often repeated, that predestination was a dogma of the theologians, not a popular doctrine. But that is only true if the people is identified with the mass of the uneducated lower classes. Even then it has only limited validity. Köhler (*op. cit.*) found that in the forties of the nineteenth century just those masses (meaning the *petite bourgeoisie* of Holland) were thoroughly imbued with predestination. Anyone who denied the double decree was to them a heretic and a condemned soul. He himself was asked about the time of his rebirth (in the sense of predestination). Da Costa and the separation of de Kock were greatly influenced by it. Not only Cromwell, in whose case Zeller (*Das Theologische System Zwinglis*, p. 17) has already shown the effects of the dogma most effectively, but also his army knew very well what it was about. Moreover, the canons of the synods of Dordrecht and Westminster were national questions of the first importance. Cromwell's tryers and ejectors admitted only believers in predestination, and Baxter (*Life*, I, p. 72), although he was otherwise its opponent, considers its effect on the quality of the clergy to be important. That the Reformed Pietists, the members of the English and Dutch conventicles, should not have understood the doctrine is quite impossible. It was precisely what drove them together to seek the *certitudo salutis*.

Notes

What significance the doctrine of predestination does or does not have when it remains a dogma of the theologians is shown by perfectly orthodox Catholicism, to which it was by no means strange as an esoteric doctrine under various forms. What is important is that the idea of the individual's obligation to consider himself of the elect and prove it to himself was always denied. Compare for the Catholic doctrine, for instance, A. Van Wyck, *Tract. de præstinatione* (Cologne, 1708). To what extent Pascal's doctrine of predestination was correct, we cannot inquire here.

Hundeshagen, who dislikes the doctrine, evidently gets his impressions primarily from German sources. His antipathy is based on the purely deductive opinion that it necessarily leads to moral fatalism and antinomianism. This opinion has already been refuted by Zeller, *op. cit.* That such a result was possible cannot, of course, be denied. Both Melanchthon and Wesley speak of it. But it is characteristic that in both cases it is combined with an emotional religion of faith. For them, lacking the rational idea of proof, this consequence was in fact not unnatural.

The same consequences appeared in Islam. But why? Because the Mohammedan idea was that of predetermination, not predestination, and was applied to fate in this world, not in the next. In consequence the most important thing, the proof of the believer in predestination, played no part in Islam. Thus only the fearlessness of the warrior (as in the case of *moira*) could result, but there were no consequences for rationalization of life; there was no religious sanction for them. See the (Heidelberg) theological dissertation of F. Ullrich, *Die Vorherbestimmungslehre im Islam u. Christenheit*, 1900. The modifications of the doctrine which came in practice, for instance Baxter, did not disturb it in essence so long as the idea that the election of God, and its proof, fell upon the concrete individual, was not shaken. Finally, and above all, all the great men of Puritanism (in the broadest sense) took their departure from this doctrine, whose terrible seriousness deeply influenced their youthful development. Milton like, in declining order it is true, Baxter, and, still later, the free-thinker Franklin. Their later emancipation from its strict interpretation is directly parallel to the development which the religious movement as a whole underwent in the same direction. And all the great religious revivals, at least in Holland, and most of those in England, took it up again.

37. As is true in such a striking way of the basic atmosphere of Bunyan's *Pilgrim's Progress*.

38. This question meant less to the later Lutheran, even apart from the doctrine of predestination, than to the Calvinist. Not because he was less interested in the salvation of his soul, but because, in the form which the Lutheran Church had taken, its character as an institution for salvation (*Heilsanstalt*) came to the fore. The individual

thus felt himself to be an object of its care and dependent on it. The problem was first raised within Lutheranism characteristically enough through the Pietist movement. The question of *certitudo salutis itself* has, however, for every non-sacramental religion of salvation, whether Buddhism, Jainism, or anything else, been absolutely fundamental; that must not be forgotten. It has been the origin of all psychological drives of a purely religious character.

39. Thus expressly in the letter to Bucer, *Corp. Ref.* 29, p. 883 f. Compare with that again Scheibe, *op. cit.*, p. 30.

40. The *Westminster Confession* (XVIII, p. 2) also assures the elect of indubitable certainty of grace, although with all our activity we remain useless servants and the struggle against evil lasts one's whole life long. But even the chosen one often has to struggle long and hard to attain the *certitudo* which the consciousness of having done his duty gives him and of which a true believer will never entirely be deprived.

41. The orthodox Calvinistic doctrine referred to faith and the consciousness of community with God in the sacraments, and mentioned the "other fruits of the Spirit" only incidentally. See the passages in Heppe, *op. cit.*, p. 425. Calvin himself most emphatically denied that works were indications of favour before God, although he, like the Lutherans, considered them the fruits of belief (*Instit. Christ*, III, 2, 37, 38). The actual evolution to the proof of faith through works, which is characteristic of asceticism, is parallel to a gradual modification of the doctrines of Calvin. As with Luther, the true Church was first marked off primarily by purity of doctrine and sacraments, but later the *disciplina* came to be placed on an equal footing with the other two. This evolution may be followed in the passages given by Heppe, *op. cit.*, pp. 194-5, as well as in the manner in which Church members were acquired in the Netherlands by the end of the sixteenth century (express subjection by agreement to Church discipline as the principal prerequisite).

42. For example, Olevian, *De substantia fœderis gratuiti inter Deum et electos* (1585), p. 257; Heidegger, *Corpus Theologiæ*, XXIV, p. 87; and other passages in Heppe, *Dogmatik der ev. ref. Kirche* (1861), p. 425.

43. On this point see the remarks of Schneckenburger, *op. cit.*, p. 48.

44. Thus, for example, in Baxter the distinction between mortal and venial sin reappears in a truly Catholic sense. The former is a sign of the lack of grace which can only be attained by the conversion of one's whole life. The latter is not incompatible with grace.

45. As held in many different shades by Baxter, Bailey, Sedgwick, Hoornbeek. Further see examples given by Schneckenburger, *op. cit.*, p. 262.

46. The conception of the state of grace as a sort of social estate (somewhat like that of the ascetics of the early Church) is very common.

Notes

See for instance Schortinghuis, *Het innige Christendom* (1740 proscribed by the States-General)!

47. Thus, as we shall see later, in countless passages, especially the conclusion, of Baxter's *Christian Directory*. This recommendation of worldly activity as a means of overcoming one's own feeling of moral inferiority is reminiscent of Pascal's psychological interpretation of the impulse of acquisition and ascetic activity as means to deceive oneself about one's own moral worthlessness. For him the belief in predestination and the conviction of the original sinfulness of every-thing pertaining to the flesh resulted only in renunciation of the world and the recommendation of contemplation as the sole means of lightening the burden of sin and attaining certainty of salvation. Of the orthodox Catholic and the Jansenist versions of the idea of calling an acute analysis has been made by Dr. Paul Honigsheim in the dissertation cited above (part of a larger study, which it is hoped will be continued). The Jansenists lacked every trace of a connection between certainty of salvation and worldly activity. Their concept of calling has, even more strongly than the Lutheran or even the orthodox Catholic, the sense of acceptance of the situation in life in which one finds oneself, sanctioned not only, as in Catholicism by the social order, but also by the voice of one's own conscience (Honigsheim, *op. cit.*, pp. 139 ff.).

48. The very lucidly written sketch of Lobstein in the *Festgabe für H. Holtzmann*, which starts from his view-point, may also be compared with the following. It has been criticized for too sharp an emphasis on the *certitudo salutis*. But just at this point Calvin's theology must be distinguished from Calvinism, the theological system from the needs of religious practice. All the religious move-ments which have affected large masses have started from the question, "How can I become certain of my salvation?" As we have said, it not only plays a central part in this case but in the history of all religions, even in India. And could it well be otherwise?

49. Of course it cannot be denied that the full development of this conception did not take place until late Lutheran times (Prætorius, Nicolai, Meisner). It is present, however, even in Johannes Gerhard, quite in the sense meant here. Hence Ritschl in Book IV of his *Geschichte des Pietismus* (II, pp. 3 ff.) interprets the introduction of this concept into Lutheranism as a Renaissance or an adoption of Catholic elements. He does not deny (p. 10) that the problem of individual salvation was the same for Luther as for the Catholic Mystics, but he believes that the solution was precisely opposite in the two cases. I can, of course, have no competent opinion of my own. That the atmosphere of *Die Freiheit eines Christenmenschen* is different, on the one hand, from the sweet flirtation with the *liebem Jesulein* of the later writers, and on the other from Tauler's religious feeling, is naturally obvious to anyone. Similarly the retention of

the mystic-magical element in Luther's doctrines of the Communion certainly has different religious motives from the Bernhardine piety, the "Song of Songs feeling" to which Ritschl again and again returns as the source of the bridal relations with Christ. But might not, among other things, that doctrine of the Communion have favoured the revival of mystical religious emotions? Further, it is by no means accurate to say that (p. 11, *op. cit.*) the freedom of the mystic consisted entirely in isolation from the world. Especially Tauler has, in passages which from the point of view of the psychology of religion are very interesting, maintained that the order which is thereby brought into thoughts concerning worldly activities is one practical result of the nocturnal contemplation which he recommends, for instance, in case of insomnia. "Only thereby [the mystical union with God at night before going to sleep] is reason clarified and the brain strengthened, and man is the whole day the more peacefully and divinely guided by virtue of the inner discipline of having truly united himself with God: then all his works shall be set in order. And thus when a man has forewarned (= prepared) himself of his work, and has placed his trust in virtue; then if he comes into the world, his works shall be virtuous and divine" (*Predigten*, fol. 318). Thus we see, and we shall return to the point, that mystic contemplation and a rational attitude toward the calling are not in themselves mutually contradictory. The opposite is only true when the religion takes on a directly hysterical character, which has not been the case with all mystics nor even all Pietists.

50. On this see the introduction to the following essays on the *Wirtschaftsethik der Weltreligionen* (not included in this translation: German in *Gesammelte Aufsätze zur Religionssoziologie.*—TRANSLATOR'S NOTE).

51. In this assumption Calvinism has a point of contact with official Catholicism. But for the Catholics there resulted the necessity of the sacrament of repentance; for the Reformed Church that of practical proof through activity in the world.

52. See, for instance, Beza (*De prædestinat doct. ex prælect.* in Rom 9a, Raph. Eglino exc. 1584), p. 133: "Sicut ex operibus vere bonis ad sanctificationis donum, a sanctificatione ad fidem—ascendimus: ita ex certis illis effectis non quamvis vocationem, sed efficacem illam et ex hac vocatione electionem et ex electione donum prædestinationis in Christo tam firmam quam immotus est Dei thronus certissima connexione effectorum et causarum colligimus. . . ." Only with regard to the signs of damnation is it necessary to be careful, since it is a matter of final judgment. On this point the Puritans first differed. See further the thorough discussion of Schneckenburger, *op. cit.*, who to be sure only cites a limited category of literature. In the whole Puritan literature this aspect comes out. "It will not be said, did you believe?—but: were you Doers or Talkers only?" says Bunyan. According to Baxter (*The Saints' Everlasting Rest*, chap. xii),

who teaches the mildest form of predestination, faith means sub-jection to Christ in heart and in deed. "Do what you are able first, and then complain of God for denying you grace if you have cause", was his answer to the objection that the will was not free and God alone was able to insure salvation (*Works of the Puritan Divines*, IV, p. 155). The investigation of Fuller (the Church historian) was limited to the one question of practical proof and the indications of his state of grace in his conduct. The same with Howe in the passage referred to elsewhere. Any examination of the *Works of the Puritan Divines* gives ample proofs.

Not seldom the conversion to Puritanism was due to Catholic ascetic writings, thus, with Baxter, a Jesuit tract. These conceptions were not wholly new compared with Calvin's own doctrine (*Instit. Christ*, chap. i, original edition of 1536, pp. 97, 113). Only for Calvin himself the certainty of salvation could not be attained in this manner (p. 147). Generally one referred to 1 John iii. 5 and similar passages. The demand for *fides efficax* is not—to anticipate—limited to the Calvinists. Baptist confessions of faith deal, in the article on pre-destination, similarly with the fruits of faith ("and that its—of re-generation—proper evidence appears in the holy fruits of repentance and faith and newness of life"—Article 7 of the Confession printed in the *Baptist Church Manual* by J. N. Brown, D.D., Philadelphia, *Am. Bapt. Pub. Soc.*). In the same way the tract (under Mennonite influence), *Oliif-Tacxken*, which the Harlem Synod adopted in 1649, begins on page 1 with the question of how the children of God are to be known, and answers (p. 10): "Nu al is't dat dasdanigh vruchtbare ghe-love alleene zii het seker fondamentale kennteeken—om de conscientien der gelovigen in het nieuwe verbondt der genade Gods te versekeren."

53. Of the significance of this for the material content of social ethics some hint has been given above. Here we are interested not in the content, but in the motives of moral action.

54. How this idea must have promoted the penetration of Puritan-ism with the Old Testament Hebrew spirit is evident.

55. Thus the Savoy Declaration says of the members of the *ecclesia pura* that they are "saints by effectual calling, visibly manifested by their profession and walking".

56. "A Principle of Goodness", Charnock in the *Works of the Puritan Divines*, p. 175.

57. Conversion is, as Sedgwick puts it, an "exact copy of the decree of predestination". And whoever is chosen is also called to obedience and made capable of it, teaches Bailey. Only those whom God calls to His faith (which is expressed in their conduct) are true believers, not merely temporary believers, according to the (Baptist) Confession of Hanserd Knolly.

58. Compare, for instance, the conclusion to Baxter's *Christian Directory*.

59. Thus, for instance, Charnock, *Self-Examination*, p. 183, in refutation of the Catholic doctrine of *dubitatio*.

60. This argument recurs again and again in Hoornbeek, *Theologia practica*. For instance, I, p. 160; II, pp. 70, 72, 182.

61. For instance, the *Conf. Helvet*, 16, says "et improprie his [the works] *salus adtribuitur*".

62. With all the above compare Schneckenburger, pp. 80 ff.

63. Augustine is supposed to have said "si non es prædestinatus, fac ut prædestineris".

64. One is reminded of a saying of Goethe with essentially the same meaning: "How can a man know himself? Never by observation, but through action. Try to do your duty and you will know what is in you. And what is your duty? Your daily task."

65. For though Calvin himself held that saintliness must appear on the surface (*Instit. Christ*, IV, pp. 1, 2, 7, 9), the dividing-line between saints and sinners must ever remain hidden from human knowledge. We must believe that where God's pure word is alive in a Church, organized and administered according to His law, some of the elect, even though we do not know them, are present.

66. The Calvinistic faith is one of the many examples in the history of religions of the relation between the logical and the psychological consequences for the practical religious attitude to be derived from certain religious ideas. Fatalism is, of course, the only logical consequence of predestination. But on account of the idea of proof the psychological result was precisely the opposite. For essentially similar reasons the followers of Nietzsche claim a positive ethical significance for the idea of eternal recurrence. This case, however, is concerned with responsibility for a future life which is connected with the active individual by no conscious thread of continuity, while for the Puritan it was *tua res agitur*. Even Hoornbeek (*Theologia practica*, I, p. 159) analyses the relation between predestination and action well in the language of the times. The *electi* are, on account of their election, proof against fatalism because in their rejection of it they prove themselves "quos ipsa electio sollicitos reddit et diligentes officiorum". The practical interests cut off the fatalistic consequences of logic (which, however, in spite of everything occasionally did break through).

But, on the other hand, the content of ideas of a religion is, as Calvinism shows, far more important than William James (*Varieties of Religious Experience*, 1902, p. 444 f.) is inclined to admit. The significance of the rational element in religious metaphysics is shown in classical form by the tremendous influence which especially the logical structure of the Calvinistic concept of God exercised on life. If the God of the Puritans has influenced history as hardly another before or since, it is principally due to the attributes which the power of thought had given him. James's pragmatic valuation of the significance of religious ideas according to their influence on life is incidentally a true child of the world of ideas of the Puritan home of that eminent scholar. The religious experience as such is of course irrational, like every experience. In its highest, mystical form it is even the experience κατ᾽ ἐξοχὴν, and, as James has well shown, is distinguished by its absolute incommunicability. It has a specific character and appears as knowledge, but cannot be adequately reproduced by means of our lingual and conceptual apparatus. It is further true that every religious experience loses some of its content in the attempt of rational formulation, the further the conceptual formulation goes, the more so. That is the reason for many of the tragic conflicts of all rational theology, as the Baptist sects of the seventeenth century already knew. But that irrational element, which is by no means peculiar to religious experience, but applies (in different senses and to different degrees) to every experience, does not prevent its being of the greatest practical importance, of what particular type the system of ideas is, that captures and moulds the immediate experience of religion in its own way. For from this source develop, in times of great influence of the Church on life and of strong interest in dogmatic considerations within it, most of those differences between the various religions in their ethical consequences which are of such great practical importance. How unbelievably intense, measured by present standards, the dogmatic interests even of the layman were, everyone knows who is familiar with the historical sources. We can find a parallel to-day only in the at bottom equally superstitious belief of the modern proletariat in what can be accomplished and proved by science.

67. Baxter, *The Saints' Everlasting Rest*, I, p. 6, answers to the question: "Whether to make salvation our end be not mercenary or legal? It is properly mercenary when we expect it as wages for work done. . . . Otherwise it is only such a mercenarism as Christ commandeth . . . and if seeking Christ be mercenary, I desire to be so mercenary." Nevertheless, many Calvinists who are considered orthodox do not escape falling into a very crass sort of mercenariness. According to Bailey, *Praxis pietatis*, p. 262, alms are a means of escaping temporal punishment. Other theologians urged the damned to perform good works, since their damnation might thereby become somewhat more bearable, but the elect because God will then not only love them without cause but *ob causam*, which shall certainly sometime have its reward. The apologists have also made certain small concessions concerning the significance of good works for the degree of salvation (Schneckenburger, *op. cit.*, p. 101).

68. Here also it is absolutely necessary, in order to bring out the characteristic differences, to speak in terms of ideal types, thus in a certain sense doing violence to historical reality. But without this a clear formulation would be quite impossible considering the complexity of the material. In how far the differences which we here draw as sharply as possible were merely relative, would have to be discussed separately. It is, of course, true that the official Catholic

doctrine, even in the Middle Ages, itself set up the ideal of a systematic sanctification of life as a whole. But it is just as certain (1) that the normal practice of the Church, directly on account of its most effective means of discipline, the confession, promoted the unsystematic way of life discussed in the text, and further (2) that the fundamentally rigorous and cold atmosphere in which he lived and the absolute isolation of the Calvinst were utterly foreign to mediæval lay-Catholicism.

69. The absolutely fundamental importance of this factor will, as has already once been pointed out, gradually become clear in the essays on the *Wirtschaftsethik der Weltreligionen*.

70. And to a certain extent also to the Lutheran. Luther did not wish to eliminate this last vestige of sacramental magic.

71. Compare, for instance, Sedgwick, *Buss- und Gnadenlehre* (German by Roscher, 1689). The repentant man has a fast rule to which he holds himself exactly, ordering thereby his whole life and conduct (p. 591). He lives according to the law, shrewdly, wakefully, and carefully (p. 596). Only a permanent change in the whole man can, since it is a result of predestination, cause this (p. 852). True repentance is always expressed in conduct (p. 361). The difference between only morally good work and *opera spiritualia* lies, as Hoornbeek (*op. cit.*, I, IX, chap. ii) explains, in the fact that the latter are the results of a regenerate life (*op. cit.*, I, p. 160). A continuous progress in them is discernible which can only be achieved by the supernatural influence of God's grace (p. 150). Salvation results from the transformation of the whole man through the grace of God (p. 190 f.). These ideas are common to all Protestantism, and are of course found in the highest ideals of Catholicism as well. But their consequences could only appear in the Puritan movements of worldly asceticism, and above all only in those cases did they have adequate psychological sanctions.

72. The latter name is, especially in Holland, derived from those who modelled their lives precisely on the example of the Bible (thus with Voet). Moreover, the name Methodists occurs occasionally among the Puritans in the seventeenth century.

73. For, as the Puritan preachers emphasize (for instance Bunyan in the *Pharisee and the Publican, Works of the Puritan Divines*, p. 126), every single sin would destroy everything which might have been accumulated in the way of merit by good works in a lifetime, if, which is unthinkable, man were alone able to accomplish anything which God should necessarily recognize as meritorious, or even could live in perfection for any length of time. Thus Puritanism did not think as did Catholicism in terms of a sort of account with calculation of the balance, a simile which was common even in antiquity, but of the definite alternative of grace or damnation held for a life as a whole. For suggestions of the bank account idea see note 102 below.

Notes

74. Therein lies the distinction from the mere Legality and Civility which Bunyan has living as associates of Mr. Worldly-Wiseman in the City called Morality.

75. Charnock, *Self-Examination* (*Works of the Puritan Divines*, p. 172): "Reflection and knowledge of self is a prerogative of a rational nature." Also the footnote: "Cogito, ergo sum, is the first principle of the new philosophy."

76. This is not yet the place to discuss the relationship of the theology of Duns Scotus to certain ideas of ascetic Protestantism. It never gained official recognition, but was at best tolerated and at times proscribed. The later specific repugnance of the Pietists to Aristotelean philosophy was shared by Luther, in a somewhat different sense, and also by Calvin in conscious antagonism to Catholicism (cf. *Instit. Christ*, II, chap. xii, p. 4; IV, chap. xvii, p. 24). The "primacy of the will", as Kahl has put it, is common to all these movements.

77. Thus, for instance, the article on "Asceticism" in the Catholic *Church Lexicon* defines its meaning entirely in harmony with its highest historical manifestations. Similarly Seeberg in the *Realenzyklopädie für protestantische Theologie und Kirche*. For the purpose of this study we must be allowed to use the concept as we have done. That it can be defined in other ways, more broadly as well as more narrowly, and is generally so defined, I am well aware.

78. In Hudibras (1st *Song*, 18, 19) the Puritans are compared with the bare-foot Franciscans. A report of the Genoese Ambassador, Fieschi, calls Cromwell's army an assembly of monks.

79. In view of the close relationship between otherworldly monastic asceticism and active worldly asceticism, which I here expressly maintain, I am surprised to find Brentano (*op. cit.*, p. 134 and elsewhere) citing the ascetic labour of the monks and its recommendation against me. His whole "Exkurs" against me culminates in that. But that continuity is, as anyone can see, a fundamental postulate of my whole thesis: the Reformation took rational Christian asceticism and its methodical habits out of the monasteries and placed them in the service of active life in the world. Compare the following discussion, which has not been altered.

80. So in the many reports of the trials of Puritan heretics cited in Neal's *History of the Puritans* and Crosby's *English Baptists*.

81. Sanford, *op. cit.* (and both before and after him many others), has found the origin of the ideal of reserve in Puritanism. Compare on that ideal also the remarks of James Bryce on the American college in Vol. II of his *American Commonwealth*. The ascetic principle of self-control also made Puritanism one of the fathers of modern military discipline. (On Maurice of Orange as a founder of modern army organization, see Roloff, *Preuss. Jahrb.*, 1903, III, p. 255.) Cromwell's Ironsides, with cocked pistols in their hands, and approaching the enemy at a brisk trot without shooting, were not the superiors of

the Cavaliers by virtue of their fierce passion, but, on the contrary, through their cool self-control, which enabled their leaders always to keep them well in hand. The knightly storm-attack of the Cavaliers, on the other hand, always resulted in dissolving their troops into atoms. See Firth, *Cromwell's Army*.

82. See especially Windelband, *Ueber Willensfreiheit*, pp. 77 ff.

83. Only not so unmixed. Contemplation, sometimes combined with emotionalism, is often combined with these rational elements. But again contemplation itself is methodically regulated.

84. According to Richard Baxter everything is sinful which is contrary to the reason given by God as a norm of action. Not only passions which have a sinful content, but all feelings which are senseless and intemperate as such. They destroy the countenance and, as things of the flesh, prevent us from rationally directing all action and feeling to God, and thus insult Him. Compare what is said of the sinfulness of anger (*Christian Directory*, second edition, 1698, p. 285. Tauler is cited on p. 287). On the sinfulness of anxiety, *Ebenda*, I, p. 287. That it is idolatry if our appetite is made the "rule or measure of eating" is maintained very emphatically (*op. cit.*, I, pp. 310, 316, and elsewhere). In such discussions reference is made everywhere to the Proverbs and also to Plutarch's *De tranquilitate Animi*, and not seldom to ascetic writings of the Middle Ages: St. Bernard, Bonaventura, and others. The contrast to "who does not love wine, women, and song . . ." could hardly be more sharply drawn than by the extension of the idea of idolatry to all sensuous pleasures, so far as they are not justified by hygienic considerations, in which case they (like sport within these limits, but also other recreations) are permissible. See below (Chapter V) for further discussion. Please note that the sources referred to here and elsewhere are neither dogmatic nor edifying works, but grew out of practical ministry, and thus give a good picture of the direction which its influence took.

85. I should regret it if any evaluation of one or the other form of religion should be read into this discussion. We are not concerned with that here. It is only a question of the influence of certain things which, from a purely religious point of view, are perhaps incidental, but important for practical conduct.

86. On this, see especially the article "Moralisten, englische", by E. Troeltsch, in the *Realenzyklopädie für protestantische Theologie und Kirche*, third edition.

87. How much influence quite definite religious ideas and situations, which seem to be historical accidents, have had is shown unusually clearly by the fact that in the circles of Pietism of a Reformed origin the lack of monasteries was occasionally directly regretted, and that the communistic experiments of Labadie and others were simply a substitute for monastic life.

Notes

88. As early even as several confessions of the time of the Reformation. Even Ritschl (*Pietismus*, I, p. 258 f.) does not deny, although he looks upon the later development as a deterioration of the ideas of the Reformation, that, for instance, in *Conf. Gall.* 25, 26, *Conf. Belg.* 29, *Conf. Helv.* post, 17, the true Reformed Church was defined by definitely empirical attributes, and that to this true Church believers were not accounted without the attribute of moral activity. (See above, note 42.)

89. "Bless God that we are not of the many" (Thomas Adams, *Works of the Puritan Divines*, p. 138).

90. The idea of the birthright, so important in history, thus received an important confirmation in England. "The firstborn which are written in heaven. . . . As the firstborn is not to be defeated in his inheritance, and the enrolled names are never to be obliterated, so certainly they shall inherit eternal life" (Thomas Adams, *Works of the Puritan Divines*, p. xiv).

91. The Lutheran emphasis on penitent grief is foreign to the spirit of ascetic Calvinism, not in theory, but definitely in practice. For it is of no ethical value to the Calvinist; it does not help the damned, while for those certain of their election, their own sin, so far as they admit it to themselves, is a symptom of backwardness in development. Instead of repenting of it they hate it and attempt to overcome it by activity for the glory of God. Compare the explanation of Howe (Cromwell's chaplain 1656–58) in *Of Men's Enmity against God and of Reconciliation between God and Man* (*Works of English Puritan Divines*, p. 237): "The carnal mind is enmity against God. It is the mind, therefore, not as speculative merely, but as practical and active that must be renewed", and, p. 246: "Reconciliation . . . must begin in (1) a deep conviction . . . of your former enmity. . . . I have been alienated from God. . . . (2) (p. 251) a clear and lively apprehension of the monstrous iniquity and wickedness thereof." The hatred here is that of sin, not of the sinner. But as early as the famous letter of the Duchess Renata d'Este (Leonore's mother) to Calvin, in which she speaks of the hatred which she would feel toward her father and husband if she became convinced they belonged to the damned, is shown the transfer to the person. At the same time it is an example of what was said above [pp. 104–6] of how the individual became loosed from the ties resting on his natural feelings, for which the doctrine of predestination was responsible.

92. "None but those who give evidence of being regenerate or holy persons ought to be received or counted fit members of visible Churches. Where this is wanting, the very essence of a Church is lost", as the principle is put by Owen, the Independent-Calvinistic Vice-Chancellor of Oxford under Cromwell (*Inv. into the Origin of Ev. Ch.*). Further, see the following essay (not translated here.—TRANSLATOR).

93. See following essay.

237

94. *Cat. Genev.*, p. 149. Bailey, *Praxis pietatis*, p. 125: "In life we should act as though no one but Moses had authority over us."

95. "The law appears to the Calvinist as an ideal norm of action. It oppresses the Lutheran because it is for him unattainable." In the Lutheran catechism it stands at the beginning in order to arouse the necessary humility, in the Reformed catechism it generally stands after the Gospel. The Calvinists accused the Lutherans of having a "virtual reluctance to becoming holy" (Möhler), while the Lutherans accused the Calvinists of an "unfree servitude to the law", and of arrogance.

96. *Studies and Reflections of the Great Rebellion*, pp. 79 f.

97. Among them the Song of Songs is especially noteworthy. It was for the most part simply ignored by the Puritans. Its Oriental eroticism has influenced the development of certain types of religion, such as that of St. Bernard.

98. On the necessity of this self-observation, see the sermon of Charnock, already referred to, on 2 Cor. xiii. 5, *Works of the Puritan Divines*, pp. 161 ff.

99. Most of the theological moralists recommended it. Thus Baxter, *Christian Directory*, II, pp. 77 ff., who, however, does not gloss over its dangers.

100. Moral book-keeping has, of course, been widespread elsewhere. But the emphasis which was placed upon it as the sole means of knowledge of the eternal decree of salvation or damnation was lacking, and with it the most important psychological sanction for care and exactitude in this calculation.

101. This was the significant difference from other attitudes which were superficially similar.

102. Baxter (*Saints' Everlasting Rest*, chap. xii) explains God's invisibility with the remark that just as one can carry on profitable trade with an invisible foreigner through correspondence, so is it possible by means of holy commerce with an invisible God to get possession of the one priceless pearl. These commercial similes rather than the forensic ones customary with the older moralists and the Lutherans are thoroughly characteristic of Puritanism, which in effect makes man buy his own salvation. Compare further the following passage from a sermon: "We reckon the value of a thing by that which a wise man will give for it, who is not ignorant of it nor under necessity. Christ, the Wisdom of God, gave Himself, His own precious blood, to redeem souls, and He knew what they were and had no need of them" (Matthew Henry, *The Worth of the Soul, Works of the Puritan Divines*, p. 313).

103. In contrast to that, Luther himself said: "Weeping goes before action and suffering excells all accomplishment" (*Weinen geht vor Wirken und Leiden übertrifft alles tun*).

104. This is also shown most clearly in the development of the ethical theory of Lutheranism. On this see Hoennicke, *Studien zur*

Notes

altprotestantischen Ethik (Berlin, 1902), and the instructive review of it by E. Troeltsch, *Gött. Gel. Anz.*, 1902, No. 8. The approach of the Lutheran doctrine, especially to the older orthodox Calvinistic, was in form often very close. But the difference of religious background was always apparent. In order to establish a connection between morality and faith, Melanchthon had placed the idea of repentance in the foreground. Repentance through the law must precede faith, but good works must follow it, otherwise it cannot be the truly justifying faith—almost a Puritan formula. Melanchthon admitted a certain degree of perfection to be attainable on earth. He had, in fact, originally taught that justification was given in order to make men capable of good works, and in increasing perfection lay at least the relative degree of blessedness which faith could give in this world. Also later Lutheran theologians held that good works are the necessary fruits of faith, that faith results in a new external life, just as the Reformed preachers did. The question in what good works consist Melanchthon, and especially the later Lutherans, answered more and more by reference to the law. There remained of Luther's original doctrines only the lesser degree of seriousness with which the Bible, especially the particular norms of the Old Testament, was taken. The decalogue remained, as a codification of the most important ideas of the natural moral law, the essential norm of human action. But there was no firm link connecting its legal validity with the more and more strongly emphasized importance of faith for justification, because this faith (see above) had a fundamentally different psychological character from the Calvinistic.

The true Lutheran standpoint of the early period had to be abandoned by a Church which looked upon itself as an institution for salvation. But another had not been found. Especially was it impossible, for fear of losing their dogmatic foundation (*sola fide!*), to accept the ascetic rationalization of conduct as the moral task of the individual. For there was no motive to give the idea of proof such a significance as it attained in Calvinism through the doctrine of predestination. Moreover, the magical interpretation of the sacraments, combined with the lack of this doctrine, especially the association of the *regeneratio*, or at least its beginning with baptism, necessarily, assuming as it did the universality of grace, hindered the development of methodical morality. For it weakened the contrast between the state of nature and the state of grace, especially when combined with the strong Lutheran emphasis on original sin. No less important was the entirely forensic interpretation of the act of justification which assumed that God's decrees might be changed through the influence of particular acts of repentance of the converted sinner. And that was just the element to which Melanchthon gave increasing emphasis. The whole development of his doctrine, which gave increasing weight to repentance, was intimately connected with his profession of the freedom of the will. That was what primarily determined the *un*methodical character of Lutheran conduct.

Particular acts of grace for particular sins, not the development of an aristocracy of saints creating the certainty of their own salvation, was the necessary form salvation took for the average Lutheran, as the retention of the confession proves. Thus it could develop neither a morality free from the law nor a rational asceticism in terms of the law. Rather the law remained in an unorganic proximity to faith as an ideal, and, moreover, since the strict dependence on the Bible was avoided as suggesting salvation by works, it remained uncertain, vague, and, above all, unsystematic in its content. Their conduct remained, as Troeltsch has said of their ethical theory, a "sum of mere beginnings which never quite materialized"; which, "taught in particular, uncertain, and unrelated maxims", did not succeed in "working out an articulate system of conduct", but formed essentially, following the development through which Luther himself (see above) had gone, a resignation to things as they were in matters both small and great. The resignation of the Germans to foreign cultures, their rapid change of nationality, of which there is so much complaint, is clearly to be attributed, along with certain political circumstances in the history of the nation, in part to the results of this influence, which still affects all aspects of our life. The subjective assimilation of culture remained weak because it took place primarily by means of a passive absorption of what was authoritatively presented.

105. On these points, see the gossipy book of Tholuck, *Vorgeschichte des Rationalismus*.

106. On the quite different results of the Mohammedan doctrine of predestination (or rather predetermination) and the reasons for it, see the theological dissertation (Heidelberg) of F. Ullrich, *Die Vorherbestimmungslehre im Islam u. Ch.*, 1912. On that of the Jansenists, see P. Honigsheim, *op. cit.*

107. See the following essay in this collection (not translated here).

108. Ritschl, *Geschichte des Pietismus*, I, p. 152, attempts to distinguish them for the time before Labadie (only on the basis of examples from the Netherlands) (1) in that the Pietists formed conventicles; (2) they held the doctrine of the "worthlessness of existence in the flesh" in a "manner contrary to the Protestant interests in salvation"; (3) "the assurance of grace in the tender relationship with the Lord Jesus" was sought in an un-Calvinistic manner. The last criterion applies for this early period only to one of the cases with which he deals. The idea of worthlessness of the flesh was in itself a true child of the Calvinistic spirit, and only where it led to practical renunciation of the world was it antagonistic to normal Protestantism. The conventicles, finally, had been established to a certain extent (especially for catechistic purposes) by the Synod of Dordrecht itself. Of the criteria of Pietism analysed

in Ritschl's previous discussion, those worth considering are (1) the greater precision with which the letter of the Bible was followed in all external affairs of life, as Gisbert Voet for a time urged; (2) the treatment of justification and reconciliation with God, not as ends in themselves, but simply as means toward a holy ascetic life as can be seen perhaps in Lodensteyn, but as is also suggested by Melanchthon [see above, note 104]; (3) the high value placed on repentance as a sign of true regeneration, as was first taught by W. Teellinck; (4) abstention from communion when unregenerate persons partake of it (of which we shall speak in another connection). Connected with that was the formation of conventicles with a revival of prophecy, i.e. interpretation of the Scriptures by laymen, even women. That went beyond the limits set by the canons of Dordrecht.

Those are all things forming departures, sometimes considerable, from both the doctrine and practice of the Reformers. But compared with the movements which Ritschl does not include in his treatment, especially the English Puritans, they form, except for No. 3, only a continuation of tendencies which lay in the whole line of development of this religion. The objectivity of Ritschl's treatment suffers from the fact that the great scholar allows his personal attitude towards the Church or, perhaps better, religious policy, to enter in, and, in his antipathy to all peculiarly ascetic forms of religion, interprets any development in that direction as a step back into Catholicism. But, like Catholicism, the older Protestantism included all sorts and conditions of men. But that did not prevent the Catholic Church from repudiating rigorous worldly asceticism in the form of Jansenism; just as Pietism repudiated the peculiar Catholic Quietism of the seventeenth century. From our special view-point Pietism differs not in degree, but in kind from Calvinism only when the increasing fear of the world leads to flight from ordinary economic life and the formation of monastic-communistic conventicles (Labadie). Or, which has been attributed to certain extreme Pietists by their contemporaries, they were led deliberately to neglect worldly duties in favour of contemplation. This naturally happened with particular frequency when contemplation began to assume the character which Ritschl calls Bernardism, because it suggests St. Bernard's interpretation of the Song of Songs: a mystical, emotional form of religion seeking the *unio mystica* with an esoteric sexual tinge. Even from the view-point of religious psychology alone this is undoubtedly something quite different from Calvinism, including its ascetic form exemplified by men like Voet. Ritschl, however, everywhere attempts to connect this quietism with the Pietist asceticism and thus to bring the latter under the same indictment; in doing so he puts his finger on every quotation from Catholic mysticism or asceticism which he can find in Pietist literature. But English and Dutch moralists and theologians who are quite beyond suspicion cite Bernard, Bona-

ventura, and Thomas à Kempis. The relationship of all the Reformation Churches to the Catholic past was very complex and, according
to the point of view which is emphasized, one or another appears
most closely related to Catholicism or certain sides of it.

109. The illuminating article on "Pietism" by Mirbt in the third
edition of the *Realenzyklopädie für protestantische Theologie und
Kirche*, treats the origin of Pietism, leaving its Protestant antecedents
entirely on one side, as a purely personal religious experience of
Spener, which is somewhat improbable. As an introduction to Pietism,
Gustav Freytag's description in *Bilder der deutschen Vergangenheit*
is still worth reading. For the beginnings of English Pietism in the
contemporary literature, compare W. Whitaker, *Prima Institutio
disciplinaque pietatis* (1570).

110. It is well known that this attitude made it possible for Pietism
to be one of the main forces behind the idea of toleration. At this
point we may insert a few remarks on that subject. In the West its
historical origin, if we omit the humanistic indifference of the Enlightenment, which in itself has never had great practical influence,
is to be found in the following principal sources: (1) Purely political
expediency (type: William of Orange). (2) Mercantilism (especially
clear for the City of Amsterdam, but also typical of numerous cities,
landlords, and rulers who received the members of sects as valuable
for economic progress). (3) The radical wing of Calvinism. Predestination made it fundamentally impossible for the State really to
promote religion by intolerance. It could not thereby save a single
soul. Only the idea of the glory of God gave the Church occasion to
claim its help in the suppression of heresy. Now the greater the
emphasis on the membership of the preacher, and all those that
partook of the communion, in the elect, the more intolerable became
the interference of the State in the appointment of the clergy. For
clerical positions were often granted as benefices to men from the
universities only because of their theological training, though they
might be personally unregenerate. In general, any interference in the
affairs of the religious community by those in political power, whose
conduct might often be unsatisfactory, was resented. Reformed
Pietism strengthened this tendency by weakening the emphasis on
doctrinal orthodoxy and by gradually undermining the principle of
extra ecclesiam nulla salus.

Calvin had regarded the subjection of the damned to the divine
supervision of the Church as alone consistent with the glory of
God; in New England the attempt was made to constitute the Church
as an aristocracy of proved saints. Even the radical Independents,
however, repudiated every interference of temporal or any sort of
hierarchical powers with the proof of salvation which was only
possible within the individual community. The idea that the glory
of God requires the subjection of the damned to the discipline of

the Church was gradually superseded by the other idea, which was present from the beginning and became gradually more prominent, that it was an insult to His glory to partake of the Communion with one rejected by God. That necessarily led to voluntarism, for it led to the believers' Church the religious community which included only the twice-born. Calvinistic Baptism, to which, for instance, the leader of the Parliament of Saints Praisegod Barebones belonged, drew the consequences of this line of thought with great emphasis. Cromwell's army upheld the liberty of conscience and the parliament of saints even advocated the separation of Church and State, because its members were good Pietists, thus on positive religious grounds. (4) The Baptist sects, which we shall discuss later, have from the beginning of their history most strongly and consistently maintained the principle that only those personally regenerated could be admitted to the Church. Hence they repudiated every conception of the Church as an institution (*Anstalt*) and every interference of the temporal power. Here also it was for positive religious reasons that unconditional toleration was advocated.

The first man who stood out for absolute toleration and the separation of Church and State, almost a generation before the Baptists and two before Roger Williams, was probably John Browne. The first declaration of a Church group in this sense appears to be the resolution of the English Baptists in Amsterdam of 1612 or 1613: "The magistrate is not to middle with religion or matters of conscience . . . because Christ is the King and Law-giver of the Church and conscience." The first official document of a Church which claimed the positive protection of liberty of conscience by the State as a right was probably Article 44 of the Confession of the Particular Baptists of 1644.

Let it be emphatically stated again that the idea sometimes brought forward, that toleration as such was favourable to capitalism, is naturally quite wrong. Religious toleration is neither peculiar to modern times nor to the West. It has ruled in China, in India, in the great empires of the Near East in Hellenistic times, in the Roman Empire and the Mohammedan Empires for long periods to a degree only limited by reasons of political expediency (which form its limits to-day also!) which was attained nowhere in the world in the sixteenth and seventeenth centuries. Moreover, it was least strong in those areas which were dominated by Puritanism, as, for instance, Holland and Zeeland in their period of political and economic expansion or in Puritan old or New England. Both before and after the Reformation, religious intolerance was peculiarly characteristic of the Occident as of the Sassanian Empire. Similarly, it has prevailed in China, Japan, and India at certain particular times, though mostly for political reasons. Thus toleration as such certainly has nothing whatever to do with capitalism. The real question is, Who benefited by it? Of the consequences of the believers' Church we shall speak further in the following article.

111. This idea is illustrated in its practical application by Cromwell's tryers, the examiners of candidates for the position of preacher. They attempted to ascertain not only the knowledge of theology, but also the subjective state of grace of the candidate. See also the following article.

112. The characteristic Pietistic distrust of Aristotle and classical philosophy in general is suggested in Calvin himself (compare *Instit. Christ*, II, chap. ii, p. 4; III, chap. xxiii, p. 5; IV, chap. xvii, p. 24). Luther in his early days distrusted it no less, but that was later changed by the humanistic influence (especially of Melanchthon) and the urgent need of ammunition for apologetic purposes. That everything necessary for salvation was contained in the Scriptures plainly enough for even the untutored was, of course, taught by the Westminster Confession (chap. i, No. 7.), in conformity with the whole Protestant tradition.

113. The official Churches protested against this, as, for example, in the shorter catechism of the Scotch Presbyterian Church of 1648, sec. vii. Participation of those not members of the same family in family devotions was forbidden as interference with the prerogatives of the office. Pietism, like every ascetic community-forming movement, tended to loosen the ties of the individual with domestic patriarchalism, with its interest in the prestige of office.

114. We are here for good reasons intentionally neglecting discussion of the psychological, in the technical sense of the word, aspect of these religious phenomena, and even its terminology has been as far as possible avoided. The firmly established results of psychology, including psychiatry, do not as present go far enough to make them of use for the purposes of the historical investigation of our problems without prejudicing historical judgments. The use of its terminology would only form a temptation to hide phenomena which were immediately understandable, or even sometimes trivial, behind a veil of foreign words, and thus give a false impression of scientific exactitude, such as is unfortunately typical of Lamprecht. For a more serious attempt to make use of psychological concepts in the interpretation of certain historical mass phenomena, see W. Hellpach, *Grundlinien zu einer Psychologie der Hysterie*, chap. xii, as well as his *Nervosität und Kultur*. I cannot here attempt to explain that in my opinion even this many-sided writer has been harmfully influenced by certain of Lamprecht's theories. How completely worthless, as compared with the older literature, Lamprecht's schematic treatment of Pietism is (in Vol. VII of the *Deutsche Geschichte*) everyone knows who has the slightest acquaintance with the literature.

115. Thus with the adherents of Schortinghuis's *Innige Christendom*. In the history of religion it goes back to the verse about the servant of God in Isaiah and the 22nd Psalm.

Notes

116. This appeared occasionally in Dutch Pietism and then under the influence of Spinoza.

117. Labadie, Teersteegen, etc.

118. Perhaps this appears most clearly when he (Spener!) disputes the authority of the Government to control the conventicles except in cases of disorder and abuses, because it concerns a fundamental right of Christians guaranteed by apostolic authority (*Theologische Bedenken*, II, pp. 81 f.). That is, in principle, exactly the Puritan standpoint regarding the relations of the individual to authority and the extent to which individual rights, which follow *ex jure divino* and are therefore inalienable, are valid. Neither this heresy, nor the one mentioned farther on in the text, has escaped Ritschl (*Pietismus*, II, pp. 115, 157). However unhistorical the positivistic (not to say philistine) criticism to which he has subjected the idea of natural rights to which we are nevertheless indebted for not much less than everything which even the most extreme reactionary prizes as his sphere of individual freedom, we naturally agree entirely with him that in both cases an organic relationship to Spener's Lutheran standpoint is lacking.

The conventicles (*collegia pietitatis*) themselves, to which Spener's famous *pia desideria* gave the theoretical basis, and which he founded in practice, corresponded closely in essentials to the English prophesyings which were first practised in John of Lasco's London Bible Classes (1547), and after that were a regular feature of all forms of Puritanism which revolted against the authority of the Church. Finally, he bases his well-known repudiation of the Church discipline of Geneva on the fact that its natural executors, the third estate (*status œconomicus*: the Christian laity), were not even a part of the organization of the Lutheran Church. On the other hand, in the discussion of excommunication the lay members' recognition of the Consistorium appointed by the prince as representatives of the third estate is weakly Lutheran.

119. The name Pietism in itself, which first occurs in Lutheran territory, indicates that in the opinion of contemporaries it was characteristic of it that a methodical business was made out of *pietas*.

120. It is, of course, granted that though this type of motivation was primarily Calvinistic it is not exclusively such. It is also found with special frequency in some of the oldest Lutheran Church constitutions.

121. In the sense of Heb. v. 13, 14. Compare Spener, *Theologische Bedenken*, I, p. 306.

122. Besides Bailey and Baxter (see *Consilia theologica*, III, 6, 1; 1, 47; 3, 6), Spener was especially fond of Thomas à Kempis, and even more of Tauler—whom he did not entirely understand (*op. cit.*, III, 61, 1, No. 1). For detailed discussion of the latter, see *op. cit.*, I, 1, 1 No. 7. For him Luther is derived directly from Tauler.

123. See in Ritschl, *op. cit.*, II, p. 113. He did not accept the repentance of the later Pietists (and of Luther) as the sole trustworthy indication of true conversion (*Theologische Bedenken*, III, p. 476). On sanctification as the fruit of thankfulness in the belief of forgiveness, a typically Lutheran idea, see passages cited by Ritschl, *op. cit.*, p. 115, note 2. On the *certitudo salutis* see, on the one hand, *Theologische Bedenken*, I, p. 324: "true belief is not so much felt emotionally as known by its fruits" (love and obedience to God); on the other, *Theologische Bedenken*, I, p. 335 f.: "As far as anxiety that they should be assured of salvation and grace is concerned, it is better to trust to our books, the Lutheran, than to the English writings." But on the nature of sanctification he was at one with the English view-point.

124. Of this the religious account books which A. H. Francke recommended were external symptoms. The methodical practice and habit of virtue was supposed to cause its growth and the separation of good from evil. This is the principal theme of Francke's book, *Von des Christen Vollkommenheit*.

125. The difference between this rational Pietist belief in Providence and its orthodox interpretation is shown characteristically in the famous controversy between the Pietists of Halle and the orthodox Lutheran Löscher. Löscher in his *Timotheus Verinus* goes so far as to contrast everything that is attained by human action with the decrees of Providence. On the other hand, Francke's consistent view was that the sudden flash of clarity over what is to happen, which comes as a result of quiet waiting for decision, is to be considered as "God's hint", quite analogous to the Quaker psychology, and corresponding to the general ascetic idea that rational methods are the way to approach nearer to God. It is true that Zinzendorf, who in one most vital decision entrusted the fate of his community to lot, was far from Francke's form of the belief in Providence. Spener, *Theologische Bedenken*, I, p. 314, referred to Tauler for a description of the Christian resignation in which one should bow to the divine will, and not cross it by hasty action on one's own responsibility, essentially the position of Francke. Its effectiveness as compared to Puritanism is essentially weakened by the tendency of Pietism to seek peace in this world, as can everywhere be clearly seen. "First righteousness, then peace", as was said in opposition to it in 1904 by a leading Baptist (G. White in an address to be referred to later) in formulating the ethical programme of his denomination (*Baptist Handbook*, 1904, p. 107).

126. *Lect. paraenet.*, IV, p. 271.

127. Ritschl's criticism is directed especially against this continually recurrent idea. See the work of Francke containing the doctrine which has already been referred to. (See note 124 above.)

128. It occurs also among English Pietists who were not adherents of predestination, for instance Goodwin. On him and others compare

Notes

Heppe, *Geschichte des Pietismus in der reformierten Kirche* (Leiden, 1879), a book which even with Ritschl's standard work cannot yet be dispensed with for England, and here and there also for the Netherlands. Even in the nineteenth century in the Netherlands Köhler, *Die Niederl. ref. Kirche*, was asked about the exact time of his rebirth.

129. They attempted thus to counteract the lax results of the Lutheran doctrine of the recoverability of grace (especially the very frequent conversion *in extremis*).

130. Against the corresponding necessity of knowing the day and hour of conversion as an indispensable sign of its genuineness. See Spener, *Theologische Bedenken*, II, 6, 1, p. 197. Repentance was as little known to him as Luther's *terrores conscientiæ* to Melanchthon.

131. At the same time, of course, the anti-authoritarian interpretation of the universal priesthood, typical of all asceticism, played a part. Occasionally the minister was advised to delay absolution until proof was given of genuine repentance which, as Ritschl rightly says, was in principle Calvinistic.

132. The essential points for our purposes are most easily found in Plitt, *Zinzendorf's Theologie* (3 vols., Gotha, 1869), I, pp. 325, 345, 381, 412, 429, 433 f., 444, 448; II, pp. 372, 381, 385, 409 f.; III, pp. 131, 167, 176. Compare also Bernh. Becker, *Zinzendorf und sein Christentum* (Leipzig, 1900), Book III, chap. iii.

133. "In no religion do we recognize as brothers those who have not been washed in the blood of Christ and continue thoroughly changed in the sanctity of the Spirit. We recognize no evident (= visible) Church of Christ except where the Word of God is taught in purity and where the members live in holiness as children of God following its precepts." The last sentence, it is true, is taken from Luther's smaller catechism but, as Ritschl points out, there it serves to answer the question how the Name of God shall be made holy, while here it serves to delimit the Church of the saints.

134. It is true that he only considered the Augsburg Confession to be a suitable document of the Lutheran Christian faith if, as he expressed it in his disgusting terminology, a *Wundbrühe* had been poured upon it. To read him is an act of penitence because his language, in its insipid melting quality, is even worse than the frightful Christo-turpentine of F. T. Vischer (in his polemics with the Munich *christoterpe*).

135. See Plitt, *op. cit.*, I, p. 346. Even more decisive is the answer, quoted in Plitt, *op. cit.*, I, p. 381, to the question whether good works are necessary to salvation. "Unnecessary and harmful to the attainment of salvation, but after salvation is attained so necessary that he who does not perform them is not really saved." Thus here also they are not the cause of salvation, but the sole means of recognizing it.

136. For instance, through those caricatures of Christian freedom which Ritschl, *op. cit.*, III, p. 381, so severely criticizes.

137. Above all in the greater emphasis on the idea of retributive punishment in the doctrine of salvation, which, after the repudiation of his missionary attempts by the American sects, he made the basis of his method of sanctification. After that he places the retention of childlikeness and the virtues of humble resignation in the foreground as the end of Herrnhut asceticism, in sharp contrast to the inclination of his own community to an asceticism closely analogous to the Puritan.

138. Which, however, had its limits. For this reason alone it is wrong to attempt to place Zinzendorf's religion in a scheme of social psychological evolutionary stages, as Lamprecht does. Furthermore, however, his whole religious attitude is influenced by nothing more strongly than the fact that he was a Count with an outlook fundamentally feudal. Further, the emotional side of it would, from the point of view of social psychology, fit just as well into the period of the sentimental decadence of chivalry as in that of sensitiveness. If social psychology gives any clue to its difference from West European rationalism, it is most likely to be found in the patriarchal traditionalism of Eastern Germany.

139. This is evident from Zinzendorf's controversy with Dippel just as, after his death, the doctrines of the Synod of 1764 bring out the character of the Herrnhut community as an institution for salvation. See Ritschl's criticism, *op. cit.*, III, p. 443 f.

140. Compare, for instance, §§151, 153, 160. That sanctification may not take place in spite of true penitence and the forgiveness of sins is evident, especially from the remarks on p. 311, and agrees with the Lutheran doctrine of salvation just as it is in disagreement with that of Calvinism (and Methodism).

141. Compare Zinzendorf's opinion, cited in Plitt, *op. cit.*, II, p. 345. Similarly Spangenberg, *Idea Fidei*, p. 325.

142. Compare, for instance, Zinzendorf's remark on Matt. xx. 28, cited by Plitt, *op. cit.*, III, p. 131: "When I see a man to whom God has given a great gift, I rejoice and gladly avail myself of the gift. But when I note that he is not content with his own, but wishes to increase it further, I consider it the beginning of that person's ruin." In other words, Zinzendorf denied, especially in his conversation with John Wesley in 1743, that there could be progress in holiness, because he identified it with justification and found it only in the emotional relationship to Christ (Plitt, I, p. 413). In place of the sense of being the instrument of God comes the possession of the divine; mysticism, not asceticism (in the sense to be discussed in the introduction to the following essays) (not here translated.—TRANSLATOR'S NOTE). As is pointed out there, a present, worldly state of mind is naturally what the Puritan really seeks for also. But for him the state which he interprets as the *certitudo salutis* is the feeling of being an active instrument.

Notes

143. But which, precisely on account of this mystical tendency, did not receive a consistent ethical justification. Zinzendorf rejects Luther's idea of divine worship in the calling as the decisive reason for performing one's duty in it. It is rather a return for the "Saviour's loyal services" (Plitt, II, p. 411).

144. His saying that "a reasonable man should not be without faith and a believer should not be unreasonable" is well known. See his *Sokrates, d. i. Aufrichtige Anzeige verschiedener nicht sowohl unbekannter als vielmehr in Abfall geratener Hauptwahrheiten* (1725). Further, his fondness for such authors as Bayle.

145. The decided propensity of Protestant asceticism for empiricism, rationalized on a mathematical basis, is well known, but cannot be further analysed here. On the development of the sciences in the direction of mathematically rationalized exact investigation, the philosophical motives of it and their contrast to Bacon's viewpoint, see Windelband, *Geschichte der Philosophie*, pp. 305-7, especially the remark on p. 305, which rightly denies that modern natural science can be understood as the product of material and technical interests. Highly important relationships exist, of course, but they are much more complex. See further Windelband, *Neuere Phil.*, I, pp. 40 ff. For the attitude of Protestant asceticism the decisive point was, as may perhaps be most clearly seen in Spener's *Theologische Bedenken*, I, p. 232; III, p. 260, that just as the Christian is known by the fruits of his belief, the knowledge of God and His designs can only be attained through a knowledge of His works. The favourite science of all Puritan, Baptist, or Pietist Christianity was thus physics, and next to it all those other natural sciences which used a similar method, especially mathematics. It was hoped from the empirical knowledge of the divine laws of nature to ascend to a grasp of the essence of the world, which on account of the fragmentary nature of the divine revelation, a Calvinistic idea, could never be attained by the method of metaphysical speculation. The empiricism of the seventeenth century was the means for asceticism to seek God in nature. It seemed to lead to God, philosophical speculation away from Him. In particular Spener considers the Aristotelean philosophy to have been the most harmful element in Christian tradition. Every other is better, especially the Platonic: *Cons. Theol.*, III, 6, 1, Dist. 2, No. 13. Compare further the following characteristic passage: "Unde pro Cartesio quid dicam non habeo [he had not read him], semper tamen optavi et opto, ut Deus viros excitet, qui veram philosophiam vel tandem oculis sisterent in qua nullius hominis attenderetur auctoritas, sed sana tantum magistri nescia ratio", Spener, *Cons. Theol.*, II, 5, No. 2. The significance of this attitude of ascetic Protestantism for the development of education, especially technical education, is well known. Combined with the attitude to *fides implicita* they furnished a pedagogical programme.

146. "That is a type of men who seek their happiness in four main ways: (1) to be insignificant, despised, and abased; (2) to neglect all things they do not need for the service of their Lord; (3) either to possess nothing or to give away again what they receive; (4) to work as wage labourers, not for the sake of the wage, but of the calling in the service of the Lord and their neighbour" (*Rel. Reden*, II, p. 180; Plitt, *op. cit.*, I, p. 445). Not everyone can or may become a disciple, but only those who receive the call of the Lord. But according to Zinzendorf's own confession (Plitt, *op. cit.*, I, p. 449) there still remain difficulties, for the Sermon on the Mount applies formally to all. The resemblance of this free universality of love to the old Baptist ideals is evident.

147. An emotional intensification of religion was by no means entirely unknown to Lutheranism even in its later period. Rather the ascetic element, the way of life which the Lutheran suspected of being salvation by works, was the fundamental difference in this case.

148. A healthy fear is a better sign of grace than certainty, says Spener, *Theologische Bedenken*, I, p. 324. In the Puritan writers we, of course, also find emphatic warnings against false certainty; but at least the doctrine of predestination, so far as its influence determined religious practice, always worked in the opposite direction.

149. The psychological effect of the confessional was everywhere to relieve the individual of responsibility for his own conduct, that is why it was sought, and that weakened the rigorous consistency of the demands of asceticism.

150. How important at the same time, even for the form of the Pietist faith, was the part played by purely political factors, has been indicated by Ritschl in his study of Württemberg Pietism.

151. See Zinzendorf's statement [quoted above, note 146].

152. Of course Calvinism, in so far as it is genuine, is also patriarchal. The connection, for instance, of the success of Baxter's activities with the domestic character of industry in Kidderminster is evident from his autobiography. See the passage quoted in the *Works of the Puritan Divines*, p. 38: "The town liveth upon the weaving of Kidderminster stuffs, and as they stand in their loom, they can set a book before them, or edify each other. . . ." Nevertheless, there is a difference between patriarchalism based on Pietism and on the Calvinistic and especially the Baptist ethics. This problem can only be discussed in another connection.

153. *Lehre von der Rechtfertigung und Versöhnung*, third edition, I, p. 598. That Frederick William I called Pietism a religion for the leisure class is more indicative of his own Pietism than that of Spener and Francke. Even this king knew very well why he had opened his realm to the Pietists by his declaration of toleration.

154. As an introduction to Methodism the excellent article *Methodismus* by Loofs in the *Realenzyklopädie für protestantische Theo-*

Notes

logie und Kirche is particularly good. Also the works of Jacoby (especially the *Handbuch des Methodismus*), Kolde, Jüngst, and Southey are useful. On Wesley: Tyerman, *Life and Times of John Wesley* is popular. One of the best libraries on the history of Methodism is that of Northwestern University, Evanston, Ill. A sort of link between classical Puritanism and Methodism was formed by the religious poet Isaac Watts, a friend of the chaplain of Oliver Cromwell (Howe) and then of Richard Cromwell. Whitefield is said to have sought his advice (cf. Skeats, *op. cit.*, pp. 254 f.).

155. Apart from the personal influence of the Wesleys the similarity is historically determined, on the one hand, by the decline of the dogma of predestination, on the other by the powerful revival of the *sola fide* in the founders of Methodism, especially motivated by its specific missionary character. This brought forth a modified rejuvenation of certain mediæval methods of revival preaching and combined them with Pietistic forms. It certainly does not belong in a general line of development toward subjectivism, since in this respect it stood behind not only Pietism, but also the Bernardine religion of the Middle Ages.

156. In this manner Wesley himself occasionally characterized the effect of the Methodist faith. The relationship to Zinzendorf's *Glückseligkeit* is evident.

157. Given in Watson's *Life of Wesley*, p. 331 (German edition).

158. J. Schneckenburger, *Vorlesungen über die Lehrbegriffe der kleinen protestantischen Kirchenparteien*, edited by Hundeshagen (Frankfurt, 1863), p. 147.

159. Whitefield, the leader of the predestinationist group which after his death dissolved for lack of organization, rejected Wesley's doctrine of perfection in its essentials. In fact, it is only a makeshift for the real Calvinistic idea of proof.

160. Schneckenburger, *op. cit.*, p. 145. Somewhat different in Loofs, *op. cit.* Both results are typical of all similar religious phenomena.

161. Thus in the conference of 1770. The first conference of 1744 had already recognized that the Biblical words came "within a hair" of Calvinism on the one hand and Antinomianism on the other. But since they were so obscure it was not well to be separated by doctrinal differences so long as the validity of the Bible as a practical norm was upheld.

162. The Methodists were separated from the Herrnhuters by their doctrine of the possibility of sinless perfection, which Zinzendorf, in particular, rejected. On the other hand, Wesley felt the emotional element in the Herrnhut religion to be mysticism and branded Luther's interpretation of the law as blasphemous. This shows the barrier which existed between Lutheranism and every kind of rational religious conduct.

163. John Wesley emphasizes the fact that everywhere, among Quakers, Presbyterians, and High Churchmen, one must believe in

dogmas, except in Methodism. With the above, compare the rather summary discussion in Skeats, *History of the Free Churches of England, 1688–1851.*

164. Compare Dexter, *Congregationalism*, pp. 455 ff.

165. Though naturally it might interfere with it, as is to-day the case among the American negroes. Furthermore, the often definitely pathological character of Methodist emotionalism as compared to the relatively mild type of Pietism may possibly, along with purely historical reasons and the publicity of the process, be connected with the greater ascetic penetration of life in the areas where Methodism is widespread. Only a neurologist could decide that.

166. Loofs, *op. cit.*, p. 750, strongly emphasizes the fact that Methodism is distinguished from other ascetic movements in that it came after the English Enlightenment, and compares it with the (surely much less pronounced) German Renaissance of Pietism in the first third of the nineteenth century. Nevertheless, it is permissible, following Ritschl, *Lehre von der Rechtfertigung und Versöhnung*, I, pp. 568 f., to retain the parallel with the Zinzendorf form of Pietism, which, unlike that of Spener and Francke, was already itself a reaction against the Enlightenment. However, this reaction takes a very different course in Methodism from that of the Herrnhuters, at least so far as they were influenced by Zinzendorf.

167. But which, as is shown by the passage from John Wesley (below, p. 175), it developed in the same way and with the same effect as the other ascetic denominations.

168. And, as we have seen, milder forms of the consistent ascetic ethics of Puritanism; while if, in the popular manner, one wished to interpret these religious conceptions as only exponents or reflections of capitalistic institutions, just the opposite would have to be the case.

169. Of the Baptists only the so-called General Baptists go back to the older movement. The Particular Baptists were, as we have pointed out already, Calvinists, who in principle limited Church membership to the regenerate, or at least personal believers, and hence remained in principle voluntarists and opponents of any State Church. Under Cromwell, no doubt, they were not always consistent in practice. Neither they nor the General Baptists, however important they are as the bearers of the Baptist tradition, give us any occasion for an especial dogmatic analysis here. That the Quakers, though formally a new foundation of George Fox and his associates, were fundamentally a continuation of the Baptist tradition, is beyond question. The best introduction to their history, including their relations to Baptists and Mennonites, is Robert Barclay, *The Inner Life of the Religious Societies of the Commonwealth*, 1876. On the history of the Baptists, compare, among others, H. M. Dexter, *The True Story of John Smyth, the Se-Baptist*, as told by himself and his contemporaries, Boston, 1881 (also J. C. Lang in *The Baptist Quarterly*

Notes

Review, 1883, p. 1); J. Murch, *A History of the Presb. and Gen. Bapt. Church in the West of England*, London, 1835; A. H. Newman, *History of the Baptist Church in the U.S.*, New York, 1894 (*Am. Church Hist. Series*, vol. 2); Vedder, *A Short History of the Baptists*, London, 1897; E. B. Bax, *Rise and Fall of the Anabaptists*, New York, 1902; G. Lorimer, *The Baptists in History*, 1902; J. A. Seiss, *The Baptist System Examined*, Lutheran Publication Society, 1902; further material in the *Baptist Handbook*, London, 1896 ff.; *Baptist Manuals*, Paris, 1891–93; *The Baptist Quarterly Review*; and the *Bibliotheca Sacra*, Oberlin, 1900.

The best Baptist library seems to be that of Colgate College in the State of New York. For the history of the Quakers the collection in Devonshire House in London is considered the best (not available to me). The official modern organ of orthodoxy is the *American Friend*, edited by Professor Jones; the best Quaker history that of Rowntree. In addition: Rufus B. Jones, *George Fox, an Autobiography*, Phila., 1903; Alton C. Thomas, *A History of the Society of Friends in America*, Phila., 1895; Edward Grubbe, *Social Aspects of the Quaker Faith*, London, 1899. Also the copious and excellent biographical literature.

170. It is one of the many merits of Karl Müller's *Kirchengeschichte* to have given the Baptist movement, great in its way, even though outwardly unassuming, the place it deserved in his work. It has suffered more than any other from the pitiless persecution of all the Churches, because it wished to be a sect in the specific sense of that word. Even after five generations it was discredited before the eyes of all the world by the debacle of the related eschatological experiment in Münster. And, continually oppressed and driven underground, it was long after its origin before it attained a consistent formulation of its religious doctrines. Thus it produced even less theology than would have been consistent with its principles, which were themselves hostile to a specialized development of its faith in God as a science. That was not very pleasing to the older professional theologians, even in its own time, and it made little impression on them. But many more recent ones have taken the same attitude. In Ritschl, *Pietismus*, I, pp. 22 f., the rebaptizers are not very adequately, in fact, rather contemptuously, treated. One is tempted to speak of a theological bourgeois standpoint. That, in spite of the fact that Cornelius's fine work (*Geschichte des Münsterschen Aufruhrs*) had been available for decades.

Here also Ritschl everywhere sees a retrogression from his standpoint toward Catholicism, and suspects direct influences of the radical wing of the Franciscan tradition. Even if such could be proved in a few cases, these threads would be very thin. Above all, the historical fact was probably that the official Catholic Church, wherever the worldly asceticism of the laity went as far as the formation of conventicles, regarded it with the utmost suspicion and attempted to encourage the formation of orders, thus outside the world, or to attach it as asceticism of the second grade to the existing orders and bring it under control. Where this did not succeed, it felt the danger that the practice of subjectivist ascetic morality might lead to the denial of authority and to heresy, just as, and with the same justification, the Elizabethan Church felt toward the half-Pietistic prophesying Bible conventicles, even when their conformism was undoubted; a feeling which was expressed by the Stuarts in their *Book of Sports*, of which later. The history of numerous heretical movements, including, for instance, the Humiliati and the Beguins, as well as the fate of St. Francis, are the proofs of it. The preaching of the mendicant friars, especially the Franciscans, probably did much to prepare the way for the ascetic lay morality of Calvinist-Baptist Protestantism. But the numerous close relationships between the asceticism of Western monasticism and the ascetic conduct of Protestantism, the importance of which must continually be stressed for our particular problems, are based in the last analysis on the fact that important factors are necessarily common to every asceticism on the basis of Biblical Christianity. Furthermore, every asceticism, no matter what its faith, has need of certain tried methods of subduing the flesh.

Of the following sketch it may further be remarked that its brevity is due to the fact that the Baptist ethic is of only very limited importance for the problem considered primarily in this study, the development of the religious background of the bourgeois idea of the calling. It contributed nothing new whatever to it. The much more important social aspect of the movement must for the present remain untouched. Of the history of the older Baptist movement, we can, from the view-point of our problem, present here only what was later important for the development of the sects in which we are interested: Baptists, Quakers, and, more incidentally, Mennonites.

171. See above [note 92].

172. On their origin and changes, see A. Ritschl in his *Gesammelte Aufsätze*, pp. 69 f.

173. Naturally the Baptists have always repudiated the designation of a sect. They form *the* Church in the sense of the Epistle to the Ephesians v. 27. But in our terminology they form a sect not only because they lack all relation to the State. The relation between Church and State of early Christianity was even for the Quakers (Barclay) their ideal; for to them, as to many Pietists, only a Church under the Cross was beyond suspicion of its purity. But the Calvinists as well, *faute de mieux*, similarly even the Catholic Church in the same circumstances, were forced to favour the separation of Church and State under an unbelieving State or under the Cross. Neither were they a sect, because induction to membership in the Church took

place *de facto* through a contract between the congregation and the candidates. For that was formally the case in the Dutch Reformed communities (as a result of the original political situation) in accordance with the old Church constitution (see v. Hoffmann, *Kirchenverfassungsrecht der niederl. Reformierten*, Leipzig, 1902).

On the contrary, it was because such a religious community could only be voluntarily organized as a sect, not compulsorily as a Church, if it did not wish to include the unregenerate and thus depart from the Early Christian ideal. For the Baptist communities it was an essential of the very idea of their Church, while for the Calvinists it was an historical accident. To be sure, that the latter were also urged by very definite religious motives in the direction of the believers' Church has already been indicated. On the distinction between Church and sect, see the following essay. The concept of sect which I have adopted here has been used at about the same time and, I assume, independently from me, by Kattenbusch in the *Realenzyklopädie für protestantische Theologie und Kirche* (Article *Sekte*). Troeltsch in his *Die Soziallehren der christlichen Kirchen und Gruppen* accepts it and discusses it more in detail. See also below, the introduction to the essays on the *Wirtschaftsethik der Weltreligionen*.

174. How important this symbol was, historically, for the conservation of the Church communty, since it was an unambiguous and unmistakable sign, has been very clearly shown by Cornelius, *op. cit.*

175. Certain approaches to it in the Mennonites' doctrine of justification need not concern us here.

176. This idea is perhaps the basis of the religious interest in the discussion of questions like the incarnation of Christ and his relationship to the Virgin Mary, which, often as the sole purely dogmatic part, stands out so strangely in the oldest documents of Baptism (for instance the confessions printed in Cornelius, *op. cit.*, Appendix to Vol. II. On this question, see K. Müller, *Kirchengeschichte*, II, 1, p. 330). The difference between the christology of the Reformed Church and the Lutheran (in the doctrine of the so-called *communicatio idiomatum*) seems to have been based on similar religious interests.

177. It was expressed especially in the original strict avoidance even of everyday intercourse with the excommunicated, a point at which even the Calvinists, who in principle held the opinion that worldly affairs were not affected by spiritual censure, made large concessions. See the following essay.

178. How this principle was applied by the Quakers to seemingly trivial externals (refusal to remove the hat, to kneel, bow, or use formal address) is well known. The basic idea is to a certain extent characteristic of all asceticism. Hence the fact that true asceticism is always hostile to authority. In Calvinism it appeared in the principle that only Christ should rule in the Church. In the case of Pietism one may think of Spener's attempts to find a Biblical justification of

titles. Catholic asceticism, so far as ecclesiastical authority was concerned, broke through this tendency in its oath of obedience, by interpreting obedience itself in ascetic terms. The overturning of this principle in Protestant asceticism is the historical basis of the peculiarities of even the contemporary democracy of the peoples influenced by Puritanism as distinct from that of the Latin spirit. It is also part of the historical background of that lack of respect of the American which is, as the case may be, so irritating or so refreshing.

179. No doubt this was true from the beginning for the Baptists essentially only of the New Testament, not to the same extent of the Old. Especially the Sermon on the Mount enjoyed a peculiar prestige as a programme of social ethic in all denominations.

180. Even Schwenkfeld had considered the outward performance of the sacraments an *adiaphoron*, while the General Baptists and the Mennonites held strictly to Baptism and the Communion, the Mennonites to the washing of feet in addition. On the other hand, for the predestinationists the depreciation, in fact for all except the communion—one may even say the suspicion—in which the sacraments were held, went very far. See the following essay.

181. On this point the Baptist denominations, especially the Quakers (Barclay, *Apology for the True Christian Divinity*, fourth edition, London, 1701, kindly placed at my disposal by Eduard Bernstein), referred to Calvin's statements in the *Instit. Christ*, III, p. 2, where in fact quite unmistakable suggestions of Baptist doctrine are to be found. Also the older distinction between the Word of God as that which God had revealed to the patriarchs, the prophets, and the apostles, and the Holy Scriptures as that part of it which they had written down, was, even though there was no historical connection, intimately related to the Baptist conception of revelation. The mechanical idea of inspiration, and with it the strict bibliocracy of the Calvinists, was just as much the product of their development in one direction in the course of the sixteenth century as the doctrine of the inner light of the Quakers, derived from Baptist sources, was the result of a directly opposite development. The sharp differentiation was also in this case partly a result of continual disputes.

182. That was emphasized strongly against certain tendencies of the Socinians. The natural reason knows nothing whatever of God (Barclay, *op. cit.*, p. 102). That meant that the part played by the *lex naturæ* elsewhere in Protestantism was altered. In principle there could be no general rules, no moral code, for the calling which everyone had, and which is different for every individual, is revealed to him by God through his conscience. We should do, not the good in the general sense of natural reason, but God's will as it is written in our hearts and known through the conscience (Barclay, pp. 73, 76). This irrationality of morality, derived from the exaggerated

contrast between the divine and the flesh, is expressed in these fundamental tenets of Quaker ethics: "What a man does contrary to his faith, though his faith may be wrong, is in no way acceptable to God—though the thing might have been lawful to another" (Barclay, p. 487). Of course that could not be upheld in practice. The "moral and perpetual statutes acknowledged by all Christians" are, for instance, for Barclay the limit of toleration. In practice the contemporaries felt their ethic, with certain peculiarities of its own, to be similar to that of the Reformed Pietists. "Everything good in the Church is suspected of being Quakerism", as Spener repeatedly points out. It thus seems that Spener envied the Quakers this reputation. *Cons. Theol.*, III, 6, 1, Dist. 2, No. 64. The repudiation of oaths on the basis of a passage in the Bible shows that the real emancipation from the Scriptures had not gone far. The significance for social ethics of the principle, "Do unto others as you would that they should do unto you", which many Quakers regarded as the essence of the whole Christian ethics, need not concern us here.

183. The necessity of assuming this possibility Barclay justifies because without it "there should never be a place known by the Saints wherein they might be free of doubting and despair, which— is most absurd". It is evident that the *certitudo salutis* depends upon it. Thus Barclay, *op. cit.*, p. 20.

184. There thus remains a difference in type between the Calvinistic and the Quaker rationalization of life. But when Baxter formulates it by saying that the spirit is supposed by the Quakers to act upon the soul as on a corpse, while the characteristically formulated Calvinistic principle is "reason and spirit are conjunct principles" (*Christian Directory*, II, p. 76), the distinction was no longer valid for his time in this form.

185. Thus in the very careful articles "Menno" and "Mennoniten" by Cramer in the *Realenzyklopädie für protestantische Theologie und Kirche*, especially p. 604. However excellent these articles are, the article "Baptisten" in the same encyclopedia is not very penetrating and in part simply incorrect. Its author does not know, for instance, the *Publications of the Hanserd Knolly's Society*, which are indispensable for the history of Baptism.

186. Thus Barclay, *op. cit.*, p. 404, explains that eating, drinking, and acquisition are natural, not spiritual acts, which may be performed without the special sanction of God. The explanation is in reply to the characteristic objection that if, as the Quakers teach, one cannot pray without a special motion of the Spirit, the same should apply to ploughing. It is, of course, significant that even in the modern resolutions of Quaker Synods the advice is sometimes given to retire from business after acquiring a sufficient fortune, in order, withdrawn from the bustle of the world, to be able to live in devotion to the Kingdom of God alone. But the same idea certainly occurs

occasionally in other denominations, including Calvinism. That betrays the fact that the acceptance of the bourgeois practical ethics by these movements was the worldly application of an asceticism which had originally fled from the world.

187. Veblen in his suggestive book *The Theory of Business Enterprise* is of the opinion that this motto belongs only to early capitalism. But economic supermen, who, like the present captains of industry, have stood beyond good and evil, have always existed, and the statement is still true of the broad underlying strata of business men.

188. We may here again expressly call attention to the excellent remarks of Eduard Bernstein, *op. cit.* To Kautsky's highly schematic treatment of the Baptist movement and his theory of heretical communism in general (in the first volume of the same work) we shall return on another occasion.

189. "In civil actions it is good to be as the many, in religious to be as the best", says, for example, Thomas Adams (*Works of the Puritan Divines*, p. 138). That sounds somewhat more drastic than it is meant to be. It means that the Puritan honesty is formalistic legality, just as the uprightness which the sometime Puritan people like to claim as a national virtue is something specifically different from the German *Ehrlichkeit*. Some good remarks on the subject from the educational standpoint may be found in the *Preuss. Jahrb.*, CXII (1903), p. 226. The formalism of the Puritan ethic is in turn the natural consequence of its relation to the law.

190. Something is said on this in the following essay.

191. This is the reason for the economic importance of the ascetic Protestant, but not Catholic, minorities.

192. That the difference of dogmatic basis was not inconsistent with the adoption of the most important interest in proof is to be explained in the last analysis by the historical peculiarities of Christianity in general which cannot be discussed here.

193. "Since God hath gathered us to be a people", says Barclay, *op. cit.*, p. 357. I myself heard a Quaker sermon at Haverford College which laid great emphasis on the interpretation of saints as meaning separate.

CHAPTER V

1. See the excellent sketch of his character in Dowden, *op. cit.* A passable introduction to Baxter's theology, after he had abandoned a strict belief in the double decree, is given in the introduction to the various extracts from his works printed in the *Works of the Puritan Divines* (by Jenkyn). His attempt to combine universal redemption and personal election satisfied no one. For us it is important only that he even then held to personal election, i.e. to

the most important point for ethics in the doctrine of predestination. On the other hand, his weakening of the forensic view of redemption is important as being suggestive of baptism.

2. Tracts and sermons by Thomas Adams, John Howe, Matthew Henry, J. Janeway, Stuart Charnock, Baxter, Bunyan, have been collected in the ten volumes of the *Works of the Puritan Divines* (London, 1845-8), though the choice is often somewhat arbitrary. Editions of the works of Bailey, Sedgwick, and Hoornbeek have already been referred to.

3. We could just as well have included Voet and other continental representatives of worldly asceticism. Brentano's view that the whole development was purely Anglo-Saxon is quite wrong. My choice is motivated mainly (though not exclusively) by the wish to present the ascetic movement as much as possible in the second half of the seventeenth century, immediately before the change to utilitarianism. It has unfortunately been impossible, within the limits of this sketch, to enter upon the fascinating task of presenting the characteristics of ascetic Protestantism through the medium of the biographical literature; the Quakers would in this connection be particularly important, since they are relatively little known in Germany.

4. For one might just as well take the writings of Gisbert Voet, the proceedings of the Huguenot Synods, or the Dutch Baptist literature. Sombart and Brentano have unfortunately taken just the ebionitic parts of Baxter, which I myself have strongly emphasized, to confront me with the undoubted capitalistic backwardness of his doctrines. But (1) one must know this whole literature thoroughly in order to use it correctly, and (2) not overlook the fact that I have attempted to show how, in spite of its anti-mammonistic doctrines, the spirit of this ascetic religion nevertheless, just as in the monastic communities, gave birth to economic rationalism because it placed a premium on what was most important for it: the fundamentally ascetic rational motives. That fact alone is under discussion and is the point of this whole essay.

5. Similarly in Calvin, who was certainly no champion of bourgeois wealth (see the sharp attacks on Venice and Antwerp in *Jes. Opp.*, III, 140a, 308a).

6. *Saints' Everlasting Rest*, chaps. x, xii. Compare Bailey (*Praxis Pietatis*, p. 182) or Matthew Henry (*The Worth of the Soul, Works of the Puritan Divines*, p. 319). "Those that are eager in pursuit of worldly wealth despise their Soul, not only because the Soul is neglected and the body preferred before it, but because it is employed in these pursuits" (Psa. cxxvii. 2). On the same page, however, is the remark to be cited below about the sinfulness of all waste of time, especially in recreations. Similarly in almost the whole religious literature of English-Dutch Puritanism. See, for instance, Hoornbeek's (*op. cit.*, L, X, ch. 18, 18) Phillipics against *avaritia*. This writer is also

259

affected by sentimental pietistic influences. See the praise of *tranquillitas animi* which is much more pleasing to God than the *sollicitudo* of this world. Also Bailey, referring to the well-known passage in Scripture, is of the opinion that "A rich man is not easily saved" (*op. cit.*, p. 182). The Methodist catechisms also warn against "gathering treasure on this earth". For Pietism this is quite obvious, as also for the Quakers. Compare Barclay (*op. cit.*, p. 517), " . . . and therefore beware of such temptations as to use their callings as an engine to be richer".

7. For not wealth alone, but also the impulsive pursuit of it (or what passed as such) was condemned with similar severity. In the Netherlands the South Holland Synod of 1574 declared, in reply to a question, that money-lenders should not be admitted to communion even though the business was permitted by law; and the Deventer Provincial Synod of 1598 (Art. 24) extended this to the employees of money-lenders. The Synod of Gorichem in 1606 prescribed severe and humiliating conditions under which the wives of usurers might be admitted, and the question was discussed as late as 1644 and 1657 whether Lombards should be admitted to communion (this against Brentano, who cites his own Catholic ancestors, although foreign traders and bankers have existed in the whole European and Asiatic world for thousands of years). Gisbert Voet (*Disp. Theol.*, IV, 1667, *de usuris*, p. 665) still wanted to exclude the Trapezites (Lombards, Piedmontese). The same was true of the Huguenot Synods. This type of capitalistic classes were not the typical representatives of the philosophy or the type of conduct with which we are concerned. They were also not new as compared with antiquity or the Middle Ages.

8. Developed in detail in the tenth chapter of the *Saints' Everlasting Rest*. He who should seek to rest in the shelter of possessions which God gives, God strikes even in this life. A self-satisfied enjoyment of wealth already gained is almost always a symptom of moral degradation. If we had everything which we could have in this world, would that be all we hoped for? Complete satisfaction of desires is not attainable on earth because God's will has decreed it should not be so.

9. *Christian Directory*, I, pp. 375-6. "It is for action that God maintaineth us and our activities; work is the moral as well as the natural end of power. . . . It is action that God is most served and honoured by. . . . The public welfare or the good of the many is to be valued above our own." Here is the connecting-point for the transition from the will of God to the purely utilitarian view-point of the later liberal theory. On the religious sources of Utilitarianism, see below in the text and above, chap. iv, note 145.

10. The commandment of silence has been, starting from the Biblical threat of punishment for every useless word, especially since

the Cluny monks, a favourite ascetic means of education in self-control. Baxter also speaks in detail of the sinfulness of unnecessary words. Its place in his character has been pointed out by Sanford, *op. cit.*, pp. 90 ff.

What contemporaries felt as the deep melancholy and moroseness of the Puritans was the result of breaking down the spontaneity of the *status naturalis*, and the condemnation of thoughtless speech was in the service of this end. When Washington Irving (*Bracebridge Hall*, chap. xxx) seeks the reason for it partly in the calculating spirit of capitalism and partly in the effect of political freedom, which promotes a sense of responsibility, it may be remarked that it does not apply to the Latin peoples. For England the situation was probably that: (1) Puritanism enabled its adherents to create free institutions and still become a world power; and (2) it transformed that calculating spirit (what Sombart calls *Rechenhaftigkeit*), which is in truth essential to capitalism, from a mere means to economy into a principle of general conduct.

11. *Op. cit.*, I, p. 111.

12. *Op. cit.*, I, p. 383 f.

13. Similarly on the preciousness of time, see Barclay, *op. cit.*, p. 14.

14. Baxter, *op. cit.*, I, p. 79. "Keep up a high esteem of time and be every day more careful that you lose none of your time, than you are that you lose none of your gold and silver. And if vain recreation, dressings, feastings, idle talk, unprofitable company, or sleep be any of them temptations to rob you of any of your time, accordingly heighten your watchfulness." "Those that are prodigal of their time despise their own souls", says Matthew Henry (*Worth of the Soul, Works of the Puritan Divines*, p. 315). Here also Protestant asceticism follows a well-beaten track. We are accustomed to think it characteristic of the modern man that he has no time, and for instance, like Goethe in the *Wanderjahren*, to measure the degree of capitalistic development by the fact that the clocks strike every quarter-hour. So also Sombart in his *Kapitalismus*. We ought not, however, to forget that the first people to live (in the Middle Ages) with careful measurement of time were the monks, and that the church bells were meant above all to meet their needs.

15. Compare Baxter's discussion of the calling, *op. cit.*, I, pp. 108 ff. Especially the following passage: "Question: But may I not cast off the world that I may only think of my salvation? Answer: You may cast off all such excess of worldly cares or business as unnecessarily hinder you in spiritual things. But you may not cast off all bodily employment and mental labour in which you may serve the common good. Everyone as a member of Church or Commonwealth must employ their parts to the utmost for the good of the Church and the Commonwealth. To neglect this and say: I will pray and meditate, is as if your servant should refuse his greatest work and tie himself

to some lesser, easier part. And God hath commanded you some way or other to labour for your daily bread and not to live as drones of the sweat of others only." God's commandment to Adam, "In the sweat of thy brow", and Paul's declaration, "He who will not work shall not eat", are also quoted. It has always been known of the Quakers that even the most well-to-do of them have had their sons learn a calling, for ethical and not, as Alberti recommends, for utilitarian reasons.

16. Here are points where Pietism, on account of its emotional character, takes a different view. Spener, although he emphasizes in characteristic Lutheran fashion that labour in a calling is worship of God (*Theologische Bedenken*, III, p. 445), nevertheless holds that the restlessness of business affairs distracts one from God, a most characteristic difference from Puritanism.

17. I, *op. cit.*, p. 242 ."It's they that are lazy in their callings that can find no time for holy duties." Hence the idea that the cities, the seat of the middle class with its rational business activities, are the seats of ascetic virtue. Thus Baxter says of his hand-loom weavers in Kidderminster: "And their constant converse and traffic with London doth much to promote civility and piety among trades-men . . ." in his autobiography (*Works of the Puritan Divines*, p. 38). That the proximity of the capital should promote virtue would astonish modern clergymen, at least in Germany. But Pietism also inclined to similar views. Thus Spener, speaking of a young colleague, writes: "At least it appears that among the great multitudes in the cities, though the majority is quite depraved, there are never-theless a number of good people who can accomplish much, while in villages often hardly anything good can be found in a whole community" (*Theologische Bedenken*, I, 66, p. 303). In other words, the peasant is little suited to rational ascetic conduct. Its ethical glorification is very modern. We cannot here enter into the significance of this and similar statements for the question of the relation of asceticism to social classes.

18. Take, for instance, the following passages (*op. cit.*, p. 336 f.): "Be wholly taken up in diligent business of your lawful callings when you are not exercised in the more immediate service of God." "Labour hard in your callings." "See that you have a calling which will find you employment for all the time which God's immediate service spareth."

19. That the peculiar ethical valuation of labour and its dignity was not originally a Christian idea nor even peculiar to Christianity has recently again been strongly emphasized by Harnack (*Mitt. des Ev.-Soz. Kongr.*, 14. Folge, 1905, Nos. 3, 4, p. 48).

20. Similarly in Pietism (Spener, *op. cit.*, III, pp. 429–30). The characteristic Pietist version is that loyalty to a calling which is imposed upon us by the fall serves to annihilate one's own selfish

Notes

will. Labour in the calling is, as a service of love to one's neighbour, a duty of gratitude for God's grace (a Lutheran idea), and hence it is not pleasing to God that it should be performed reluctantly (*op. cit.*, III, p. 272). The Christian should thus "prove himself as industrious in his labour as a worldly man" (III, p. 278). That is obviously less drastic than the Puritan version.

21. The significance of this important difference, which has been evident ever since the Benedictine rules, can only be shown by a much wider investigation.

22. "A sober procreation of children" is its purpose according to Baxter. Similarly Spener, at the same time with concessions to the coarse Lutheran attitude, which makes the avoidance of immorality, which is otherwise unavoidable, an accessory aim. Concupiscence as an accompaniment of sexual intercourse is sinful even in marriage. For instance, in Spener's view it is a result of the fall which transformed such a natural, divinely ordained process into something inevitably accompanied by sinful sensations, which is hence shameful. Also in the opinion of various Pietistic groups the highest form of Christian marriage is that with the preservation of virginity, the next highest that in which sexual intercourse is only indulged in for the procreation of children, and so on down to those which are contracted for purely erotic or external reasons and which are, from an ethical standpoint, concubinage. On these lower levels a marriage entered into for purely economic reasons is preferred (because after all it is inspired by rational motives) to one with erotic foundations. We may here neglect the Herrnhut theory and practice of marriage. Rationalistic philosophy (Christian Wolff) adopted the ascetic theory in the form that what was designed as a means to an end, concupiscence and its satisfaction, should not be made an end in itself.

The transition to a pure, hygienically oriented utilitarianism had already taken place in Franklin, who took approximately the ethical standpoint of modern physicians, who understand by chastity the restriction of sexual intercourse to the amount desirable for health, and who have, as is well known, even given theoretical advice as to how that should be accomplished. As soon as these matters have become the object of purely rational consideration the same development has everywhere taken place. The Puritan and the hygienic sex-rationalist generally tread very different paths, but here they understand each other perfectly. In a lecture, a zealous adherent of hygienic prostitution—it was a question of the regulation of brothels and prostitutes—defended the moral legitimacy of extra-marital intercourse (which was looked upon as hygienically useful) by referring to its poetic justification in the case of Faust and Margaret. To treat Margaret as a prostitute and to fail to distinguish the powerful sway of human passions from sexual intercourse for hygienic reasons, both are thoroughly congenial to the Puritan standpoint. Similar, for instance, is the typical specialist's view, occasionally put forward by very distinguished physicians, that a question which extends so far into the subtlest problems of personality and of culture as that of sexual abstinence should be dealt with exclusively in the forum of the physician (as an expert). For the Puritan the expert was the moral theorist, now he is the medical man; but the claim of competence to dispose of the questions which seem to us somewhat narrow-minded is, with opposite signs of course, the same in both cases.

But with all its prudery, the powerful idealism of the Puritan attitude can show positive accomplishments, even from the point of view of race conservation in a purely hygienic sense, while modern sex hygiene, on account of the appeal to unprejudicedness which it is forced to make, is in danger of destroying the basis of all its success. How, with the rationalistic interpretation of sexual relations among peoples influenced by Puritanism, a certain refinement and spiritual and ethical penetration of marital relationships, with a blossoming of matrimonial chivalry, has grown up, in contrast to the patriarchal sentimentality (*Brodem*), which is typical of Germany even in the circles of the intellectual aristocracy, must necessarily remain outside this discussion. Baptist influences have played a part in the emancipation of woman; the protection of her freedom of conscience, and the extension of the idea of the universal priesthood to her were here also the first breaches in patriarchal ideas.

23. This recurs again and again in Baxter. The Biblical basis is regularly either the passages in Proverbs, which we already know from Franklin (xxii. 29), or those in praise of labour (xxxi. 16). Cf. *op. cit.*, I, pp. 377, 382, etc.

24. Even Zinzendorf says at one point: "One does not only work in order to live, but one lives for the sake of one's work, and if there is no more work to do one suffers or goes to sleep" (Plitt, *op. cit.*, I, p. 428).

25. Also a symbol of the Mormons closes (after quotations) with the words: "But a lazy or indolent man cannot be a Christian and be saved. He is destined to be struck down and cast from the hive." But in this case it was primarily the grandiose discipline, half-way between monastery and factory, which placed the individual before the dilemma of labour or annihilation and, of course in connection with religious enthusiasm and only possible through it, brought forth the astonishing economic achievements of this sect.

26. Hence (*op. cit.*, I, p. 380) its symptoms are carefully analysed. Sloth and idleness are such deadly sins because they have a cumulative character. They are even regarded by Baxter as "destroyers of grace" (*op. cit.*, I, pp. 279–80). That is, they are the antitheses of the methodical life.

264

27. See above, chap. iii, note 5.

28. Baxter, *op. cit.*, I, pp. 108 ff. Especially striking are the following passages: "Question: But will not wealth excuse us? Answer: It may excuse you from some sordid sort of work by making you more serviceable to another, but you are no more excused from service of work . . . than the poorest man." Also, p. 376: "Though they [the rich] have no outward want to urge them, they have as great a necessity to obey God . . . God hath strictly commanded it [labour] to all." Chap. iv, note 47.

29. Similarly Spener (*op. cit.*, III, pp. 338, 425), who for this reason opposes the tendency to early retirement as morally objectionable, and, in refuting an objection to the taking of interest, that the enjoyment of interest leads to laziness, emphasizes that anyone who was in a position to live upon interest would still be obligated to work by God's commandment.

30. Including Pietism. Whenever a question of change of calling arises, Spener takes the attitude that after a certain calling has once been entered upon, it is a duty of obedience to Providence to remain and acquiesce in it.

31. The tremendous force, dominating the whole of conduct, with which the Indian religious teaching sanctions economic traditionalism in terms of chances of favourable rebirth, I have shown in the essays on the *Wirtschaftsethik der Weltreligionen*. It is an excellent example by which to show the difference between mere ethical theories and the creation of psychological sanctions with a religious background for certain types of conduct. The pious Hindu could advance in the scale of transmigration only by the strictly traditional fulfilment of the duties of the caste of his birth. It was the strongest conceivable religious basis for traditionalism. In fact, the Indian ethic is in this respect the most completely consistent antithesis of the Puritan, as in another respect (traditionalism of the caste structure) it is opposed to the Hebrew.

32. Baxter, *op. cit.*, I, p. 377.

33. But this does not mean that the Puritan view-point was historically derived from the latter. On the contrary, it is an expression of the genuinely Calvinistic idea that the cosmos of the world serves the glory of God. The utilitarian turn, that the economic cosmos should serve the good of the many, the common good, etc., was a consequence of the idea that any other interpretation of it would lead to aristocratic idolatry of the flesh, or at least did not serve the glory of God, but only fleshly cultural ends. But God's will, as it is expressed (chap iv, note 34) in the purposeful arrangements of the economic cosmos, can, so far as secular ends are in question at all, only be embodied in the good of the community, in impersonal usefulness. Utilitarianism is thus, as has already been pointed out, the result of the impersonal character of brotherly love and the

repudiation of all glorification of this world by the exclusiveness of the Puritan *in majorem Dei gloriam*.

How completely this idea, that all idolatry of the flesh is inconsistent with the glory of God and hence unconditionally bad, dominated ascetic Protestantism is clearly shown by the doubts and hesitation which it cost even Spener, who certainly was not infected with democracy, to maintain the use of titles as ἀδιάφορον against numerous objections. He finally comforted himself with the reflection that even in the Bible the Prætor Festus was given the title of κράτιστος by the Apostles. The political side of the question does not arise in this connection.

34. "The inconstant man is a stranger in his own house", says Thomas Adams (*Works of the Puritan Divines*, p. 77).

35. On this, see especially George Fox's remarks in the *Friends' Library* (ed. W. & T. Evans, Philadelphia, 1837), I, p. 130.

36. Above all, this sort of religious ethic cannot be regarded as a reflex of economic conditions. The specialization of occupations had, if anything, gone further in mediæval Italy than in the England of that period.

37. For, as is often pointed out in the Puritan literature, God never commanded "love thy neighbour more than thyself", but only as thyself. Hence self-regard is also a duty. For instance, a man who can make better use of his possessions, to the greater glory of God, than his neighbour, is not obliged by the duty of brotherly love to part with them.

38. Spener is also close to this view-point. But even in the case of transfer from commercial occupations (regarded as especially dangerous to virtue) to theology, he remains hesitant and on the whole opposed to it (*op. cit.*, III, pp. 435, 443; I, p. 524). The frequent occurrence of the reply to just this question (of the permissibility of changing a calling) in Spener's naturally biassed opinion shows, incidentally, how eminently practical the different ways of interpreting 1 Corinthians vii were.

39. Such ideas are not to be found, at least in the writings, of the leading Continental Pietists. Spener's attitude vacillates between the Lutheran (that of satisfaction of needs) and Mercantilist arguments for the usefulness of the prosperity of commerce, etc. (*op. cit.*, III, pp. 330, 332; I, p. 418: "the cultivation of tobacco brings money into the country and is thus useful, hence not sinful". Compare also III, pp. 426–7, 429, 434). But he does not neglect to point out that, as the example of the Quakers and the Mennonites shows, one can make profit and yet remain pious ; in fact, that even especially high profits, as we shall point out later, may be the direct result of pious uprightness (*op. cit.*, p. 435).

40. These views of Baxter are not a reflection of the economic environment in which he lived. On the contrary, his autobiography

shows that the success of his home missionary work was partly due
to the fact that the Kidderminster tradesmen were not rich, but
only earned food and raiment, and that the master craftsmen had
to live from hand to mouth just as their employees did. "It is the
poor who receive the glad tidings of the Gospel." Thomas Adams
remarks on the pursuit of gain: "He [the knowing man] knows . . .
that money may make a man richer, not better, and thereupon
chooseth rather to sleep with a good conscience than a full purse . . .
therefore desires no more wealth than an honest man may bear
away" (*Works of the Puritan Divines*, LI). But he does want that
much, and that means that every formally honest gain is legitimate.

41. Thus Baxter, *op. cit.*, I, chap. x, 1, 9 (par. 24) ; I, p. 378, 2.
In Prov. xxiii. 4: "Weary thyself not to be rich" means only "riches
for our fleshly ends must not ultimately be intended". Possession in
the feudal-seigneurial form of its use is what is odious (cf. the remark,
op. cit., I, p. 380, on the "debauched part of the gentry"), not possession in itself. Milton, in the first *Defensio pro populo Anglicano*, held
the well-known theory that only the middle class can maintain
virtue. That middle class here means bourgeoisie as against the
aristocracy is shown by the statement that both luxury and necessity
are unfavourable to virtue.

42. This is most important. We may again add the general remark:
we are here naturally not so much concerned with what concepts
the theological moralists developed in their ethical theories, but,
rather, what was the effective morality in the life of believers—that
is, how the religious background of economic ethics affected practice.
In the casuistic literature of Catholicism, especially the Jesuit, one
can occasionally read discussions which—for instance on the question
of the justification of interest, into which we do not enter here—sound
like those of many Protestant casuists, or even seem to go farther in
permitting or tolerating things. The Puritans have since often
enough been reproached that their ethic is at bottom the same as
that of the Jesuits. Just as the Calvinists often cite Catholic moralists,
not only Thomas Aquinas, Bernhard of Clairvaux, Bonaventura,
etc., but also contemporaries, the Catholic casuists also took notice
of heretical ethics. We cannot discuss all that here.

But quite apart from the decisive fact of the religious sanction of
the ascetic life for the layman, there is the fundamental difference,
even in theory, that these latitudinarian ideas within Catholicism
were the products of peculiarly lax ethical theories, not sanctioned
by the authority of the Church, but opposed by the most serious
and strictest disciples of it. On the other hand, the Protestant idea
of the calling in effect placed the most serious enthusiasts for
asceticism in the service of capitalistic acquisition. What in the one
case might under certain conditions be allowed, appeared in the
other as a positive moral good. The fundamental differences of the

two ethics, very important in practice, have been finally crystallized, even for modern times, by the Jansenist controversy and the Bull *Unigenitus*.

43. "You may labour in that manner as tendeth most to your success and lawful gain. You are bound to improve all your talents." There follows the passage cited above in the text. A direct parallel between the pursuit of wealth in the Kingdom of Heaven and the pursuit of success in an earthly calling is found in Janeway, *Heaven upon Earth* (*Works of the Puritan Divines*, p. 275).

44. Even in the Lutheran Confession of Duke Christopher of Württemberg, which was submitted to the Council of Trent, objection is made to the oath of poverty. He who is poor in his station should bear it, but if he swore to remain so it would be the same as if he swore to remain sick or to maintain a bad reputation.

45. Thus in Baxter and also in Duke Christopher's confession. Compare further pasages like: " . . . the vagrant rogues whose lives are nothing but an exorbitant course; the main begging", etc. (Thomas Adams, *Works of the Puritan Divines*, p. 259). Even Calvin had strictly forbidden begging, and the Dutch Synods campaigned against licences to beg. During the epoch of the Stuarts, especially Laud's regime under Charles I, which had systematically developed the principle of public poor relief and provision of work for the unemployed, the Puritan battle-cry was: "Giving alms is no charity" (title of Defoe's later well-known work). Towards the end of the seventeenth century they began the deterrent system of workhouses for the unemployed (compare Leonard, *Early History of English Poor Relief*, Cambridge, 1900, and H. Levy, *Die Grundlagen des ökonomischen Liberalismus in der Geschichte der englischen Volkswirtschaft*, Jena, 1912, pp. 69 ff.).

46. The President of the Baptist Union of Great Britain and Ireland, G. White, said emphatically in his inaugural address before the assembly in London in 1903 (*Baptist Handbook*, 1904, p. 104): "The best men on the roll of our Puritan Churches were men of affairs, who believed that religion should permeate the whole of life.'

47. Here also lies the characteristic difference from all feudal view-points. For the latter only the descendants of the parvenu (political or social) can reap the benefit of his success in a recognized station (characteristically expressed in the Spanish *Hidalgo = hijo d'algo = filius de aliquo* where the *aliquid* means an inherited property) However rapidly these differences are to-day fading out in the rapid change and Europeanization of the American national character, nevertheless the precisely opposite bourgeois attitude which glorifies business success and earnings as a symptom of mental achievement, but has no respect for mere inherited wealth, is still sometimes represented there. On the other hand, in Europe (as James Bryce once remarked) in effect almost every social honour is now purchasable

for money, so long as the buyer has not himself stood behind the counter, and carries out the necessary metamorphosis of his property (formation of trusts, etc.). Against the aristocracy of blood, see for instance Thomas Adams, *Works of the Puritan Divines*, p. 216.

48. That was, for instance, already true of the founder of the Familist sect, Hendrik Nicklaes, who was a merchant (Barclay, *Inner Life of the Religious Societies of the Commonwealth*, p. 34).

49. This is, for instance, definitely true for Hoornbeek, since Matt. v. 5 and 1 Tim. iv. 8 also made purely worldly promises to the saints (*op. cit.*, I, p. 193). Everything is the work of God's Providence, but in particular He takes care of His own. *Op. cit.*, p. 192: "Super alios autem summa cura et modis singularissimis versatur Dei providentia circa fideles." There follows a discussion of how one can know that a stroke of luck comes not from the *communis providentia*, but from that special care. Bailey also (*op. cit.*, p. 191) explains success in worldly labours by reference to Providence. That prosperity is often the reward of a godly life is a common expression in Quaker writings (for example see such an expression as late as 1848 in *Selection from the Christian Advices*, issued by the General Meeting of the Society of Friends, London, sixth edition, 1851, p. 209). We shall return to the connection with the Quaker ethics.

50. Thomas Adams's analysis of the quarrel of Jacob and Esau may serve as an example of this attention to the patriarchs, which is equally characteristic of the Puritan view of life (*Works of the Puritan Divines*, p. 235): "His [Esau's] folly may be argued from the base estimation of the birthright" [the passage is also important for the development of the idea of the birthright, of which more later] "that he would so lightly pass from it and on so easy condition as a pottage." But then it was perfidious that he would not recognize the sale, charging he had been cheated. He is, in other words, "a cunning hunter, a man of the fields"; a man of irrational, barbarous life; while Jacob, "a plain man, dwelling in tents", represents the "man of grace".

The sense of an inner relationship to Judaism, which is expressed even in the well-known work of Roosevelt, Köhler (*op. cit.*) found widespread among the peasants in Holland. But, on the other hand, Puritanism was fully conscious of its differences from Hebrew ethics in practical affairs, as Prynne's attack on the Jews (apropos of Cromwell's proposals for toleration) plainly shows. See below, note 58.

51. *Zur bäuerlichen Glaubens- und Sittenlehre*. Von einem thüringischen Landpfarrer, second edition, Gotha, 1890, p. 16. The peasants who are here described are characteristic products of the Lutheran Church. Again and again I wrote Lutheran in the margin when the excellent author spoke of peasant religion in general.

52. Compare for instance the passage cited in Ritschl, *Pietismus* II, p. 158. Spener also bases his objections to change of calling and

pursuit of gain partly on passages in Jesus Sirach. *Theologische Bedenken*, III, p. 426.

53. It is true that Bailey, nevertheless, recommends reading them, and references to the Apocrypha occur now and then, though naturally not often. I can remember none to Jesus Sirach just now (though perhaps by chance).

54. Where outward success comes to persons evidently damned, the Calvinist (as for instance Hoornbeek) comforts himself with the reflection, following the theory of stubbornness, that God allows it to them in order to harden them and make their doom the more certain.

55. We cannot go farther into this point in this connection. We are here interested only in the formalistic character of Puritan righteousness. On the significance of Old Testament ethics for the *lex naturæ* there is much in Troeltsch's *Soziallehren*.

56. The binding character of the ethical norms of the Scriptures goes for Baxter (*Christian Directory*, III, p. 173 f.) so far that they are (1) only a transcript of the law of nature, or (2) bear the "express character of universality and perpetuity".

57. For instance Dowden (with reference to Bunyan), *op. cit.*, p. 39.

58. More on this point in the essays on the *Wirtschaftsethik der Weltreligionen*. The enormous influence which, for instance, the second commandment ("thou shalt not make unto thee a graven image") has had on the development of the Jewish character, its rationality and abhorrence of sensuous culture, cannot be analysed here. However, it may perhaps be noted as characteristic that one of the leaders of the Educational Alliance in the United States, an organization which carries on the Americanization of Jewish immigrants on a grand scale and with astonishing success, told me that one of the first purposes aimed at in all forms of artistic and social educational work was emancipation from the second commandment. To the Israelite's prohibition of any anthropomorphic representation of God corresponds in Puritanism the somewhat different but in effect similar prohibition of idolatry of the flesh.

As far as Talmudic Judaism is concerned, some fundamental traits of Puritan morality are certainly related to it. For instance, it is stated in the Talmud (in Wünsche, *Babyl. Talmud*, II, p. 34) that it is better and will be more richly rewarded by God if one does a good deed for duty's sake than one which is not commanded by the law. In other words, loveless fulfillment of duty stands higher ethically than sentimental philanthropy. The Puritan ethics would accept that in essentials. Kant in effect also comes close to it, being partly of Scotch ancestry and strongly influenced by Pietism in his bringing up. Though we cannot discuss the subject here, many of his formulations are closely related to ideas of ascetic Protestantism.

But nevertheless the Talmudic ethic is deeply saturated with Oriental traditionalism. "R. Tanchum said to Ben Chanilai, 'Never alter a custom'" (Gemara to Mischna. VII, i, 86b, No. 93, in Wünsche. It is a question of the standard of living of day labourers). The only exception to this conformity is relation to strangers.

Moreover, the Puritan conception of lawfulness as proof evidently provided a much stronger motive to positive action than the Jewish unquestioned fulfillment of all commandments. The idea that success reveals the blessing of God is of course not unknown to Judaism. But the fundamental difference in religious and ethical significance which it took on for Judaism on account of the double ethic prevented the appearance of similar results at just the most important point. Acts toward a stranger were allowed which were forbidden toward a brother. For that reason alone it was impossible for success in this field of what was not commanded but only allowed to be a sign of religious worth and a motive to methodical conduct in the way in which it was for the Puritan. On this whole problem, which Sombart, in his book *Die Juden und das Wirtschaftsleben*, has often dealt with incorrectly, see the essays referred to above. The details have no place here.

The Jewish ethics, however strange that may at first sound, remained very strongly traditionalistic. We can likewise not enter into the tremendous change which the inner attitude toward the world underwent with the Christian form of the ideas of grace and salvation which contained in a peculiar way the seeds of new possibilities of development. On Old Testament lawfulness compare for example Ritschl, *Die christliche Lehre von der Rechtfertigung und Versöhnung*, II, p. 265.

To the English Puritans, the Jews of their time were representatives of that type of capitalism which was involved in war, Government contracts, State monopolies, speculative promotions, and the construction and financial projects of princes, which they themselves condemned. In fact the difference may, in general, with the necessary qualifications, be formulated: that Jewish capitalism was speculative pariah-capitalism, while the Puritan was bourgeois organization of labour.

59. The truth of the Holy Scriptures follows for Baxter in the last analysis from the "wonderful difference of the godly and ungodly", the absolute difference of the renewed man from others, and God's evident quite special care for His chosen people (which *may* of course be expressed in temptations), *Christian Directory*, I, p. 165.

60. As a characterization of this, it is only necessary to read how tortuously even Bunyan, who still occasionally approaches the atmosphere of Luther's *Freiheit eines Christenmenschen* (for example in *Of the Law and a Christian, Works of the Puritan Divines*, p. 254), reconciles himself with the parable of the Pharisee and the Publican

(see the sermon *The Pharisee and the Publican, op. cit.*, p. 100). Why is the Pharisee condemned? He does not truly keep God's commandments, for he is evidently a sectarian who is only concerned with external details and ceremonies (p. 107), but above all because he ascribes merit to himself, and at the same time, like the Quakers, thanks God for virtue by misuse of His name. In a sinful manner he exalts this virtue (p. 126), and thus implicitly contests God's predestination (p. 139). His prayer is thus idolatry of the flesh, and that is the reason it is sinful. On the other hand, the publican is, as the honesty of his confession shows, spiritually reborn, for, as it is put with a characteristic Puritan mitigation of the Lutheran sense of sin, "to a right and sincere conviction of sin there must be a conviction of the probability of mercy" (p. 209).

61. Printed in Gardiner's *Constitutional Documents*. One may compare this struggle against anti-authoritarian asceticism with Louis XIV's persecution of Port Royal and the Jansenists.

62. Calvin's own standpoint was in this respect distinctly less drastic, at least in so far as the finer aristocratic forms of the enjoyment of life were concerned. The only limitation is the Bible. Whoever adheres to it and has a good conscience, need not observe his every impulse to enjoy life with anxiety. The discussion in Chapter X of the *Instit. Christ* (for instance, "nec fugere ea quoque possumus quæ videntur oblectatione magis quam necessitate inservire") might in itself have opened the way to a very lax practice. Along with increasing anxiety over the *certitudo salutis* the most important circumstance for the later disciples was, however, as we shall point out in another place, that in the era of the *ecclesia militans* it was the small bourgeoisie who were the principal representatives of Calvinistic ethics.

63. Thomas Adams (*Works of the Puritan Divines*, p. 3) begins a sermon on the "three divine sisters" ("but love is the greatest of these") with the remark that even Paris gave the golden apple to Aphrodite!

64. Novels and the like should not be read; they are "wastetimes" (Baxter, *Christian Directory*, I, p. 51). The decline of lyric poetry and folk-music, as well as the drama, after the Elizabethan age in England is well known. In the pictorial arts Puritanism perhaps did not find very much to suppress. But very striking is the decline from what seemed to be a promising musical beginning (England's part in the history of music was by no means unimportant) to that absolute musical vacuum which we find typical of the Anglo-Saxon peoples later, and even to-day. Except for the negro churches, and the professional singers whom the Churches now engage as attractions (Trinity Church in Boston in 1904 for $8,000 annually), in America one also hears as community singing in general only a noise which is intolerable to German ears (partly analogous things in Holland also).

Notes

65. Just the same in Holland, as the reports of the Synods show. (See the resolutions on the Maypole in the Reitmaas Collection, VI, 78, 139.)

66. That the "Renaissance of the Old Testament" and the Pietistic orientation to certain Christian attitudes hostile to beauty in art, which in the last analysis go back to Isaiah and the 22nd Psalm, must have contributed to making ugliness more of a possible object for art, and that the Puritan repudiation of idolatry of the flesh played a part, seems likely. But in detail everything seems uncertain. In the Roman Church quite different demagogic motives led to outwardly similar effects, but, however, with quite different artistic results. Standing before Rembrandt's *Saul and David* (in the Mauritshuis), one seems directly to feel the powerful influence of Puritan emotions. The excellent analysis of Dutch cultural influences in Carl Neumann's *Rembrandt* probably gives everything that for the time being we can know about how far ascetic Protestantism may be credited with a positive fructifying influence on art.

67. The most complex causes, into which we cannot go here, were responsible for the relatively smaller extent to which the Calvinistic ethic penetrated practical life there. The ascetic spirit began to weaken in Holland as early as the beginning of the seventeenth century (the English Congregationalists who fled to Holland in 1608 were disturbed by the lack of respect for the Sabbath there), but especially under the Stadtholder Frederick Henry. Moreover, Dutch Puritanism had in general much less expansive power than English. The reasons for it lay in part in the political constitution (particularistic confederation of towns and provinces) and in the far smaller degree of military force (the War of Independence was soon fought principally with the money of Amsterdam and mercenary armies. English preachers illustrated the Babylonian confusion of tongues by reference to the Dutch Army). Thus the burden of the war of religion was to a large extent passed on to others, but at the same time a part of their political power was lost. On the other hand, Cromwell's army, even though it was partly conscripted, felt that it was an army of citizens. It was, to be sure, all the more characteristic that just this army adopted the abolition of conscription in its programme, because one could fight justly only for the glory of God in a cause hallowed by conscience, but not at the whim of a sovereign. The constitution of the British Army, so immoral to traditional German ideas, had its historical origin in very moral motives, and was an attainment of soldiers who had never been beaten. Only after the Restoration was it placed in the service of the interests of the Crown.

The Dutch *schutterijen*, the champions of Calvinism in the period of the Great War, only half a generation after the Synod of Dordrecht, do not look in the least ascetic in the pictures of Hals. Protests of the Synods against their conduct occur frequently. The Dutch concept of *Deftigkeit* is a mixture of bourgeois-rational honesty and patrician consciousness of status. The division of church pews according to classes in the Dutch churches shows the aristocratic character of this religion even to-day. The continuance of the town economy hampered industry. It prospered almost alone through refugees, and hence only sporadically. Nevertheless, the worldly asceticism of Calvinism and Pietism was an important influence in Holland in the same direction as elsewhere. Also in the sense to be referred to presently of ascetic compulsion to save, as Groen van Prinsterer shows in the passage cited below, note 87.

Moreover, the almost complete lack of *belles lettres* in Calvinistic Holland is of course no accident (see for instance Busken-Huet, *Het Land van Rembrandt*). The significance of Dutch religion as ascetic compulsion to save appears clearly even in the eighteenth century in the writings of Albertus Haller. For the characteristic peculiarities of the Dutch attitude toward art and its motives, compare for example the autobiographical remarks of Constantine Huyghens (written in 1629–31) in *Oud Holland*, 1891. The work of Groen van Prinsterer, *La Hollande et l'influence de Calvin*, 1864, already referred to, offers nothing important for our problems. The New Netherlands colony in America was socially a half-feudal settlement of *patroons*, merchants who advanced capital, and, unlike New England, it was difficult to persuade small people to settle there.

68. We may recall that the Puritan town government closed the theatre at Stratford-on-Avon while Shakespeare was still alive and residing there in his last years. Shakespeare's hatred and contempt of the Puritans appear on every occasion. As late as 1777 the City of Birmingham refused to license a theatre because it was conducive to slothfulness, and hence unfavourable to trade (Ashley, *Birmingham Trade and Commerce*, 1913).

69. Here also it was of decisive importance that for the Puritan there was only the alternative of divine will or earthly vanity. Hence for him there could be no *adiaphora*. As we have already pointed out, Calvin's own view was different in this respect. What one eats, wears, etc., as long as there is no enslavement of the soul to earthly desire as a result, is indifferent. Freedom from the world should be expressed, as for the Jesuits, in indifference, which for Calvin meant an indifferent, uncovetous use of whatever goods the earth offered (pp. 409 ff. of the original edition of the *Instit. Christ*).

70. The Quaker attitude in this respect is well known. But as early as the beginning of the seventeenth century the heaviest storms shook the pious congregation of exiles in Amsterdam for a decade over the fashionable hats and dresses of a preacher's wife (charmingly described in Dexter's *Congregationalism of the Last Three Hundred Years*). Sanford (*op. cit.*) has pointed out that the present-day male

hair-cut is that of the ridiculous Roundheads, and the equally ridiculous (for the time) male clothing of the Puritans is at least in principle fundamentally the same as that of to-day.

71. On this point again see Veblen's *Theory of Business Enterprise*.

72. Again and again we come back to this attitude. It explains statements like the following: "Every penny which is paid upon yourselves and children and friends must be done as by God's own appointment and to serve and please Him. Watch narrowly, or else that thievish, carnal self will leave God nothing" (Baxter, *op. cit.*, I, p. 108). This is decisive; what is expended for personal ends is withdrawn from the service of God's glory.

73. Quite rightly it is customary to recall (Dowden, *op. cit.*) that Cromwell saved Raphael's drawings and Mantegna's *Triumph of Cæsar* from destruction, while Charles II tried to sell them. Moreover, the society of the Restoration was distinctly cool or even hostile to English national literature. In fact the influence of Versailles was all-powerful at courts everywhere. A detailed analysis of the influence of the unfavourable atmosphere for the spontaneous enjoyment of everyday life on the spirit of the higher types of Puritan, and the men who went through the schooling of Puritanism, is a task which cannot be undertaken within the limits of this sketch. Washington Irving (*Bracebridge Hall*) formulates it in the usual English terms thus: "It [he says political freedom, we should say Puritanism] evinces less play of the fancy, but more power of the imagination." It is only necessary to think of the place of the Scotch in science, literature, and technical invention, as well as in the business life of Great Britain, to be convinced that this remark approaches the truth, even though put somewhat too narrowly. We cannot speak here of its significance for the development of technique and the empirical sciences. The relation itself is always appearing in everyday life. For the Quakers, for instance, the recreations which are permissible (according to Barclay) are: visiting of friends, reading of historical works, mathematical and physical experiments, gardening, discussion of business and other occurrences in the world, etc. The reason is that pointed out above.

74. Already very finely analysed in Carl Neumann's *Rembrandt*, which should be compared with the above remarks in general.

75. Thus Baxter in the passage cited above, I, p. 108, and below.

76. Compare the well-known description of Colonel Hutchinson (often quoted, for instance, in Sanford, *op. cit.*, p. 57) in the biography written by his widow. After describing all his chivalrous virtues and his cheerful, joyous nature, it goes on: "He was wonderfully neat, cleanly, and genteel in his habit, and had a very good fancy in it; but he left off very early the wearing of anything that was costly." Quite similar is the ideal of the educated and highly civilized Puritan

woman who, however, is penurious of two things: (1) time, and (2) expenditure for pomp and pleasure, as drawn in Baxter's funeral oration for Mary Hammer (*Works of the Puritan Divines*, p. 533).

77. I think, among many other examples, especially of a manufacturer unusually successful in his business ventures, and in his later years very wealthy, who, when for the treatment of a troublesome digestive disorder the doctor prescribed a few oysters a day, could only be brought to comply with difficulty. Very considerable gifts for philanthropic purposes which he made during his lifetime and a certain openhandedness showed, on the other hand, that it was simply a survival of that ascetic feeling which looks upon enjoyment of wealth for oneself as morally reprehensible, but has nothing whatever to do with avarice.

78. The separation of workshop, office, of business in general and the private dwelling, of firm and name, of business capital and private wealth, the tendency to make of the business a *corpus mysticum* (at least in the case of corporate property) all lay in this direction. On this, see my *Handelsgesellschaften im Mittelalter* (*Gesammelte Aufsätze zur Sozial- und Wirtschaftsgeschichte*, pp. 312 ff.).

79. Sombart in his *Kapitalismus* (first edition) has already well pointed out this characteristic phenomenon. It must, however, be noted that the accumulation of wealth springs from two quite distinct psychological sources. One reaches into the dimmest antiquity and is expressed in foundations, family fortunes, and trusts, as well as much more purely and clearly in the desire to die weighted down with a great burden of material goods; above all to insure the continuation of a business even at the cost of the personal interests of the majority of one's children. In such cases it is, besides the desire to give one's own creation an ideal life beyond one's death, and thus to maintain the *splendor familiæ* and extend the personality of the founder, a question of, so to speak, fundamentally egocentric motives. That is not the case with that bourgeois motive with which we are here dealing. There the motto of asceticism is "Entsagen sollst du, sollst entsagen" in the positive capitalistic sense of "Erwerben sollst du, sollst erwerben". In its pure and simple non-rationality it is a sort of categorical imperative. Only the glory of God and one's own duty, not human vanity, is the motive for the Puritans; and to-day only the duty to one's calling. If it pleases anyone to illustrate an idea by its extreme consequences, we may recall the theory of certain American millionaires, that their millions should not be left to their children, so that they will not be deprived of the good moral effects of the necessity of working and earning for themselves. To-day that idea is certainly no more than a theoretical soap-bubble.

80. This is, as must continually be emphasized, the final decisive religious motive (along with the purely ascetic desire to mortify the flesh). It is especially clear in the Quakers.

Notes

81. Baxter (*Saints' Everlasting Rest*, p. 12) repudiates this with precisely the same reasoning as the Jesuits: the body must have what it needs, otherwise one becomes a slave to it.

82. This ideal is clearly present, especially for Quakerism, in the first period of its development, as has already been shown in important points by Weingarten in his *Englische Revolutionskirchen*. Also Barclay's thorough discussion (*op. cit.*, pp. 519 ff., 533) shows it very clearly. To be avoided are: (1) Worldly vanity; thus all ostentation, frivolity, and use of things having no practical purpose, or which are valuable only for their scarcity (i.e. for vanity's sake). (2) Any unconscientious use of wealth, such as excessive expenditure for not very urgent needs above necessary provision for the real needs of life and for the future. The Quaker was, so to speak, a living law of marginal utility. "Moderate use of the creature" is definitely permissible, but in particular one might pay attention to the quality and durability of materials so long as it did not lead to vanity. On all this compare *Morgenblatt für gebildete Leser*, 1846, pp. 216 ff. Especially on comfort and solidity among the Quakers, compare Schneckenburger, *Vorlesungen*, pp. 96 f.

83. Adapted by Weber from Faust, Act I. Goethe there depicts Mephistopheles as "Die Kraft, die stets das Böse will, und stets das Gute schafft".—TRANSLATOR'S NOTE.

84. It has already been remarked that we cannot here enter into the question of the class relations of these religious movements (see the essays on the *Wirtschaftsethik der Weltreligionen*). In order to see, however, that for example Baxter, of whom we make so much use in this study, did not see things solely as a bourgeois of his time, it will suffice to recall that even for him in the order of the religious value of callings, after the learned professions comes the husbandman, and only then mariners, clothiers, booksellers, tailors, etc. Also, under mariners (characteristically enough) he probably thinks at least as often of fishermen as of shipowners. In this regard several things in the *Talmud* are in a different class. Compare, for instance, in Wünsche, *Babyl. Talmud*, II, pp. 20, 21, the sayings of Rabbi Eleasar, which though not unchallenged, all contend in effect that business is better than agriculture. In between see II, 2, p. 68, on the wise investment of capital: one-third in land, one-third in merchandise, and one-third in cash.

For those to whom no causal explanation is adequate without an economic (or materialistic as it is unfortunately still called) interpretation, it may be remarked that I consider the influence of economic development on the fate of religious ideas to be very important and shall later attempt to show how in our case the process of mutual adaptation of the two took place. On the other hand, those religious ideas themselves simply cannot be deduced from economic circumstances. They are in themselves, that is beyond doubt, the most powerful plastic elements of national character, and contain a law of development and a compelling force entirely their own. Moreover, the most important differences, so far as non-religious factors play a part, are, as with Lutheranism and Calvinism, the result of political circumstances, not economic.

85. That is what Eduard Bernstein means to express when he says, in the essay referred to above (pp. 625, 681), "Asceticism is a bourgeois virtue." His discussion is the first which has suggested these important relationships. But the connection is a much wider one than he suspected. For not only the accumulation of capital, but the ascetic rationalization of the whole of economic life was involved.

For the American Colonies, the difference between the Puritan North, where, on account of the ascetic compulsion to save, capital in search of investment was always available, from the conditions in the South has already been clearly brought out by Doyle.

86. Doyle, *The English in America*, II, chap. i. The existence of iron-works (1643), weaving for the market (1659), and also the high development of the handicrafts in New England in the first generation after the foundation of the colonies are, from a purely economic view-point, astounding. They are in striking contrast to the conditions in the South, as well as the non-Calvinistic Rhode Island with its complete freedom of conscience. There, in spite of the excellent harbour, the report of the Governor and Council of 1686 said: "The great obstruction concerning trade is the want of merchants and men of considerable estates amongst us" (Arnold, *History of the State of Rhode Island*, p. 490). It can in fact hardly be doubted that the compulsion continually to reinvest savings, which the Puritan curtailment of consumption exercised, played a part. In addition there was the part of Church discipline which cannot be discussed here.

87. That, however, these circles rapidly diminished in the Netherlands is shown by Busken-Huet's discussion (*op. cit.*, II, chaps. iii and iv). Nevertheless, Groen van Prinsterer says (*Handb. der Gesch. van het Vaderland*, third edition, par. 303, note, p. 254), "De Nederlanders verkoopen veel en verbruiken wenig", even of the time after the Peace of Westphalia.

88. For England, for instance, a petition of an aristocratic Royalist (quoted in Ranke, *Engl. Geschichte*, IV, p. 197) presented after the entry of Charles II into London, advocated a legal prohibition of the acquisition of landed estates by bourgeois capital, which should thereby be forced to find employment in trade. The class of Dutch regents was distinguished as an estate from the bourgeois patricians of the cities by the purchase of landed estates. See the complaints, cited by Fruin, *Tien jaren uit den tachtigjarigen oorlog*, of the year 1652, that the regents have become landlords and are no longer merchants. To be sure these circles had never been at bottom strictly

Calvinistic. And the notorious scramble for membership in the nobility and titles in large parts of the Dutch middle class in the second half of the seventeenth century in itself shows that at least for this period the contrast between English and Dutch conditions must be accepted with caution. In this case the power of hereditary moneyed property broke through the ascetic spirit.

89. Upon the strong movement for bourgeois capital to buy English landed estates followed the great period of prosperity of English agriculture.

90. Even down into this century Anglican landlords have often refused to accept Nonconformists as tenants. At the present time the two parties of the Church are of approximately equal numbers, while in earlier times the Nonconformists were always in the minority.

91. H. Levy (article in *Archiv für Sozialwissenschaft und Sozial-politik*, XLVI, p. 605) rightly notes that according to the native character of the English people, as seen from numerous of its traits, they were, if anything, less disposed to welcome an ascetic ethic and the middle-class virtues than other peoples. A hearty and un-restrained enjoyment of life was, and is, one of their fundamental traits. The power of Puritan asceticism at the time of its predominance is shown most strikingly in the astonishing degree to which this trait of character was brought under discipline among its adherents.

92. This contrast recurs continually in Doyle's presentation. In the attitude of the Puritan to everything the religious motive always played an important part (not always, of course, the sole important one). The colony (under Winthrop's leadership) was inclined to permit the settlement of gentlemen in Massachusetts, even an upper house with a hereditary nobility, if only the gentlemen would adhere to the Church. The colony remained closed for the sake of Church discipline. The colonization of New Hampshire and Maine was carried out by large Anglican merchants, who laid out large stock-raising plantations. Between them and the Puritans there was very little social connection. There were complaints over the strong greed for profits of the New Englanders as early as 1632 (see Weeden's *Economic and Social History of New England*, I, p. 125).

93. This is noted by Petty (*Pol. Arith.*), and all the contemporary sources without exception speak in particular of the Puritan sectarians, Baptists, Quakers, Mennonites, etc., as belonging partly to a property-less class, partly to one of small capitalists, and contrast them both with the great merchant aristocracy and the financial adventurers. But it was from just this small capitalist class, and not from the great financial magnates, monopolists, Government contractors, lenders to the King, colonial entrepreneurs, promoters, etc., that there originated what was characteristic of Occidental capitalism: the middle-class organization of industrial labour on the basis of private

property (see Unwin, *Industrial Organization in the Sixteenth and Seventeenth Centuries*, London, 1914, pp. 196 ff.). To see that this difference was fully known even to contemporaries, compare Parker's *Discourse Concerning Puritans* of 1641, where the contrast to promoters and courtiers is also emphasized.

94. On the way in which this was expressed in the politics of Pennsylvania in the eighteenth century, especially during the War of Independence, see Sharpless, *A Quaker Experiment in Government*, Philadelphia, 1902.

95. Quoted in Southey, *Life of Wesley*, chap. xxix (second American edition, II, p. 308). For the reference, which I did not know, I am indebted to a letter from Professor Ashley (1913). Ernst Troeltsch, to whom I communicated it for the purpose, has already made use of it.

96. The reading of this passage may be recommended to all those who consider themselves to-day better informed on these matters than the leaders and contemporaries of the movements themselves. As we see, they knew very well what they were doing and what dangers they faced. It is really inexcusable to contest so lightly, as some of my critics have done, facts which are quite beyond dispute, and have hitherto never been disputed by anyone. All I have done is to investigate their underlying motives somewhat more carefully. No one in the seventeenth century doubted the existence of these relationships (compare Manley, *Usury of 6 per Cent. Examined*, 1669, p. 137). Besides the modern writers already noted, poets like Heine and Keats, as well as historians like Macaulay, Cunningham, Rogers, or an essayist such as Matthew Arnold, have assumed them as obvious. From the most recent literature see Ashley, *Birmingham Industry and Commerce* (1913). He has also expressed his complete agreement with me in correspondence. On the whole problem now compare the study by H. Levy referred to above, note 91.

97. Weber's italics.

98. That exactly the same things were obvious to the Puritans of the classical era cannot perhaps be more clearly shown than by the fact that in Bunyan Mr. Money-Love argues that one may become religious in order to get rich, for instance to attract customers. For why one has become religious makes no difference (see p. 114, Tauchnitz edition).

99. Defoe was a zealous Nonconformist.

100. Spener also (*Theologische Bedenken*, pp. 426, 429, 432 ff.), although he holds that the merchant's calling is full of temptations and pitfalls, nevertheless declares in answer to a question: "I am glad to see, so far as trade is concerned, that my dear friend knows no scruples, but takes it as an art of life, which it is, in which much good may be done for the human race, and God's will may be carried out through love." This is more fully justified in other passages by mercantilist arguments. Spener, at times in a purely Lutheran strain,

designates the desire to become rich as the main pitfall, following 1 Tim. vi, viii, and ix, and referring to Jesus Sirach (see above), and hence rigidly to be condemned. But, on the other hand, he takes some of it back by referring to the prosperous sectarians who yet live righteously (see above, note 39). As the result of industrious work wealth is not objectionable to him either. But on account of the Lutheran influence his standpoint is less consistent than that of Baxter.

101. Baxter, *op. cit.*, II, p. 16, warns against the employment of "heavy, flegmatic, sluggish, fleshly, slothful persons" as servants, and recommends preference for godly servants, not only because ungodly servants would be mere eye-servants, but above all because "a truly godly servant will do all your service in obedience to God, as if God Himself had bid him do it". Others, on the other hand, are inclined "to make no great matter of conscience of it". However, the criterion of saintliness of the workman is not for him the external confession of faith, but the "conscience to do their duty". It appears here that the interests of God and of the employers are curiously harmonious. Spener also (*Theologische Bedenken*, III, p. 272), who otherwise strongly urges taking time to think of God, assumes it to be obvious that workers must be satisfied with the extreme minimum of leisure time (even on Sundays). English writers have rightly called the Protestant immigrants the pioneers of skilled labour. See also proofs in H. Levy, *Die Grundlagen des ökonomischen Liberalismus in der Geschichte der englischen Volkswirtschaft*, p. 53.

102. The analogy between the unjust (according to human standards) predestination of only a few and the equally unjust, but equally divinely ordained, distribution of wealth, was too obvious to be escaped. See for example Hoornbeek, *op. cit.*, I, p. 153. Furthermore, as for Baxter, *op. cit.*, I, p. 380, poverty is very often a symptom of sinful slothfulness.

103. Thomas Adams (*Works of the Puritan Divines*, p. 158) thinks that God probably allows so many people to remain poor because He knows that they would not be able to withstand the temptations that go with wealth. For wealth all too often draws men away from religion.

104. See above, note 45, and the study of H. Levy referred to there. The same is noted in all the discussions (thus by Manley for the Huguenots).

105. *Charisma* is a sociological term coined by Weber himself. It refers to the quality of leadership which appeals to non-rational motives. See *Wirtschaft und Gesellschaft*, pp. 140 ff.—TRANSLATOR'S NOTE.

106. Similar things were not lacking in England. There was, for example, that Pietism which, starting from Law's *Serious Call* (1728), preached poverty, chastity, and, originally, isolation from the world.

107. Baxter's activity in Kidderminster, a community absolutely debauched when he arrived, which was almost unique in the history of the ministry for its success, is at the same time a typical example of how asceticism educated the masses to labour, or, in Marxian terms, to the production of surplus value, and thereby for the first time made their employment in the capitalistic labour relation (putting-out industry, weaving, etc.) possible at all. That is very generally the causal relationship. From Baxter's own view-point he accepted the employment of his charges in capitalistic production for the sake of his religious and ethical interests. From the standpoint of the development of capitalism these latter were brought into the service of the development of the spirit of capitalism.

108. Furthermore, one may well doubt to what extent the joy of the mediæval craftsman in his creation, which is so commonly appealed to, was effective as a psychological motive force. Nevertheless, there is undoubtedly something in that thesis. But in any case asceticism certainly deprived all labour of this worldly attractiveness, to-day for ever destroyed by capitalism, and oriented it to the beyond. Labour in a calling as such is willed by God. The impersonality of present-day labour, what, from the standpoint of the individual, is its joyless lack of meaning, still has a religious justification here. Capitalism at the time of its development needed labourers who were available for economic exploitation for conscience' sake. To-day it is in the saddle, and hence able to force people to labour without transcendental sanctions.

109. Petty, *Political Arithmetick, Works*, edited by Hull, I, p. 262.

110. On these conflicts and developments see H. Levy in the book cited above. The very powerful hostility of public opinion to monopolies, which is characteristic of England, originated historically in a combination of the political struggle for power against the Crown—the Long Parliament excluded monopolists from its membership—with the ethical motives of Puritanism; and the economic interests of the small bourgeois and moderate-scale capitalists against the financial magnates in the seventeenth century. The Declaration of the Army of August 2, 1652, as well as the Petition of the Levellers of January 28, 1653, demand, besides the abolition of excises, tariffs, and indirect taxes, and the introduction of a single tax on estates, above all free trade, i.e. the abolition of the monopolistic barriers to trade at home and abroad, as a violation of the natural rights of man.

111. Compare H. Levy, *Die Grundlagen des ökonomischen Liberalismus in der Geschichte der englischen Volkswirtschaft*, pp. 51 f.

112. That those other elements, which have here not yet been traced to their religious roots, especially the idea that honesty is the best policy (Franklin's discussion of credit), are also of Puritan origin, must be proved in a somewhat different connection (see the following essay [not translated here]). Here I shall limit myself to

repeating the following remark of J. A. Rowntree (*Quakerism, Past and Present*, pp. 95–6), to which E. Bernstein has called my attention: "Is it merely a coincidence, or is it a consequence, that the lofty profession of spirituality made by the Friends has gone hand in hand with shrewdness and tact in the transaction of mundane affairs? Real piety favours the success of a trader by insuring his integrity and fostering habits of prudence and forethought, important items in obtaining that standing and credit in the commercial world, which are requisites for the steady accumulation of wealth" (see the following essay). "Honest as a Huguenot" was as proverbial in the seventeenth century as the respect for law of the Dutch which Sir W. Temple admired, and, a century later, that of the English as compared with those Continental peoples that had not been through this ethical schooling.

113. Well analysed in Bielschowsky's *Goethe*, II, chap. xviii. For the development of the scientific cosmos Windelband, at the end of his *Blütezeit der deutschen Philosophie* (Vol. II of the *Gesch. d. Neueren Philosophie*), has expressed a similar idea.

114. *Saints' Everlasting Rest*, chap. xii.

115. "Couldn't the old man be satisfied with his $75,000 a year and rest? No! The frontage of the store must be widened to 400 feet. Why? That beats everything, he says. In the evening when his wife and daughter read together, he wants to go to bed. Sundays he looks at the clock every five minutes to see when the day will be over—what a futile life!" In these terms the son-in-law (who had emigrated from Germany) of the leading dry-goods man of an Ohio city expressed his judgment of the latter, a judgment which would undoubtedly have seemed simply incomprehensible to the old man. A symptom of German lack of energy.

116. This remark alone (unchanged since his criticism) might have shown Brentano (*op. cit.*) that I have never doubted its independent significance. That humanism was also not pure rationalism has lately again been strongly emphasized by Borinski in the *Abhandl. der Münchener Akad. der Wiss.*, 1919.

117. The academic oration of v. Below, *Die Ursachen der Reformation* (Freiburg, 1916), is not concerned with this problem, but with that of the Reformation in general, especially Luther. For the question dealt with here, especially the controversies which have grown out of this study, I may refer finally to the work of Hermelink, *Reformation und Gegenreformation*, which, however, is also primarily concerned with other problems.

118. For the above sketch has deliberately taken up only the relations in which an influence of religious ideas on the material culture is really beyond doubt. It would have been easy to proceed beyond that to a regular construction which logically deduced everything characteristic of modern culture from Protestant rational-

ism. But that sort of thing may be left to the type of dilettante who believes in the unity of the group mind and its reducibility to a single formula. Let it be remarked only that the period of capitalistic development lying before that which we have studied was everywhere in part determined by religious influences, both hindering and helping. Of what sort these were belongs in another chapter. Furthermore, whether, of the broader problems sketched above, one or another can be dealt with in the limits of this Journal [the essay first appeared in the *Archiv für Sozialwissenschaft und Sozialpolitik*—Translator's Note] is not certain in view of the problems to which it is devoted. On the other hand, to write heavy tomes, as thick as they would have to be in this case, and dependent on the work of others (theologians and historians), I have no great inclination (I have left these sentences unchanged).

For the tension between ideals and reality in early capitalistic times before the Reformation, see now Strieder, *Studien zur Geschichte der kapit. Organizationsformen*, 1914, Book II. (Also as against the work of Keller, cited above, which was utilized by Sombart.)

119. I should have thought that this sentence and the remarks and notes immediately preceding it would have sufficed to prevent any misunderstanding of what this study was meant to accomplish, and I find no occasion for adding anything. Instead of following up with an immediate continuation in terms of the above programme, I have, partly for fortuitous reasons, especially the appearance of Troeltsch's *Die Soziallehren der christlichen Kirchen und Gruppen*, which disposed of many things I should have had to investigate in a way in which I, not being a theologian, could not have done it; but partly also in order to correct the isolation of this study and to place it in relation to the whole of cultural development, determined, first, to write down some comparative studies of the general historical relationship of religion and society. These follow. Before them is placed only a short essay in order to clear up the concept of sect used above, and at the same time to show the significance of the Puritan conception of the Church for the capitalistic spirit of modern times.

INDEX

absolution, sacrament of, 116, 134

acquisition, as principle of economic action, 63

acquisition, impulse to, 16, 56

Adams, Thomas, 223, 237, 258, 259, 266, 267, 269, 272, 281

adaptation, 72
(*see* selection)

adiaphora, 256, 274

administration, 25

adventurers, capitalistic, 20, 24, 58, 69, 76, 166, 174, 186, 199, 279

after-life, idea of, 97, 109

Alberti, Leon Battista, 194, 202, 262

Anglican Church, 82, 99, 179

Anthony of Florence, 73, 83, 197, 201, 202

anthropology, 30

Anti-authoritarianism, 167
(*see also* asceticism)

architecture, in West, 15

aristocracy, antagonism to, 150

aristocracy, commerical, 37, 65, 74

Aristotle, 14, 235, 244, 249

Arminians, 200, 217

Arnold, Matthew, 191, 280

Arnold, Samuel G., 278

art in West, 14

Arte di Calimala, 203

arts, Puritan attitude to, 168, 272

asceticism, anti-authoritarian, tendency of, 167, 255

asceticism, definition of, 193-4

asceticism, monastic, 80, 121, 253-4

asceticism, sexual, 158

asceticism, tendency of capitalism to, 71

asceticism, types of, 118

asceticism, worldly, 149, 154

Ashley, W. J., 280

Augsburg Confession, 102, 206, 209

Augustine, St., 101

Aymon, Jean, 190

Bailey, R., 106, 129, 132, 222, 228, 231, 233, 238, 245, 259

Baird, Henry M., 219

Bank of England, 186

baptism, 145, 222

Barclay, Robert, 148, 156, 171, 252, 257, 269

Barebones, Praisegod, 243

Bartholomew's day, St., 156

Bax, E. Belfort, 253

Baxter, Richard, 106, 155, 181, 218, 224, 226 ff., 245, 259 ff.

Becker, Bernhard, 247

begging, 177, 268

believers' church, 122, 144
(*see also* sect)

Below, Georg von, 283

Benedict, St., 118

Bernhard, St., 230, 236, 238, 241, 267

Bernhard of Siena, 197, 201, 202

Bernstein, Eduard, 219, 256, 258, 278, 283

Berthold of Regensburg, 208

Beruf, 79, 204 ff.

Beruf, translation of, 194

Beza, Theodore, 110, 230

bibliocracy, 123, 146

Bielschowsky, Albert, 283

Bohemian Brothers, 197

Bonaventura, St., 236, 242, 267

Bonn, M. J., 217

book-keeping, 22, 67

book-keeping, moral, 124, 238

Borinski, Karl, 283

bourgeoisie, 23, 24, 176

Brassey, Thomas, 198